NIGHT SPEAK

August Sands

ISBN-13: 979-8-218-50463-2

Book Cover Design by ebooklaunch.com

Printed in the United States of America

CONTENTS

Part I

Prometheus in Exile

CONTENTS

Part I

Prometheus in Exile

REEVE I

Their apartment overlooked a cemetery.

The mourners woke Reeve in the early afternoon on weekends when their muted voices would saturate the walls in displaced misery. It felt to him almost like an intrusion into something private. His twin brother, Ephraim, liked to hear them speak. He would curl up at the head of his bed and press his ear to the wall and eavesdrop if the rites were held close enough to be overheard, looking equal parts eager and mischievous.

Reeve thought it was a little funny to Ephraim—death, that was.

That day began the same. Ephraim had two fingers inserted between the blinds to try and peer out into the lot adjacent, squinting in concentration. He stood balanced on a chair he had taken from the kitchen, baseball cap askew. Reeve was on the floor, preoccupied with a set of matchbox cars, listening as Ephraim provided the occasional commentary on the proceedings.

"Reeve," Ephraim said, then turned when the other boy didn't respond.

"Hey, Reeve, c'mere. I think it's for Miss Barnett—I saw her in the obits this past week."

Reeve set the cars down. "Eph, you're so bad," he said.

"Yeah, sure. There's got to be only 'bout five people out there. I just can't see well enough to check," Ephraim continued, interest peaking. "It's too bright. We need to get closer. The pool should work."

He shifted his gaze back to Reeve, and there was a familiar glint there. The one that made Reeve squirm, feel pinned in a way he could not explain.

"But Dad got so mad the last time he caught us down there. You know he doesn't like us being out by the pool. Especially not to spy on the funerals. They're *private*," Reeve told him, putting an emphasis on the word "private."

Mom and Dad sometimes used other words to describe Ephraim's fixation with the cemetery when they thought he couldn't hear. Reeve, for his part, thought Ephraim was just bored. If there had been other kids in the complex, or if they owned bikes, or lived closer to their friends, then maybe things would be different. But it was just them, their scant neighbors, and the graves. Reeve didn't blame Ephraim for being the way he was. He didn't think their parents should, either.

"He can screw off," Ephraim scoffed. "Mom, too."

"You shouldn't say that."

"Alright, kid. Jesus. They just need to mind their own, that's all I'm getting at. Now, let's book it before Mom and Dad notice."

Reeve glanced between his cars and Ephraim, whose face now bore an expectant look. He bit his lip and then abandoned them for good, following the other boy out the door. The living area was steeped in their parents' voices, carried over from their bedroom, which were edged with something Reeve could not quite name. Something sour.

Ephraim was already tense by the time they crossed the threshold, shoulders up by his ears, and Reeve knocked their hands together to try and settle him. His brother didn't spare him even a backwards glance.

Outside, it was an ugly evening.

Reeve slit his eyes against the sun, which burned bright and hot as he and Ephraim each took the steps two at a time downstairs. The pool area was deserted, the water's surface caked with brittle leaves and dried-out cicadas. Reeve could almost cut the humidity with his teeth. It wasn't long before sweat began to gather at his temples, slipping along his cheeks to wet his lips.

The funeral was being held on the other side of the wire fence that separated the complex from the cemetery, which wilted beneath the heat.

The service was louder here, as Ephraim had predicted, and it was indeed for Miss Barnett, the elderly, bad-tempered clerk who worked the register at Al's General Store. She'd had it out for Ephraim ever since she'd caught him red-handed with several candy bars shoved down the front of his jeans last year. Dad had been so mad that Ephraim walked funny the next two days, welts up and down his back and sour-faced with shame. After that, the older woman never failed to spare their family either a sneer or veiled remark whenever they shopped there.

Yeah, Reeve couldn't say he was too sorry she was dead.

He didn't feel good about it, but it was the truth. Ephraim didn't seem to feel any different, either. He just laughed and reclined back on a lounge chair to watch the proceedings unfold.

As the procession wore on, Ephraim withdrew a pack of cigarettes and lit one. It was his newest rebellion. He'd bought them off some older boys who sold them by the track at the junior high for extra cash. Reeve didn't like them, but if his brother was going to have one, then he was, too.

Ephraim handed him one and they sat there and smoked together as the sky darkened in slow gradations, while the figures that surrounded the grave opposite became ever more indistinct. As though they were shapes, rather than people. It made the scene look all the lonelier for it, and Reeve's earlier callousness now seemed to him somewhat cruel. He could compare it only to the way he'd felt after Ephraim had squashed a small toad beneath his heel while they were out at the quarry together earlier in the summer. That dirty, wrung out feeling. The shame. How the poor little toad had done nothing to deserve it other than be in the path of the wrong giant. The bad fortune of it all.

His brother had laughed then, too.

"Christ, Reeve," Ephraim said, finally, "let's go in. I'm getting bored, and 'sides, Mom and Dad are probably winding down by now."

He put out his cigarette into the concrete, and Reeve did the same. He did not look back at the silhouettes cloistered around Miss Barnett's grave. He knew he wouldn't like what he saw.

They walked back around the pool, and Ephraim had that look on his face again. The one that never meant any good for Reeve, or the toads of the world for that matter. Reeve waited for what felt like the inevitable foot to drop. Ephraim chose that moment to sling an arm over his shoulders, and Reeve tensed up even more at that.

Ephraim's grip tightened. "There, kid, look, they've all left. She's all alone now, just like she deserves."

Reeve turned to watch the procession of shadows across the lawn. It really did look lonely. Unbearably so. His earlier disdain evaporated entirely then, and in its place was that dirty feeling from before, which rose up and out of him like a sickness.

Ephraim leaned in closer, and he heard his brother laugh. It was a mean, ugly noise, and reminded Reeve of their dad at his worst. "God, you always fall for this shit," he barked out, and pushed him backwards into the pool.

He fell. The suddenness of it was more terrifying than the pain. In between one breath and the next, the sun was gone. Then all he knew was chlorine.

He inhaled on reflex and felt his throat tighten around an influx of water. It burned. More than anything, it burned. Reeve thrashed, unable to get a good enough rhythm to break the surface and felt Ephraim's heel press his head further down. There was another laugh, distorted by the water in his ears.

Maybe he didn't realize how scared Reeve was. Or maybe he did, and just didn't care. It didn't matter; his gut rolled with blind panic regardless. Reeve reached out, grasping for something, anything, to hold onto, and when that just so happened to be a leg, he accidentally pulled his brother into the pool.

He heard a dull thud as Ephraim's head cracked against the side. Reeve continued to gasp and retch as he latched onto his brother, trying to get his head above water. But even then, he couldn't seem to quite make it, and black began to encroach at the edges of his vision. The last thing he could recall was his mother's pale arms reaching towards him as he sank, ghost-like, and the feeling of weightlessness as she carried him upwards—

***

His hands fumbled for the tap.

Reeve let out a low, shuddering breath. He didn't know how long the faucet had been on, or how long he'd been there, in the restroom at work, only that he'd been paralyzed over the sink for some time. His fingers were cold, pruned.

He thought back to that evening so long ago, over sixteen years now. Miss Barnett's newly tilled grave. The sunset. Ephraim's laughter. The bitter echo of their parents' voices. The past, he'd learned, was inescapable.

He exhaled and stared down at the soap that circled the drain. It was the water, he thought. There was something about it that had the ability to transport him elsewhere, lost in his memories, which would come on suddenly and overwhelm him. They were so, so real. Even the feeling of moisture on his skin, faint as it was, would sometimes take him back to that day. He'd hear cicadas, smell the pool, and Ephraim's voice as it drowned alongside him.

Reeve would always be reminded of how he had killed his brother. It was impossible to forget when the suggestion was around him every day.

"Hey, Scarlet," a voice called out. "You going to finish sometime today or what?"

Reeve jerked at the noise. It was one of his coworkers—a man in his late twenties with neatly-parted hair and small, almost colorless eyes. *Hoyt.* They had gone to high school together. He'd been popular then and popular now, having just vacillated from keggers to dinner parties.

It was funny, Reeve thought, how they couldn't have been more different. If Hoyt embodied the quarterback turned sales jockey, then Reeve had become the town's own bad myth. The face in the dark. When people remembered he was there, that he existed, their thoughts invariably turned to Ephraim's death. Reeve may not have been punished by the law, but that didn't mean he'd emerged unscathed in the court of public opinion. Everyone made it obvious what they thought of him. Always.

And yet he, like Hoyt and so many others, had remained fixtures within Carthage. No leaving, no nothing. Reeve was but a minor character in the mundane pantheon of bookkeepers and secretaries who drifted throughout Gadfly Industrial each day. He tried to imagine how it felt to be Hoyt, or any other guy like him for that matter. The picture didn't materialize.

Hoyt cleared his throat. Reeve realized then that the other man had been waiting for him to respond. He was still hunched over the restroom sink, palms poised above the tap as if in prayer. Hoyt's eyes roved over him until a crease formed between his brows. His face shifted. It was that look. The one where people saw him, really *looked* at him, and wished they hadn't.

"Freak," Hoyt muttered when he received no response, knocking shoulders with Reeve as he left. The door swung shut behind him with a decisive *click.*

Reeve turned over the word "freak" in his head. How many times had he been called that, he wondered; by his parents, by Ephraim, and by every other goddamn neighbor, classmate, and coworker he'd known over the years. The only person who'd ever used it without malice had been Neal.

But after the mess with his dad, and then later with social services, Neal had disappeared. The last Reeve saw him had been that final June afternoon they'd spent out beneath the bleachers together, where everything had been good and right in his life for the first and last time. Neal could be dead for all he knew. He'd never been able to track him down, not then and not now, with a decade gone by. He'd tried, though. If he ever met him again, he'd tell Neal that he'd tried.

He left the restroom with a heavier gait than he'd entered with and felt eyes on him as he returned to his desk. There was laughter, too, and he guessed that Hoyt must have considered their brief encounter strange enough to be conversation worthy. Reeve felt his shoulders slump forward and busied himself with some overdue invoices. The chatter around him ebbed and flowed from then on, and he tried not to listen for his name in it. He knew from experience he wouldn't like what he heard.

Reeve's felt himself grow more sullen and withdrawn the longer the workday wore on, and he tried to distract himself with ledgers and numbers as much as he was able. Reeve's scheduled smoke breaks were his sole respite, and when the time came for lunch, he ate in his car alone.

As usual, he was the last to leave that evening, kept behind by quarterly reports and a preference for avoiding the daily exodus of workers. When he finished, Reeve was greeted by a deserted parking lot. It was darker than usual for the hour, and bitterly cold. The first snow of the year hadn't yet arrived, despite being over a week deep into November. Only day after day of near-freezing rain. The single working streetlight present guttered in and out, bathing the area in shadow figures.

Reeve lit a cigarette and smoked it until the filter burned hot between his fingers. The routine was its own relief, and he supposed, an homage to Ephraim, whom he still associated with the taste, the scent. He moved to discard it and watched the still-lit end work itself out on the asphalt until all that remained was him and the anemic black.

The silence in this place, his home, his life, was so absolute, so impenetrable, that there were days when Reeve wondered whether he was even alive. He was nothing. A nothing person. Sure, people would look at Reeve, and talk about him, his family, but their eyes saw right through him—regarding him either with clinical detachment or something he could interpret only as disgust. The same disgust directed at house vermin or insects. Things both unwanted and feared.

The message was so clear it was physical; it pressed in all around him until his head felt so full it could pop. *You do not matter. You are the dirt on my boots. The mold in the kitchen grout. You exist, but you are not like us. Not at all.*

Reeve was caught between that hunger for kinship, its pain, and fear at what being known would mean, still wondering which was worse—their hate or their indifference?

He slouched back to his car, parked in an isolated spot behind the office building. Here the gravel was pitted and uneven, and just beyond the parking lot's northernmost edge, past the brush, the ground deepened into a pit.

The occasional sinkhole would sometimes open in town, eat a vehicle or invert a yard. It was commonplace enough. Carthage, Oklahoma was built around a mine system, after all, and sinkholes were just another side effect of many in the Tri-State Mining District that comprised the eastern intersection of Oklahoma, Missouri, and Kansas. There had been lead and zinc in the ground not too long ago, and for decades, everyone and their families worked as subterranean vampires until it was sucked dry and abandoned.

Then came the mass departure of ex-miners to the meatpacking plant in nearby Maidenhead. After, what remained was a skeletal network of tunnels that spiderwebbed beneath the entire town like a minefield, and the leftover debris known as "chat" that surrounded Carthage's perimeter, invaded its parks and streets. The byproducts of their own underworld.

Reeve ground out his cigarette and exhaled.

If Ephraim was here, he'd fill the quiet up with his dirty jokes and laughter. He'd say something, anything. The air would never be dead. For his part, Neal would comfort him, bring up the latest NASCAR race or local gossip to entertain him, distract him. He'd do the talking, and Reeve would be the conversation's quietly pleased recipient.

His current and only acquaintance was Maze, but she was nearly as much a mystery to him as everyone else was. Sometimes, he thought she visited him just to feel better about her own life, and in a way, he didn't blame her.

Reeve drove home in silence. No music, no radio programs. Just the engine, and his own subdued breaths. This lasted until he heard raised voices when he pulled into his driveway. If Reeve were a more expressive man, he would have groaned. Zebadiah and Heddie, his neighbors, were at it again.

Their trailer homes were near enough to where he could hear every argument they had as if it were held in the room over. Not to mention their kids and animals, too. Tonight, the two mutts were chained to a post in what passed for their backyard, barking at anything that so much as twitched. Loud cartoons and children's laughter bled out onto the street, punctuated by an errant shriek. *Again*, he thought. He laid his head on the steering wheel and counted to ten.

There were books on grief. How to cope. He had a stack in his kitchen. They emphasized therapy. Self-actualization. Multi-step processes. Religious enlightenment. Maze had given them to him after reading through each at the recommendation of her boyfriend, some older guy who was into philosophy. Reeve tended to run his fingers along the creases where she'd once dog-eared the pages, and tried to let whatever she had found so meaningful on the page set in.

Diffusion, he'd been told, was the word for it.

He was still reading, and still waiting. Wondering what it was she saw in them. He wanted, desperately, to understand how he could fix himself. He wanted there to be a book out there, somewhere, that held all the secrets he'd been looking for. Reeve wanted to not feel broken for once in his life.

Heddie screamed at Zebadiah again. It was something about being home late, or whether she'd seen him out by the Blue Room Club when he was supposed to be at work. Then the low, rough intonation of Zebadiah's voice. After a moment, a plate shattered against a wall. Heddie began to cry, a high-pitched whine. Reeve would pity her more had he not seen her take it out on the animals and the kids, not to mention himself whenever she got the chance.

Jesus, don't they get tired of this? Reeve rubbed his eyes, exhausted and feeling irritation slip through. Yet he knew from experience there was nothing to be done.

Reeve had confronted the couple. Once. Years ago, back when they'd first moved to Carthage. It had been late, he recalled. The TV was turned to some old cowboy movie for his dad, who'd been house-bound ever since he got the oxygen tank. Even past the gunfire and heavy orchestral cues, their arguments had seeped into the living room and oozed between the slats in the walls like water from the pores of a sponge.

His dad stared, unaffected, at John Wayne and Robert Duvall onscreen, while drool pooled and coagulated into a pale crust at the corner of his mouth. The cancer meds had him more out of it than usual. Where was the proud man of his youth, he'd wondered. The one his mom had once called "baby" and "Amon, darling."

But he couldn't relax. Not like this. Reeve peeked through the curtains and watched their silhouettes bleed into each other over and over, and how hers would inevitably yield to his every time. He'd heard around that their names were Zebadiah and Heddie. That they'd just moved to Carthage from someplace further west, like T-Town or Muskogee. Maybe they didn't know about his past. Maybe they'd listen to him. If he was polite about it, that was. They could even be… something. Acquaintances, maybe.

He got to his feet and was outside before he could talk himself out of it, disturbing a few of the stray cats that loitered around the front steps. There had been a town-wide infestation ever since the pound shut down, but Reeve liked having them around. He fed the growing cluster whatever extra food he had on hand, and there was one particular black tabby that stuck close by. Reeve called her Selene, whereas the others were collectively referred to as "Cat."

He walked across the lawn and onto Zebadiah and Heddie's porch, where he lingered for a moment, mouth dry with—something. Anxiety, he supposed. It was sour. Metallic, even. Like a bad penny. Reeve swallowed.

He waited for someone to notice him. For Zebadiah to emerge as a tall shadow in the doorway, or an appearance from Heddie, whose eyes would be pale and searching. But nothing happened.

The tension he'd built up over the past half-hour seeped out of him the longer he stood there, an unwanted ghost, until Reeve was left feeling empty and somewhat sick. His hands trembled where they were fisted at his sides.

He was better off for not saying anything. Had to be. Carthage was a poisoned well for Reeve. The entire town knew about what he'd done to Ephraim, or were soon made aware, and no one besides Neal had ever tried to look beyond his past. He was a fool for thinking they would be any different.

He almost left, then. His dad wasn't lucid enough at that point to call him out if he walked home without getting into it. He'd be in that same damn chair, with that same damn look on his face. There would be no consequences. No dirty looks or muttered remarks. No hushed, quietly furious, "Rephidim Elwood Scarlet" from him, his Christian name laced with disappointment. His dad hadn't even noticed him leave to begin with. It would be easy, even.

In his distraction, Reeve hadn't noticed that Zebadiah had finally come to the door. The other man cleared his throat and leveled him with an appraising look when his appearance was registered. This close, there was something about him that immediately put Reeve on edge.

"Evening, hoss. Mind telling me what you're doing on my porch?" Zebadiah said coolly.

He didn't unlatch the screen divider. There was dip caught in the crook of his mouth, and when his lips pulled back into a smile, it revealed crowded, nicotine-stained teeth.

Behind him, Heddie could be seen further back in the trailer's common area, but the kids were noticeably absent. Reeve's frustration evaporated and was replaced by the same dull panic from before. He wanted nothing more than to leave. Zebadiah's eyes were heavy upon him.

Reeve swallowed. "I was just fixing to knock."

"Sure." Zebadiah sipped at his beer.

He had a funny way of speaking. Each time Zebadiah sucked in a breath and released it, his tongue flicked out a staccato *tht tht tht* against his teeth before words emerged.

"I, uh, live next door." he said. "Name's Reeve."

"Zebadiah," the other man said after a long pause. "I'd say it's good to meet you, but I don't exactly know what you want. And it's a little late for a welcome, don't you think?"

"I apologize. I know the time ain't exactly the best. I just wanted to ask if you could keep it down, is all."

Zebadiah paused at that. He looked amused. There was an animal cunning in his gaze. "Look neighbor, I know I'm new around here, but that don't make it your business what I do in my home. Now leave us be."

"It's just that my dad's sick—"

"That sure is awful. Still ain't your business."

"I understand, but—"

"*Reeve*," Zebadiah tested the name. Tasted it. "Like I said before, I'm new to Carthage. I think I know who you are, though. I've heard about you, Mister Reeve Scarlet. You're that guy who killed his brother." His voice was calm with a sinister edge.

Reeve felt something in his expression shift at the accusation. Fracture. It seemed Ephraim's death was a weakness he could not help but expose to the world.

Natural-born opportunist that he was, Zebadiah picked up on this at once.

"Yeah, you are. I can see it in your face. How's your old man feel about living with you? Not too great, I'd reckon. Not after that. So, I think y'all got bigger problems than us. I don't want to see you over here again, or else I'll call the good people over at the sheriff's office. I'm sure you're familiar by now after everything."

Zebadiah was still smiling. He had the look of a man who knew he'd won hand over foot with little effort. Further back, Heddie's eyes glittered knowingly. Reeve's throat closed at that and worked around an aborted breath. He jerked his head in Heddie's direction in an attempt at cordiality before returning once more to the suffocating dark—back to the house where his dad's remnants awaited him.

He said nothing to Amon as he passed through their living room. The end credits to the movie flashed across the TV screen. Reeve put in a new tape. Wiped the spittle from his dad's mouth. Thought about how old and small he looked sitting there. How pathetic. Reeve remembered how his dad's presence used to dominate every room he entered. The strong timbre of his voice and the power in his hands. He wondered what that man would think of this one, or if he'd even want to live like this.

In that moment, Reeve could no longer bear to look at Amon anymore or listen to his neighbors' renewed arguments. He didn't want to think about how right Zebadiah had been about him. About everything. Because he *was* right, and that's what hurt the most.

His dad may not have hated him, but he'd never forgiven him for what he'd done. The town's memory ran long, too. It was an old grudge, the kind of wound that had scabbed over but never healed. The kind that was still picked at just enough to draw blood. He was the guy who killed his brother, and no one would ever forget. Even years later, he felt watched. Always watched.

There were eyes everywhere.

He felt it, then. The familiar urge. It began somewhere deep in his chest and soon migrated to his throat, where it remained until he nearly asphyxiated with need.

11

Reeve clutched at the door frame. His hands trembled. He bit his tongue so hard he drew blood, but the call persisted still. He was caught somewhere between dread and ecstasy at what he was about to do, as he had never been able to deny himself. It was an itch in his brain to which surrender was inevitable. He released the frame and stumbled towards the bathroom, feet dragging along the carpet.

He heard the tap squeak before he identified the obscene slip of water across his skin, and he shuddered and twitched beneath the shower spray. Ephraim returned to him upon contact, like he always did when Reeve punished himself like this, his dark laughter echoing off the tiles. And it was almost like his brother was alive again, if only for a moment, brought back in pieces as the humid air suffused the room.

Reeve didn't understand why he needed this. Why grief seemed so impenetrable, inescapable, necessary. Maybe there was no reason. Just that his brain was corrupt, and that its savage turnings could only be quelled by pain.

After his clothes were soaked through, and Ephraim's presence had faded until all that remained was the cold and the wet and the shame, Reeve turned the tap off and collapsed in a heap in the tub. He leaned over, reached into the cabinet, and withdrew a discarded cigarette carton and a crumpled matchbook. He compulsively chain-smoked through the five that remained, crushing the ends into his loafers.

The *skitch* of the match being struck was the only sound besides the word that reverberated throughout his head in the aftermath. Pathetic.

Now, three years later, Reeve considered that night yet again. What he had called himself in the aftermath. *Pathetic.*

He exited the car and trekked through the overgrown grass. The moon was a waning crescent. The drooping double-wide that had been his home for the past fifteen years did not welcome him. It never had, not since it had come to replace the apartment with too many rooms, too many memories.

His family moved here after Ephraim died, but it wasn't long before his mom left, too. She hadn't said a thing to Reeve about it being his fault, not directly, and his dad never spoke about the fight they'd had the night she stormed out the door, never to return. But he knew he was responsible.

Reeve saw her a few times after, each visit held at a Dairy Queen in Okmulgee, where she'd moved following the divorce. These ended when

Reeve got to be in the eighth grade, substituted with phone calls until she got hit by a drunk driver while changing a tire off the side of I-35.

Like Ephraim's death and Neal's departure, that night dominated most other memories. It had been his sophomore homecoming, and the whole town was adorned in lights and streamers and filled with girls and boys wearing elaborate mums and garters on their chests and biceps, respectively. Reeve attended the proceedings as a perfunctory attempt at normalcy, standing in the back of the gym wearing his dad's too-big sport coat and bolo tie. He stared at his feet and tried not to think about how much he'd rather be anywhere else, though it grew on him a little the longer he stayed.

Attending had been an impulsive move. Reeve had mentioned the dance without thinking, but the surprised, almost pleased look that crossed his dad's face when he told him he might go cemented his decision, though, and he purchased a ticket at the door from a pimple-faced girl who sat behind him in Geometry. She turned her nose down at him but could do nothing more.

Inside, it was dark in the gymnasium, lit only by flashing, multihued lights. Students were hustling along to a woman's voice that crooned "Barracuda" over the speakers. The few staff members present congregated in the corner, looking tired and entirely disinterested in the bodies entwined together on the gym floor. The punch was colored neon blue, the snacks powdery, stale.

And for a while, it was almost as though he was normal, drinking punch and tapping his heels to the music. He didn't even hear the group approach until it was too late. There was a push on his back, suddenly, and Reeve stumbled, turning towards the source on instinct. It was the usual suspects: Hoyt, Lynda, Trinity, and Dillon.

Reeve made a move to get closer to where the teachers were, but was stopped by Lynda, who dragged her nails up and down his shirtfront with a coy expression. "Heya," Lynda said, simpering, before pushing him towards the others.

Hoyt stuck his leg out and tripped him, causing Reeve to plunge forward and collide with the edge of the punch table. He then tumbled onto the floor and gasped for air, the room spinning around him.

The other boy loomed over Reeve, smiling. His friends joined in, too, until a circle had formed around him. Glitter snowed down like rain.

"No hard feelings, Scarlet. We just don't want you getting any ideas."

Hoyt leaned in and set one shiny oxford onto his chest. "No ideas," Reeve gasped when the heel dug in expectantly. "None."

The music swelled and ebbed into something pulsating, intense, weird. Soon, a male voice warbled out about psychos and murderers. This caused laughter to erupt amongst the group, and they began crooning along at him.

He took the opportunity to stagger upright and drag himself away from them. Reeve clutched at his front and limped out the side door, collapsing against the wall and feeling the brick cut into his back as he sat there and heaved. The mocking chorus stalked him into the night. Tears pricked at his eyes, and he rubbed them away, angry at himself for letting it get to him.

I wasn't even doing nothing, he thought. *I was just there.*

He heard a clatter from around the turn, back where the walkway led to the baseball field and outdoor restrooms. Reeve poked his head around the corner, hoping that it wasn't more of Hoyt's crowd.

It wasn't any of them; instead, he saw a dark figure hunched over a trashcan, lit match in hand. A second later, flames emerged from within, illuminating the only other person with a reason to ditch the dance. Back before he was Neal, *Reeve's Neal*, he had simply been Vásquez. And there Vásquez was.

Vásquez tipped his head back and took a long drink from a flask, which he tucked back into his jacket before lighting a cigarette in the blaze. And that wasn't the end of it, either, because he picked up a handful of loose gravel off the ground to throw at the chain-link fence. He kicked at the metal links after, swearing and muttering to himself. He had a familiar directionless energy about him.

I see you, Reeve wanted to say. *I think I even get you a little.*

His abdomen twinged, and Reeve was pulled back to reality. He couldn't take another beating, not tonight, and certainly not from Vásquez.

His dad said nothing when he returned home, but he nonetheless handed Reeve an ice pack and helped him out of the suit jacket and tie. They watched *Jeopardy* together until the phone rang. It was unusual; hardly anyone ever called them, and certainly not at this time of night. His dad rose to answer, and that was it.

Reeve watched the grief play out in real time, felt its physical presence encroach upon the trailer. His dad, who'd never remarried or even dated after his mom, just slid down the wall by the phone hook and began sobbing hysterically. Reeve had never seen him cry before or since, not even when Ephraim died.

His thoughts rolled to a stop, pulling him back to this current lonely night in what could have been any other winter of his adulthood. There was no point in thinking any more about these things. He banged his head once against his front door, sighing, and then let himself in.

Inside, it was quiet. His dad was dead now, had been for years. There was no program on the TV or record spinning slow and sweet on the turntable. Reeve disliked music for the most part. He didn't watch tapes or cable anymore.

For his part, Reeve didn't own much. The items that took up most of the space had belonged to his dad, and his dad alone. It was hard to throw dead people's things away, though, especially when they were all you had left of them.

Things began to accumulate inside the trailer after his mom first packed her bags. It had always been cluttered, but it was different in her absence; where before the books, tapes, and records had been relegated to boxes and shelves around the rooms' perimeter, they then began invading the living area, kitchen, and master bedroom. New items appeared, too, nonsensical finds like baby toys his dad found abandoned outside, emptied cardboard food containers, and plastic grocery bags.

He didn't understand the *whys* or *hows* behind the behavior. Reeve just knew that they were important, meaningful in some weird, obscure way, and so he resolved to maintain the collection as best he could even in his dad's absence. It was the least he could do.

Enough of the hoard had been relocated from the living area to Reeve's former bedroom for him to move around semi-comfortably. There was no room for him inside, so he'd set up shop in the attached garage.

His own relics were few: one poster of Cale Yarborough, faded with age; one solitary shelf; a few milk crates; and, most importantly, books. Hundreds of them, situated in neatly organized columns wherever he had space. Each had been annotated to some degree, and bookmarks, paper scraps, and notecards yellowed with age protruded from within the pages.

Throughout them one title was ubiquitous: *Prometheus in Exile*. The cover was that of a man posed in contrapposto, face half-smothered by shadow. There was the suggestion of grief in his features. All harsh lines and twisted, inverted grooves.

He had at least six copies of the novel, presiding over them like a dragon its gold since it had gone out of print last year. If asked, Reeve could not articulate what, exactly, drew him so strongly to this novel. It was important to him in a way that was difficult to explain.

He set his briefcase and coat on the kitchen counter. Sleep would not come for hours yet, even without his neighbors' ruckus. Reeve deliberated between reading and working on his car—not the Honda Civic he drove to and from work, but, rather, the dark red 1976 Chevrolet Chevelle Laguna that had long since been abandoned to perpetual restoration.

The far side of the attached garage was its current purgatory.

Reeve didn't think he'd ever get behind the driver's seat again, not when he wanted it so badly. But Neal loved that car. He couldn't destroy something Neal loved. No matter how much he needed to suffer.

Before he could set to work, he proceeded with his nighttime routine. Reeve checked every window latch and doorknob three times, and then again because he wasn't sure whether he counted right the first time, and not getting it right meant he'd be thinking about it until he made sure the locks were done right.

He knew it didn't make sense. Objectively, logically. In this dark, old trailer, he could acknowledge it as necessary, but on the outside, it felt a little like superstition. The truth, however, was that giving into his compulsions was so much easier than fighting them.

Besides, Reeve had learned what happened when he left things to chance.

He returned to the kitchen and fixed a perfunctory meal, steepling his hands and when he was finished. If he'd just stayed underwater that day, maybe things would be different, and Reeve wouldn't have set these cosmic events into motion. Perhaps his parents would still be here, and Ephraim would be married with a family of his own.

He unfastened his tie and rolled up his shirtsleeves, brushing back his untidy hair from his eyes. The car beckoned him.

As he laid his hands on the Laguna's engine block in a gentle near-caress and began the familiar care of a car that would never again be driven, Reeve wondered, not for the last time, if he was even alive. That maybe he had died in that pool with Ephraim, and now haunted Carthage like an uncommon ghoul—one that faded in and out of the afterlife, with neither present nor destiny. Just the murder, the past. His own bad luck.

Neal had been different, though. Not like Hoyt, Zebadiah, Heddie, or even Maze. Neal had made him feel real.

MAZE I

The thing about Waylon was he had to be a secret. He told Maze that people wouldn't understand if they knew, and he was right. Waylon so often was. It was a little strange, she thought, to go about her days and nights as though nothing changed when so much, in truth, had. Then again, everyone was entitled to a little selfishness sometimes.

Maze popped her gum. Douglas H. Cooper Senior High School dwindled in her rearview mirror, and when she turned a corner at the next light, it disappeared entirely. The world looked bleak in the ebbing afternoon: marked by dead trees, shrubs, and further back, chat piles that loomed large in the distance. Home wasn't far, and she pulled into her neighborhood with a rough twist that had her tires groan from the effort.

The street parking in her cul-de-sac was choked with familiar cars, and she could see their owners milling about inside through her front window. Maze's grip on steering wheel tightened, and she ground her teeth. *Vultures.* The air settled cold and heavy in her chest as she disembarked, gravel and leaves crushed beneath her boots. The atmosphere was almost funereal.

Maze could admit the house was a sorry sight.

Intricate weeds poked through cracks in the drive, and the lawn was dry, overgrown. Her garage-door hoop was rusted, its net half-desiccated. Maze hadn't touched a basketball in months, not since what happened with her dad, and she wondered whether it would feel the same between her hands, or whether the sense-memory had gone away with everything else.

They had to muddle through the repairs alone now, just she and her mom. Maze felt there was a lot to appreciate about someone in their absence, or, at least, that's what she had come to understand throughout the past six months. There was something to be said for such unlearning.

Maze rested her head against the doorframe and sighed. It wouldn't be long, she told herself, before she could leave and see Waylon again. Not long at all. Her watch beckoned to be examined, but she ignored it. The hands would only taunt her.

Thursday evenings were reserved for Reverend Gould alone.

The door snapped shut behind her and Maze was greeted by the familiar floral-patterned and box-dyed ornaments arranged throughout her living room. It had become the women's custom in recent months to congregate here to watch Gould's weekly sermons on KLO-TV.

Courageous Grace was exactly what one might expect from local broadcast televangelism. The public access set with overexposed lighting gave the program an awkward slant that was made worse by the sycophantic audience members that gasped or cooed on cue. The *Full House* laugh track would have been preferable. Anything else would've been, really.

The preacher and his wife weren't from Carthage, but they were kicking around the area—the station was over in nearby Maidenhead, and they hosted live events on their off days, everything from tent revivals to visiting sermons in local churches. These had become more frequent over eastern Oklahoma, with the next revival set to be held in Carthage.

Maze heard they were hoping to get a nationally syndicated slot on Christian Unified Network Television. *Hah.* There were already so many self-proclaimed preachers out in the world that it was hard to imagine these people had a place in any of it. Then again, here they all were, gathered in her living room week after week.

Putting on a brave face, she made her way to the kitchen, hooking her keys on the rung before returning to her usual viewing spot. No one had deigned to speak to her yet. They rarely did. Her presence was only tolerated because her mom had wanted Maze to get involved with the group.

Each Thursday after school, she slunk in like a dark-clad blight and folded herself into the most unobtrusive corner she could find to watch, seething, as someone preached a religion she did not and would not follow.

Her mom, Jessica, was a super fan, and even had Maze tape the sermons so they could rewatch them. Maze remembered when it had just been something to put on while her mom was knitting or doing a Bible study. Then she got more and more invested over time, mailing in checks to help fund whatever thing it was Reverend Gould needed, meeting up with the other mothers in the neighborhood that were likewise interested, until, well, *this.*

Maze herself had developed a Pavlovian-style hatred in response to the show; whenever she heard the little jingle or Gould's name called out, her teeth would be set on edge, and she'd get so mad she could spit.

Maze cut her gaze around the room, coming to rest on Jessica. They were mirror images of each other, with the same dark, curling hair and cool gray eyes. Her mom couldn't have been more than a foot away, yet the gap between them seemed to stretch wider, and Maze was struck by how easy it was to feel lonely without being alone. *I miss how well we knew each other,* she thought. *I was your mind reader; you were mine. And now it's all gone blank.*

Jessica, of course, said nothing.

Her mom and the women presided over their coffee table, which was dominated by pamphlets, flyers, letters, and half-finished signage, all promotional material for the congregation. Their husbands and sons were gathered over at some other sap's place two doors down. Not that this would have been rendered somehow more bearable with their presence.

It was almost funny, Maze thought. Just how much time and money these people spent on useless shit. But it wasn't. Not when she had to live with it. Not when it was her life.

Maze had seen cults on the news and read about them in the paper. Jonestown. The Manson Family. Rajneeshpuram. It was supposed to be crazy, out-there stuff. Esoteric groups filled with addicts, hippies, or desperate idiots. People who lived and died on the fringes. Not store clerks and housewives eating tuna sandwiches and discussing their kids' grades after work. Maybe that's how they all were in the beginning, she thought, normal. Right up until everyone around you started drinking the Kool-Aid.

After her dad's funeral, the church-folk had descended on them with grief casseroles and smiles. It was nice, so nice. To feel supported by people, their neighbors, and for them to see how much they were really going through it.

The weird shit had flown under the radar at first. It was the way things worked out in the boonies; people took up for Jesus every chance they got and didn't care whether anyone else wanted to hear about it. Then came the televangelism, and the sermons, and these weekly meetings. Her mom rolled into the loom of the spider's web.

Now there was this weird, desperate air about the group, a tension that was so palpable she could feel it grit between her teeth. Maze found no comfort in their faces or the words in their mouths. Just exhausted, angry. So, so angry. It was the kind of anger that never went away.

If it was up to Maze, she'd be in her room watching *Sleepaway Camp* on VHS or listening to Brain Dead's new album on her Walkman. Anything else, really. But even in her worst, most pissed-off moments, she hadn't been able to give up on her mom. And this was one of those things that, for whatever reason, was truly important to Jessica.

Maze glared at the wall. There were three portraits set above the mantle: Jesus Christ in his solemn, lenticular glory; a signed photograph of a genial-looking Ronald Reagan from his cowboy days; and, most prominently, the esteemed Reverend Aaron Gould.

Even in print, he projected a larger-than-life figure.

Gould was a tall, round man with a look on his face like butter wouldn't melt in his mouth. His eyes were a near-colorless blue, pupils two dark stars suspended between his grinning moon cheeks. His clerical collar was stark against the black of his shirt, which peeked through the lapels of a pristine white suit. This was the man who was supposed to lead them to salvation, somehow. Maze didn't quite get the appeal.

It was just something about him. Gould, that was. Maze's unease eked out from between her ribs every time she saw him emerge on screen. He was one slick-tongued televangelist among many, and by all rights, he should have been just another silly man in a flashy suit, strutting around as he belted out Bible verses to his audience.

But there was something about him that put her off. Maybe it was how empty his words were. The way he stared through her and everyone else as if they weren't even there. The hunger he cultivated in his audience until they were starved for his words.

This time last year, Jesus had yet to enter their home. Not as anything more than a man. Now he was much more. They had been Jews, once. Her mom wasn't one anymore. Maze didn't know what to call herself.

Her family had never been particularly observant even before Gould. Secular at worst, Reform at their most religious. There were no *shuls* close enough to warrant more than biannual trips to Temple Israel in Tulsa for Rosh Hashanah and Yom Kippur. The *Shabbat* was any other Friday evening. No *minyan* to *daven* with, either.

When she and her dad placed a hannukiah in the front window to observe the holiday a few years back, they woke in the night to a tremendous crash after a brick had been thrown through the glass. There was no message on it; there didn't need to be for them to understand.

It never left the basement after that.

"It's starting," an excited voice exclaimed, and Maze returned her attention to the TV and its acolytes.

When Gould's ecstatic face at last appeared onscreen, reflected in the rapt gazes of the other women, Maze wondered how they could be so certain. That Gould was the real deal and not another garden-variety quack. They all made promises it seemed difficult to deliver upon.

The man in question stepped onto the stage. He was dressed in his usual bone-colored suit, clerical collar, and cowboy boots. His bald head gleamed beneath the stark lighting. Dollar signs practically flashed in his eyes like a cartoon character. Maze rather thought he resembled a bowling pin on legs.

"Good evening, everyone," Gould announced with a genial look. Then he began the sermon how he always did. "Now, open your eyes. Your heart. More than that, your soul, too. And everything in turn will be opened to you. This is God's way.

He cleared his throat. "The Bible is clear about the end. It's coming. You could even say it's past due." Gould paused and a few chuckles echoed throughout the studio. "But what folks don't know is *when*. That's the real question. It's all in here, though," he continued, tapping the Bible's cover one, two, three times. "They just weren't being guided by the right shepherd. I told you the truth was coming. The truth that no one else will or can tell you. I'm here today to get into that answer.

"The numerology in Revelation is guided by three key numbers: four, twelve, and seven. The four corners of the earth; the four living creatures by God's throne. The seven seals. Twelve angels at the twelve gates. Four, twelve, seven. Twelve and seven equals nineteen. Nineteen and four equates to nineteen ninety-four.

"That's the year. Ten represents totality in the book. Ten diadems on the ten horns of the beast. Ten, ten. October 10, 1994. The date is set.

"I warn you now: get your affairs in order. You've got the next two years to do so. Everything around us—our jobs, our money, our things… it ain't coming with us into the Kingdom, so please, consider tithing to the ministry so that we can better spread the Word."

Nice to see you citing your sources, Maze thought.

After that, she tuned him out from then on and tried not to pay her watch any mind, feeling a little self-conscious about how much she was looking forward to seeing Waylon. Near the end, her mom and the other women had their checkbooks at the ready to service him like good little concubines in this bizarre "whores for Christ" scenario. It was more than money to them, she'd since intuited, these were seeds planted in the hopes that one day divine favor would be reaped.

No sickness had yet been healed, nor wealth gained. Their lives remained the same. Yet still they gathered here like clockwork each week to watch Gould beg for cash and talk nonsense. Maze sometimes got the sense that so long as they thought they were going to heaven, what happened here didn't matter as much anymore.

After all, they were the ones who had lobbied the town to put up money for Gould to make an appearance, renting out the old fairgrounds to him for the event. The gathering of women spent their time together and apart working on signs, leaflets, and other various forms of advertising for the event. Maze had seen them posted over lost dog notices and even over the announcement for the canned food drive Cooper S.H.S. was holding.

The hour continued to elapse slow and miserably, with Maze's baseline irritation evolving into full-bodied discontent. When Gould exited the stage with a grandiose little two-step and a honeyed farewell, the group began to disperse. Maze rushed to leave.

Heddie, a newer member, one that Maze was less familiar with, set her dixie cup down and approached Jessica. Her hair was pulled into a severe bun near the base of her neck, which made her face appear almost skeletal. Just skin stretched tight over bone.

"They're trying to suppress the Word. They know it's the truth, that it could change things," her mom was telling another member seriously when the woman interrupted them.

"Jessica—phone?" Heddie asked, gesturing towards the kitchen. Ever since she first joined, she'd always called her husband around this time to check in.

"Go on ahead," Jessica said, after which Heddie nodded and walked away.

Maze unfolded herself from the chair and went to grab her car keys. The kitchen light hadn't been turned on. Heddie had the phone cord tangled in one thin hand. Her face was pressed up against the wall, features set in chiaroscuro. Maze could see the faint outline of a bruise around her left eye where it peeked through her makeup. Must've fallen or something.

"—Gould'll be here the Sunday after next. That should be the time to do it, I reckon. Half the town will be out to see him."

There was a low noise of assent on the other line.

"Yeah, I think—"

The keys jangled in Maze's hand. Heddie jumped at the noise and cut herself off. Then she licked her lips and smiled at Maze. It was a flash of teeth in the dark like the edge of a knife.

"—I'll be home a little later than usual. Bye now, honey," Heddie continued and hung up the phone with a loud *clink*. "Can I help you, Maze?"

Maze realized she'd been staring. "Uh, no. Sorry," she said and held up the keys to indicate why she was there.

When she passed by the counter on her way out and noticed the stack of bills, she sighed. Maze would need to go through them when she got back. Her job at the Burger Barn was bringing in more money, but she'd still need to bust out her mom's checkbook to balance out the rest. *Ugh.*

Maze meandered back out into the living area, where she gave her mom a peck on the cheek. Jessica withdrew a little from the gesture, not leaning into it, not pausing her conversation once. The sole indicator as to her continued displeasure was the slight thinning of her lips. So, she was still mad.

It wasn't enough for her just to be here, as she'd realized in recent weeks. Jessica needed more from her. Things she couldn't give. Like real belief in this insane televangelism shit. A smiling face free from makeup.

Christ. Why was she stupid enough to think things would change? No one could freeze her out quite like her mom. Maze wondered when the thaw would come, if ever.

"See you," she muttered under her breath and left without further comment.

The sun burned low as she crossed the lawn back to where her car was parked. The '88 wood-paneled Chrysler LeBaron was a damn eyesore, that was for sure, but it had belonged to her dad, so Maze felt obliged to take care of it now. Reeve was good about helping her out with that, even though he despised the station wagon. He could be particular about certain things, with cars being first and foremost among them.

Maze slid behind the wheel and deposited her purse in the passenger seat, next to her Burger Barn uniform and backpack, which presided over a sundry collection of lipstick tubes, vigorously worn-down eyeliners, novelty sunglasses, and, somewhat incongruously, a faded OU sweatshirt (also her dad's). She slipped on a purple, star-shaped pair and turned the key in the ignition. Pantera's *Vulgar Display of Power* immediately saturated the car, and the song "Fucking Hostile" was her parting gift to the women as she set off for the evening.

Her mom thought she was spending the night at her friend Oralene's house. She wasn't. At least not in the way Jessica expected.

Oralene had agreed to cover for her on when asked, even though she still had no idea it was Waylon that Maze had been visiting. Her friend wouldn't approve—of that she was certain. Oralene was still holding out hope she'd get back together with Dean, her ex-boyfriend, and was reluctantly assisting in the charade out of loyalty as opposed to anything else.

Maze made the perfunctory gesture of parking her car out front and walking up the neatly paved path to her friend's front door. There was a "Coming!" from the inside, and then the lovely door with the lovely fall wreath swung open. Oralene pulled Maze down into a hug and led her to the dining room.

Oralene's placid nuclear family sat there, eating casserole at their nice dinner table, looking at the watercolor paintings Mrs. Kennedy had produced herself on the walls, their pristine China set spread laid across the table. Maze was suddenly, profoundly jealous that Oralene got to have this, that she had this and didn't even get how good she had it. But then Oralene showed Maze the seat they'd saved for her, and her two younger brothers smiled toothily at her, and Mrs. Kennedy rubbed her shoulder when she sat down, and Maze felt like the rottenest person on earth for ever having wished them ill will.

The food was still hot, thankfully, and delicious despite its relative blandness. Maze made small talk with them until it was time to do the washing-up, after which she and Oralene left for the latter's room. The two girls spent a few minutes fixing Maze's makeup, reviewing the clothes she'd chosen for the outing, and braiding her hair back before Oralene went in for the kill.

"You're all moony-eyed over this guy," she remarked, adjusting a bobby-pin on Maze's temple.

"Sure, if that's what you want to call it."

"I guess I just don't get why you're so zipped up about things. I can keep a secret, believe it or not."

Maze sighed. "I know. It's just... he wants it kept quiet. He has his reasons. And it's kinda nice, it being this way—like he's just for me."

"As long as you're sure," Oralene said after a pause, something serious flitting across her face.

Oralene knew that she was seeing someone older, someone she probably shouldn't be, and that there was more Maze wasn't telling her. The truth was that she was seeing *two* older guys, just for different reasons. Waylon was her man; Reeve was... well, she didn't really know what to call him. Her mentor? Friend? A Mr. Miyagi type? The guy she vented to every week like he was some therapist rather than Boo Radley?

Maze shrugged on a dark sweatshirt and pulled the hood over her head. "Yeah. I'm sure."

"If you say so."

Oralene hugged her and opened the window, which Maze hopped out of and ran around back to where the other girl's bike was locked up. As she pedaled away from her best friend and the perfect, wonderful family she got to have, under a near-moonless sky, Maze tipped her head back and let the wind drag itself up and down her face.

How could she tell anyone what was really going on? Maze didn't want to come off like a slut or get into why she did the things she did. Being questioned, talked down to—she hated it.

The trip was short.

Waylon lived in a shotgun-style house several streets over, which sat squat and unassuming beneath the stars. Maze turned onto the back end of the property and parked her bike close to the tree line. He was expecting her, leaving the back door cracked open with a stack of Ayn Rand doorstoppers. He was really into them, and even though Maze wasn't much of a reader outside self-help books and magazines, she found it wasn't so bad when they did it together.

He must have heard her arrive since he wandered out of the bedroom. Waylon was shirtless, smoking a joint, and had a copy of *Anthem* clasped in hand.

"Hey there," he called out, smiling a not-quite smile.

Maze unzipped her hoodie and let it fall to the floor, shaking out her braids. She met his gaze but didn't walk over, instead making her way to the gleaming Fender Stratocaster lounging on a stand in the corner. The guitar was named "Lucky." She was the only other female currently competing for Waylon's attention.

"Still haven't tuned this old broad?" Maze asked, flicking one of the strings. Then she stared at Waylon head-on, trying to look up at him through her lashes despite being taller.

"Hey," he said, mock hurt, "she's a lady. And you know damn well she's taken care of."

"Then she's the only lady here," Maze told him, looking at his bedroom meaningfully.

The tension between them turned hot in an instant, and Waylon pulled her into his room and bore her down hard into the mattress. Maze let herself be manhandled, situated to his liking. There was a tight, swooping discomfort ballooning within her chest that she ignored in favor of baring her throat to him.

"I can't believe you let me do this to you," he murmured against her skin. "Because you do, don't you? Let me have this."

Maze jerked out a nod, but it seemed he wanted her to go on and say it since his grip on her wrists turned painful during her silence. "I let you do this," she whispered.

"That's right, Bright Eyes."

The nickname scraped through her brain. He worked a rubber down his length, then he fucked her hard, dry, fast.

Maze grit her teeth and rubbed her clit until she clenched around him when she climaxed, causing Waylon to come and flop forward onto her chest. His breath was damp and warm where his cheek lay smushed against her sternum, and Maze shifted in discomfort. His slow-softening cock was still inside her. Eventually he got the memo and pulled out, tying off the condom and tossing it to the side.

He settled back into place, star-fishing over Maze and pulling his arms tight around her waist. Maze sighed and said nothing, trying to enjoy the mood. She knew she should just be happy someone like him put up with someone like her, but there were times when she just... struggled to get into it. The sex, some of the things he was interested in. The fact that everything had to be on his terms. Maze had always liked sex because sex came with intimacy, and it wasn't a dealbreaker that he couldn't make her come her brains out like her last boyfriend had, so long as they could share the afterglow.

Their connection was real. Mind to mind type stuff. They would talk about life and dreams and people while bathed in a shroud of smoke from a shared joint, laid back in his bed together. He'd push her, and she'd give in. Maybe Maze needed it, though, to be pushed like that. And Waylon was good about pushing her.

Waylon told her she was mature, an old soul, and that it was good she'd realized she needed to be around like-minded people. He understood she wasn't the same person she'd been before what happened with her dad, that in some ways it had rendered her as much of an adult as he was. Maze was certain she had some catching up to do when it came to him, and then it would all settle into place.

The day couldn't come fast enough.

"You're so easy," Waylon said, snaking an arm around her. "You never need anything."

"Thanks," she said because she *was* grateful, in a way. It was nice not to feel like a burden for once.

"I don't want to be the person who makes their problems other people's problems," Maze told him.

"Mm. That's what makes you so great."

Soon he fell asleep wrapped around her, Maze still awake and only somewhat sated from rubbing herself off. Their evenings together often ended this way. Maze wanted to talk with him, even if that meant hearing about some author older than dirt, but that could wait until next time. These topics were reserved for him the same way her feelings were reserved for

Reeve and Oralene, but Waylon didn't need to know that. The lines needed to be clear.

Turning towards Waylon, she examined his slack features and thought back to earlier, when Gould announced his forthcoming presence in Carthage. *Is it weird to invite your not-boyfriend to a tent revival?* The silence was answer enough.

Dean would have gone. He'd have hated it, but he would've gone. She was no "Bright Eyes" to him, though, and he'd made his choice. He chose *them,* not his own girlfriend—and, beyond that, best friend. Her hands clenched. Yeah, she was still hopping mad at him. Their time apart had dulled nothing.

Maze picked at a loose thread on the sheets. Reeve didn't have anything planned. He never had anything planned. Maybe she could ask him. Anything was preferable to facing the crowd alone. Obviously, they couldn't go together, but if they just so happened to run into each other, then… well, wasn't it her Christian duty to make sure he was welcomed to the fold? And the best part would be that her mom couldn't do anything about it without looking like a hypocrite.

Sure, Reeve was a weird one. He lived alone at the end of a desolate road near the town's southernmost edge. He had no real neighbors, just Heddie and her husband on one side, and some nameless elderly woman on the other. The lawn was bare. No crosses, no gnomes, no nothing.

He'd been difficult to approach. Not just on account of his history or whatever, but because there was something *off* about him. Maze couldn't really articulate what it was, something felt but not seen.

This is what she'd learned about him in the months since making his acquaintance: he had a routine. A monotonous daily routine that he adhered to without fail. Feral cats were the closest things he had to friends (besides her). He liked working on cars. It was perhaps the only thing he had any real passion for.

Reeve had these round, dark eyes. Crow's eyes. They were the only expressive thing about him. Everything else was subdued, severe; the heavy brows, scar-like mouth. His skin was so white it was almost tinged with blue, like cold milk.

Truthfully, Maze was waiting for the guy to go full-on Dahmer. But, hey, she'd take what she could get at this point. And maybe one day Maze would even get to be the star witness at his trial.

Maze had told him such one night while making a sandwich for herself in his kitchen. His single-wide was packed with shit, and the air inside had a heavy, undisturbed feeling about it, as though no one living had entered in some time. "Hey, you know Dahmer," she'd said, buttering a bread slice. When he gave her a blank look, she continued, "The cannibal? The guy who killed and ate a bunch of poor schmucks in Milwaukee?"

"What about him?"

I don't know, she didn't say. *Everything?*

"Nothing. Just thought of him for some reason."

Reeve's expression didn't change. "Alright," he said. And then they sat together in a not-uncomfortable silence.

They often ended up like that. Reeve couldn't really empathize with her. And neither did he have anything to offer her advice-wise. Maze would just stop by and talk to him—well, at him, most times—or they would sit there and *not* talk. Reeve was good at that, she thought. The not-talking. It could even be nice. Her mom was big on the nagging and the preaching and the apologies. She was always sorry for all the wrong things.

Reeve made her feel heard without having to say a word.

Despite this, she wondered whether she'd end up just like him if she didn't figure things out. Lifeless by choice, or whatever. Reeve wasn't as bad as everyone made him out to be, but he was a certified shut-in with more problems than all head shrinkers in the world could deal with.

Not that anyone could stop her from seeing him or Waylon. Maze was sixteen now, had been since this past February. Seventeen loomed on the horizon. She wasn't a girl anymore.

Sure, she might still be in high school and live with her mom, but there was more to her than people knew. Way more. And while she wasn't stupid enough to think that she could hide her boys forever, she'd try and keep a good thing going for as long as possible. You couldn't have a secret like this in a town this size for too long. Good thing her rep had been trashed for months.

It was midnight when she left Waylon's.

The ride back to Oralene's was quick, but she wasn't ready to turn in yet, so Maze produced her keys and slid into her station wagon for a ride around town. She bump started it and rolled down the street before letting the engine turn over for real.

Maze tugged her Sherpa-lined jacket tighter around her shoulders and shivered in the front seat until the LeBaron heated up. The stars burned darkly overhead as she drove aimlessly around Carthage, trying not to think about Waylon's hands, the play of light across his features, or her mom, whom she knew was curled up alone on their couch with a TV dinner, watching *Dynasty* reruns or taped *Courageous Grace* sermons. Alone, just like her.

Maze continued to drive. She passed the Burger Barn, Carthage's own answer to McDonald's and the reason her clothes reeked like grease four days out of seven; the illustrious Palace Movie House, purveyor of both stale popcorn and candy alike; the Blue Room, a club backlit by radioactive neon signs advertising "GIRLS GIRLS GIRLS" and "LIVE NUDES"; and, once she approached the edge of town, the Mirage Motor Inn, a motel past its prime that somehow managed to eke out a continued half-life time and time again.

The Blue Room still being open was truly a testament to how starved the town was for entertainment. Dingy and more than a little rough now, it had been a real hotspot a decade ago, and even had live bands that would play while women danced and rode poles and served drinks. And it was all good for a while. That was, until some bad pyrotechnics ignited the acoustic foam and lit the place up like a tinderbox.

She'd heard people didn't realize what was happening at first, figuring it was part of the show, so they didn't make a break for it until it was too late. The exit doors were all blocked off save for the front entrance, which people squeezed themselves through, with more and more getting stuck as those at the back kept pushing even as friends and coworkers got crushed into corners and trampled underfoot. The result was a stacked mass at the front, bodies upon bodies that thrashed, screamed, pulsated like an organ.

They would have felt the night air on their faces while they burned at the back.

This town had a history with fire. If she was superstitious, she'd say it was cursed. And some days, Maze thought she believed it was.

Maze figured that maybe, if she learned everything she could about this place, that one day she would find a way to escape it. The mine. The pollution. Everyone just taking what little they could get out of life.

Her grip on the wheel tightened. If she were to keep going, she would come across the old mining operation and see it unfold like a poisonous flower across the brush.

Most of the money from it was gone. She didn't know how long this—the remnants—would last. What had once been a modern and beautiful company town had descended into disrepair. Most work was found at the nearby meat packing plant over in Maidenhead, or at Gadfly Industrial Supply here in town. There were still boys at her school that planned on being miners, girls aiming to be their wives. To her, these people had been raised for a future that no longer existed.

Maze watched a sleek black car pull into the Mirage Inn's parking area, which idled there for a moment before its driver disembarked. His skin flashed deep bronze beneath the streetlights, which illuminated a tattoo that twined up his throat. Maze didn't recognize him. The Inn catered to truckers and the occasional lost, west-bound family on vacation, but he didn't appear to be either. He bled into the shadows like he belonged there.

As she turned around at Carthage's outer limits and wound back through its asphalt veins, Maze turned up Corrosion of Conformity's "Mad World" until she felt it in her teeth. The dirty vocals and convulsive gnashing and snapping of each instrument eroded the bad thoughts in her head until she could breathe again.

Maze rolled to a stop before her house. Just to check in before returning to Oralene's. The TV was on. It bled through the curtains in faint strokes, and she could hear Reverend Gould's voice spill out onto the lawn.

Maze rubbed at her forehead. Her mom exhausted her. Made her feel old and young at the same time. It wasn't that Jessica was a bad or mean person. She was sad. Just so, so sad. And Maze didn't know how to help her. The enormity of her grief was too much.

In books, movies, tragedy made people more than they were. It tested them, sure, but they always seemed to emerge better, braver, stronger. Maze was about the same as before, just broken in ways that let some innate ugliness that she'd managed to conceal up until now seep out.

Her dad would have known what to do, but he wasn't here, and wasn't that the fucking problem?

Back when her beliefs had first grown roots, Jessica had cried to her one night, reeking of cheap wine, that her dad was burning in hell. That him burning up was all she could think about; how she couldn't let Maze go the same way. *I don't believe in your hell* was all Maze could think, but she bit her tongue like a good daughter should.

How could Maze help her mom when she didn't even know how to help herself? They were both lost. Two people belonging to nothing and no one. Not really. What that preacher was selling a nice dream, and, in a way, she didn't even blame her mom for falling for it. She was after the same thing, in the end.

Maze just wanted something to believe in.

NEAL I

Neal was in town for a little over three days before he saw Reeve again.

He pulled into Carthage late Thursday night as the evening light guttered out around him, the once-familiar shops and houses passing by in a haze. The moon was but a thin sliver in the sky. There was a fierce wind out. The grind of the Road Runner's engine was a rich backdrop against the occasional rumble of rundown cars and trucks. It was beautiful in a way he could not explain.

The desk clerk recoiled at his appearance when he walked into the Mirage Motor Inn's lobby. Neal recognized her from high school. Lynda, he thought. Her hair had begun to fray at the temples, and there was some extra weight around her middle. The wedding ring on her finger was tarnished, cheap, and she worried at it each time she looked at him askance. Funny. He mostly remembered her being a two-faced bitch. How she'd laughed at him and called him *"Mutt"* like it was a joke. Lynda didn't seem to be laughing now.

"Neal Vásquez," she blurted out, flustered, then straightened herself. "You're back. Here, that is."

"Evening, Lynda," he said by way of reply, and inclined his head to her.

He watched with subdued amusement as she fought back the urge to interrogate him. She had been a notorious gossip back in high school, and it seemed nothing had changed. Neal wouldn't give her the satisfaction.

After the realization he didn't intend to divulge anything further, Lynda twisted her ring again. "Well, then. How can I help you tonight?"

"I'll take a single. Make it a week," he said, and put down a wad of cash between them. Her eyes widened at the amount but said nothing and handed him a set of keys after counting it out and keeping the change at his request. As he walked away, he heard her dial up the phone and launch into a discussion about him. God. She was so damn predictable he couldn't help but roll his eyes.

"You'll never believe it. Vásquez is—"

The door cut her off. He went and fished out his duffle bag from the Road Runner's trunk and drifted towards Room 18. It was small and musty smelling, but clean enough. The ceiling was mirrored, and the walls were papered in lurid blue and red fractals. There were sconces affixed at random intervals around the room, each shaped in the vague suggestion of an outstretched hand. He'd make do. Neal wouldn't be in town for long, besides. Ruth and Joseph were waiting for him back home, not to mention all the work he'd be missing in the interim.

He showered and dressed for bed perfunctorily. The TV had cable, thankfully, and Neal flipped through a few more serious channels before realizing he couldn't handle the heavy shit before bed. There was a UFF attack in Belfast. A mom set her baby on fire, claiming it was possessed by the devil. Then the coverage turned to the Lindhurst High School Shooting. Jesus, he didn't need this.

Neal instead settled for watching *Erotic Confessions* on Cinemax, which turned out to be the most tedious softcore porn he'd ever seen. He ignored the whining, lingerie-clad woman and tried instead to focus on the man's face, his glistening chest, his blissed-out expression while he rubbed one out.

After, Neal scrubbed a restless palm over his jaw and turned over onto his side, unsatisfied. He knew what tomorrow meant. It made his throat close. He'd see Reeve again. Neal had come back because Reeve deserved an explanation. Even now, well over a decade later. He wanted to give Reeve everything. He just wasn't sure if Reeve would let him, or if he even wanted the same things Neal did.

***

They had first met—really met, that was—not too far from the Inn, on a dirt-packed access road that led to nowhere and nothing, one cold Sunday morning late in the autumn of his junior year. His car had been pitched nose-first down a drainage ditch, the hood saturated in smoke, when Reeve Scarlet arrived.

Neal was still wasted from the night before, his face and hands covered with cuts that had yet to scab over. His whole body felt like a fresh bruise. He'd been too out of it to maneuver the car back onto the road and was at first content to drink what remained in his flask and languish there until someone drove by. But his jean jacket wasn't enough to keep out the chill, and the whiskey could only provide so much warmth. By the time he heard a car pass, Neal had become miserable and somewhat desperate.

"Hey," he yelled, "down here."

There was the sound of an engine being put into reverse. He wasn't quite sure how to explain his predicament, though, or how to convince whoever was up there to help him out. Most folks around Carthage had already written him off as some thug just one major fuck-up away from jail time. Like it was some forgone conclusion.

They didn't want to get involved, and if any one of them saw Neal now, drunk and beat to hell, it would be like living up to every bad thing that was expected of him. The thought burned. God, it burned.

His reputation was mostly unwarranted. It was as if he was out and about every day on a merry-go-round of petty theft, arson, and vandalism. The most he'd ever done was throw rocks at trains or some of the abandoned buildings downtown. He'd figured he may as well get in on the action if he was going to get blamed, but it never made him feel better; it just made him feel even more like a piece of shit.

When he stumbled out of the car and got turned around, Neal was shocked to find it was the kid-killer who had stopped for him. Scarlet loomed overhead and looked almost like a walking corpse in the weak-pre-dawn light with his colorless hair and skin. He had the death stare to match, too, and Neal felt discomfited beneath his unyielding dark gaze. It was weird. His eyes weren't brown but black, like coal or ditch water, and dilated in the extreme—as if his pupils had seen fit to devour both iris and sclera, leaving nothing but a thin ring of white behind.

Neal swallowed his unease. "Scarlet, you gon' help me out or what?" he said, voice thick, and gestured at the smoking front-end of his car.

Scarlet said nothing, just shrugged and climbed down the slope until they were level with each other. He wore a faded flannel shirt and jeans, with an oversized winter coat thrown haphazardly overtop. There was an old scar that turned the crook of his mouth down into a permanent grimace. This close, he seemed even more out of place than before, so out of sync with the world around him he was almost unreal.

Scarlet popped the hood without asking. "I can fix this," he murmured, more to himself than Neal. He had a voice like broken glass. "There's a toolbox in my trunk, go get it."

"The hell'd you say to me?" Neal said. He was somewhat taken aback by Scarlet's forwardness, and still just drunk enough to get pissed off about it.

"You heard me," Scarlet said, "Go get my toolbox."

"Hey, just who the fuck d'you think you are, talking to me like that? No one talks to me like that," he said, discarding the flask, and tried to sucker punch Scarlet in the gut.

The other boy sidestepped it with surprising ease, which made the swing go wide and caused Neal to lose his footing and fall flat on his ass. Scarlet looked underwhelmed by whatever threat Neal may have posed to him, and he deflated at that. He felt too tired, suddenly, to put up much of a fight.

"You're pathetic," Scarlet said, not looking at him, but rather the car. His whole demeanor was cold and flat as ice. Though his eyes were half-obscured by lid and lash, the contemptuous look he issued Neal was unmistakable.

"Yeah," he breathed out, exhausted, "tell me something I don't fucking know." Then he laughed and laughed, sprawled out in the dirt. It was so funny he could have cried.

Scarlet's face shifted, as though he wasn't sure if he was being mocked or not. He must have decided Neal was worth sticking around for, though, because he extended a hand to Neal and helped him up. Why the kid saw fit to do so, Neal couldn't even begin to guess at. If he had been in Scarlet's position, he would have kicked dirt and ants into his own stupid face and then abandoned himself to the winter.

Neal sighed and resigned himself to... whatever this was. "Where's the toolbox?"

"In my trunk."

Scarlet went back to examining the engine block. Neal ascended the slope somewhat haphazardly and stumbled a little once he reached the top. Scarlet's infamous car was a damn sight to behold, its red coat glittering like the carapace of an exotic beetle beneath the slow-rising sun. The horizon was euphoric. Neal imagined himself behind the wheel, leaving Carthage never to return.

It was a nice dream.

He found the toolbox and carried it back down to Scarlet, who had discarded his jacket and rolled up his sleeves despite the weather. There was grease on his hands and forearms, which were corded with lean muscle. He touched his tools with a familiarity that almost approached the intimate. Neal looked away. After a while, Scarlet made a displeased noise and stepped back. He wiped his hands on a rag he'd pulled from the box and jammed it in his pocket.

"I'm almost done. There's one more thing I need to work on, but it looks like my pry bar and coolant are at the house. I'll have to swing by and get them."

"Alright," Neal said.

He would just wait here then. No smokes, no whiskey, and nothing to do besides stand around and stare at shrubs. Lie back on the mine tailings. *Hah.* Fine by him.

Scarlet paused, contemplative. "Y'know," he said, "you can come if you want."

"You sure?"

"I wouldn't have asked if I wasn't."

What a damn freak. There was nothing to be done, though, so Neal followed him to the car, and they drove back through Carthage before rolling to a stop before a squat double-wide at the other end of town. It was set on cinderblocks with an attached garage that looked to be an add-on. The whole thing looked apt to blow away the next time a twister rolled through. But to Scarlet, he supposed, this was home, and it wasn't like his was much better, besides.

He made to go after the other boy but stopped himself at first, unsure whether to do so or stay put. *Fuck it*, he thought. Just fuck it. When he caught up to him, Scarlet gave Neal a searching, dark-eyed look in response.

The door swung shut behind them with a shudder, and even in the entryway he sensed that there was something off. It was the oppressive silence. How quiet everything was. No laughter, no noise. As if all the air had been sucked out of the room. He wondered, then, how his old man was with him. Scarlet's mom had skipped town soon after the dead kid's funeral, and as far as he knew, it was just the two of them now: the father and the son.

The inside was choked with shit. Junk had been stacked from floor to ceiling with only a narrow path carved through, leading first to the couch and then further in, he'd discover, to the kitchen. It didn't smell bad, per se, just like old things. Stale.

When they navigated their way to the living area, they found Scarlet's dad sprawled in an armchair that had seen better days, beer in hand and gaze glued to the small box across from him. Charlie Chaplin danced on screen with the volume turned low. He set down the beer and lit a cigarette, coughing after the first inhalation. He didn't acknowledge either of them, not even Neal. Blood and dirt and all.

So that's how it is, huh, he thought.

Scarlet's bedroom was small and windowless. There was a sleeping bag on the floor in the corner, and several milk crates filled with books, tools, and packaged car parts. There were no posters, no records, or anything that would have given it some semblance of personality. It may as well have been a prison cell.

Neal lingered in the doorway while Scarlet fished out a half-empty jug of coolant and something that resembled a cross between a screwdriver and a crowbar.

"Let's get outta here," Neal said quietly.

When he spoke for the first time, it was like a spell had been broken. He could breathe again. The sound of his own voice was a relief.

The crook of Scarlet's mouth, the one with the scar, quirked up. "Yeah," he agreed, "okay."

The house soon became a beige smear in the rearview mirror as they sped off back the way they came. Neal sank into the seat as the heat washed over him, feeling wrung-out and worked over.

When they passed by the Nite Lite diner, his stomach let out a sad growl which made Scarlet look at him askance. Neal had maybe five bucks to his name, and there was nothing more substantive than a sleeve of crackers waiting for him back at home. Grocery day wasn't till next Tuesday, and he was already in the doghouse from last night. Not that he could even head there now, with the car trashed. His dad—God, Neal didn't know what he'd do if he saw him like this. He twisted a hand through his hair.

Scarlet sighed and pulled into the parking lot. Neal tensed up at that and felt himself go on the defensive. Why was he doing this? Any of it, really.

Was it to rub in his face just how much of a joke he was? That there was no one lower, more hated, or less than himself. Not even the kid-killer. People didn't give something for nothing.

"The hell are you doing, man?"

"Getting some breakfast."

"Y'know what I damn well mean."

Don't make me say it, he thought.

Scarlet's hands flexed on the wheel. "No, I don't know," he ground out. "Is that what you want me to say?"

"I don't fucking know what I want you to say. I don't even know why you're doing this. We ain't friends, we don't know each other. So, I don't think—"

Scarlet cut him off. "Don't think, then."

"I—I don't have any money," Neal said in desperation, after a moment, sagging back into the seat.

"I do."

"Great, I'll just watch you eat then. Just sit there with my hands in my pants, all casual-like. I'm sure everyone will be keen on that."

"Don't play dumb, Vásquez. It don't suit you. I'll pay for you because I reckon someone should take pity on you every once in a while. So, take it or leave it."

Neal stared at Scarlet. Took in his black eyes and serious expression. The slight nervousness at his own bold invitation. He was being real. Neal felt his neck grow hot, and he licked his lips.

"Fine."

They exited the car and walked into the diner together. The effect was instantaneous. Every head in the diner swiveled towards them, shocked, and the two took a seat in the corner farthest from the door—their pariah's throne. The mutters then began in earnest, and Neal could not help but duck his head a little. Scarlet remained impassive. The solemn crease between his pale brows was the only indicator as to his discontent. It was a hell of a thing, Neal thought, to be despised together. More new material for the soap opera of their lives.

Twenty long, silent minutes later, a waitress appeared. He recognized her from school. Frances, a redhead with a mile-long mean streak. Her mouth was drawn and expression pinched, voice an annoyed sigh when she "greeted" them. Frances had drawn the short straw on serving them, apparently.

"What can I get you two?"

"Just coffee," Scarlet said.

"The Classic, coffee on the side," Neal said. Then, after she left with an uppity sway to her hips, muttered to Scarlet almost conspiratorially, "Bet you it'll take another twenty before we see any damn food, and then it'll be fucking cold."

That actually got a laugh out of the humorless bastard. It made him look as young as he was. Almost as if he'd been unburdened from something. He could stand to do it more often.

"What's that about?"

"You ain't got two bucks to bet."

That should've stung. And maybe if it had been even moments before, it would have. But Scarlet's expression didn't seem mean or bad, just like he was trying his best to play along with Neal but had zero brain-to-mouth filter.

"You caught me," Neal said. "So, uh, what kinda wheels you got?"

"A '76 Chevelle Laguna. Like the one Cale Yarborough drove for NASCAR," Scarlet said, growing livelier as he launched into the single longest string of words he'd ever heard from the other boy. Neal watched the minute shifts in Scarlet's face as he talked.

Eventually Scarlet trailed off, leaving the pair to sit in silence. Maybe it was normal for Scarlet, but it made Neal anxious, and he searched for something else to keep them going in the interim. When he dredged up nothing, Neal returned to picking at the Sweet N' Low packets in the canister until Frances made another pass, steadfastly not looking their way.

"Ain't that crazy?" Neal said.

"What?"

"Her just ignoring us like that."

"I've seen stranger."

Jesus Christ, Neal thought. *Trying to talk to this guy is like pulling teeth.*

"Doesn't matter, I guess. Frances would be a bitch to us no matter if things were different."

"I'm not too good with names."

"You don't talk to anyone, you mean."

"That, too. Not that you do, either. You just watch."

Scarlet was right. Neal did watch. He watched people's hands, in particular. It was an old instinct.

Neal forced a grin. "I guess I can't argue with that," he said, leaning back in his seat. "But it can be interesting. Women, especially—they talk without talking. They can cut you without lifting a single hand. They don't say what they mean and let it be done. When they get mad, they simmer," Neal said.

He knew this because his mom was like that. There was this duality to her that he didn't understand. Irena was funny and a little cruel. If he was interesting enough some days, they could talk and drive around together for hours. But that was only some of the time. Irena drained him, was difficult to please. Whenever he got exhausted or needy, she would up and disappear. Sometimes even for days at a time. His dad hated when she did that, and blamed Neal for it. Like if he was better then things wouldn't be the way they were. Sometimes Neal even believed him.

The leash his dad had on her had tightened in recent months with the sale of their second car, so she was around more than ever before, blistering with discontent. This was better and worse. Better, because she was there for him, could even distract his dad; worse, because Neal knew she was, in her own way, suffering.

Torn between the brief kindness she'd show him, and the longer, more expansive periods of apathy, he clutched at whatever affection was offered. His mom was the good parent. The one who didn't yell at him or smack him around. If he didn't have her, he had nothing.

Neal was reminded, then, of the theater masks he'd learned about last week in his English class: *Melpomene* and *Thalia.* The Tragedy Mask and the Comedy Mask. It fit. The idea, that was. The two-sidedness. His mom would smile at him one minute and discard him the next. And anything was better than being ignored. He thought Scarlet would understand.

They were quiet again for a moment. Scarlet was used to it, though. He had to be. He was in that house all the time, alone, except for the father who didn't talk to or even look at him. Then there was the town that mythologized him as this malevolent *thing*. People would part around him like the Red Sea when he walked past, like he was a leper, like there was something contagious about his supposed evil. As if what had happened hadn't just been some tragic accident.

What Neal saw was a boy, distant and a little weird, but a boy all the same. His flannel shirt hung too large on him, and grease lingered in the creases of his knuckles and palms. When the light hit his eyes, they did not flash gold or brown; they remained an impenetrable, inescapable black. He wondered what Scarlet thought about him. Maybe there would even be time to figure it out, if he could keep from driving him off.

He realized that they had been staring at each other and not speaking. He felt himself go red and he scratched at his neck.

"You're unhappy," Scarlet said without prompting.

"The hell d'you know about me?"

"I don't need to know you to see you."

"Is there a problem?" Neal asked, voice rough.

Scarlet folded his arms. "The problem is that you've got a damn Dodge Aspen, Vásquez. But there's nothing we can really do about that. At least it's not a Pinto. You'd be dead, then, with the way you're driving."

Neal threw his head back and laughed. "It's Neal," he said, feeling lighter than he had for a while. "Not Vásquez."

"Reeve."

"Alright, Reeve," he said. The name felt intimate in his mouth. It was good though. Reeve suited him. Red suited him even better, so he continued, "Red."

They spent the time until their food arrived making stilted conversation, but it was more lighthearted than it had been before. Normal guy shit. The breakfast managed to be both cold and overdone, but a little Tabasco Sauce made it edible enough. The warmth from his first full meal in days and Reeve's company followed him back to his car, where he watched as the other boy migrated back under the Aspen's hood.

He heard metal grind against metal, a *click*, and then Reeve emerged with a look of satisfaction on his face. It was visceral. Real. Neal liked how real he was.

"It's done," Reeve said.

"Thanks, man."

Reeve nodded. He closed his eyes and looked up at the sun. He was so white he seemed like he could use more of it.

"You don't talk much, do you?" Neal said.

"Not really."

"That's okay, I don't mind," he said, even though he kind of did. "Maybe we could, I don't know, do this again sometime."

"Like fix your car?"

"*No*. I mean, sure, if you want. I'm talking about us, uh, hanging out."

"Oh, alright."

"Okay?" Neal said.

"Yeah."

"Cool."

Neal scratched his head. He didn't want to leave but knew his dad would come looking for him soon. It was time to head out if he wanted dinner.

"Well, I'll see you around then," he said.

Reeve's expression was inscrutable. "You will."

After they put the Aspen into neutral and pushed it out of the ditch, the two went their separate ways. Reeve sped off towards the main drag through town, while Neal headed home with a pit in his chest.

It was almost midday by the time he got back, the sky bright and the air still cold. He lingered at the front steps. His breath caught in his throat, and he swallowed, trying to talk himself into going inside.

They know I was out all night. But it won't be as bad as it could've been. Better than it would be if I hadn't run into Reeve. Then, his mind re-circled. *He knows I've been out all night—*

The front door opened. Neal flinched back on instinct, but it was only his mom, who wore a disappointed expression. Yesterday's makeup was smeared beneath her eyes. Irena said nothing and ghosted back inside. Neal smoothed his hair and took a steadying breath before he followed.

His mom seated herself on the couch next to his dad, curling into his side. Gabriel's palm splayed possessively around her hip. Neal felt his dad's eyes rove over his face, torso, legs, lingering where he knew he'd left marks. Gabriel was good about knowing where to hide them. His mom motioned for him to come join and smiled at Neal, slow and strange and sad.

His dad turned to him. "Heard you were at Nite Lite's," he said. His voice was deceptively soft, a light tenor.

He tensed. It was an innocuous enough statement. But Neal knew better. Nothing was safe. All it took was one wrong answer. Sometimes it felt like his dad, Gabriel, was just waiting for him to mess up. Neal never disappointed.

"Yeah," Neal said, mouth dry. "I was."

Gabriel *hmm*'d. "You shoulda come back last night. I don't like you out there by yourself. Not when it's dark."

"Baby, your daddy's right. You never know what could happen," Irena cut in.

"I'm sorry."

"You shoulda known better, right?"

His dad put his hand on the back of Neal's neck. He thought back to the night prior, when that same hand had cracked across his back, his sides. When he had been chased out into a more preferred darkness.

"Right."

"J.D. from the barber's called me up. He said you were with that Scarlet boy. The one that drowned his brother."

"Yeah. We're, uh, friends."

"I heard he's a killer."

Neal said nothing. There was no good answer. His dad continued to speak.

"I won't tell you to stay away from him. I know you ain't the type to listen," Gabriel murmured to him, grip tightening. "Just make sure I don't hear about any funny business, and I won't have to step in. I don't think you'll like that much."

Funny business. His dad had known what he was long before Neal even realized himself. He wasn't sure how, or why, just that he did. And he'd never let him forget it, no matter how much Neal tried to prove he wasn't what he thought.

"No, sir."

Irena threw her head back and laughed. There was some variety show playing on the TV across from them, and her attention returned to it when a clown got pied in the face. His dad joined in and clapped him on the back. He gave him a look that told him to go along with it or else. Neal did. He fixed his eyes on the screen and tried to disappear into the show.

Everything was bright and oversaturated. Men and women twirled around each other with plastic smiles. The host was a short, insincere-looking man dressed in a yellow plaid suit. The clown's makeup was a rictus of pain and ecstasy as he danced and threw more pies at the contestants. Neal was reminded again of the masks, and how complicated people could be.

He'd later take to driving around the town's outskirts, splitting his time between loitering in the parking lot of an abandoned gas station and tossing bricks through windows on the industrial side of town.

It was quiet there. Nobody looked at him or spoke his name. He didn't have that heavy anticipation slung over his shoulders. No shoe to drop or whatever. The absurd reality was that this condemned building felt safer to him than the walls of his own bedroom.

But he wasn't out; he was there, in his house, eyes roving over the oversaturated pixels that made up the clown and its victims.

They sat there for the rest of the afternoon and well into the evening. Then his parents retreated to their room and Neal to his. He laid in bed and thought back to his breakfast at Nite Lite's. Reeve had called it pity, and that much was true. But Neal was so touched by his unexpected kindness that he could not put the incident out of his mind. He wanted to see him again. Maybe learn how to fix up the Aspen on his own terms. Make Reeve smile and feel unburdened, even if just for a moment.

The next day at school, he found the other boy during his lunch block. Usually, he smoked in his car and ate a candy bar or two in the parking lot, but knew Reeve tended to skulk around beneath the bleachers and decided to track him down. As expected, he was there, book in one hand and sandwich in the other. It was a slim, teal volume that bore the title *Mourning Becomes Electra* in faded lettering.

Neal was immediately overcome by the same unexpected fondness he'd felt the other day. He wanted so badly for Reeve to give him something, anything, even a look that acknowledged he was there at all. He felt a lot like a dog asking to be pet.

"Red," he said.

His dark eyes flicked upwards. There was a calculating glint to them that made him nervous. "Neal."

Not quite sure if he was welcome yet, Neal stood above Reeve where he was reclined in the dead grass. They stared at each other until Reeve removed the other half of his sandwich from its wrapper and offered it to him. Neal's relief was so palpable he felt his knees go weak. He accepted the gift and tried to savor it. Their silence was companionable, he realized.

They would sit together in that spot beneath the bleachers from then on, unbothered aside from the occasional freshmen who would stumble across them by mistake and scurry off just as quickly as they had arrived. Even if the air was thick with cold or sweltering heat, their presence remained ubiquitous. Reeve was often quiet, content to let Neal fill the silence, unless drawn into conversation about either books or cars; it was almost funny how quickly he'd flip and let an unseen feeling—passion, he guessed the word would be—bleed out into the world, and his characteristically expressionless features would gravitate into something almost approaching excitement.

Those brief glimpses were to Neal as gentle touch was to a stray, and he treasured the privilege their appearances implied. Maybe he didn't know it, but they did have value, and were valuable because they were so rare and so sweet. Neal could never tell him that. His—whatever this was—could live only in a gaze that lingered, words unspoken, and how his thoughts were pulled into Reeve's current, at first submerged, and then resolved into a tortuous roll around him. His brutish voice, his bluntness, their shared kinship... everything.

Neal smiled. The memory was bittersweet, like most from back then. His time in Carthage was mostly viewed through a lens corrupted by misery, but Reeve had been one of the few good, uncomplicated things to come of it, and Neal wondered how he'd turned out. Did he have a girlfriend or a wife? Kids? Was he a mechanic like he'd sometimes talked about? God. Neal was desperate to figure him out. To apologize. To be friends again. He knew Reeve was still here—he'd checked the phone book to make sure. He even lived in the same single-wide.

Why he hadn't left the town that hated him, Neal didn't understand. The people who lived in Carthage were circling the drain. And Reeve deserved so much more than that.

The thing about it was they didn't get along at the onset. Reeve had come off like a creep, and Neal himself had been a bastard to deal with. He didn't know how it worked out that they became friends.

Now, though, looking back, Neal realized that he'd felt seen. He hadn't ever been real around anyone before that, but the other boy never turned away or looked down on him. Neal was unable to articulate quite what that had meant to him as a teenager, a period where he mostly remembered being overwhelmed by his own life, its hopelessness, and his inability to do anything about either. What he'd known was that when Reeve held his gaze while speaking, or helped him work on the Aspen, or included him in his strange conversations, his strange interests, he'd been almost happy.

And there were times, though, times when Reeve would flash him something approaching a smile or regard him with complex fondness, times which to Neal felt a little like having his own want reflected at him. Then the question would lodge in his throat, unbidden, and die soon after, "Do you see this? What we could be?" But the other boy would invariably return once more to his usual dispassionate self, and Neal would be left empty, aching, still torturing himself with *what-ifs*.

Later, in the cell that had been his home for more of his life than he liked to think about, he'd wonder if those moments—the special ones—were something his younger self fabricated because he'd needed so badly for it to be true. If it was a way to whet his thirst for comfort. It was pathetic, how he'd turn over those smiles and touches in his head, creating meaning out of nothing. Had he been a normal man, Neal doubted the idea would have ever come up. But he wasn't a normal man.

Neal knew what it was to feel like he could never be forgiven. He prayed for it every night. He wondered how it would be to move through the world unburdened.

He slept little that night and did not dream. When he woke the next morning, it was to the lingering taste of insomnia. By the time he threw on his coat and started the Road Runner, the unease from the night prior had taken hold again. Neal found himself at a loss for how to approach Reeve. It had been over ten years since he left, and there was a good chance his return wouldn't be welcome. Not that he would blame him for being mad. He deserved it after not saying goodbye.

Neal pressed his face to the steering wheel and fingered the medal around his neck. Not even Maria Goretti could bring comfort to him now. It hadn't even been one day yet, and he'd already lost his nerve. How predictable. Rather than call or pay Reeve a visit, Neal drove aimlessly around Carthage for a few hours before rolling to a stop right at the edge of town. The horizon was dominated by a billboard featuring a large man dressed in a white suit and sunglasses.

Beyond the withering storefronts, corrugated metal buildings, and unused industrial space, the area bled into emptied-out houses and shrubs; this is where the billboard had been placed. In bold block lettering it read:

"JUDGMENT DAY IS COMING. SEE AARON GOULD LIVE AT THE CARTHAGE FAIRGROUNDS ON 11/22/92."

The man—who Neal figured had to be a kind of local celebrity preacher or something—was everything he disdained rolled into one package. Liar, hypocrite, somebody who took advantage of people's faith.

He felt a familiar hatred grip him. For the sign, the town, the people in it, and, above all, his own stupid cowardice. How everything felt unchanged. He'd been a fool to think he was ready to come back to this place. But Ruth and Joseph had supported this, made him feel like his need to revisit a childhood best left forgotten wasn't as pathetic as it seemed. He supposed he should just be glad that his parents were long gone from Carthage. His dad, prison. His mom—elsewhere.

His bad mood followed him back to the Mirage Motor Inn, as well as the collective gaze of Carthage's residents. He picked up dinner at the Burger Barn drive-thru on his way back, which was served to him by a sullen girl wearing too much makeup. When she handed him his food, it was with a look that could have curdled milk. He bared his teeth at her and ate fries by the handful until he got back to the motel. He paced around his room until dark and then slept poorly again, feeling even more unfulfilled than before.

"Fuck it," he said on Saturday, knowing they were the same words that had brought him and Reeve together the first time. "Just fuck it."

He jammed his sunglasses on his face and left the lot with a squeal. He wound through the familiar path to Reeve's place, settling behind the fence that sectioned off the abandoned lot across the street and idling there, waiting for the best moment to approach him. Hours passed, and nothing happened. The windows were dark, lined with newspaper, and a sad-looking Honda Civic occupied the front drive, rather than the beautiful Laguna that dominated his memories.

Neal pulled his Road Runner off into the trees across the street, near an old barn that had long since been abandoned. It was getting darker now. The longer he sat there, the less he felt like he could leave, figuring he'd invested so much into this escapade already. So, he sat there, waiting and waiting, wondering whether Reeve could feel his eyes on him, and whether he would even care.

The silence inside had to be even worse now, he thought.

The idea gripped his chest like a vise, and the unease Neal felt at this became more oppressive the longer he watched them. This area was cold, dark, unpopulated—well-suited for a voyeur.

The occasional stray cat wound beneath the single-wide. Reeve had to be feeding them. The only real soft spot he'd even shown Neal was for animals. There was a local feline infestation even back in the day, ever since the pound closed in '81; Reeve must have been leaving food out for them.

He rubbed his hands together and blew on them for warmth. It was then that he saw a figure emerge from the darkness. He picked out that it was a bike, which they pulled around back before surreptitiously hefting themselves through a side window.

Soon he saw two shadows flit through the trailer through the newspaper where there were gaps in the hoard; one of them looked like a woman, maybe. It was something about the way she carried herself. The motions her hips and arms made as she moved about the living area. *Are they...?*

He dismissed the idea at first, but the longer he sat and watched them, the sicker he got.

What did you expect? He asked himself finally. *For him to be like you? Or that he would be alone forever? Are you so selfish that you'd rather he not have anyone just because you want him for yourself?*

Neal was honest enough to know he wouldn't like the real answer to any of them.

No one came in or out until around two, when the figure slipped out the same window as before. This time, though, the light from inside illuminated her properly, revealing the same teenager from the Burger Barn who'd served him yesterday.

He had a better look at her now. The girl was tall in the extreme, with an athlete's physique. Her hair had been cropped unevenly around her chin, where it framed her face in dark waves. If not for the aggressive eyeliner and lipstick, she could have almost passed for a boy. But she wasn't a boy; worse, she couldn't be older than seventeen.

There was no sign of Reeve other than one pale, outstretched hand bidding her farewell. Neal leaned back in his seat. What the hell was he doing with a teenager? If he'd been anyone else, Neal would have assumed the worst. But Reeve would never do that. He was a good man. There had to be something else going on.

Neal watched the trailer even after the girl left. He didn't know why he'd stuck around to torture himself further. But just when he was about to leave, the front door swung outward, and the man of the hour materialized.

Not much had changed; he was still blond and lean and serious. Gaunt was maybe a better word for how he looked now. He now wore a thin pair of wire-framed glasses. He had a small bowl of cat food that he sat down, standing guard until one, two, three strays emerged from the darkness to feed. When he turned to go back inside, the dim interior light illuminated a ragged gray streak near his left temple. His eyes were so, so dark. The sight was like water to a man dying of thirst. Neal wanted—

He put the car into first and drove off, feeling strange and fearful. The Inn's neon sign soon eclipsed the skyline, backlit by velvet night and endless flat earth broken only by chat mounds. When he returned to his room, Neal kicked off his boots and gnarled his hair between his hands. Reeve was here. Everything he wanted was right within his grasp. Reconciliation. Closure. The chance to get to talk to his best friend again.

The phone book was open and turned to Reeve's name before he could change his mind. He dialed the number and sat there, poised over the phone in anticipation until he heard the other man pick up.

"Hello?" The familiar voice was a low rasp—like smoke and gravel, dragged across a ruptured larynx.

At that, Neal choked. He didn't know what to say. *Sorry I left. Sorry I never called. Sorry it's been so long. Did I mention I'm in love with you? That I have been since we were kids.* The words lingered and then died on his lips. He touched his medal and muttered a prayer.

"Hello?" Reeve asked again.

He said nothing and slammed the phone back on the receiver. His throat crawled with nerves, and his hands ached to hit something. No—he didn't do that anymore. He got up and paced instead. Neal wondered if it was better to let things be. To let the past remain as it was. It couldn't be tainted that way, destroyed.

He stared up at his reflection in the ceiling. His eyes were wide, posture tense and angry. He looked like his dad. Neal cut his eyes back to the phone, recalling Reeve's faint smile all those years ago. The one that was beautiful and empty at the same time. He was helpless against it.

Neal wasn't certain he could stay away, not for long, but he didn't know what the truth would mean.

REEVE II

"**N**eal," they said. "Neal Vásquez is back."

The name lived in the sneering mouths of his coworkers and neighbors for the next three days. Reeve hadn't known what they were talking about at first. He'd just been dogged by whispers at work until dusk. They had taken on a newfound significance, one he couldn't quite parse, and it escalated as the day wore on. He felt little desire to interpret the vagaries of their interactions at first. Fine. It was fine. Let them talk. There was nothing he could do.

But then Neal's name surfaced for real, and suddenly, everything made sense. Reeve had been so shocked by the initial mention of Neal's reappearance that his mind went completely blank. He'd sat at his desk with white noise in his ears until he'd reentered the stratosphere and found that half the day had passed.

Reeve struggled whether to believe them. It couldn't be Neal, not really, because if he was here, then he would have come to him. Neal would have knocked on his door right when he got in. They would have embraced like old friends. Reeve wouldn't be hearing about this secondhand.

The parking lot was silent when he left work the third night. That much, at least, was normal. He'd felt watched more than ever over the weekend, and Reeve now half-expected a voyeur around every corner. Yet despite this heightened awareness and apprehension, nothing had so far come of it. He supposed it could be just another byproduct of his corrupted mind.

Reeve smoked a cigarette and thought about the route the evening would take: is neighbors' arguments. The car. The inevitable restless edge into sleep sometime in the morning's early hours. Ephraim's death featured often in these dreams, from which Reeve would awake in a stale sweat with a blanket tangled between his legs. Then there was always the water. God, the water, the pool. His hands clenched.

He just wanted the thoughts to stop.

If he went home, he knew he wouldn't be able to keep himself from returning to the shower, where he would drown once more in his memories. Not going meant only postponing the inevitable, though, and the prospect of diverging from his routine was a discomfort that pooled heavily in his stomach. But it would also pose a momentary reprieve. Yeah, he decided. He would do it. Before he could back out, Reeve forced himself into motion.

The drive was quick, and soon he pulled onto the main drag through town, parking a few blocks down from his destination. Reeve opened the glovebox and withdrew another well-worn copy of *Prometheus in Exile*, pocketed it, and set off for what passed for Carthage's downtown area. It was Monday, which meant there was even less foot traffic than usual. Most of the businesses had closed hours ago, besides the check-cashing and bail bond place.

Nite Lite's was the only food joint still open, sandwiched between corrugated metal buildings and withered storefronts. It was cold and winter wind howled through the streets. His sole company was to be the familiar characters secreted away in the pages of his favorite book.

Although the night was quiet, and the people infrequent, the feeling that he was being watched began to creep up his spine. At first, Reeve resolved to pay it no mind, knowing how he could get, but when the sensation grew so strong as to be almost physical, his resolve broke and he pivoted around to search for the source and found nothing. Just darkness, the occasional passerby.

Ducking into his coat, Reeve had just about neared the diner when the culprit resolved into focus. They had taken up residence in the payphone parallel to him on the opposite sidewalk, fiddling with the phone but without any real intent. There was a certain purposeful slant to their body in relation to where Reeve stood bathed in neon.

The shape was indeterminate for only a moment, though, until the silhouette moved, features becoming clear even while half-enveloped in the slow-falling darkness and distorted by dirty glass panels.

It's Neal. The breath rushed out of him. His feet began their forward march before he'd even decided to approach the other man, and Reeve came to a stop before the booth. If even for a moment Reeve thought he'd mistaken a stranger for his friend again, the recognition he saw mirrored in the other man dispelled that notion at once.

He forgot he could be anything other than silent sometimes, so the sound of his own voice shocked him when he breathed out, *"Neal."*

The man stepped out into the street. He was broader than Reeve remembered, and older. There were faint lines around his eyes. Inked fire twined up his throat to frame his jaw. But his cheeks still dimpled when he grinned, and he kicked his heels like he'd done so often in high school when nervous, so it was Neal all the same. Reeve could hardly believe it.

"Hey, Reeve," he said. His voice was deep as a grave.

Reeve felt an acute pain twist in his chest. He sagged a little and fisted a hand in his shirtfront.

The afternoon Neal had left was still clear, still gutting. He was there one day and gone the next. Reeve heard around town what had happened, that the whole family was in the hospital. He wasn't permitted to see Neal but thought the other boy might call. It was a call that never came.

Only later did he learn Neal had been taken by social services and that his dad was locked up in the county jail. There was no letter, no visit—not even long after he should have been able to make contact. Then Reeve once more returned to the solitary existence.

The pill had been hard to swallow, ground glass in his throat. Now, seeing him again, the forgiveness surprised him with how easy it came. It was instant, warm, as if it were sunlight poured from cupped hands.

"Neal," he said again. "You're here."

Neal laughed, "Yeah, I am."

Reeve licked his lips. He didn't know what this feeling was inside him. The joy coupled with disbelief. He wanted to reach out and touch Neal, just to make sure he was really there.

"You've been watching me."

Neal looked embarrassed and scratched his head. "Um, yeah, sorry 'bout that. I didn't really know what to say."

"I don't mind, Neal. It's *you*."

"Oh, okay."

"Did you," Reeve began, tentative, "come back to see me?"

Neal's face did something complicated at that. Then he nodded.

"I did. I, uh, wanted to see the town, too."

That was surprising. "Why?"

"It's just something people talk about, y'know. Going back to where everything started."

"No, I don't know."

Neal laughed again. "I don't reckon you would," he said, then, when Reeve said nothing in response, continued, "Look, let' s get some food. We can catch up and get out of the cold. Well, I mean, unless you're busy."

Yes, absolutely, Reeve wanted to say. He was still in disbelief over Neal's reappearance, and it felt like the other man was liable to vanish at any moment. But his tongue got thick with nerves, and for a moment he was afraid that he would stand there, paralyzed, until he was left alone on the street. It was that image of Neal walking away from him that got Reeve to spit the words out.

"I'm not busy."

"Nite Lite's, then?"

"Nite Lite's," Reeve agreed.

Never mind the fact that he'd already been on his way there, or that maybe Neal had guessed, and wanted to ask without making him feel like a loser for going there alone—to a place saturated in their memories, their once-friendship. He was lonely. That was the truth. It had been his truth since Neal left. So, when the other man sauntered towards the diner, Reeve was helpless to follow.

It was bright inside Nite Lite's, and the air smelled like cigarette smoke and overcooked eggs. There were several older men seated at the counter, while a young couple presided over two half-empty plates at a secluded table. All heads turned to them upon their arrival, and it was then Reeve was reminded why everyone had been whispering that week. They had known Neal was back before he did. How long, Reeve wondered, had he been in town? Why did he feel the need to watch but not approach? Had Neal found him pathetic, wanting, not like the old friend he knew?

They slid into a corner booth nearest to the window, which faced the street. The blue-black night was broken only by the occasional neon sign and streetlight. Rain began to fall. Reeve withdrew a cigarette and lit it, relaxing back into his seat once he had some nicotine in him and something for his hands to do.

Reeve held out the open carton to Neal. "You want one?"

"Nah, I quit a few years back."

"For the best, I s'pose."

"God, tell me 'bout it."

Reeve had a better look at Neal now that they were inside and stationary. He had aged over the past decade, but in a good way. More well-worn than anything. His black hair had been shorn into a sleek undercut, slicked back where it was longer on top. Reeve was used to the animal pelt-like shaved head he'd borne back in high school, though he noted how this seemed to suit him more. His clothes were clean, expensive. A supple leather jacket, new, dark jeans, and black cowboy boots. The ornamental stitching was done in indigo.

Neal had always liked cowboys. He'd liked James Dean, Steve McQueen, and terrible Italian action movies, too.

There was a certain louche elegance about him. His expression was languid, easy despite his earlier anxiety. Easier than Reeve had ever seen him. He smelled like an old memory, and when he smiled at their waitress, left cheek dimpling, Reeve could see that his left eyetooth was now chipped. He wanted, more than anything, to know what happened. Was it an accident? Another fight? His dad's handiwork?

Neal's eyes were different too. The right iris had collapsed and collided with the pupil, and there was a faint starburst of a scar cutting through the skin beneath. The color was familiar, something like sea-glass; a strange intersection of blue and green that reminded him of bottles licked by the ocean. The kind of blue that was cruel and gentle all at once.

Reeve wanted to know where he'd been, almost desperately, but felt like he couldn't ask. Not yet. Surely it was more interesting than his own life.

He hadn't felt this seen, exposed, in a long time. It pricked at him, but in a good way. It wasn't cutting or impersonal like most people's glares were, people who had known his family and liked Ephraim, or the clinical disdain with which everyone else examined him. It was the stares people exchanged with those whom they saw as worthy of their time.

Their coffee arrived, along with a plate of steak and eggs for Neal. Reeve took his black, scalding. He ground out his cigarette and lit another one. Neal stirred some sugar from the dispenser into his cup, then doused his food in Tabasco.

"I'd say we could people watch like we used to, but it looks like they're all just eavesdropping, so there's no real point," Neal said. "Not to mention we actually got our food on time for once."

Reeve cut his eyes around the diner. Yeah, they were all watching, muttering. Was it because Neal had come back? His new well-to-do look? The two of them being seen together again? Or just him, like usual. He hadn't become any more well-liked in the past decade.

Maybe it was what it had always been; that Neal was brown and poor and different from them. It was funny, in a way. The things that made Reeve like him were the same things he was disdained for by others.

"When did you get in?" Reeve said finally. His tongue felt thick in his mouth, stupid. It hurt, too. Like fingering an open wound.

Neal paused. "Thursday. I was, uh, busy. I planned to stop by your old man's place tomorrow. Heard you were still there."

"That's fine." It wasn't.

"No. I shoulda come to you first. I was just, I dunno, worried you didn't want to see me? That you'd have every damn right to hate me for what I've done."

"Why would I not want to see you?"

"I was—" Neal began, then cut himself off. "Jesus, why bother arguing the point if you ain't mad. Anyways, I wanted to apologize."

"Why?"

"I was... I wasn't always a good person, I guess. And I don't think I was always a good friend, either."

"You gave me everything I needed."

"Still, I'm sorry. I had a lot going on and took it out one you more often than I'd have liked." Neal picked at his napkin. "Now tell me what you've been up to."

"Nothing, really."

"Extrapolate."

"Elaborate, you mean."

"Sure, whatever. Just give me a little more than *nothing*."

Reeve actually laughed at that. Though barely audible, it rang out like the hinges of a door that hadn't been used in some time. Rusty and in want of use. Neal looked pleased by this.

It's quotidian, Reeve didn't say. *The same all the time.* But he wanted to give Neal something more than that.

"Okay. As you thought, I live in the same house. It was easier that way since my dad got sick spring of senior year—"

"Sick?"

"Cancer."

"Shit."

"Yes," Reeve agreed. "I took care of him. Through high school, through college, up 'til I got the job at the regional branch here for Gadfly Industrial Supply. He was proud of me, I think. Maybe. Because it was a "real job." Even if he didn't live to see much of my success." The word "success" was laced with sarcasm.

Neal leaned forward. "You didn't go to technical school?"

Reeve had wanted to. However, his dad had left a pamphlet out for the community college a few towns over, earmarked where their accounting program was advertised. That was that. Reeve signed up the next week.

"It didn't work out."

"Is that so."

"Yes."

"What'd the old man say?"

"He didn't have to say anything."

Neal leaned back and took another drink. The flames on his throat shifted as it worked, up, down, like they were crackling with heat. Would they feel hot to the touch, too? Reeve bit back the absurd urge to reach out and lay his hand in the fire.

"You were gonna become a mechanic."

"I wanted to. I did. But he had something different in mind for me. I respected that."

"Bastard," Neal remarked, taking a vicious stab at his food. "So, what— you do books now for that place?"

Reeve nodded.

"I'll be honest with you, Red—" Neal began, then cut himself off. "Is it, uh, still alright to call you that?"

"I don't mind. It's the name you gave me."

He liked the way Neal said his name. "Red" made him feel more than himself. He never wanted Neal to stop; he just didn't know how to tell him.

Neal turned his head into his hand and smiled at him. "You really haven't changed much, have you?"

"No, I don't think so."

"Hell, yeah. Anyways, well, your job sounds awful."

"It's—" Reeve said. The word *fine* was about to leave his mouth. But that wasn't right. He hated his job. He hated his coworkers. Why pretend otherwise with Neal? "—boring. You're right. I hate it there."

"Damn. Haven't you thought about, I don't know, leaving?"

"No."

Like many unpleasant things about his life that could change, Reeve hadn't really even considered it. He was bound by duty. To his dad, his mom's memory, Ephraim. Why be selfish?

Neal looked perplexed by this. Reeve tensed. How could he explain to him that suffering could, and often was, necessary? That it had become a comfort, in its own way. Reeve needed it as much as he hated it.

He acted quickly. "Forget it. I want to know what happened to you. Up 'til now you could've been dead for all I knew," Reeve said.

"Definitely not dead, that's for sure."

"Where'd you go?"

"After everything went downhill with my dad, I got sent to foster care. Moved around 'til I aged out."

"You could've called me," he said. "I thought I was your friend."

"Reeve, you were my *only* friend. I just thought it'd be better not to hear from me. I was... so angry. All the time. I was awful to you more than I was good, and I couldn't stop it. Not then. Not the way I was. You deserved better."

"I didn't mind."

Neal glanced down at his hands, face inscrutable. The shadows threw his handsome features into harsh relief. "I wanted something from you that you weren't ready to give," he added quietly.

"What," Reeve began, feeling something unravel in his chest. It was something he could not yet put a name to but made him ache. "What d'you mean by that?"

"Maybe I'll tell you one day." There was a funny look on Neal's face, then, like he was in on some private joke at his own expense.

Reeve sat for a moment, digesting the oblique confession before he pivoted the conversation. "They weren't bad, were they? The people who took you in."

"The homes were okay. The foster parents weren't bad or anything, just indifferent. Cold, y'know? Like they saw right through me. Better than my dad, though. You know how he was."

"I'm glad. I didn't want you to suffer."

"I never forgot about you, Red. Even after it'd been years and years."

The admission made Reeve feel less self-conscious about how often he turned Neal's face over in his mind. That maybe it wasn't weird how he'd fixated on their friendship for so long. When Neal said he felt like those people saw through him, Reeve got that. He felt that way all the time.

"Me, too," he said.

Neal leaned forward and smiled. His teeth were very white and straight. Reeve loosened his tie. He'd always liked it when Neal looked happy.

"After you graduated, what happened?" Reeve asked.

"I hitchhiked around for a year or so. Settled down in Des Moines, of all places. Started my own business there. Glass installation. Turns out the pay ain't bad, believe it or not. People always need glass, you see. It's like death, taxes. However the saying goes," Neal said. "That's who I was talking to earlier, my business partner. Joseph. He's, uh, on four wheels now, but still as sharp as a damn tack. A good guy. And his wife, Ruth, has been amazing to me, too."

So the phone call that had been a ruse for his voyeurism did have real purpose.

"You're doing well for yourself, then. That's good."

"I guess so."

Reeve sipped at his coffee and withdrew one final cigarette before placing them back into his coat pocket. Neal followed the movement with his eyes and looked questioningly at the book he'd tucked away in there earlier.

"*Prometheus in Exile*," Neal read, whistling. "Hell of a title."

"It's nothing complicated. I think you'd come 'round to it if you tried," Reeve said. His hands tightened around the book. The frayed cover gazed up at him, agonized. He felt the need to make Neal understand how important this book was to him. What were the words that would make him see this was something worth his time? His teeth grit together.

There are two friends who live in a little town in Arkansas. Near the mountains, where it's beautiful, remote. And these guys, they may as well be brothers. But they aren't. They can't even really be friends, either. There are horrible things in their world. In ours. Things set on keeping them apart.

"Hey, don't worry," Neal said, setting his fork down, "I believe you."

Reeve turned to the window again. His drawn, gray-colored face stared back at him. He was old, nearly thirty now. When had that happened? Where had all the time gone? How could he be a man and still struggle with the very things he'd been promised he'd grow out of?

It was Ephraim's face, too. They had been identical twins. His mom had told him not long after he passed, "When you miss him, all you have to do is look in the mirror." The only difference was the scar on his mouth.

When he turned back to his—friend—Reeve could almost see his reflection's gaze follow him, smiling. He refused to meet its eyes.

He pushed the book across the table to Neal. The other man picked it up with gentle hands. "I can give it a try. I'll be sure to return it before I leave."

Neal was good about that; understanding him, that was. It was a relief to not have to try and fail to explain himself. He relaxed back into his seat.

"Thanks," Reeve said finally.

"Anytime," Neal said, before trailing off into silence.

"Do you, uh, still...?" Neal trailed off, his intent evident. *Do you still watch people the way you did back then? The way I told you not to do.*

"Not anymore. I want to, but I don't."

They had done it together once, after he'd alluded to his extracurricular nighttime activities to Neal. The other boy had asked him about it, and he'd told him, "I go out" in return.

"You go out?"

"Did you not hear me?"

"No, Jesus, 'course I did. I just don't know what the hell that's s'posed to mean. What d'you even do, man?"

"I go into houses and watch people."

"You're breaking and entering? What's wrong with you, Red? That's an actual crime—a serious one. You could get locked up for that. Or worse, popped by a homeowner."

"I don't take anything. Not usually. Nothing they'll miss."

"I don't think that matters to the damn pigs!"

"Come with me then. You'll see. I don't hurt no one when I do this."

And he did. It was so special, that night. It was maybe the most special night of his entire life. He chose a house he'd been eyeing for a while, one with a nice fenced-in yard and garden statuettes. Reeve slipped a knife between the window frame and the lock to ease it open, soon hefting himself through it.

The house was dark, still. He caught flashes of history as moonlight rippled across picture frames and handcrafts. The pair—a smiling blond man and woman—looked perpetually content, whether it be on the lake, a hunting trip, or vacation. He stopped once they reached their room. He and Neal listened to the couple, then took two fishhooks from the garage on their way out.

Reeve could still feel the adrenaline rush. He could still see the sweat on Neal's brow. He still had his fishhook from that night back home, along with everything else he'd ever taken.

When the town was at its blackest, its most empty, and his insomnia had reached its climax, Reeve would emerge from his trailer and out into the soundless night. There, he'd wander the streets until a house beckoned him inside. He answered, he always did. The welcoming was easy; he had an affinity for locks and latches, which seemed to give way beneath his hands.

This thing, his hauntings, it wasn't about money. Reeve had little use for that. What he did was walk the halls and slip into the rooms, standing vigil over the inhabitants' beds as he listened to them breathe. The soft dreamtime sounds.

If no one was home, sometimes he would even lay atop their sheets, run their sinks, and move around kitchen implements. *Will they notice?* He'd wonder. *Will they feel the difference?* Maybe they didn't because, in a way, one not yet understood by them, they knew he belonged there. That an invisible man meant no harm.

The only things he ever took were special. They were special things, taken at special times. A child's toy, well-loved enough to where the paint had eroded along the edges. Or two mismatched earrings—unsought heirlooms. People would suppose these items simply lost or misplaced. That happened, right? It was not some uncommon occurrence. But the truth was that he, Reeve Scarlet, was responsible.

He'd become the god of lost things.

Trinkets in hand, he'd return to his trailer and secret everything away into a safe place before at last settling onto his pallet in the attached garage. It was there that Reeve would fall asleep, still dressed and dreaming about those people's breathing, the homes he'd violated.

He supposed he could trace it back to when he'd spied through people's windows as a kid, even before everything that happened with Ephraim and his mom, drinking in tantalizing glimpses into other lives. They were his initial comparison for what normal was intended to be, and what families looked like that weren't his own. In some, he saw echoes of familiar dysfunction, whereas most just made him yearn for something he'd never had.

He'd stopped when he went to college, but like his self-imposed exposure to water, the urge never really went away.

When Reeve said nothing in response, Neal cleared his throat and checked his watch. "Looks like it's almost nine. We can catch up some more tomorrow?"

"'Course."

The other man motioned for the check. They paid and then got up to leave. Reeve felt a strange loss when the diner door closed behind him. The rain had lessened to a light mist and would soon fade entirely. His skin prickled at the contact, and he tried not to react. Neal looked at him askance anyway.

"Mind if I walk you back to your car?"

"No."

"Lead the way."

The night was deep and cold. Familiar. Neal sauntered alongside him with insouciant ease. They reached the parking lot, and Reeve took a moment to stop and breathe in deep.

"What is it?" Neal asked.

Reeve inhaled and exhaled. "Petrichor," he said. "It's the smell in the air after it rains. Try it."

"Try, uh, what?"

"Breathe. You'll see."

Neal half-closed his eyes and tipped his head back, mouth open. The brown column of his throat flexed around a breath and his lips turned up at the corners. This close, Reeve could see where the blue and green collided around his pupil.

"Good?"

"Good," Neal said.

They stood there facing each other in silence, after, and Neal moved towards him. It was an abortive gesture. "Can I—" he began, arm outstretched. He'd done the same thing often when they were in high school. Reeve knew what he wanted.

"Yeah."

Neal embraced him for real this time. The contact was almost painful. Reeve felt turned inside out, all his raw insides exposed. No one had touched him like this in years. His arms hung limp at his sides until he reached up to brush his palms against Neal's back once before the two parted.

"We can meet tomorrow after you get off work."

"Tomorrow," Reeve said. The word had a certain finality to it. "I'm home at seven. You know where it is."

"Seven, great. See you then, Red," he said with a wave, and disappeared back into Carthage like he'd never been there at all.

Reeve drove home in a near-daze, thinking about how much he had enjoyed being able to see Neal again. He wasn't dead, or worse. He was good. Better than good, even. Well-to-do. And he'd come back for him.

The lights in Zebadiah's house were on, but Reeve heard nothing from them while he pulled up. Maze's bike was parked along the side, and he could see her outline slumped inside. He opened the door and was immediately assaulted by the combination of weed, fast food, and perfume that marked her presence.

Maze was slumped on his couch, a half-smoked joint in hand.

When the girl registered his presence, she put it out and staggered to her feet. Even slouched, Maze stood about half a head taller than him. Her red work shirt was stained with grease, and her eyeliner had started to run. He wanted to know why she wasn't at home, or at her boyfriend's place. Anywhere else, really.

"Hey, old man," she said, "Can I stay?"

"Why're you here?" Reeve asked after he'd taken off his shoes and coat.

Maze had flopped back down onto the couch, long legs stretched out in front of her. The novelty cow ears on her hat were jammed up against the wall. He neatly folded his coat underneath him and sat next to her. Reeve knew her well enough now to tell she wanted to talk.

"I needed to get out of the house for a little while," she said, gray eyes cutting towards him. "Also, I brought more weed if you want some."

He didn't want weed and told her that.

"Your loss, man," she informed him, lighting the joint back up. "Ugh. Today has been so bogus."

"Bogus," he echoed. "What does that mean?"

"Well, y'know, like, 'This is stupid.'"

"Okay."

"Yeah?"

He paused. "It's... "bogus" that you felt the need to ask again."

Maze laughed deep and long. "You're so weird, Reeve." Then she got quiet, contemplative. "Hey, you want to hear a joke?"

He didn't but let her continue.

"Why do you never hear a pterodactyl go to the bathroom?"

"Why?"

"'Cause the "pee" is silent," Maze finished, grinning at him.

When he didn't react, she groaned dramatically. "I think you're a total psycho for not even pretending to think that's funny," she told Reeve, almost gently, "but don't worry—I still like you plenty."

Reeve stared at her face, the open affection spread throughout its features, and let himself smile.

Maze's mouth had parted at that, maybe because she'd never seen him express this degree of amusement before, and then closed it after a short while to smirk. He was struck by a certain fondness for her in that moment, reaching out to scrape a knuckle across her forehead.

The girl did not stay for much longer after that, chattering about her day before leaving Reeve to his nighttime routine. Completing it was like scratching an itch deep within the folds of his brain. Doors, windows, water.

When he at last lay down to sleep, he could not keep himself from thinking about Neal. He reached over to the small metal bowl he kept beside his pallet to hold his keys and other necessities and pulled out an old latch, running his fingers over it.

He had taken shop class back in high school. It didn't come easy to him, art. The surety the lines and grooves required seemed at first beyond him, and his hands would shake each time he held a saw or sander. Making something, he'd found, was a heavy burden to bear. So was eking out whatever creative spirit not yet stifled by the people around him, the town, Ephraim. But Reeve had always had a knack for working with his hands, so when the spring semester neared its end, he could see the progress.

Then came May.

Their final project was to make a box, any box, as long as it came complete with its own latch and hinges—"It could even be a gift you'd give to someone in your life," Mr. Billings had said, smiling at the class. At everyone but him. "Someone special"—and get up in front of the class and explain the woodworking process and any significant details they chose to include.

Neal, he'd thought. *Neal-Neal-Neal.* No other name came to mind. There was no one else. It took him time to figure out what he should add to personalize it, and he started to try and pay the other boy more mind while he worked. He'd go with a cowboy-boot themed exterior design since he liked westerns so much, wouldn't stop talking about them or force-feeding them to Reeve, and a blue corduroy lining at the bottom. The stitch-like patterns on the outside soon began to appear as though they were flames. They licked at each edge, each flat surface, each other.

He pulled it close to his chest when he'd finished, chest twisting in on itself, and the overwhelming urge to possess made him sneak the box from the classroom and spirit it home. It was the most beautiful thing he'd ever made. He couldn't stop stroking it. There was an atmosphere about it that magnetized him.

He wanted to give it to Neal, wanted to give the box to him so badly he could hardly stand it. Reeve didn't know what it meant, only that it scared him. It scared him so bad he couldn't handle it.

He burned the box and watched until the fire worked itself to nothing. Then he took the half-melted latch and pocketed it, just to know it had ever existed at all.

He showed up to class empty-handed, saturated in Mr. Billings' disappointment as well as the failing grade he knew he'd receive.

"Mr. Scarlet, where's your project?"

"I lost it."

"Uh-huh."

Reeve had returned to his station in shame.

The fire lingered. It lingered every time he ran a thumb across the ridged latch in his pocket. He could still feel its heat.

MAZE II

"**H**e's staring at you again."

He was. Maze cut her gaze to the other side of the cafeteria and looked Dean up and down, hunched over two tables away in a windbreaker and picking at his lunch tray. Her gut twisted unpleasantly, and she stabbed at her free lunch: soggy green beans and potato mash.

"So, what?"

"So, stare back any harder, and you'll burn a hole in him."

"And nothing of value would be lost," Maze sneered, fork skittering across her tray. She wrote the meal off as a wash.

Dean sat with his buddies and some girls, Tandy and Amber, the ones who really got on Maze's nerves even before she fell out with everyone earlier that year. Oralene was the only one who stuck it out with her. Maze knew she didn't make it easy; Oralene didn't always make it easy, either. When Maze looked at her, she saw everything she wanted to be but couldn't. Oralene didn't even *know*, and that was the worst part. Petite and blonde, with straight, white teeth. A family that was happy, together.

It was the two of them at the table.

Well, the two of them and *Cricket*. Cricket sat with them for a lack of alternative options. She was a lesbo, so even the fat kid, "Bitch Tits," bullied her. People called her Cricket because her voice emerged as a weird, cricket-like chirp whenever she dared to speak. Her real name was Corliss Fields, and her daddy was the Ottawa County Sheriff.

Across the cafeteria, Tandy threw her head back and laughed. *Ah-hah-hah.* Cricket's shoulders hunched forward at the sound.

Tandy had made a pass at Cricket back in the spring as a joke. The pair were the last to leave one day when the locker room cleared out, having prolonged their showers, and maybe Cricket's gaze had lingered just a little too long on her, or maybe it was just bully's intuition, but Tandy noticed something. It was enough to interest her in a game.

Cricket went to meet her later that night at the Pit—a secluded asphalt lot down by the mineshaft where people went to drink and have sex—only to be met with two cars filled with Tandy's friends, armed with buckets filled with trash taken from the girl's restrooms. They held her arms behind her back and dumped the contents over her head, and used pads, tampons, toilet paper, and dirty gray water that had collected at the bottom tumbled down around her. Then they left her there alone.

Now she didn't sit with the band kids anymore; Cricket had been excommunicated to their table, where all she did was listlessly push around her food. No eye contact, no comments. To Maze, it was like eating lunch with a corpse.

People still laughed about it. And Maze herself had been guilty, too. Sometimes you had to take shots at those beneath you to lift your own spirits a little, remind yourself you're not at the bottom of the food chain, but it got to the point where Maze felt a little sick at how just... cruel the group was to her. If Cricket didn't make things weird, she was okay to be around. Maze knew what it felt like to be collateral damage in that crowd's endless search for entertainment.

The bell rang, and Maze and Oralene stood to leave.

As she was gathering her things, Lee knocked into Maze as he and the rest of his crowd walked by. He was one of Dean's friends, one she wasn't as familiar with. He was the kind of guy who always took a joke too far. The kind of guy who couldn't take what he dished out. Maze didn't like the way he looked at girls—especially little Cricket.

"Watch it, fugly," he said to her.

Maze already pulled shifts at the Burger Barn. She didn't have time for another job pretending he was funny. Her temper flared hot and quick.

"Tell that to me again, you limp-dick little fuck," she shot back, squaring her shoulders and looking him dead in the eye when he pivoted.

"What'd you just say to me?"

"Should I try using smaller words?"

Maze and Lee got up in each other's faces until Mr. Brown stepped between them and told them to cut it out. Lee and the others regarded her sourly before backing off, with Dean being the sole exception. He couldn't quite meet her gaze.

Dean was cool. He had been, at least, until he hurt her bad. Now Maze hated the sight of him.

For his part, Dean was Vietnamese by way of OKC. His great-grandparents had come over decades ago and first settled in Texas before migrating north. Beverly, his mom, cooked chicken-fried steak better than anyone else Maze knew. They made Vietnamese food, too, like *xôi gà* and *bánh cuốn*; Maze had been fed well at his house, and they played board games and watched old French movies together after dinner. Beverly had this weird obsession with some old Parisian actor called Alain Delon, so *Purple Noon* and *Le Samouraï* were often on their TV.

The actor really was easy on the eyes, enough so that Dean would lean in close, elbow Maze and ask her if she was going to leave him for "Monsieur Delon," as he called him, drawl lengthening the vowels out. She'd cross her legs and whisper coquettishly, "Dean-o, your parents are here."

He was loved. At the end of the day, Dean was so, so loved. And Maze had gotten scraps of that love while they were together, even if his parents had never quite known what to make of her. So what if she missed them, missed all of it but Dean?

Waylon was mature, too grown for nonsense. He really got her. He didn't pull stupid shit like Dean had, when he'd stuffed her locker full up with packing peanuts the day before a big game. He didn't jerk her around when it came to her feelings. Waylon took her side when it was important.

After her dad's funeral, Maze had laid in bed for days. It was like she'd taken a melon baller to the gut. That period in her life was a haze: all she could recall were shadows, just shadows moving in the darkness.

She'd look at family photo albums, pictures on the wall and the icebox, and wonder what the hell was the point in keeping them anymore. Maze drifted through the days that followed, and when she returned to school, everything seemed different, pointless. She couldn't bring herself to care about things in the same way she had before—not that Maze had ever been all that interested in school to begin with.

Athletics were where she'd excelled. She'd played basketball, thrown discus and shot put for the track team, and ran cross-country in the off season. It had been easy to make friends when she'd taken the school to state for three different sports two years running. More than that, it had been her best chance at going to college. Basketball, that was. But then she'd dropped out before the final state game and hadn't returned to the court since. No games, no recruiters, no scholarships. Just Carthage.

That, and the Burger Barn.

Nothing had quite prepared her for the existential horror of working a dead-end job with a nasty boss and coworkers who either didn't or were incapable of doing their jobs. The Burger Barn, as a rule, smelled like grease, ball-sweat, and deep-fried human misery. But she couldn't quit. $4.25 was shit pay, but it was still more than what she'd have otherwise. Money was her ticket out of here and a way to keep she and her mom afloat in the meantime. So, she plastered on her best customer service smile and tried to let the bullshit slide off her for five hours every other day.

Maze kept her head down from then on, speaking to no one besides Oralene. It was easier that way. Oralene was still cool with their old friend group, but she and Maze had known each other for as long as Maze had lived in Carthage. It was some real best friend loyalty. Sure, they worked each other's nerves, but that was par for the course.

So when Oralene told her that Tandy was hosting some kind of party next week, and she'd been invited, Maze agreed to tag along. Maybe getting back out there wouldn't be so bad. The only caveat was that Cricket, for whatever horrible reason, had been invited too, and they were supposed to pick her up on the way. Weird.

The day concluded with the final bell. As Maze peeled out of the parking lot, Douglas H. Cooper Senior High School could not disappear fast enough behind her.

The sunset was toxic orange and ringed in gut-colored cirrus clouds. Her mouth moved around air laced with dust. The chat mounds became shadowed palisades in the descending night, and the Hiram Evans riverbed was a glittering streak of dried blood beneath the bridge. Iron hydroxide deposits from the mine discharge upstream had stained the bottom red. There were no fish, no algae; they were long since dead. The mine was mostly closed, but its ghost remained.

Things were worse than people liked to say. The chat and sinkholes were commonplace, accepted even, but the EPA had been a constant presence for years now, working with the state and the sheriff's office to test the groundwater and sample soil and chat residue. They had even begun to cap the abandoned mine shafts. The suits wouldn't be here unless there was something seriously bad going on.

It made a certain kind of sense to her, this decay.

The earth was dying all around them. There was poison in the dirt, the air, in the mouths of those who were supposed to love her. Maybe it was in Maze, too. Maybe it sought out the cracks in people to burrow inside. Or maybe she was just being dramatic.

Maze detoured towards Reeve's house like she sometimes did, just to scope it out in the daylight. It seemed different during the day, less real. Reeve was one of those people who gave off the impression of existing only at night.

Today was different, though. There was a car loitering down the street from his place, secluded just enough to where she would have missed it had she not been so relentlessly nosy. It was a sleek muscle car, and the guy behind the wheel was as sleek and muscular as his vehicle. You didn't see men like that too often in Carthage.

Maze first wrote it off as being a cross-country traveler trying to rest after a long drive, as some tended to do on their way through town. But then he was there again, and again, and again.

After the car's presence at the house had persisted for three consecutive days, Maze decided she couldn't wait any longer to intercede. When he left the drive that fourth afternoon, Monday, Maze followed Reeve's visitor in her station wagon until he noticed his tail and pulled over onto a secluded shoulder. Maze parked right behind him, defiant.

He threw open the door and disembarked. This close, he appeared even more threateningly symmetrical than before. "Alright, who the hell are you and why are you following me?" The man asked. His voice was deep and accented with an unmistakable Okie drawl. "Sonuvabitch—you're that girl who was at Reeve's place."

Stalker, she thought.

"Maze," she said, walking towards him. He was a tall man, like Reeve, but still stood only at nose-level with her. Most everyone did. "And I followed you 'cause I was curious. I don't know who you are or how you know Reeve. I mean, people here ain't exactly jumping at the chance to hang 'round him."

"I'm his friend."

"He doesn't have friends."

"Consider me an exception, then," he snapped at her. "What are you to him, anyways? You're a kid."

"Do I look like a kid to you? I'm seventeen. Well—I'll be seventeen three months from now."

His face did something complicated at that. "Sure, whatever you say," he said, with a tone that made her suspect he was rolling his eyes behind the aviators. "Name's Neal. Maybe he's mentioned me."

The name was familiar. Maze was reminded of the few times Reeve had divulged anything noteworthy about his childhood, and he'd always sounded fond when "Neal" came up. The man didn't usually do fond, so it stuck out.

"Yeah, a little. I'm usually the one doing the talking, though, so don't feel too bad about it. I got the feeling y'all were familiar."

"Familiar, huh?"

"We're familiar, too. Kinda."

"You're his friend?"

"Hey, he doesn't do friends, remember? We're, like, confidants. Not to mention Mr. Perfectly Fine needs some occasional human contact."

"Good to know."

They lapsed into awkward silence. Maze and Neal continued to assess each other warily. Whatever she had expected, it hadn't been him.

Reeve would give her these abrupt, one-word answers that brooked little flexibility. There was work, home, and the car. That was it; that was his life. And Maze realized there was no room for anyone or anything else in it—her presence was long-sufferingly tolerated by Reeve at best, though she liked to think he was slowly warming to her.

Neal was in for a surprise. Maybe things wouldn't be like he'd expected. At least she hadn't deluded herself into thinking Reeve was anything more than what he was. To tell Neal that, though, when his lips were turned up into something that yearned so openly, and his gaze seemed so fond, well, it just seemed cruel.

"This has been fun and all," Neal said at last, turning on his heel, "but I got things to do."

Shit, he was going to leave. "Wait—we could talk more if you wanted," Maze blurted out, trying not to sound too eager. Letting a golden opportunity like this slip through her fingers would end any chance she had at getting to know Reeve better.

"Look, you seem nice and all, but I'm not taking jailbait back to my motel or anywhere else, for that matter. I don't care if you and Reeve are "confidants," but I ain't getting picked up for that. Not to mention us even being together is more than a little untoward."

"I told you it's nothing weird like that, man! I meant at, like, a restaurant or something."

"Still weird."

"Whatever."

"Look, kid, what would you even get outta this? You don't even know me."

Info on your childhood friend turned my personal confidant. That probably wouldn't go over well with Neal, however, so Maze quickly reviewed her options.

"Look, you're not ready to talk to Reeve. I, however, do want to talk to you. Play nice with me for an hour, and I won't let slip that you've been lurking around," she told him.

Neal got a look on his face like he felt very old and wasn't sure why he was bothering with her. "This is extortion," he grit out.

"If that's what you want to call it."

"A spade's a spade. And this spade is some goddamn extortion. But I guess I'll bite. Where're we headed?"

Maze slipped her sunglasses on. "Just follow me."

***

From her rearview mirror, Maze watched as Neal trailed her out of Carthage and into the barren flatlands that marked the space between their town and Maidenhead. She imagined he was still wearing the same pissed-off expression as earlier, magnified further by the fact he'd been conned into doing her bidding.

Well, too bad. She did things she didn't like all the time.

The station wagon kicked up dust when she skidded into town. Maidenhead wasn't a large place by any means, but it had actual chain restaurants and even a strip mall, which is all it really needed to get a leg over on Carthage.

Maze turned the next corner.

Piggy's Pizza Palace was a squat brick building presided over by a towering neon sign that flashed the titular Piggy's face at five-second intervals. The pizza was greasy, and the inside stank like old vomit, but those things didn't matter when it was saturated in nostalgia.

Neal glared at her when they faced off in the parking lot. She was right: same pissed-off look.

"You promised me a hot meal, didn't you?"

"God, I hate kids," the man said by way of reply.

"Gee, thanks," Maze said, leading him in.

The red and black and white checkered interior took her back more than she expected. Even the smell affected her. Maze was reminded of the times when her dad brought her there growing up. Playing games, mocking the stupid mascots, splitting a pie between them—she missed him so much.

How was it that she felt him more here than in her own home? He'd died there, even, and now it was as though his essence had been bled from the walls until nothing was left. It was her mom's fault, she thought. It seemed like everything was her mom's fault nowadays.

"Can I seat y'all or what?" The bored voice of someone not getting paid enough to deal with the public intoned.

"Please," Neal said.

"Great," the hostess said, extending the "r" unenthusiastically. She led them to a corner table. "Piggy will be by to help in a sec. 'Til then, enjoy our complimentary water, straight from the trough."

And with that, she departed, leaving Maze and Neal to sit in awkward silence. They were separated by a laminate countertop bearing another Piggy rendition. Now that she was no longer an object in motion, and she had actually gotten Neal here, Maze found that all questions, all lines of interrogation had left her. For his part, Neal regarded her with a *well, what are you waiting for* look.

The bib-wearing pig mascot had made the rounds and just arrived at their table in time to break the ice. "Welcome to Piggy's Pizza Palace! My name is Piggy, and that there's my pizza you're eating today!" The mascot—Piggy—exclaimed loudly, oblivious to their mood and evident childlessness.

"Excited to be here," Maze said. "I'll have the Piggy Pie and a Dr. Pepper." Piggy was undeterred by her sarcasm and turned to her guest.

Neal leaned back in his seat. "Nothing for me," he said shortly. "Leave us be, please."

"Get over yourself," Piggy muttered under his breath as he walked off.

Neal made a face at his retreating figure before refixing his gaze on Maze, who suddenly felt a little bad about dragging this poor bastard out to Maidenhead for nothing except her company and pizza that he wasn't even going to eat.

Maze supposed she'd thought he would understand she needed to vent, just as Reeve had. Maybe she even needed him to. For someone, anyone, to just listen and get her. What kept him loyal to a killer for this long? And how could Maze replicate or likewise bottle that loyalty? Reeve and her mom were the only ones who knew what she'd done. The part she'd played in her dad's death.

It had destroyed her relationship with Jessica; it brought her and Reeve together. Maze wanted to know how to keep others in her orbit if she ever felt comfortable enough to confide in them.

Neal sighed and scrubbed a hand over his face. "Alright, spill," he said.

"Spill?"

"Yeah, spill. You clearly got something on your mind. God knows why I'd even be on the list of people to talk to, though."

Maze opened and closed her mouth. Now that she'd been given the opportunity to speak, she found the words she needed were right out of reach.

It had to do with a question she'd often asked herself in recent memory. What had drawn her to Reeve? He was a bad luck charm, and old-ish, besides. But she'd wondered if he knew what it was like to feel this kind of grief. That she could divine some secret from him that would render her whole again. Maze wanted to ask him if the pain would ever stop, or the guilt. The constant reminder of her dad enveloped everything around her, and she wondered whether it would ever dissipate. More than anything else, Maze needed normalcy. When would she go back to being what she was, rather than the girl no one could stand anymore. It did not take long after meeting Reeve to realize that for him, nothing had been the same since.

His bluntness ranged from comedic to downright uncomfortable. He really didn't know he was doing it, either. It had taken Maze a little while to get that. In the beginning, she'd been put off by him, his demeanor. When she'd played some Iron Maiden for him one day, he'd grimaced and requested that she "shut the goddamn noise off." Or if Maze went overboard with the eyeliner, he'd examine her face with intent, and then ask very seriously whether she'd gotten into a fight. At this point, she didn't expect to learn from or change him. It was just nice, she supposed, to be around someone who got where she was coming from.

Maze could feel his patience eroding whenever she overstayed her welcome, which was often. He wouldn't try to excommunicate her anymore, but his mouth would thin, and he would busy himself around the trailer while pointedly not looking her way. It was funny, odd. Maze got better at taking the hint, and she liked to think he'd warmed to her in turn.

"Well?" Neal inquired further.

"It's complicated," was what she settled on.

Even though she was turned away, she could practically feel his eye roll from across the table. "Uncomplicate it, then," he said.

"Don't—" she began, cutting herself off, "don't say that like it's easy."

Neal's expression shifted into something more serious. "Alright, why don't we talk about why the hell we're in this shithole."

"I haven't had their pizza in forever," she told him, grateful for the subject change despite it being, in truth, unearned.

"And *this* is good enough to drive to Maidenhead for?"

"Hey, it's the best I got to work with around here."

"I can't believe I got blackmailed by a teenager."

"At least you can afford it," Maze muttered, shooting his expensive jacket a significant look.

Piggy took that opportunity to give Maze her meal, rebuffed from offering any further service by Neal's glare. The irony of a Jew being served food by a pig wasn't lost on her.

"How is he? Really," Neal asked once he'd driven off whatever poor soul was trapped in that costume. There was only one *him*—Reeve.

Maze searched for the word to best describe him. *Stasis*, she decided. That was it. He sought stasis in all things.

The old box cars in his kitchen among the miscellaneous clutter were just one of many examples she could name. It was a peculiar and sad detail. Another piece of his broken life.

Attempting conversation with him seemed at times almost futile, and she would ask herself why she even bothered with Reeve. When she turned the image of her dad over in her head, she knew the answer. It was then she remembered they were the same. The sole difference was that her mom made sure she was the only one who knew what Maze had done. He'd been afforded no such anonymity.

People didn't know what to do with him, so it seemed to her like it was easier for them to pretend like he wasn't there at all. Those who didn't were just cruel.

He carried himself like a background fixture—Reeve, the living wallpaper, Reeve, your friendly neighborhood lampshade. Maze could not imagine Reeve relaxing with a TV show or listening to the radio; he probably stared at the wall in silence for a couple hours and wrote it off as his daily amusement intake.

Even despite this, she still didn't really get why he'd stayed. Maze was getting the hell out of dodge as soon as she could. When that day would come, she wasn't sure.

"Uh," was all she said, and that hesitance was enough for Neal to groan and grind his knuckles into his temples.

"I knew this would happen if he didn't get out. God, I knew it."

"Good luck getting that guy to do anything he doesn't want to. And for some reason, Carthage is where he wants to be."

"Don't you think I know that? Even though that place is killing him!"

It was then that Maze realized that Neal cared about Reeve. Like, really, *really* cared about him.

"He's like a frog, y'know," Maze offered.

"A frog?"

"Yeah, a frog. You put one in a pot of hot water, and it'll jump out. If you slip one in all easy-like, though, when the water is still lukewarm, it won't realize it's been brought to a boil 'til it's as good as dead."

"This a metaphor or something?"

"Or something," Maze agreed, then continued, "You haven't talked to him yet."

"No."

"I know you've been here for at least four days. You're stalking him outside his house. So, what's the holdup?"

"I got my reasons. Jesus, why am I even explaining myself to you?"

"'Cause I got the inside scoop on your boy," Maze said, paying close attention to the twitch he gave at the words "your boy."

"He's not my boy, bitch," Neal spat, his anger dying out as quickly as it fared up. "Apologies. Didn't mean to—"

"Not my first time hearing it," Maze informed him.

He smiled thinly. "Surprise, surprise. Finish your pizza."

When she cleared her plate, Maze fisted the napkin in her hands, picking at it until little white pieces littered the tabletop and her jeans.

"This has been fun."

"Not really."

"Yeah," she said, "guess I'll see you around, then."

Maze left him there, a bronze statue in the evening light outside the pizzeria and headed home. Their conversation lingered in her mind. Neal's devotion to Reeve, and her own—as she'd called him earlier—companion's solitary existence. How could Neal not have told Reeve about being back? What reason could he have to hide? There was no issue, no situation she'd gleaned from him so far that would point to any kind of falling out or rift. There was something he wasn't telling her.

There was something he wasn't telling Reeve.

NEAL II

Wherefore, be it by the vicissitudes of fortune, or by the acidic intent of some now ill-favored and long forgotten god, Eliot Barnes and Ezrah Bell were destined to be separated in this life. They had been born just minutes apart in a small town deep in the Ozarks known as Scythe, and soon became fast friends. This is their tale.

Eliot's tortured gaze followed him from the cover as he set the book down. Neal shuddered and turned it over. He'd never been one for novels; this one was no exception.

Reeve's eyes had disturbed Neal, too. It was something about them, their blankness, maybe, or how they seemed to absorb light rather than reflect it. He couldn't remember it being this bad before. Maybe he was just kidding himself.

He moved through the town like he didn't touch it, couldn't. Neal reflected on how stupid he'd been to think he could just slide back into Reeve's life without consequence. But God. He'd missed that brutish voice, his dark gaze, Reeve's unthinking honesty. It was a comfort, familiar, his homecoming.

They had always done better when together than apart.

When they were kids, he and Reeve would hang out beneath the bleachers, mostly, or out near the Pit late in the evening. Their homes were both off-limits. It didn't even require discussion. Reeve had his tools, his books, his view on the world. Neal's only real hobbies were avoiding his dad and the occasional small-scale property crime, so if the other boy felt like a change of pace, the pair would take a baseball bat out to the junkyard and smash the windshields in on beaters until everything sick and awful was squeezed out into the open.

Some days, they would light up a public trashcan or throw bricks through the windows of foreclosed houses. He recalled his childhood anger as a dark, jagged shape that intruded into and dominated even the few good things in his life. It ached for release, to be sated, and then packed back inside, until it boiled over once more.

Neal thought Reeve was above it, that he didn't really need it in the same way he seemed to. That their activities were more for Neal than him. Then he let him in on his "hauntings," and Neal realized he was much, much worse.

It was different—it was real crime. It was some serial killer shit.

Neal remembered feeling so sick with nerves he'd almost wretched the moment they entered the darkened kitchen. Sweat beaded along his fringe, trickled down to pool above his lips. Each footstep was an earthquake, each breath a guttering exhale. Reeve, though—for such an awkward, nervous guy, he was preternaturally silent. It was a corpse-like silence. The silence of a dead man. His friend seemed to be more in his element here than in the daylight world.

Reeve moved through the house like he didn't even touch the floor. His fingers brushed the owner's things, almost touching but not, and when he floated upstairs and into the bedroom, he hovered over her bed and stared down at her supine form with an unblinking gaze. It wasn't a fetish; it wasn't sexual. Reeve seemed impervious to sexuality, which somehow made everything all the weirder for it.

He was the same person he'd been back then, Neal thought. These things he was doing, the compulsions—they had just been magnified, the cracks deepened. He didn't think he'd expected to change or even need him to. This, him, Neal had missed it. Knowing someone like that, so intimately, was its own comfort. He wanted Reeve to know him, the new him, and to see how far he'd come.

He let these thoughts roll over, turn, until they emerged the next day when he saw Reeve again after work. They were at his place, wedged together on the couch amidst the clutter and records and books everywhere. The other man was a line of heat beside him. Reeve looked like he would be cold, but Neal knew better.

Their conversation was stilted and as laden with words unspoken as it had the day before. Work. Interests. Friends and lack thereof. Neal's trip to Piggy's. He skirted around the years in between leaving the foster system and starting up his business. Eventually, they came to a pause. He couldn't put it off any further.

Neal swallowed, not able to hold his gaze. "These things you do," he began, tentative, "is there a reason?"

He felt Reeve tense. Then his black gaze roved over him with palpable weight. Neal's mouth went dry.

"Bad things happen when I don't."

"What, uh, do you mean?"

"They protect me," he said. "I know it doesn't make much sense. I need to, though. I have to do them."

"But *why,* then?"

"I try, sometimes. To keep from giving in. But then my brain talks back to me. It asks me, "What if?" What if I don't go through with it and something goes wrong? Something I could've stopped? So, I do it. I do it and do it and do it. It's the only way I can live in peace."

"Oh."

"Yeah."

Neal searched for comfort but came up empty. What words could he give him? There was nothing. He had nothing.

Reeve stepped in, sidestepping Neal's attempt to shift their talk into less dangerous waters. "I wish I had taken it for you. I would've taken that pain like a bullet."

There was no other *it* in their lives other than the night that had driven them apart, seemingly forever. When Neal's dad lost his mind and ruined what good he'd found in this mundane, horrible town. The night that got Neal bedridden in the hospital and run out for good.

Neal sighed and sagged back into the cushions. "It's not the kind of thing you can share."

Reeve's face twitched at that.

Neal wanted to reach out and comfort him, even as just his friend, hand twisting in on itself to keep from reaching out. Was comfort something Reeve would accept? He wasn't sure. The boy—man, he reminded himself— who sat across from him now was at once both strange and unfamiliar. Maybe he'd gone blood simple.

There were still moments to this day where he'd get sickened by his own want, feel the familiar companion choke his lungs and twine around his stomach. Why couldn't he flip some switch that would allow him to offer

Reeve a friendly palm on his forearm, a clap on the back? But he couldn't; his motives would never be pure.

He'd been afraid to let it mean something. The shame had scalded his throat like bile for the longest time, and he could not separate it from the act until well after he got out. He could fuck men, but he could not love them.

Eventually, Neal settled on asking, "You see the National 500 last Sunday?"

"It was a good race," Reeve said.

"Not the same without Yarborough."

"No, it's not."

A lot of things were different now.

Neal searched for something to break up this goddamn awkward conversation, saying, "Hey, let's put in a tape since I'm over. I know you got some stored here,"

Reeve did. It was an ancient western he and his old man had probably watched a dozen times over. They were so close, and the couch may have been sagging, stained in places, but it was soft and well-loved.

And before he knew it, his eyes fluttered shut.

***

His first thought was that he was warm. In a distant, dreamy way, it was nice. But then the warmth shifted, breathed, and Neal realized it was a person he was lying on. Neal jerked awake.

Reeve's hard planes and angles were drowned in flickering light from the TV, which was still playing the film they'd selected. His gaze wasn't on the screen, though; no, it was fixed on Neal, heavy and full.

Neal's face and chest went hot. He didn't want to move. In fact, he could have died there, comfortably, in what was effectively Reeve's embrace. Well, the closest he'd ever get to it.

Neither man moved for a long moment, two statues caught between the motion and the act. It was Reeve who broke first, which shocked some sense back into Neal.

"Uh, sorry, man," he stuttered. "I must've been more tired than I thought. Can't believe I used you as a pillow, Jesus."

Reeve's strange, almost perplexed expression deepened. "I didn't mind," he informed him entirely without guile.

God, you have no idea what you do to me.

"Really?"

"I don't say things I don't mean."

"I guess you don't," Neal agreed. "Anyways, I had better leave. It's late."

Reeve led him all the way to the door before making an aborted grab for Neal's arm. Neal let him. He could count on one hand the number of times the other man had touched another human of his own free will.

"If you wanted, you could stay," he said.

Neal licked the inside of his mouth. "You sure?"

"What did I tell you earlier?"

That you don't say things you don't mean.

And with that, he followed Reeve inside again, back through the maze-like hoard, its memories, until they had reached the attached garage. It was more personable in there, less heavy. It contained Reeve's actual belongings. He even had up the old Cale Yarborough poster Neal had given him in high school, which graced the room with a presence not unlike Jesus', especially with the way he smiled down at what passed for Reeve's bed.

"I know it's not much."

"It's fine, Red."

"I have some things for you to sleep in, if you need," he said, rifling through his dresser and tossing Neal a worn, soft shirt and some sweatpants when he nodded in assent.

He tried not to be too obvious about tangling the clothes between his fingers to feel the fabric, scent its detergent. "Uh, how should we do this? I'm guessing I'll take the couch."

"If you want. I don't mind sharing, though. It'll be more comfortable for you."

Neal wondered if he should say no not only for his own sake, but Reeve's as well. It felt to him like he was taking advantage of his ignorance; this meant different things to them, even though Neal wanted so desperately to believe he wasn't alone in his want.

"Sounds good," he stuttered out.

After a torturous period where he had to turn his back on the other man as he changed, Neal got settled in for the night without further incident. The pair lay next to each other, wrapped in their respective comforters on the pallet.

"Good night," he told Reeve, just to have something to say.

Reeve huffed out a low breath in response. Then everything got quiet, and the comfort Neal felt on all sides set in, and he was somewhere else before he even really understood what was happening.

Neal dreamed about his dad. He dreamed about his parents a lot, he found. And this dream was a familiar one because it was a memory that he'd rehashed so many times in retrospect.

The evening had started off normal enough.

He'd been watching NASCAR with his dad when the program switched to commercial and an ad for beer came on. A man was surrounded by couples on a beach, reclining alone on a towel with a cooler at his feet. But he didn't look sad, or angry, just expectant, and when he opened the cooler to reveal it was full up with beer bottles, the women abandoned their boyfriends to converge on him.

Neal's eyes lingered on the water droplets glimmering on the man's collarbone, their sinuous movements as they trickled down his chest, and then beneath the hem of his swim trunks—

"Skin," his dad remarked suddenly, "look at her skin. So beautiful."

"Yeah," Neal replied, mouth dry. He turned towards his dad.

Gabriel's gaze was fixed on the girl beside the man drinking the beer, some tiny blonde thing in a bikini with her tits and ass hanging out. Neal could see what made her so special, in theory, but he did not feel it. He never had.

Even if it had always existed somewhere within him, acknowledging to himself that what he was felt different, more real, and Neal wondered whether people would be able to look at him and *see*. And the word for men like him, men who liked other men… Neal could not use that word, not even in his own head. It seemed to connote a whole way of being, of living, that bore only a superficial resemblance to his own.

He wished that there was something in his past that he could point to, some trauma that explained why he was this way. A funny uncle. Something. Because he sure as hell didn't choose this.

Gabriel was a perceptive man, perhaps far more than people outside his family gave him credit for. Neal and his mom knew this well.

His dad had always tried to make him act more like a man, like he knew without being told what Neal was. He gave Neal beer for the first time when he was eight; had him shoot cans out back when he was ten. By eleven, they were blowing critters up with Tannerite in the woods over by Maidenhead.

These things may have brought them closer in the short term, but mostly it made Neal feel so small. Like he could never be what the people in his life wanted him to. He was being punished for something invisible but irrevocable about himself.

The two men said nothing for the rest of the afternoon, and the images in his memory were fractured—he couldn't recall whether the day ended with a fight or more quality time with his dad. It was dominated by skin, skin, skin—

Neal woke the next morning to Reeve's alarm. They had migrated towards each other in the night, though his friend still lay flat on his back like a corpse. It was almost endearing. And when his eyes opened, it was an instantaneous shift from rest to wakefulness.

The pair separated for the day, for which Neal felt pathetically grateful. He needed to get some space between himself and Reeve. More than anything, he worried he would do something he'd regret.

He drove around, thinking back to what the hell had even motivated him to come here to begin with. The urge to speak with Ruth or Joseph surfaced again, just like it had when Reeve had found him. Neal drifted back to a payphone and leaned up against the glass. He slipped a quarter in and dialed the number he'd memorized by heart.

"Neal," Ruth said by way of greeting.

"Heya, Ruth," he said, slouching into the payphone.

"How are things?"

"The same as they were the last time you called," she told him. "Now, why are you calling me, honey?"

"Oh," he said, "y'know."

"No, the hell I don't," she replied, an undercurrent of humor present in her tone.

"I just miss y'all, I guess."

"Well, sure. But you'll see us again soon, son. We aren't going anywhere. We're still waiting for you—no matter what happens there. Even if—God forbid—that boy of yours cuts you out, curses you, whatever, we'll be here to welcome you back. Just like we talked about before you left. And if you think this would be the thing to tear us apart, then you've forgotten all you, me, and Trev have been through together."

"I haven't, Ruth," Neal said, "I promise."

"With that settled, why don't you tell me what's been going on."

So, he did, retracing the past day's events until he felt more settled in his skin, Ruth's familiar laugh washing over him like a calm shroud. She was a visceral reminder that he had changed since his time here in Carthage, that he wasn't the same person he'd been all those years ago.

He placed the phone back on the receiver with a loud *click*. About only thirty or so minutes had passed, which meant he still had time to kill before returning to Reeve's. Around him, he could see people in his periphery going about their business: shopping, clustering together in conversation, or out for a walk to enjoy the day. Some, he noticed, were in clear discussion over him, pointing and whispering to each other.

It became even more obvious that he was still living in quasi-infamy here when the people nearest to him pivoted to pretend being otherwise occupied. Neal rolled his eyes and returned to the Mirage Inn, intentionally avoiding his old house. Neal didn't know what he would do if he saw it. Lose his shit, probably. The last time he was there was the single worst day of his life.

He itched for a drink but resisted, instead opting for fast food to take back to his motel room. Joseph and Ruth helped keep him on the wagon, but they were back in Des Moines. His mom had warned him about it when he was a kid, but he'd acted the way most kids do.

"Don't touch that shit," Irena had told him, eyes dark and watchful.

Neal reared back. "Why?"

"You know why," she said. "Not to mention you'll wind up like your daddy."

"That's rich. You tolerate him well enough."

Irena pulled him by the collar down to her level. "I've seen this destroy lives, families. It's not a joke. It's the furthest thing from it. You know what people are gonna say about you. About us."

"Good thing I'm a mutt. Maybe I got enough white in me to get away with it."

"Gabriel thinks that just 'cause he looks white that he is. He isn't. Those people see it. Even we see it. He'll never be what they are, not fully. And if he ever forgets his place, they'll damn well make sure he never does again. It's just a matter of time.

"You'd do right to not forget it, either. Doesn't matter how mixed you might be. They'll always see you as whatever the other half is. And that other half is me."

His mom had told him she didn't want him to know what it felt like to carry that. Their history. Her blackness. But that wasn't her choice to make, and it didn't matter anyways.

"Thanks for nothing, mama. Least I got *Vásquez* going for me."

"I gave you all the names that matter. Neal, for Neal Cassady. I read "On the Road" while hitchhiking. It's what gave me the courage to leave as a child. Sören, for your farmor's daddy. Blue, for my favorite color. The kind of clear, easy blue that marks an early morning."

"Look where those names got me," he told her, unable to watch her sigh and purse her lips at his insolence. "Nowhere."

Irena bared her teeth. "So you say."

In the present, Neal tipped his nape back against the headboard and sighed. He regretted how things went down between them. They were so often pitted against each other in the court of Gabriel's favor.

He almost made an excuse to not go over to Reeve's again, but then the thought of being needlessly separated from him when they were so close pricked deep in his throat, almost as though he were a man dying of thirst. Neal could no more deny himself this than water. However, he did return to the Mirage Inn to clean up, wash and slick back his hair with gel, apply cologne—something expensive he'd treated himself to—and a clean shirt and jeans.

After it was said and done, Neal felt a little silly, a little like a high school girl getting ready for her first date. His face got hot, and his nails bit into each palm. There wasn't anything weird about two guys hanging out together. He was allowed to want to look nice. Friends did it all the time. And they had a lot of time to make up. But it wasn't Reeve who was making it weird, though, it was him, like always, ruining and twisting the good in his life until it was as messed up as he was.

The numbers on the complementary digital clock caught his eye: it was six-thirty in the evening. Reeve would be home by now, expecting him. It was one thing to get caught up in himself; it was another to make his own problems Reeve's. He'd done that enough already. Ruth and Joseph taught him that.

Throwing on his sherpa-lined jacket, Neal exited the motel and wound back through Carthage to Reeve's place.

The neighbor's porch was lit up when he arrived, and the man—Zeke or Zachariah or something—stepped out into the light, which rippled across his face like water. Neal could tell right away that this man was cold-blooded. He'd seen that kind of man before, in prison and growing up. There was something distant, reptilian about his gaze. Those pale, bulbous eyes. The way they imparted the feeling of being examined under a microscope.

Neal moved to knock, but Reeve opened the door before he even had a chance. Neal's hand wavered in the air for a moment, arm aloft, so close to Reeve's chest that had he been any closer, they could've touched. Neal withdrew as if he'd been burned.

"Hello," Reeve said in his low, rasping voice.

"Hey, Red."

"Would you like to come in?"

What am I, Neal thought, *a vampire?*

"That's why I'm here."

Reeve spared no more words and instead stepped aside to make room for Neal like a gentleman. His irrational heart pounded. He recovered quickly, tipping his head in mock assent. Reeve did not smile, but his lips twitched upwards. For him, that may as well have been a full-on belly laugh.

They didn't put on another movie like last night. No, that was too dangerous. Rather, Neal browsed through the meticulously ordered junk Reeve's old man had left behind and that his friend still maintained. It was clean, too—no dust. How much time did Reeve spend in here looking after this useless shit? Did it take up his otherwise lonely nights and weekends? Was it all he had?

There was a record scratch, then—

"Voodoo Chile" by Jimi Hendrix moaned to life.

Oh, I remember this one, Neal thought to himself. It was the last LP they had listened to together before things changed between them, seemingly forever. Why had Reeve put this on? He wasn't a particularly sentimental person; at least, not on his own.

Hendrix crooned deep and low on the speakers.

"You still got this record?"

"Yes."

"We listened to this one 'fore I left."

"We did."

"You remembered."

"You didn't expect me to?"

"I guess not."

"Then you assumed wrong."

"Jesus, Red," Neal laughed awkwardly. "Guess I was. I'm the kinda guy who's wrong about a lot of things."

Reeve's mouth cracked open for real. "Oh, I wouldn't say that."

Neal rubbed the back of his neck. The he reentered foot-in-mouth territory by saying thickly, "Anyways, you settin' the mood or somethin'?"

"I don't know what that means."

Of course, you don't, Neal thought hysterically.

"Never mind, man," he said. "Why don't you show me what your life looks like nowadays? Gimme the run-down."

"If you insist."

"Oh, I'm insisting, alright."

Reeve then proceeded to guide him through the motions. It was as he'd suspected: his friend would arrive home late to this goddamn empty trailer, meander through the towering horde until he reached what little space he'd carved out for himself in the place supposed to be his home.

There was the couch and area that encircled it, encompassing the TV set, rug, and record player; and, naturally, the attached garage that doubled as Reeve's bedroom and workspace.

Neal nearly asked *why? Why the hell d'you insist on suffering like this?* to Reeve but kept his mouth shut. It was another one of those—things he felt compelled to do without any logical rhyme or reason.

Then, absurdly, he almost asked Reeve to dance. There was music on, after all. The idea of grim, silent Reeve who had no real fondness for what anyone in their right mind would consider "fun" getting down to a beat was so comical it made him laugh out loud.

"What's so funny?"

"I don't really know. Just happy, I s'pose."

"I'm glad, Neal. I missed you."

I missed you more than you will ever know, Neal thought. *I've tortured myself over you. I've tried to be a better man because of you. I don't think I even know who I am without you. I thought I did, but I was wrong. I needed you so bad.*

"Missed you too, Red."

Part II

In the Lethe

REEVE III

There had once been a dog. More of a mutt, really, he recalled, with a sad, sloe-eyed look about it and droopy, folded ears. The runt of the litter. Sad.

Reeve had found it one hot afternoon while playing out near the back of the apartment complex, where it whimpered and pawed at itself. Someone had poured glue all over it, the kind that came in a bucket, and knotted a rope around its neck, tying it to the fence separating the apartment complex from the trees beyond. This was the side opposite to where the pool was, away from the cemetery, the pool.

But what Reeve remembered more than anything was the *sounds*. The strange, baby-like sounds warbling up and out from its throat. Somewhere between human and animal.

Reeve instinctively reached out to touch it, offer comfort, but the little thing yipped and snapped at him in fear. They were primitive reflexes. It was alright. He understood; he had his own.

He'd seen Ephraim leave the apartment with a can in hand earlier that day, and it was with a sinking feeling that Reeve contemplated the prospect that his brother had left this dog to die in the summer heat. Nearby, people were out by the pool, playing and laughing, but none had stopped to help.

Had they even noticed?

Then, from behind, a hand appeared on his shoulder, and he jumped. Ephraim grinned down at him, eyes glittering like the edge on metal. The switchblade he always carried was held aloft.

"Look at it," he said, gripping Reeve's jaw in his hand to twist it back towards the dog, "this little thing. It's just sitting there now, waiting to die."

The dog whimpered again, trying to blink as its eyelids caught on each other as they tried to open and close. It never managed more than a sliver of terrified pupil.

"You hurt it," Reeve said.

Ephraim scoffed. "You think I'm supposed to feel sad?"

"I-I don't get it. Why're you doing this? What's the point in making it hurt? It's just a dog. It never did nothing to nobody."

"That's the point, Reeve. What I've been trying to tell you for so long," he said, almost laughing. "A dog can't tell on you or complain. It gives in, submits because it has to. In that way, it knows its place. Submission is second nature. Kind of like you, really. There's an animal in us all. It's the part that doesn't think or talk—just feels, needs. Some of us are closer to that than others."

Reeve tried to shake his head, still caught in his brother's unrelenting grip.

"You don't see it? Maybe you should prove me wrong then," Ephraim told him, pressing the switchblade into Reeve's palm. "It won't feel like anything. No more than cutting into meat from the butcher's shop would. It's already as good as dead, after all."

Reeve grunted out a "No," and wouldn't let his fingers wrap around the handle, even when his brother interlocked their hands to make him.

"Guess I was right," Ephraim said eventually, voice laden with faux disappointment, wrenching the knife from his grasp to hook it into the left crook of Reeve's mouth. "Looks like you're a gutter dog bitch, too. Ain't even man enough to take care of this."

"But I love you, Eph."

"I love you, Eph" sounded more like "Why are you doing this to me?"

His brother said nothing to that, but an expression crossed his face that bordered on pity. *Oh, Reeve,* the look seemed to say, *don't you know anything? Anything at all?*

The metal rested on his tongue for a moment, and Reeve thought that Ephraim was maybe psyching him out, playing another sick joke on him, but then he felt a tug to the left and suddenly tasted hot blood. He registered the shock before the pain and uttered a broken noise from between ruined lips.

Ephraim murmured in his ear, "Now they'll always be able to tell us apart."

Reeve didn't need to see his brother's face to know he was smiling.

When Ephraim released his hold on him, Reeve fell to his knees and clutched at the severed flap of skin. He did not cry, and nor did he feel sad, really—his chest just felt heavy, he thought. Heavy and empty at the same time.

"The animal can die quick, or it can die slow. You decide," his brother said, tossing the knife down beside him. "And don't forget what I told you."

Ephraim left him there at some point after that, a distance that Reeve felt but did not see. There were footsteps, the smothered crinkle-crunch of grass in his periphery, each sound growing softer and softer by the second.

The dog was still alive—still crying, still convulsing. The noises it made now were less like a baby's, rawer, more scraped-open. The glue was in its throat, too, Reeve realized. Laying thick to the esophagus' inner walls, trickling down.

Could Ephraim be right?

The switchblade had been discarded on the ground by his knees, wet metal glinting beneath the sunlight. It intimidated him. Not because he knew what it meant to be at its end, or even that his brother had been the one to use it, but because of the slow-dawning understanding that he was going to be the next one to wield the blade. And it would mean something, he thought, doing this. What that was, he wasn't sure yet.

Slow, fast. Slow or fast.

He lifted the hem of his shirt and packed it into his mouth to staunch the blood dribbling from the open slit gauged into the side, then picked up the knife with one small, trembling hand. When he leveled it at the dog, bile rose in his throat, and Reeve nearly lost his nerve right then and there.

"I-It's," he began, tenuous, "it's, uh—shit. Sorry, I'm so sorry. If you could talk, you would thank me for this. I promise."

Reeve crawled forward and petted its head once, twice, before pressing the flat of the blade against its throat. He closed his eyes and hugged the dog close to his chest, head turned into its body, then turned the switchblade and slashed it in a downward arc as deep and hard as he could. The animal jerked in his arms and continued to cry out, only now it sounded weirdly distorted. Reeve held on tighter and kept stabbing until the crying stopped. At this, he let the blade slip from his fingers and collapsed forward onto the dead mutt, stroking its matted fur and murmuring, "I'm sorry, I'm sorry, I'm sorry."

He lay there for a while—he wasn't sure how long, really—but when the sun nearly completed its descent, he knew it was time to leave. He got up on unsteady legs while the dog remained motionless at his feet. No one had come across them or intervened, despite the close echo of children's laughter and adult conversation.

When he turned to head back inside, Reeve hesitated. He hesitated because if it were him, he wouldn't want to be abandoned like this. So, he unwound the rope and gathered the dog into his arms, nuzzling it again as he wandered through the back end of the complex and out onto the road. Reeve didn't know what he was looking for at first, wandering until he was drawn towards a small, forested area right off the main drag.

It was an easy place to imagine a dog enjoying, he thought.

The grave was dug with his bare hands. Little more than an uneven dirt hole in the end, marked only by disturbed earth. But it wasn't nothing, either.

Later, when he returned home that night to his parents' identical concerned expressions, and was asked what the hell happened, Reeve told them under Ephraim's watchful gaze that he'd been playing with a knife.

In the coming years, he would visit this otherwise unremarkable clearing time and time again to stare at that spot where the nameless dog lay, withered, slept. He never brought flowers or anything so sentimental. His presence was a contemplative one, and he'd finger the thick scar that extended out from his lip while in repose.

He'd haunted that gravesite more than his dad's, his mom's, or even his brother's. It was funny, Reeve thought, because he couldn't explain why. Maybe Ephraim had been right about another thing, too—that they were the same.

His mom, Alana, had been hopping mad at him for weeks after. He and Ephraim were special, her first live ones; she'd gone through one miscarriage after another and named every one of their unborn older siblings. Alana made them both recite those names at night when they prayed before bed. They prayed for their souls in heaven, and that they would watch over them as they suffered on this earth.

Then Reeve took a son from her. And after, when he sat in Sunday school with the stained-glass triptych of Mary, Joseph, and the Son bearing down on him, he felt too disgusting to be there. It was under their gazes that he formed the first of many habits—picking at his nails until they bled, counting things out in threes. He'd spend those mornings staring at them, trying to work out why it was he that survived, and Ephraim didn't, especially since it seemed everyone wished it had been the other way around.

"How am I supposed to love you," his mom had murmured into his neck some indeterminable day after Ephraim's death, holding him close, "when I can't even stand to look at you anymore?"

They were twins. Apart from the scar, they had been identical. That meant that each time Alana saw him, she was seeing double.

How it took him by surprise that she left, he wasn't sure. But it did, and it hurt. He hurt more because he knew he was at fault. Reeve declared himself an atheist the day his dad told him she wasn't coming back. The existence of God didn't trouble him daily anymore, really. He'd just quit caring.

He supposed he stopped caring about everything else too along the way.

***

Now, deep into the daily cleaning process he followed for the items within the trailer, he sighed. Reeve had passed by the gravesite earlier that evening; Neal was busy or whatever, so he'd paid it a visit before driving home. As for his things, he had nothing better to do and knew it would bother him if he tried to resist his routine: clean, adjust, count, windows, doors, rinse, repeat.

He couldn't explain why he needed things to be this way. There were thought loops he could not think his way out of, and he spent more time arguing with his own brain than he had in conversation with any other human being.

If he didn't check the window latches, he would be set upon by the ominous premonition that someone would break in. The same went for when he contemplated the alternative to caring after his dad's stuff; the idea to him felt like a violation to the extent where he became certain, even though he did not believe in God, that Amon would somehow take notice and return from the dead to give him a piece of his mind.

Even letting Maze into his house ground against his every instinct. The most difficult time had been the first, but it bothered him less and less the more she frequented the trailer. He supposed he was just folding her into said routine as the days elapsed.

Maze had initially knocked on his back door late one evening back when Carthage was in the throes of summer. Reeve, who did not entertain visitors as a rule, had been so taken aback by her presence on his property that he did not react for several long moments. He pulled back the curtain once more at the window and found that yes, she was still there, and had not made some bizarre mistake as to a friend's address. Why she was here, he couldn't even begin to guess.

The girl turned to face him. "Hey, I see you!" She shout-whispered, pointing at where he'd been exposed by the curtain. "So, you might as well come out."

Reeve understood it would be best to oblige her and get whatever this was over and done with. But the prospect of someone new intruding into his home disturbed him. His palms were clammy. He loosened his tie. He touched the lock three times before unlatching it, then let the door swing open.

The girl fixed him with a dolorous stare when he emerged. Tall, muscular, and dark-haired, she easily had three inches on him in height even while slouched. Her arms were folded across her chest and her tennis shoes tapped out a rapid beat as he assessed her.

"What do you want?"

"Oy, some greeting that is," she said, then rubbed the back of her neck. "I, uh, don't really know how to explain why I'm here."

He said nothing to that and made no attempt at pleasantries. The girl shifted on her feet. Her makeup was beginning to run in the heat, and it streaked down her face in irregular black and brown lines.

"Look, can we take this inside? Your weird neighbors can't mind their own, and neither of us want them getting up into our business."

Reeve poked his head out further. Sure enough, Heddie was posted by her front window and inspecting the neighborhood as she directed her brood to do various chores. Fine, he thought. Fine, fine. He didn't need to borrow trouble.

"Fine."

The girl had to duck her head just to get inside, and it soon became clear that the trailer had not been designed with people of her stature in mind. He gestured for her to follow, and they navigated the labyrinth until the pair reached the kitchen, where he cleared a space for her at the table. He removed the books and set them on the counter, where he took care to ensure their spines were aligned. The girl's gray eyes tracked the movement.

There was a tightness in his chest when he sat down. Everything felt disturbed, in a way. Reeve recalled an experiment his first-grade science teacher, Miss Smith, had conducted in class once. She had filled a plastic tub with water and added objects until liquid was splashing over the brim. Water displacement, she had called it.

To his artless child-self, it had been magnificent. It was before he had cause to fear what water could do to him. This girl—whoever she was—was doing the same thing now as those objects had so long ago; her very presence in his home was an exercise in displacement.

"This is… nice," she said finally.

"Not really."

"Yeah, not really," she agreed, then leaned forward after he did not offer further comment. "You're wondering why I'm here, right? I get it. You don't know me, but I've heard of you. And I need your help."

Reeve blinked. "In what way?"

"It's complicated," she said. The girl picked at her t-shirt. "Well. You killed your brother. That's a fact. People see you and think "murderer." That's also a fact. But it was an accident, right?"

Reeve was rendered momentarily speechless by how damn forward she was. Then he said, "Yes."

"Okay, cool. Good."

"Is that all?"

"Hey, wait. No can do. I haven't even got to the point yet."

There's a point to this conversation? Reeve thought, then told her to get on with it.

"I, uh, did it too," she blurted. "The same thing you did. Hurt somebody. And you seem like you're doing alright for yourself."

"Really."

"I don't know. But you've grown up with this, and I'm a fucking mess, so I figured talking to you wouldn't hurt."

That was interesting. "Get your head screwed on straight," people would tell him. *I'm trying,* he'd think. *Can't you see I'm trying?*

"I don't reckon I'll be much help."

Her features turned pleading. "Please? I'll just pick your brain."

"Fine. Ask your questions."

The girl did, and she proceeded to inquire after every detail involved in Ephraim's death and Reeve's subsequent appointment as murderer. He saw no reason to lie or likewise obscure the truth, so he answered every question honestly. Yes, he had knocked Eph so badly he drowned. No, he didn't mean it. Yes, people still called him a murderer. No, life wasn't particularly good here, but it could be worse, and the chatter about him had somewhat eased up with time.

"You said you did something similar."

Maze—which was her surname, according to her, but the mononym she insisted on being called—sighed. In that moment, the look in her eyes aged her beyond her years. "Yeah," she began, reflexively knuckling her temple. "It was my dad. I could've helped him. But I didn't, and now he's gone forever. I think about it all the time. I'm not even myself anymore, really."

Reeve understood the feeling intimately. He regarded the girl with less reserve, then, and tried his to comfort her as best he knew how.

"It's a feeling no one will know unless they've been there. I can't describe it. Not to people who aren't like us. I hope they never understand."

Maze wiped at her face and smiled at him. It transformed her; it reminded him that she was so, so young. Reeve offered her a towel to clean up before sending her off to wherever she usually spent her days.

"Can I come back?" Maze asked by the door.

He paused, considering. "If you want."

"I might, uh, need to sneak in. Don't need people spreading our association around and all, especially since it could look weird."

"Weird in what way?"

"I'm sixteen. You're, like, thirty-five or something."

"I'm twenty-seven."

"Same difference."

"I don't understand."

"You're hopeless, man. It'd look like we were doing, *y'know*, which wouldn't be good for either of us," she entreated, sighing when his expression didn't shift. Maze elaborated with, "Having sex, Reeve. That's what I mean."

"Oh, right."

And she left him there, off to do whatever teenage girls did in their free time. Reeve would not see her for another week until he heard tapping on his rear window one late weekday night. He finished what he was doing before peering around the newspaper and through the glass. It was her, trying to act discreet. He sighed but let her in.

Then emerged the new routine. Each time she returned, Reeve thawed more and more towards her. Maze would bring tidings from school and work—gossip, that was. He didn't mind.

He learned about her estranged ex-boyfriend, Dean, who was a basketball star and a coward. She'd ended things with him on account of the last part. Maze had a new man in her life now. Emphasis on "man." Reeve didn't know his name or really anything significant other than the fact that he was older. He likewise didn't know what to make of the relationship but figured that due to what she'd mentioned during their first encounter, he wasn't in a position to judge.

There was her friend Oralene, too. The picture she painted was one of opposites: Oralene was pretty, Maze was not; she was soft and inviting, Maze all hard planes and angles. Maze seemed to regard her with a strange mixture of love and jealousy. Reeve couldn't recall ever speaking to or about Neal in such a manner, not even when the wound from his absence had gaped open and throbbed endlessly in his chest. Was there something fundamentally different about female friendships? Or was there just something different about him and Neal?

If there was one thing he could pin down about her, though, it was that her life was complicated, just like she'd said. Neal had arrived at a similar realization during their fateful excursion to some idiotically named restaurant called Piggy's Pizza Palace. The other man had told him little else of their encounter aside from that, but Reeve could tell something more had transpired between them.

As for work, it continued to be awash with whispers. Where before he had been a kind of peculiar, if not outright detestable non-entity, he had been once again sublimated into something interesting. And not much interesting usually happened in Carthage. Reeve was either inundated with questions or the unwilling recipient of gossip almost daily, and it was all because of Neal.

"Heard Vásquez is back in town."

"He was seen 'round your place, Scarlet. Y'all still friends or what?"

"Saw him in a nice, nice car, dressed to the nines. Who's he trying to impress? We all know what he's like."

"Lynda said he didn't have a ring on when he checked in."

"He said why he's come by Carthage again? There's nothing for him here, and it can't just be for his butt-buddy, Scarlet."

More women than men inquired about Neal; Reeve wasn't sure as to why. They were concerned primarily with his marital status—"He doesn't have a wife," he'd informed them when questioned—whereas the men commented on Neal's new clothes, his car, and his friendship with Reeve in a strangely dark tone. He had begun to despise the interactions, as they were evidently laden with something he couldn't parse properly, and he had thus ceased responding at all.

When Reeve complained to Neal about this phenomenon, he'd just laughed. It confirmed that he was indeed missing something, but Reeve didn't press further and instead let them lapse into their usual arrangement—listening to a record and not talking, just being. Sometimes Neal stayed over, sometimes he didn't. His absence on such nights was an open wound.

About a week had passed since Neal returned, and that Tuesday night, Reeve returned home at his usual hour with the anticipation of his friend's visit. He spared a glance for his neighbors, taking in the new clutter. Zebadiah and Heddie had recently purchased expensive items like TVs, video game consoles, and ATVs that they stored in the shed nearer to the trees that bordered their property to the south.

He stood on the steps and watched while Heddie and Zebadiah circled their own property with Kodak FunSavers, snapping photos and occasionally directing one of their four sons to stand in frame. It was a bizarre sight.

Noticing his voyeur, Zebadiah turned and smiled at him. He uttered that skittering *tht-tht-tht* laugh. The message was clear: *What are you gonna do about it?* Nothing. Reeve didn't give a shit about what he got up to so long as it didn't involve him.

He closed the door behind him decisively. Reeve didn't open it again until Neal arrived at what had become his usual time, rapping out a neat little knock.

"Your neighbors sure are weird, Red," he said by way of greeting.

"I'm aware."

Neal laughed and clapped him on the back like it was easy, like reaching out to touch another person wasn't akin to crossing the Atlantic.

"I'm talking *up to something* weird," the other man continued.

"I don't care."

Neal exhaled loudly. "'Course you don't. But, Red, this is happening next door. Ain't you even a little bit curious?"

"I see no point in involving myself," Reeve informed Neal, thinking about all the good "getting involved" had ever done him.

They ceased speaking for the moment, letting the record Neal put on spin out between them instead. Today's fare was Chet Baker's *Witch Doctor*. Neal was still testing out different albums with the hope to one day indoctrinate him into liking music in general and jazz in particular. It was fine. He hadn't found anything that stirred some deep, heartfelt emotion within him yet.

"Hey, Red," Neal said suddenly, cutting into the song. "Tell me something about yourself."

"What do you want to know?"

"Anything. I feel like I always talk about myself. I want to know you again. I want my friend back."

His features were open and earnest. The look lodged itself deep in Reeve's chest. He couldn't help but respond, opening his mouth to tell him:

"It wasn't always Scarlet. Our surname, I mean. My grandparents were Czech, from the old country, and when they came here, no one spoke their language. Not their names, either. It was beyond them, I s'pose. Tereza and Matyáš became Tess and Matthew; Červený became Scarlet. My grandma told me she thought it was beautiful, the way it rolled off the tongue, and that if she had to change, she may as well keep something of it for herself.

"Rostislav Červený would have been my name there. It's what they called me those few times I got the chance to visit. It was… it was nice. *Můj malý vnuk. Můj malý Rastík.* That's what they would call me. *My little grandson. My little Rastík.* Dědeček and Babička were good. I'm glad they didn't live to see this part of me."

"Červený—what does it mean?"

"Don't you know, Neal," he said, quiet, "it's red."

Later that night, Reeve fell into a restless sleep. It had been nine days since Neal began visiting him and twelve days total since the other man had returned. His dreams were strange, tortuous. Neal had declined to stay over, their conversation ending not long after he'd delved into what "Scarlet" meant to him. He couldn't put a name to the feeling his absence evoked; it was nebulous, difficult to grasp. The fact that Neal's absence correlated with this event was negligible—it had to be.

In his dream, he was in a forest draped in shadow. The sky hung heavy and pendulous above, almost indistinguishable from the horizon in its darkness. Nightbirds rested in the boughs of trees that wept blood as opposed to sap. Reeve was not any more human here than he was in the real world, and he floated through the underbrush upon crow's wings.

Traveling onward, dark filaments of fog whipped past him as he went deeper into the forest. The trees were thicker here, more concentrated. It gave the impression that the sun was someplace completely beyond his reach.

But then the growth broke, and Reeve came upon a meadow ensconced within this wilderness, overgrown with wildflowers in varying shades of indigo, violet, and burgundy. They were none like he had ever seen before.

Among these sumptuous blooms was Neal, pillowed on his back in the nude with one arm hooked behind his head. His hair was loose from its gel and curled gently around his ears. The flame tattoo licked down his neck and onto his shoulder, terminating down by his wrist in an inky black swirl.

"Red," he murmured. "Red, Red, Red."

I'm here, he wanted to say. Nothing emerged save for an animalistic *caw* like a crow's call, but Neal smiled as though he understood.

"C'mere," he said.

And he would have, Reeve realized, if not for his sudden inability to breathe. His heart thudded behind his breastbone; it was incomprehensible, what he was feeling. He had no idea what it was or how to explain himself. It ebbed, eddied, then surged forward, as inevitable and devouring as a pyroclastic flow. For once, he cracked open with heat and want, which followed him out of the dream and into bed when he awoke, wet with sweat and an ache between his legs.

He clutched at his hair, his throat, Neal's handsome features still burning darkly in his mind.

MAZE III

There had been a time when Maze would do whatever it took to be noticed.

Her grades may not have been perfect, but they were good, all A's and B's, and her parents would smile when they signed off on her report cards. She was the first freshman to make varsity in over two decades, and Maze carried the team to state in back-to-back seasons. And her social life thrived, too: she hung out with the other basketball players, their boyfriends, and anyone popular enough to join them. Dean, her equal and opposite, played for the boy's team; he was their starting point guard and would smile a small and secret smile whenever he locked eyes with her. Shooting hoops turned into backseat make out sessions, which then turned into making love in the bed of his truck beneath the stars.

That was back before everything stopped making sense. It felt so long ago now, funnily enough, even though she recognized that only mere months had passed since everything changed. To her, being invisible was looking better and better by the day.

Her Tuesday had started off promising enough.

Maze chugged half a pot of coffee and picked out the mini marshmallows from her cereal bowl before rushing out the door, swiping on mascara and lipstick at the first and only stop sign she passed through on her morning commute. Douglas H. Cooper may as well have been the Death Star for all the joy it inspired in her as she rounded the corner and pulled into its student lot.

It wasn't until gym class that things boiled over.

The trouble began with a game of basketball. On one side of the court, the girls were playing five on five while sharing a basket; on the other, a disorganized jumble of boys argued over who was on whose team. Dean was among them, and Maze watched his lean figure maneuver throughout the packed bodies, features gleaming with sweat. He threw his head back and shook his damp hair out, eyes half-closed to the light—

106

Maze turned just in time to feel something whisk past her face and then subsequently slam into the wall behind her. The basketball ricocheted and bounced to a stop at her feet.

"Sorry 'bout that," Lee called out, not sounding sorry at all.

"Sure you are," she told him sweetly, returning the favor with a chest pass so hard it knocked the breath from him. "Keep an eye on your shit, alright?"

Lee's expression shuttered, went angry, but before he could shout something at her that probably rhymed with "witch," Dean took the opportunity to intercept the ball and divert Lee's attention elsewhere.

"Hey, man. Let's just play," she heard him say. He made a clean three-pointer to further punctuate this.

Lee scoffed and made a *gong* sound. "You're whipped, Short Round. Y'all aren't even together anymore, and you're still whipped."

Dean's shoulders tightened but he maintained his easygoing façade; however, Maze knew him well enough to tell the comment had bothered him. Like, really, really bothered him. If Lee was supposedly his friend, why didn't he say something? Dean wasn't some pushover, but more and more he seemed to cede ground to Lee and his kin.

When their teacher blew his whistle and waved them off the court, she ducked into a corner and watched the other students leave one after another until she was sure she could get Dean alone.

Maze crept inside the boy's locker room. She could hear the shower running but continued forward, finding Dean beneath the showerhead with his neck tipped back to let shampoo suds sluice off his hair and down between the jut of his shoulder blades.

The sight stopped her short, and she momentarily forgot why she was even there. The sight was familiar, sensual.

"Jesus Christ, Maze," he snapped when he noticed her, scrambling to cover himself. He ended up with a bottle of generic bodywash carefully situated over his junk. "What the hell are you doing in here?"

"That ain't nothing I haven't seen before," she waved him off, leaning back against a locker. "We need to talk."

"And *now's* the best time?"

"Don't act like there's ever a good time for us. Tell me what the hell was that back there with Lee."

"I'm trying to keep my head down, is what."

Maze laughed bitterly and went for the jugular. "Don't you have any self-respect? I get not standing up for me, but yourself? C'mon."

Dean dispensed with the pretense of the bodywash and advanced on her in the nude, incandescent with rage.

"Just where d'you get off lecturing me? You're not my girlfriend. You're not anything to me."

"Nice of you to bring that up."

"You're the one who ended things, not me."

"And why was that, Dean? If I gotta explain that to you, then you're more behind than I thought."

"Jesus, Mazie. I get it. I do. I was wrong when I looked the other way with you, but that doesn't give you the right to hate me or run my life."

"I ain't tryin' to run your life. I just care enough about you still to hate seeing you roll over and... and take this from them. You play better. You're smarter. You're tough enough to take those bozos even if they ganged up on you."

"Believe it or not, those "bozos" are my friends. They were yours, too, not that long ago. Or have you forgotten?"

"Oralene's my friend. Those guys were convenient. Decoration."

"You ever stop and think about why I might need some decoration?" Dean spat, jamming a finger into her sternum. "You think you got it bad here? I'm the one damn Asian guy in the whole school. I put up with people's shit every day. If I get good grades, it's a given. If I got a girlfriend, she's got "yellow fever." I'm good at basketball "for an oriental." At least you look like them. But you're so dead set on being victimized that you won't even try to figure a way out.

"The Klan still marches in the fourth of July parade. The people out there, they see their history, their family. I know what *we* see. My parents work hard just so me and my sister can have it better than they did. Everything I do here, it's 'cause I got to think about them. I piss off the wrong person, what happens when they go home and say somethin' to their daddy? Doesn't matter if he's on the town council or the grand fucking wizard of the Klan—my family's screwed either way.

"'Sides, there's no point in tryin' to argue. I won't change their minds. I'll just make things harder on my family. You got your way, and I can respect that. But this is mine. When Lee knocks up Tandy for the first time, gets work at the plant like everyone else does, and rots away in a double wide, I'm gonna be playin' ball for UCLA. All this, here—I'm just doin' time."

"Don't act like this has been easy for *my* family, either."

That made his jaw snap shut and do a full-body eye roll. "And here we go again with you intentionally missing the damn point. C'mon, Mazie. You know what I'm trying to get at here."

Maze felt her throat close up. "Fine," she said, furious and sad. "Just don't let them push you too far. You're worth more than that."

She hated how much sense he made in that moment. Dean was in survival mode; Maze was, too. They were just different animals. And neither needed to hear anyone in Carthage say, "You're not like us," to feel it. *Hah.* As if that was the worst thing a person could be.

The bell rang, jolting the pair apart. That was definitely her cue to leave. Maze stepped back towards the exit, sparing him one last lingering glance as she did so. "By the way, I never hated you. I thought I did at first… but I was just mad. And I needed someone else to be mad at besides myself, I guess."

He paused. "Thanks, Mazie. Really."

The two didn't speak again after that. Even when they passed each other in the hallway, both were too heated to do anything save for let their eyes meet.

Her afternoon dragged on. There was more school. Work. Time at home, languishing in her mom's silence—or so she thought.

The fact that there was a special broadcast on today didn't hit her until she arrived home to a crowded street and voices spilling out onto the drive. *I can't take this today,* she thought to herself, breath eeking out from between her teeth. *If I don't get a break from the religious B.S., I'm gonna explode.* The safety of her room beckoned, but Maze had a role to play. Putting it off would only make it worse.

She disembarked from the car and let her feet take her inside.

Gould's nasal intonation hit her right off the bat. "And with the help of you all, our dearest flock, we've managed to outgrow our airtime at this station. Central Oklahoma, Limited has kindly extended us an offer to join their Sunday slot from nine to eleven. Of course, there are bigger aspirations, aspirations that I have faith we will achieve thanks to the spiritual power this congregation has."

His wife stepped in then, looking like Nancy Reagan after she'd had a nice, relaxing formaldehyde bath. Maze could smell the Aqua Net through the screen.

"Yes. Faith is a funny little thing, isn't it? It can bring great joy or great pain depending on how God chooses to test us. But such is his will. We're prepared to mee whatever he sees fit to challenge us with. So let us walk on unto tomorrow with faith that, one day, our hopes of joining the Christian Unified Network of Truth will one day become a reality. After all, to everything there is a season."

And so it went on, the show's muted palette blending out into a smear, its stars dim parodies. Maze made nice with the ladies in the meantime. She subsisted on subpar lemonade and deviled eggs during the sermon and the discussion after, her ass fusing with the couch cushions in a concerted effort to avoid human interaction and being forced to exert any real critical thinking skills.

She'd just get mad if she tried.

Heddie was the last to leave that evening and lingered at the door while Jessica conversed with Judy and Martha outside. Maze waited for her to turn, walk down the front steps, but she just stood there, watching. Her eyes were pale, ringed in off-color base makeup, and edged with an intensity that discomfited Maze.

Leave, she thought. *Leave, so I can get some damn time alone.* It had been a long day, and she felt drained in more ways than one. Maze just wanted to go lay in bed and listen to Slayer on her Walkman.

"Is there, uh, something you need?"

"No," Heddie said eventually, gaze never once leaving her face. "I wanted to have a talk with you in private."

Maze rocked back on her heels. "You and me? Why?"

"I've seen you out at that... man's house. Coming by all hours and playing that vile music." Heddie said *that man* with a sneer, like she hadn't been neighbors with Reeve for years. Like she didn't just admit to spying on him.

Maze could recall the flicker of a curtain across the lawn, and a thin, pale hand shifting the fabric. Her attempts at subterfuge had clearly only delayed the inevitable, so she decided to lay her cards out on the table.

"Reeve's a friend," she admitted. "What of it?"

"What of it?" Heddie echoed with a breathy laugh. "I'll tell you. It ain't right. Not you, not him. Not even your mama. You people can't change. She might believe in Jesus now, but the blood's the same.

"Adonai," she went onto remark, "it's the name of God, isn't it?" Heddie's thin lips fluttered around the vowels. There was a strange, glittering ill humor in her eyes. "Oh, I forgot—y'all don't say his name."

Maze ground her teeth together. The Almighty's name was Holy. It was used when reading the Torah or in prayer. She might not practice, but she had some respect for where she came from. This exceeded ignorance; it was disgust, hate. Heddie had shoved a hand into her intestines to root around in them.

"Why're you here?"

"You know why."

"Dammit, lady, who hurt you to make you like this?"

Heddie scoffed. "There's no reason. I've had a good enough life. I was never beaten or starved. No man laid a hand on me that I didn't want. My parents love me. They loved me then, and they love me now. You think I must've been... deprived in some way, to turn out like this. I see it every time you look at me.

"It's a joke—you trying to figure me out. And when I feel it, see it, I almost want to laugh. I know it's not pity, but it's something near to it. So, don't. It's a goddamn waste of your time, honey. Don't pity the people who despise you.

"I come to this house—and sit there, right there, on that couch—each week and try not to think about how sad it is that your mama ever got it into her head that she could be something else. You know it ain't the case, so it's almost sweet that she's even trying to get herself outta the muck. Bless her heart.

"There's gotta be a punchline here. Three Jews walk into a bar: one's dead, one's a convert, and the other spits in the face of her own God every day. Your music, your clothes. That Rephidim Scarlet and who knows else.

"It's not about race or religion, though, not to me. Not really. Zeb believes in it; I follow him. He's usually right about the world, anyways. If Zeb was here, I'd tell you you're a roach. That your people are worth as much as the dirt beneath my feet. But he's not, so I'll give you some advice instead: watch yourself."

Maze had been stunned into silence up until this point. "So, you what, just enjoy dragging people around?" Her voice was small.

"Something like that. Don't worry. It's not personal."

Feels pretty fucking personal to me, Maze thought.

Her mother returned through the door, and Heddie plastered on her bland expression once more. "I apologize for taking up your time, Maze," she said, with such false sincerity Maze's teeth clenched. "Good night, ladies. I'll see y'all around."

The placid look she'd fixed on her face had slipped off by the time Jessica came upon them. It was probably closer to downright murderous at this point. Heddie's weird eyes flicked back and forth between mother and daughter with barely restrained mirth. As always, her mom ignored everything suspicious about Heddie in favor of zeroing in on Maze. Typical.

"Bye now," Heddie announced with satisfaction.

Maze flipped her retreating figure off, only to have her hand slapped away by Jessica, whose lips had pinched into an unhappy line. *Great,* Maze thought, *I'm in for it now.*

"What was that?" Her mom asked.

"What d'you mean?"

"Don't play dumb with me. I wasn't born yesterday," Jessica snapped. "We've got a good thing going here. We need this. And these people haven't been anything but kind and welcoming to us. Why can't you respect that?"

I could respect it if it was anywhere near being real or true. They're not our friends. We just happen to be living in the same place at the same time. And I think it's sad you feel any different.

"Sorry, mom," she ground out.

"You're always sorry."

Her emotions boiled over at that point, the exhaustion from the day, her life, everything finally getting to her. "If I need to say more to get the point across, I can. I wanna make this go away," Maze said.

"You're unbelievable."

"More like tired. I want to go to bed."

"*You*—ugh!"

"Tell me what you really think, mom," Maze burst out. "You blame me, right? You think what happened to dad was my fault. That's why you've been acting this way to me. Let's get it all out in the open."

Jessica glared up at her. "And if I told you that, yes, I did blame you, what would you do then? Would it help anything? I can't change the way I feel. It exists in me regardless of whether it makes sense or not, so why ask? To humiliate me? To make me feel like the bitch you clearly think I am? You'll have to force me, Maze. You'll have to force me to say it so you can't blame me for the answer. You blame me for everything else wrong in your life— why wouldn't you blame me for this, too?"

Maze was quiet for a moment. Then she asked, "Do you?"

"What?"

"Blame me?"

Her mom said nothing, but the strained pull at her eyes and mouth told Maze enough.

"I guess this is the part where I force you to come out and say it, just like you told me. Tell me the real truth," Maze said.

"I..."

"Tell me!"

"Fine, yes. I do! Is that what you wanted to hear? I do blame you. Every time I look at you, it's all I can think about. I can't stand you!"

There it was, she thought, the disgust. A look that scorched. Although she'd expected this and had maybe even known from the moment they drove home from the hospital that horrible day, neither prepared her for the inexplicable hurt that rose within her in that moment. Maze felt wounded in a way she could not explain.

Jessica continued, "And I wonder how you can live with yourself. After j-just doing nothing!"

Not easily, Maze thought. She'd asked herself the same questions and had no answers. It didn't seem like there were answers to anything in her life anymore.

Maze's throat felt tight, and she clenched her jaw to keep from letting anything more than a curt, "I see," through. She'd asked for this, yeah, but it had become evident that there was a difference between assuming something and knowing it to be true.

The anger had been squeezed from her like a rag, leaving behind a wrung-out emptiness in her chest. Maze hadn't realized how far it had carried her, sustained her, until it was gone.

"You're exhausting," her mom said. Maze could see her white-knuckle grip around the stem of the wine glass, the red pooled between the corners of her mouth. "Why… can't you just do this one thing for me. Be with us, here, let the love of our Lord wash over you. It would be so easy."

Maze swallowed. "No, mom. It ain't easy. Not this. You're asking me to give up everything I am. I can't do that—not even for you."

"I just don't want you to be in hell. I want to see you up there once all this is over. That can't happen if you don't believe in Jesus," her mom said with a tremulous lip.

"I don't believe in hell. Not yours, at least."

"You will when you're there!"

"Then I'll burn that bridge when I come to it."

"There will be burning, Maze, 'cept it will be quite literal. And don't expect me not to care about that. Because believe it or not, I love you enough for it to matter."

"I can't hear about this shit anymore, mom. I wanna talk about how I feel for once: I hate how unfair everything is all the time! And I hate that I'm expected to deal with it because that's just the way things are!" Maze burst out.

Jessica laughed bitterly. "You have no idea what my days and nights are like now. I sleep in an empty bed. I go to work at a job I hate. People still stare, even now. Then I come home to a daughter who looks at me like she can't stand me, like she doesn't respect me. And the worst part is how *hard* I'm trying. Because I am, okay? I'm trying so hard. I'm—I'm suffering, too. It's not just you."

Maze felt her insides twist up at that, and her mind shrieked at her, *"Look, you've made your mother cry again."*

"I'm sorry, mom. I really am. Promise."

"Good," she said. "That's good, because sometimes… sometimes I need a reminder that you actually love me."

Me too, Maze thought.

"Yeah, 'course, mom. You know I do."

Did her voice sound as tired to Jessica as it did to her? She pulled the shorter woman into her arms, tucking her mom's head into the crook of her neck. The smell of shampoo and roses was familiar.

When a parent dies, you lose a piece of your past; but what was this, here, with her mom? It felt like some kind of purgatory. A murky present.

Maze hated that she could never manage to find the right thing to say, and she pitied her mom so much it was just easier to give in than fight. When they got like this, she always cried. She cried and cried and cried. Jessica's cheeks would redden, her eyes swelled, and makeup smeared everyone in dramatic fashion.

Maybe Maze wanted to be the one who got to be sad every once in a while.

With her heart feeling like it had been rooted out and trampled on, Maze left for the very place she had sought out since school had ended—her room. She didn't even bother to wipe off her makeup or change before flopping face-down onto the mattress, groaning. Maze languished there in abject exhaustion but eventually made a blind grab for her Walkman off the nightstand to break up the silence.

Black Sabbath exploded into existence. "War Pigs" reverberated out, overtaking her errant breaths and elevated heartrate. It also reminded her as to why she loved music so much. The right song could just spirit her away from a terrible place and into somewhere better.

Maze turned onto her side. Jessica bringing up hell, the afterlife, and her dad were each one low blow after another. It had been made abundantly clear that her mom also blamed her for her dad's death, too, which confirmed what Maze suspected ever since March.

In her mind, his features began to emerge: a prominent, straight nose; dark and curling hair identical to her own; and his omnipresent blinding grin. She could hardly recall a time when he wasn't smiling. It seemed as if it embodied every memory she retained, making what happened all the more devastating. Why would someone so happy, so full of love and life do this to her? To her mom? People who enjoyed life didn't kill themselves. Or so she'd been told.

But that's what happened, and it was all her fault.

Needy, she thought. *I'm just needy. Again.* But it was so total, so encompassing, that it felt vital, as much a part of Maze as her ribs, her blood. More than what her mom said it was.

Maze couldn't stop thinking about what happened or thinking about him. The grief shrink had told her that it was okay, that it was normal. He advised she needed to time to come to terms with him being gone. Jessica hadn't agreed. Her mom didn't think she should go anymore, and that what she really needed was to find Jesus. Then she would be fine, just like that.

Maze didn't want to remember her dad like as some dead body, though—she sought to fix her interest on times when they had played ball together, or board games, or sat next to each other and laughed themselves sick at Jerry Springer. He was neither a martyr nor a deadbeat. He was just Levi Maze, her dad.

On some nights, though, she'd think about how it had already been months since he'd been gone, and would soon be years, and that then there would come a day when she had gone longer without him than they'd ever been together.

It made her sick, really. The anger, the sadness. The dark things that had taken up residence in her chest ever since the spring.

I miss you so much. And you left me. I needed you, and you left anyway. It's not right. None of it. The image of that cord, his eyes—it would never leave her.

And then she thought about the beginning of the universe: how everything emerged from the cast-out remnants of some weird cosmic explosion that scattered everything they knew across the universe. There were primordial elements in the air, the earth, space. They were supposed to be woven into the fabric of the universe and in themselves. Maze liked that idea—that they too must be stardust.

It made her hope that he would become one with it too, in whatever beautiful place he went. Whether that be *Olam Ha-ba,* the World to Come, or some realm likewise as beautiful, where his *neshamah* had returned to after death, Maze knew he was somewhere better than Carthage, Oklahoma.

That's why their people's burials—at least, in her experience—were undertaken with the greatest care. There was a connection between the body and *neshamah*, the spark of the divine, which was released to a peaceful eternity after death. The catch was that suicide violated Jewish law; it was incompatible with their beliefs on life's importance, its sanctity. Despite the bleak realization he'd have to be buried in a separate part of the cemetery, and then the even bleaker reality, she still held out hope that he was out among the stars.

Maze had been too angry to say the *Kaddish* over his casket. Because he'd killed himself, she wasn't even really supposed to. No one else did. However, there was a part of her that was still so torn up about not doing it that she hadn't recited the prayer yet, not even when she visited his grave each month. Oh. She loved him and hated him and wanted the pain to go away.

Maze blinked back tears.

Bye, dad.

NEAL III

It was dark out when he saw her again. His second Wednesday. There was a familiar run-down station wagon parked outside the Burger Barn, with a long-limbed figure sprawled atop the hood. Neal slowed to a crawl and turned into the lot before he could think twice about it. He needed a distraction. Reeve's smell—cold wind, damp leaves—lingered. His presence did, too. He was everywhere.

When Neal pulled up next to her, he watched the girl groan at his arrival. Maze was dressed in her requisite red uniform, complete with the absurd cow-eared ball cap. A joint was pinched between her fingers, and the lit end was a lightning bug in the night. Even the sign had been shut off. He wondered what she was doing here so late; she had school tomorrow.

He got out of the car and joined her on the hood. "Shove over," he said, a statement to which she sneered at but complied with. "The hell is all this? Don't you got better places to be?"

The girl was quiet at first. "Speak for yourself," she said after a moment.

Neal scraped a palm through his hair. "Not really. Not tonight, at least."

"Funny."

"So I've been told."

Maze gave him a jaunty little wave with the joint. "You got it."

He glanced back at the station wagon's windshield. It ran well, was detailed on the outside, but the interior made it look a little like a crack rental. There were lipstick tubes, sunglasses, and clothes piled on almost every available surface. It was probably the most normal "teenage girl" thing about her.

He turned to embrace the stars again, and let the silence settle over him. Neal pulled out and flicked the zippo on, off. It would catch, ignite, and perish with each revolution. He had long since worn away at the pattern, leaving a flat, burnished divot in its middle.

"Tell me—why are you really here?"

"What?"

"Be honest with me, Neal. This can't be some hometown, trip down memory lane bullshit. It—it don't make any sense. And don't sit there and tell me you're just *visiting a friend*. You could've looked him up in the phonebook. You could've sent him a letter. You could've done anything. But you came here instead. Why?"

Neal said nothing to her at first. He felt his neck heat, exposed, and his shoulders migrate up towards his ears. The question as to why he'd even pulled over to begin with reared its head, turning over and over, setting its teeth into the fleshy contours of his brain.

Maze seemed to pick up on his mood, and her eyes shifted nervously between him and the joint pinched between her fingertips. The girl licked her lips. "I'll, uh, leave off it," she said quietly.

"There's nothin' weird 'bout what I'm doin' here," he forced out.

"Neal…" she began, hesitant now, "I *know*. Least, I think I do."

It echoed what Ruth had told him not even two weeks ago, *"Neal, we know."* And Maze had that same intent, almost pitying look, too. The hair on the back of his neck prickled. Neal thought he'd moved past fearing this; how could he, if he sought to make peace with what he felt for Reeve? He considered posturing and brushing her off—and he could do it, too, real good—but something stopped him.

Maybe it was something about the way she'd said it, with the same almost-tender intonation Ruth had, that made him crack. He'd been pried open for public viewing. More than that, he wanted, paradoxically, to eradicate her kindness.

Instead, all he said was, "Why do you even care?"

"I guess I just can't imagine anyone loving him."

Neal didn't understand how anyone couldn't. There was no love known to him other than this. Thinking about some other place, one where he'd never met Reeve or understood what it meant to feel wanted, left him with the certain, ominous realization that he'd have ended up in an even worse hole than he had in this one.

"It's the easiest thing I've ever done."

Her nose scrunched up at that. "Is your head screwed on straight, or what?"

"There's nothing straight about this," he said, wresting a laugh from her. "And I, uh, think I'm still tryin' to figure that out."

"Good luck," she remarked, smoking before continuing, "So, you're... a queer? Bisexual?"

"I'm not either of those," he said, fists clenched at his sides. "I'm gay. That's it. I don't care if everyone thinks it's some kinda joke. It ain't that to me. It's the furthest fucking thing from a joke I can think of. And damn anyone who says otherwise!"

It felt silly, almost, that it had taken him so long to say these words, even to himself, when now they fell so readily from his tongue. Being known for what he was felt both strange, ecstatic, even though Maze was little more than a stranger to him, and a teenage girl at that. Whatever people wanted to call what he was—it wasn't a personality defect. Or a sickness. He was gay long before his mom died, and he was gay before his dad got locked up.

It was just him, Neal.

These things sometimes went deeper than his own opinion of himself, indefinable, known to him as echoes of what he'd heard people say about men like him. He recalled his dad's fateful words uttered: *It's not what I would choose for you. You got a hard road ahead, but if this is who you are, I can't change that. Not even to ease your way.*

There was so much longing, want, shame bottled up inside him he felt fit to burst. Would it leak out his eyes, he wondered. Spill from them like tears? Would he immolate from within, combust, and be splayed outside himself for all to see? Or would he find the words—the right ones, intimate—to articulate the starvation that had cannibalized his chest since the first time Reeve said his name?

He turned the question over in his head. *Why?* It wasn't as though Reeve was perfect, or even particularly kind. His stare was cold and at times even cruel. He stood removed from everything and everyone. But he never raised his voice. He said what he meant. He knew what it meant to suffer. He'd given Neal a chance.

He looked at him like he was worth something.

Maze interrupted his reverie with, "I wouldn't have guessed otherwise. You don't act fruity or nothing."

"Fruity?"

"You know," she said, then made an effete hand gesture. "Like Elton John, George Michael. Those guys. You're manly."

"I have sex with men. That gay enough for you?" Neal snapped. "I'm not any less of a man for that."

Maze went red in the face but admitted, ducking her head, "Alright, I had that coming."

"Yeah, you did."

"Sorry, I shouldn't have called you that. I didn't mean anything by it, honest." "It's fine," he said, even though it wasn't. He was sensitive about this topic probably more than about anything else in his life, but he also recognized that Maze was a girl, and that she was putting forth a genuine effort to be understanding.

"That tattoo," she began, gesturing at his neck, "I've been wondering about it ever since I saw it. Fire—why?"

Neal reached up towards his throat.

"All my life I've walked through fire. I wanted something to show for it."

"Figures," she said. Maze leaned forward and shifted her legs, exposing a grease-stained paper bag laden with fries. She pulled out a handful and offered some to him, which he accepted, then stuffed the rest into her mouth. They poked out as she chewed with open-jawed deliberation.

He opened his lips. They were cold, salty, perfect. He felt a strange and undeniable fondness for this girl.

"Perks of the job," she said, voice muffled. "Well, the only perk, really."

"Worst job I ever had was doing roofing in Utah for a summer. We were in some fancy suburb north of Salt Lake, and it was hot up there, hotter than hell. Those roofs may as well have been frying pans. But when I got a break and could make a pass at the cooler, it would hit me. How good it was, I mean. It had the best damn water, I swear. I don't think water had ever tasted as good as it did then."

"I've heard it's beautiful there."

"It really was."

"You've been other places, too, right?"

"All over. Never made it to the west coast, though. Much as I wanted to."

"Did you ever find somewhere that fit you? Better than anything else. The place you'd stay if you could."

Neal's mind drifted back to California, his and Reeve's proposed dream. "I don't think I've been there yet."

"I can't wait to get outta this town. Sometimes it's all I can think about, even if I was being real with myself, I don't have a future. Not like that. My life is right now."

He was struck in that moment by how much he saw himself in her. Maze possessed similar raw, un-sanded edges and hands that took too easily to fists. These were things she'd just have to learn to live with.

Maze changed the subject after that, and he wondered whether she picked up on his disquiet. "About that tat, where'd you get it done? I don't think I've ever seen anythin' like it. I mean, it's no butterfly tramp stamp, but still."

Neal paused and touched a hand to the tattoo. Maze and he were strangers still, and yet she felt moved enough by—what, some shared affinity—to speak freely.

His breath emerged in a long rush. "I got it done in the pen, then cleaned up a little at a place in Des Moines after I got out. The lines were bleeding. Had been for a while by then."

That got her attention. "Hell, really?" Maze asked, sitting straight up and twisting to face him. He took it she understood "pen" to mean "penitentiary."

"Yeah."

"I don't s'pose Reeve knows anything about this."

"No, he sure as hell don't. And it'll stay that way 'til I'm ready."

If I'm ever ready, he didn't add. Telling Reeve was different. Everything about him always was. Losing his attention, affection… Neal feared it would destroy him.

Maze seemed to chew on that. "It is what it is," she said. "No judgement. We've all made bad choices. So, unless you're about to tell me you shot up a chicken joint, we're cool."

It was, weirdly, the most comforting thing she could have said to him.

"No, uh, shootouts at KFC," he said. "Like you said, just bad choices."

Rather than make small talk or seek further insight, Maze pivoted to the next heavy topic. "That cross on your neck—it's a rosary, ain't it?"

Neal almost sighed. He nodded, grasping it without thinking.

"Your people, suicide's a sin to you. A crime. It's something to be punished for."

"That's what they say," he said diplomatically, discomfited by the direction the conversation was taking.

"So, if we suffer here, suffer so bad in our lives or minds that there's nothing else but the ground, we get to go suffer down there too?"

This was personal, he realized.

"I'm not a priest. I can't answer that for you."

"Why even bother with being a Catholic at all then, since you don't seem to get clear answers about anything?"

That did it.

"Don't you take that tone with me, girl," he snapped. "Look… I can't really get into why I believe what I believe. It's personal. And that doesn't mean everything's perfect or that I don't have questions. Because I do. I got so many. But when I go to bed at night or drive down a dark highway, I'm not alone. There's someone out there watching me, loving me without strings attached. I need that—that love. I need to be needed. I've got something to live for. Don't you feel the same way?"

Maze exhaled. "Sometimes," she said.

Neal continued, "I thought I'd feel different about it when I was older. But it's funny. So much of who I am is the same. I'm still struggling with what I was then. I'm not wise. I'm not complete, either. Not even close. But I'm better than I was. Maybe one day I'll come to terms with everything. That I won't feel so—less. Just dirt beneath the heels of the people around me. Maybe it's impossible. I gotta try, though. Things don't seem so hopeless when I do.

"And it got me thinking that moving on ain't as straight as everyone makes it out to be. This—unlearning. Moving past all the awful shit that happened to me. What I did to others. Who I am now. These are just things that've happened to us, I think. It's not who are. And it's not forever.

"It ebbs, flows. Some days are better than the rest. I'm okay with that. I think you should be, too. You don't need to be so hard on yourself. You're young. You're a good kid, all things considered. This is just the beginning."

Maze chewed at her lip. "You've been wondering why I'm friends with Reeve. It's like…" she began, trailing off, seemingly searching for the right words, "it's like being in a dark place. There, when me and him are together. I can be the ugliest, most disgusting version of myself. I can be hateful, jealous. I can crawl in the mud like a worm. There's no judgement between us. It'd be hard since we've both done the same thing: hurt people we cared about."

Neal was speechless. "That's, uh, heavy," he said after the moment dragged long and out.

Maze took another pull from the joint and smiled at that, but the look in her eyes was somewhere between amusement and grief.

"My dad is... He's, uh, dead. Killed himself six months back. It was pretty bad. I had it thrown in my face. People here hated him, y'know? I mean, they just hated him. I guess I didn't realize how much until he died," she said, looking away. "When we first moved to Carthage from Tulsa, it'd been because he'd been promoted to management in United Beef and got transferred to oversee the plant in this area. I s'pose it must've seemed like the thing to do at the time.

"But we're Jews. So 'course he couldn't have gotten the job for being the right man or a good worker. It had to be some damn conspiracy that kept a nice boy from these parts from getting his just due. I mean, if we're in the government and the banks, then we may as well have gotten to the meatpackers, right? It's funny, really. I can't even name a time where we haven't been treated like shit or looked at different, but they're somehow the ones being hurt by us. *Hah.*

"I'll say this. My dad deserved everything he got. He was a good man. The best man. I-I wish people could've seen that in him. They never did. Even up 'til he died. And that moment—his worst moment—is how everyone'll remember him now. The Jew who hung himself in his garage. No one'll know anything else about him. They won't care to. He's been erased. He's nothing.

"My mom's gone away, too. I don't even know who I live with anymore. It's like some other person wearing her skin. And this person is less than a stranger to me. She doesn't talk about him. Took down all out photos, too. Even got in with this Christian group. They've convinced her to throw out everything that was important to us. To our religion, our culture. To *him.* I watched her throw away his journal, his Tanakh.

"The only reason it ain't rotting out in some landfill right now is 'cause I was quick enough to grab 'em before the can got picked up. They're boxed up now like junk to keep 'em safe. It was the cruelest thing I'd ever seen, what she did then. And she's so delusional she doesn't even realize how bad it's gotten to be. I just... I really hate her. I don't want to, but I do. And I guess I just had to tell someone that," she trailed off.

Maze's voice had become thicker as the deluge went on, and he could see where tears had begun to pool in her eyes. Neal didn't know what to say. He'd watched what felt to him like every human emotion inhabit her expressions during their conversation: grief over her dad's death; the joy at his memory; disgust and fear with the town, its people; and, more than anything, a pure, seething rage it seemed only a kid fed up with the world could manage to muster.

He was reminded, suddenly, of himself. Neal saw in her the pain produced by having to deny everything you were. It was impossible to lie for that long without self-destructing.

Neal said, "The people who're s'posed to give us these things don't always have it in 'em. There's somethin' missing. It doesn't make 'em evil or bad, exactly, but it sure doesn't mean they're good parents."

When she didn't respond, he began tentatively, "Maze..."

"It's Hezyr, actually."

"*Heh-zuhr?*"

"Yeah. Hezyr Sigalit Maze," she said, taking one final hit from her joint before flicking it onto the asphalt. "I don't think I need to explain to you why I go by "Maze" instead."

No, she didn't. It was the same reason his dad had took him and told him, almost gently, "You got too much of your mama in you, boy," thumb pressed to the skin beneath Neal's eye. "It's a shame; I can't do nothing about this."

What lived in Neal's insides was something Gabriel could, in fact, do something about, or so he'd thought.

"I saw you," his dad said one day after Neal returned home from work. It was mentioned in a casual tone, almost offhandedly.

There was a beer languishing beside his hands, which were unfolded and set palm-down on the table. His features were shadowed in gradated red-orange evening light.

"Saw me?" Neal repeated, mouth dry.

"Don't play stupid, boy. You know what I mean."

He swallowed and blinked. Then he did it again. There was a heavy pressure behind his eyes and his hands were pulled taut against his sides.

"No," he said, "I don't."

His dad uttered a low, almost careless sigh and got to his feet. He sauntered over to where Neal stood frozen. They were the same height now, but it didn't seem to matter. His dad always seemed to be bigger than him in every way.

"Idiot," Gabriel said.

"What?"

"Idiot. I said it because it's clearly what you think I am."

"No—that ain't right at all."

"So, I'm a liar?"

"Wait—"

Gabriel' hand darted out to grasp Neal's jaw and force their eyes to meet. His gaze was cold, mercurial. It gleamed with a light he couldn't understand.

"Which is it, then. Idiot or liar?"

"N-neither."

"Am I right?"

"Yes," Neal admitted. "You're right."

"I know," he said, releasing him and half-turning away, only to pivot and strike Neal across the cheek.

He stumbled back and clutched at his face. Gabriel didn't even look at him now, and instead stared out the window in a contemplative manner. "I didn't like what I saw today. I don't like the man you're becoming."

I don't like the man you are, Neal thought.

"If you want to act like a girl, I'll treat you like one," he sneered at Neal before throwing the lipstick on the carpeted floor. "Now pick it up."

Neal hesitated.

"I said *pick it up.*"

He leaned forward and grasped the tube between shaking hands, waiting for further instruction. The worst part was Irena, his mom, watching from the kitchen table.

"Tell me, son, what do girls do with shit like that?"

Neal's breath hitched as he replied, "Wear it. They wear it."

"Go on, then."

God, he felt sick. His stomach rolled unpleasantly as he uncapped the lid and screwed the base until pink poked through. He could see the shimmer catch in the light, a taunt. Neal pressed it to his lips with an unsteady hand and dragged the tube around once. But when he began to withdraw, his dad shook his head and said, "Keep going." There was an implicit, *"Until I tell you to stop,"* laden in the ensuing silence.

So, Neal did.

He kept applying more and more until the bullet had eroded to little more than a nub and his mouth was caked in product. It got everywhere—his chin, his teeth, his tongue. The waxy, almost saccharine tase nearly made him gag.

"That road is a dead-end, son. You'll think you're in love. Maybe you even will be. Whatever the closest thing you people have to it. But there's no future there, boy. There's nothing. So, save yourself the grief and be a man," Gabriel informed him before departing for his bedroom, taking Irena with him.

His dad may as well have been God to him then, and since he couldn't fight God, he'd fought everybody else. The problem with being raised by an asshole was that you usually turned out the same way.

"Hey," Maze ventured, cutting into his reverie. "Where'd you go?"

"Nowhere."

"Sure," she said.

"I used to drink, he admitted, mouth dry. "A lot. Did some, uh, other stuff, too. And I was so—ashamed. It felt like a trap I was born to fall into. I knew how people saw me. What they thought. I couldn't have personal shit. It couldn't be that I failed on my own. I drank and messed around 'cause I was *her* son. Black. Not for any other reason.

"I was bored and lonely. My parents were—Jesus, I dunno—not good to me. Reeve was my only friend. I was so damn angry all the time, and I couldn't handle it. I wanted to be anything other than what I was. Drinking was easy. It meant that for a little while, I didn't have to deal with my life.

"I'm not Christ; I'm just a man, even though it feels more and more like I don't get to be one since I'm not white."

Maze looked pained. "I'd tell you I understand, but I can't. Not really, I guess. I used to think we were all the same. Jews, Indians, Asians, whatever. We're not. Even if we're all looking in on the same world that ain't ours," she said. "And you know what—you're a real gift, Neal. I thought I wouldn't like you. I was wrong."

"… thanks?"

"And I don't care that you're gay or whatever. I don't think Reeve would, either. You came back for him, right?"

"I love him," Neal confessed.

His dad had never felt love, but he understood it. Love was a tool to wield against them, to keep them in line. Neal had even believed him at one time. But that hadn't been love; it was possession. Ruth and Joseph taught him so. That didn't stop Neal and Irena from wanting it to be real.

"Wow," was all she said.

"I've never said that out loud 'til tonight," Neal said, clarifying he meant "gay" at Maze's questioning look.

"Are you gonna tell him? You're keeping a lot from him right now. I know he ain't the easiest to talk to, believe me, but you're running out of time to come clean, right? I mean, you won't be here forever."

Maze was right, maybe more right than she knew. He had enough money and stability to hang around for a while longer, but he couldn't stand this place, and Neal wouldn't endure it forever—not even for Reeve.

"It's late, kid. We should get you going," he said.

Maze shifted away from him and groaned. "Fine, fine," she said. "But only if you listen to some of my music. I never get to share it anymore."

"One song," Neal agreed. "*One.*"

"Hell, yeah."

"Alright, let's see about this 'Slayer' tape."

He rolled off the hood and leaned in through the open window, breath a slow fog in the cold, ready to listen to whatever the hell it was she had to show him.

Maze flashed him a black cassette case with a skull on the cover, open-mouthed and done up in thick paint strokes that faded inward from black to ectoplasm green. *Seasons in the Abyss,* it read.

"This is their album from a few years back. It totally topped *South of Heaven,* which was bogus. Here's the title track for a taste."

Music spiraled out from the speakers in eerie, atmospheric riffs and nihilistic refrains. It was… interesting, but Neal would stick with Sonny Rollins and Cab Calloway.

"Not for you?" Maze asked.

"Uh, not really," Neal said, to which she laughed.

"It's fine, man. I'll clear out. And you should catch some Z's, too, for real."

"Sure, kid."

"Don't "sure, kid" me, Neal. 'Sides, I got some advice for you: talk to Reeve. He deserves that much. I get that I don't fully understand all that y'all have been through together, or what it means to be gay, but I know that you'll regret not speaking to him more than if you do and it goes sideways."

Maze's gaze had turned unexpectedly serious while she said this. Neal felt himself melt a little at the sight, and he reached forward to clasp her on the shoulder. "I'm sorry you're having such a tough go of it. No matter what anyone tells you, nobody deserves that."

Maze choked back something like a sob and wiped at her eyes. "It's just, um, an eyelash," she said.

"Sure," he agreed magnanimously.

Eventually she spoke again, saying, "You've seen the billboards around, right?"

"The ones advertising that TV preacher?"

"Yeah, those. He's fixin' to be here this Sunday."

"...Alright."

"He's the guy my mom's obsessed with. She and all her friends, that is. A bigshot, hotshot type of preacher."

Neal quirked a brow. "Maze, what's this about?"

"You got anything better to do this weekend?"

Yeah. Anything was preferable to palling around with a bunch of nutjobs in a tent while collection tins got passed around. He'd already missed mass last weekend and skipping it again in favor of attending a tent revival setup for a religion he didn't even follow with a bunch of people he didn't even like seemed borderline sacrilegious. But with Maze looking at him with those searching gray eyes, he felt almost obliged to say yes.

"I'll need to check my horoscope first. See if Protestantism is something the stars have lined up in my favor," he said to her, laughing a little when she clapped him on the back.

"You do that," she said. "I hear Mercury is in retrograde."

"Well, God forbid. Yeah, yeah. I'll show up to this party. Can't let you be the only heretic there, after all. And I'll try and bring your "confidant," too."

For the first time since they met, a genuine smile spread across her face.

They shared the night together more easily from then on, listening to another song on Maze's tape until both recognized it was well and truly time for her to head home. The two parted on good terms, leaving Neal alone in his car yet again.

He resumed his drive through Carthage, passing by the old cemetery where Ephraim Scarlet was interred. Ephraim has never been more than a lingering memory to him, seen through Reeve's eyes. He knew, rationally, that a human boy had been buried there, but he held no more attachment to that corpse than any other. Whatever role his friend had played in his death, he'd paid for it ten times over.

How much Maze knew about what happened, though, he still wasn't entirely sure. Not to mention her own claims about having a hand in her dad's suicide. And for all he'd been honest with the girl, he still hadn't told her about Joseph, or Ruth, or delved into deep well of bad decisions that had defined his early twenties. Although the two were as close as family to him, he'd done more wrong by Trev and Ruth than right.

He'd gone west after jumping the foster care ship. Lived out of his car, motels, and took odd jobs that paid him under the table in the little backwater towns he frequented. Neal drank, too, and fought. He fucked women even though he could never love them, because it was easier than the alternative. He was alive, but not living.

The want, the shame, they were so twisted up in each other that he couldn't untangle them at first when he started giving in. He got off on it. The swooping, breathless, *oh, God, I'm in bed with another man* feeling. Meeting another guy's eyes in a darkened bar, their mutual appraisal of each other, and then the covert nod towards the men's restroom or slipping of a motel key into his palm. He'd expected it to feel different. There was no momentous change, or realization, or becoming; Neal woke the next morning the same man he'd always been. But the newness had abated with time and experience, even more so when he'd really started to settle into his own skin.

Still, when other—normal, that is—men spoke to him about breasts, lipstick, curls, Neal saw only a woman; beautiful, sure, but beautiful in the way a painting was beautiful. He admired them coldly, distantly. *God*, he'd ask himself, *I know I can choose. So why is the choice so hard?*

There had been one time, after another failed attempt at sex with a woman in his early twenties, when he'd hit rock bottom. The rock bottom before he experienced what real rock bottom was like. Neal hadn't been able to finish, and he sat, tense, on the edge of the bed and chewing on a cigarette filter.

He remembered the woman—her name escaped him now; Blondie, he'd call her—leaning forward to brush her hand over his collarbone. The gesture's sweetness grit between his teeth, and maybe it was how she'd intended to comfort him, or because she'd gotten off and he hadn't, or even her obvious, torturous good looks, whose appeal he feared he could never possess, but he couldn't take it.

He ground the filter to a pulp and leaned over to the nightstand to stub it out. There was a pressure forming behind his forehead. It had to be deep, he reasoned, since that was how far this wrongness went in him. Blondie touched him again then, and when Neal rebuffed her, she murmured, "It's alright, y'know? You don't have to pretend—"

"Quit talking 'bout shit you don't know nothin' about, goddammit," he told her, feeling his anger catch and spark without anywhere to go but out. It wasn't her fault, exactly, but she sat so close on the bed, looking at him with the most horrible, piteous expression on her face. He wanted to wipe it off; he wanted to be able to make her twist with pleasure.

"Are you for real? Don't speak to me like that—" Blondie said, outraged, before being cut off by Neal, who grabbed her hand and reared back to slap her without thinking.

"The hell did I just tell you, you fuckin' whore?" He felt his voice emerge as a hoarse shriek, and he was so startled by this he at last registered what he was about to do. Neal froze and stared at his open palm. So did Blondie.

He felt himself puncture and then decompress, arm lowering slow until it hung limp at his side. This… this was… Neal had never been delusional enough to think he was a good man, but this was different. He was acting like his dad.

"No need for that, cowboy," she said after a while, motioning for a cigarette. He handed one to her without question.

They didn't attempt to have sex again and instead watched a terrible action movie and fell asleep together while the credits rolled. When he woke, she was gone. Blondie had been decent enough not to roll him for his wallet.

That should have been enough of a sign that he was toeing the line and on the verge of crossing it. But no. Neal didn't learn his lesson until later.

Neal had been drunk and miserable the night it happened, hands worked raw from steel wool after a double shift washing dishes earlier at the restaurant, when the guy approached him. They were in some dive in downtown Des Moines, its walls papered with graffiti and piss stains. Terrible soft rock music buzzed in his ears, along with low chatter and the distinct sounds of a game of pool being played.

He'd been chasing shots with beer at the bar when some guy knocked into him from behind, causing Neal to spill Modelo down his front. "Jesus Christ," he said, stepping down from the stool and wiping himself off with a towel the bartender passed him. "You gonna at least apologize or what?"

"Not my problem, man," the other guy—white with bad acne and greasy, wispy hair—told him, his friends laughing as they passed by.

It wasn't just that slight. It was also every other slight that came before it. Every slap from his dad, every "mutt" and "faggot" thrown his way, everything. He felt a switch flip in his brain.

Neal set his bottle down, tipped the bartender, and then turned around to punch the man square in the face. He went down like a stone, one friend catching him before he hit the floor, while the others converged on him. The ensuing fight was quick, dirty, and ended up outside after the owner threw them out on their asses. Neal didn't stop, though, and he instead kept going after the group even after he'd gotten knocked down a few times. He was possessed, furious, and had twenty-one years of pent-up anger behind him.

What he didn't notice was the older couple, black and well-dressed, who'd evidently been walking home from a nice dinner when the brawl had spilled into the street. He didn't see the man step forward to shield his wife from them, and Neal didn't see him when he got pushed back into the man's body, sending them both toppling over the curb in a tangle of limbs. There was a sickening *crack,* followed by a thump, and Neal was so dazed from the fall that he barely realized the other guys had taken off.

"Joseph!" A woman's voice called out, growing closer. "Jesus, Mary, and Joseph—Joseph!"

Her small hands rolled Neal over, pushed him away before he could stagger onto his feet. The world around him was still unclear, and he was confused about the sudden shift in atmosphere. Then he turned, saw the awkward angle the man's neck was twisted into, and heard his labored breathing.

"I didn't mean to… I'm sorry… I'm not going anywhere," Neal said in a slow, shocked voice, barely registering the sirens and arrival of emergency services until two police officers shouldered him to the ground and cuffed him.

The ensuing hours were a blur, mostly bright lights and uncontested admissions on his part, until Neal woke up in a holding cell the next morning, dead sober, to find out he'd ruined his life and two others'.

How he could tell Reeve anything about what happened, Neal wasn't sure. Maze was right about him having to give up the truth at some point, but the prospect of Reeve looking at him differently, whether it be because he loved him or for what he had done to Joseph all those years ago, made him sick. The intervening decade had blunted his recollection as to just how intensely he sought Reeve's approval, his affection, but now that he was here and had seen him again, those feelings had resurfaced with a vengeance.

He cupped a hand to his own cheek—just to, he didn't know, feel something. Maybe. Like it was possible, even remotely, infinitesimally, that there could exist a person capable of loving him that way.

Neal imagined Reeve's dark eyes. They cut through him like he was being fucked. Then the latent want reemerged. *I love him.* It was the hot ache behind his navel, the thrill that flit up his spine whenever he saw the other boy, the way his brain felt tenderized at the barest touch.

His dream was to brush that hair from his brow, then move his palm down, lower, until he could cup Reeve's jaw in his hand. Tender, it would be tender. To feel his skin cool with perspiration, give to his palm, their shared longing unspoken but present. He tried to imagine being trusted with that proximity. He wanted it so much it was almost palpable, tangible.

He'd felt this way for so long he didn't know what it meant to live without it, even when he hadn't been able to put a name to what it was.

It had been another mundane afternoon when he'd first realized this. Reeve had been laid out beneath the bleachers with a book in hand. When the light cascading down from between the slats caught his features, the contrast was like night. Neal's heart did a funny little flip in his chest. *I never knew I could feel this close to somebody,* he thought, surprising himself by how raw his want was.

Reeve hadn't done anything special or different that day. He'd just been the same as he always was. That's all Neal needed from him. The urge to reach out and touch burned inside. He just wanted to be loved so bad. And he wanted Reeve to be the one to give it to him.

Love, hah. His mom had so often used it as a fix-it for their problems. *He loves you. He doesn't mean this.* Neal had needed to believe her. And his dad had always told them both the most beautiful things, things that were beautiful in the moment but never lasted. Just empty promises in their dysfunctional, endless playing at house.

Even now, Neal would sometimes hear a car backfire, or a firework go off, and he'd be taken back to that final day in his childhood home, a place where he would freeze and flinch because it wasn't just a car or a toy—it was a gun, and he was about to die.

There was something about the visceral sense memory that rendered it bigger and more terrible. Gunshot, glass, orange peel. His mother's face.

Neal had lain there in his own blood, eye fucked to hell and half out of his mind with pain. Irrationally, he'd thought what he always did when he was on the ground, and his dad was above him. *Aren't you supposed to love me? Out of all the people in this world, aren't you the one who's supposed to love me the most?*

He remembered staring up at his dad like a man caught in some strange dream. He remembered Irena putting herself between them. Irena had never stood up for him before that day. And Neal learned why she'd done so in quick and brutal fashion. His mom had only ever been brave for him that once.

His mom had hurt him, but she'd been a victim, too. And wasn't that just the rub? That she could do bad things and yet still be hurt? Irena hadn't deserved to be treated like that by his dad; Neal hadn't deserved her cold and capricious treatment or his dad's heavy hands, either. It had taken him until that moment to get that both could be true at the same time.

He had something to prove. Born with a chip on his shoulder and fire in his heart. It had burned up inside him for so long, but now, he wondered what it had all been for. The fire is in his heart. The hatred for people who didn't give less than a damn about him.

He thought back to the paperback languishing atop the motel's bedside table. Its intrinsic misery.

When Ezrah was born, it was not with his mother's blue eyes or fair hair; he emerged into the world dark like night, head crested with tight curls and his eyes burning black. His was the spitting image of Isaiah Bell, the butcher's son. Jude saw at once it could not be his boy and left the room in a piteous furor, all the while Dierdre's parents cried rape. For rape was all it could be. How else would a woman like her lay with a man like that?

Neal was a man like that.

He headed back to the motel under a strange spell, contemplative and in such a daze that he didn't recall having missed his standing appointment with Reeve. The other man was sat rigid in the driver's seat of the infamous Laguna in the motel parking lot. He was characteristically silent, but his lips twitched into something approaching a smile when he registered Neal's presence. That, there—that smile. Or as much as one could extract a smile from Reeve. It was so special.

The pair migrated towards the motel door and settled just across the threshold. In this light, Reeve was set in a red-blue gradient from the sign, merging into violet at the midpoint. His glasses reflected Neal's own reflection back at him.

Neal felt something tender, raw rise inside him. The vulnerable underbelly of his being. That thing in him that everyone else demanded be excised. What would it be like, he thought, to reach out and touch Reeve? That same fondness from before reared its head again. It was buoyant, so much so that he could not halt the hand that reached towards the other man. The initial press of his palm against Reeve's jaw was a shock. Neal could not move. Neither, it seemed, could Reeve. And thus they stood there, paralyzed, two sculptures caught between the motion and the act.

Feeling like someone gets you, really gets you—it's the best feeling in the world, he thought. *Can't you see? Please.*

"What are you doing?" Reeve's deep voice rasped. He hadn't moved, but his expression was wrought in confusion. His eyes flit back and forth across Neal's face.

Where could he even begin?

I want you to know me. I want you to know me, all of me, and not flinch. I want you. I want us, together. I want to tell you everything. I want you to fuck me. I want you to love me.

The desperation so strong it was almost physical, and he feared that the other man could somehow sense it, like heat off asphalt. Neal felt sick with how far gone he was.

"I love you, Red," he confessed. "I'm *in* love with you."

Reeve stumbled back at that as if scorched. His usual level features were smeared open with shock. It was clear this was the last thing he'd been expecting Neal to say.

Then he turned, soundless, and disappeared into the dusk.

When it became clear that Reeve had left for good, and that he did not intend to return, Neal let out a dry sob. He was alone again.

His eyes lingered on the closed door.

REEVE IV

Reeve fled into the darkness.

Neal's phantom touch followed him, and he saw the other man's accusation reflected in his own gaze each time he glanced at the rearview mirror. His grip was tight around the steering wheel. The radio had been turned to Neal's favorite jazz station, and Chet Baker played sweet and low over the speakers. He was drowned in its familiarity. Reeve cut the knob, after which the only sounds in the cab were his rapid heartbeat, his own half-strangled breaths.

It was not long until he found himself pressing a palm to his own cheek in a facsimile of Neal's earlier motion and flinched. It was too much, too soon. The skin there still felt warmer and more over-sensitized than the rest, as if some part of Neal had stayed even after he had gone.

Reeve's throat closed up and heat pooled in his gut. It was want, he thought. Undeniable want. The realization was like cold water to the face.

He changed gears and reversed course, the Laguna's tires kicking up gravel and loose chat as he spun. Reeve had migrated south with the intent to trace aimless circles near where the main drag would connect to the interstate but was now pulled back through town to the last place he should be. The Blue Room Club.

The air settled cool and bitter in his lungs when he got out. He noosed his tie and pawed at his hair to smooth it. Reeve tilted his head back and examined the club's half-dead neon sign, which was backlit by a waxing gibbous moon and fetal stars.

He had driven by the Blue Room before but never went in, had no reason to, so he now walked towards the entrance with no small amount of trepidation. The bouncer, some nameless Gulf War Vet he recognized only in passing, gave him a curious once-over but waved him in without comment. Reeve was then assaulted by multihued blue light, smoke, and a sick, downtempo beat that turned him inside out.

He quickly took the most secluded seat he could find, but his arrival had not gone unnoticed. There were a few guys he recognized from work gathered near the front where the dancers were concentrated, and Reeve picked out Zebadiah's and Hoyt's faces among the crowd further in. Unsurprising, if unfortunate. Zebadiah made a gesture at Reeve and the men laughed.

If only they knew why he had come; it would have been even worse. He chewed on his nails and the surrounding cuticle. The things they had said about him had never cut so deep as they did now—perhaps because he recognized they had never been so true before. Had Neal always felt this way? Was their friendship ever real? Or had he always just wanted something from him? Though, Reeve supposed, if he really was certain he could never return those feelings, then he wouldn't feel the need to come here. He wouldn't have something to prove to himself.

He ducked his head, hands folded in his lap. The music continued to rattle him. Reeve thought about his childhood home, its inexhaustible silence. He hated it at first, its purpose escaping him. Not anymore. Reeve longed for that peace to return.

His gaze drifted towards the bar, tracked the patrons and cocktail waitresses who frequented it. He didn't drink often, but he gave it a lasting look nonetheless; he thought that liquor might make him feel a little more at ease.

The women continued to orbit different sections around the stage, where two half-naked girls gyrated on a gleaming pole that distorted and reflected the club around it. They looked young, old, empty.

The floor was dirty, and sweat glistened on their torsional bodies, on the open foreheads of the men whose heads were tipped back to watch them dance. They tossed the dancers crumpled singles every now and then, which they collected in a rush after their performances ended. When Reeve breathed in, out, he found the air thick with stale beer and unwashed clothes.

This was the view from Olympus.

It had never been clearer that he did not belong here. Not with the other men or even in the town itself. He was looking in on a world that didn't belong to or welcome him, and once again he wished desperately that wasn't the case.

Reeve did not have much time to spare for that last thought before he was approached by a slender, scarlet-haired woman in a deep red slingshot thong and lucite heels. There were crystal-encrusted pasties adorned by ruby tassels covering her nipples. They stared at each other in silence at first, and she appraised him coolly until her expression shifted into something that almost approached friendliness.

"God," she remarked, voice dry, "we must be doing something wrong if you're that damn tense."

He looked down at himself. His arms were held taut at his sides, fingers curled into fists. Reeve tried to relax back into the chair. It didn't work. He knew it wouldn't—his unease was as much a part of him as the breath in his lungs, the blood on his hands.

The woman threw her head back and laughed. The lights caught her face properly then, and he recognized her. Her name was Jane, and she'd been in the year above him back in school. Jane and her friends had egged his house and defaced his locker with spray paint. KILLER. PSYCHO. LOSER. Those were the words that lived in the mouths of everyone, then and now.

"Hey there," she said, drawing closer. "I'm Destiny."

It was a perfunctory nod to anonymity. Everyone knew each other. Carthage was too small for anything else. But they could pretend, he supposed. Let the fantasy invade for a little while, until the music faded with dawn, when everyone would scatter, ant-like, back into their daylight places.

"Reeve."

"*Mm.* Never heard of you."

"Sure."

Reeve could see how face powder had settled into the lines around her eyes, lipstick bleeding a little around her lips. The mouth before him became an open sore rather than an invitation. He wanted to poke at it to see if blood would well up underneath.

Jane—no, Destiny—regarded him with interest. "I don't know what to make of you."

"There's not much to say."

Her grin widened into something realer. "Now, we both know that's not the case."

"Just—give me whatever the guys usually pay you for," he said, withdrawing several twenties from his billfold and inexpertly tucking them into her thong.

Destiny's eyes widened at the amount and her smile crept upward. "You're in for a real treat tonight, *stranger*. Let's take this show somewhere more private."

Then she motioned for him to follow her, and Reeve got to his feet. Destiny was a glittering red smear backlit by neon, leading him through the tables, couches, and past the main stage into a secluded back area. The other men's eyes tracked him as he went, and Reeve looked away to escape their scrutiny.

Even more than the main floor, this room smelled like sweat and salt. The walls and floor were done in deep indigo gradations, and a mirrored platform with a pole jutting up from it dominated the small space. Further back was a velvet lounge that Destiny motioned for him to sit on. The music here was different, slower, almost hypnotic in its intensity.

His teeth were on edge.

Destiny stepped up onto the mirror and made one graceful rotation around the pole. There was a distinct athleticism to the performance that impressed Reeve despite the tension curdling in his gut, especially when she maneuvered herself upside-down to face him.

"I guess you wouldn't know what this is. It's for VIP's. I thought you might relax more if we were alone," she said, shifting her legs to invert into a different yet similarly intricate position, "but I can tell that ain't the case. Maybe a lap dance would get you into it. You did pay the big bucks, after all."

Then she flipped backwards off the stage and sauntered over to him, putting on a show as she did so. Destiny was lithe and sinuous, and when she turned around to circle her hips over his groin, he could tell she had practiced this game many times over. It was intimate, discomfiting.

Despite this, Reeve soon got hard. It came as an insane relief. He could do it. He could want her. But Neal was never far from his thoughts, even while bathed in Destiny's body heat, her too-sweet perfume. His image persisted still.

What does it mean? Reeve wondered. *To want both. Men, women.*

Reeve didn't know. He'd sought answers but everything had instead remained gray, nebulous. He was more at odds with himself than before.

Destiny continued to grind. Her long hair swayed with each concentric movement, and she flipped it over one shoulder, exposing the lean lines of her back. There, situated between her shoulder blades, was a tattoo that had been only half-visible before. A murder of crows twisted and shimmered across her spine.

"You ain't much of a talker, are you?" Destiny remarked after a while, looking back at him. The tassels on her chest swayed.

Reeve cleared his throat. It was already difficult to hold a conversation on his better days, and this certainly wasn't one of them. "Not particularly," he said. "But you knew that."

"The guys here, when they come to this room, they talk, but you're sitting there like there's something on your mind. There's not usually a whole lotta distraction on that couch," she murmured.

Reeve didn't know what to say.

"Do you even wanna be here? No? I can tell," she continued, expression less amused than it had been earlier. "I'd offer to suck you off for an extra twenty, but I don't think that would solve your problem. There's something else. Or someone."

He stared at Destiny's heavy-lidded eyes, as though it would render him able to interpret the direction of her thoughts, or that he could pull them forth from her head. Reeve adjusted his glasses. The lap dance ended, and her smile dissipated entirely.

"I never forgot about you. "Kid-Killer," or whatever. I was cruel to you. We all were. Most still are. If it makes you feel any better, the world's been cruel to me, too.

"Take a look around," she said, "it's new. Almost all of this place is. You've lived here your whole life, so you remember. There was a fire in '87. God—it was bad. Whatever you've heard about it, imagine worse.

"Live music used to play on Fridays sometimes, and there was this band that brought pyrotechnics. Gerbs, other fireworks. It was fun, y'know. Different. But one night they ignited the egg crates behind the drummer's spot and the flames spread like nothing I'd ever seen. It was too quick for most to even realize it wasn't part of the show at first. They just stood there, cheering, while I ran out the back.

"Then everything began to burn. The firemen called it flashover. Even now, I still think about it. I remember the smell best. It was like cooked meat. People were stuck in the front door, literally stuck, packed so close together no one could get out. Bodies stacked on bodies. They were wriggling and screaming and burning. It'd been busy that night. The club was black with smoke.

"Men died, sure. But my girls did, too. Nobody put a gun to their head and made them work here, but I don't know how much of a choice it was either. And they died scared. They deserved it even less than the guys did.

"Nobody did it on purpose or outta evil intent. It was just a mistake. A horrible, horrible mistake. So, yeah, you could say I've gained some perspective. Makes me wish I'd done things differently."

Reeve could see that Destiny had meant what she'd said. He realized also that, had things been different, he could have come to care for someone like her. His inability to do so now had nothing to do with being gay or broken, but because his heart had belonged to Neal since that first odd, bitter morning when they first met so long ago, their shared breaths clouding the air like smoke under a slow-rising sun.

He felt light-headed and in need of escape. "I can't do this," he ground out, jerking back. He nearly tripped over his own feet in his effort to extricate himself from her.

Destiny watched him leave with a strange light in her eyes. Soon, her erotic contours bled into shadow, then disappeared entirely as he rounded the corner leading from the VIP room back to the main area.

His own cowardice curdled in his gut. The strobes had intensified, and his feet were unsteady beneath him. He loosened his tie, feeling sweat pool in his collarbone and at the nape of his neck. The walls closed in around him.

Reeve went out the first door he could find—a side entrance marked by an acid-green EXIT sign—and was greeted by the cold night. The asphalt crackled beneath his shoes. He wound his hands through his hair and tugged. Between clenched teeth emerged a low, strangled groan. He had never felt so lost.

He resented Neal for changing things, for being so open. Nothing would ever be the same again. He'd deprived Reeve of the last uncomplicated thing in his life.

He thought he wouldn't understand how to want Neal. He'd misjudged himself. It came easy to him, now, and the feeling welled up inside him from someplace he hadn't known existed, resplendent, clean, echoing through dark halls to fill them with light, and it was easy as anything, easy as breathing.

Reeve felt overcome. He may as well have been crawling on the ground for how lightheaded it made him. He bent over to try and catch his breath. His fingers twitched. *One, two, three.*

He didn't hear the door swing open behind him. Not at first. It was the familiar laughter that had him turn on his heel, in a daze, to find that Zebadiah and Hoyt had joined him in the alley. The former had his head tilted to the side. His gaze was half-lidded, hands tucked loosely into his pockets. Ever the lackey, Hoyt lurked in the background. The two had carried the stench of booze outside.

"The way you ran out, boy," Zebadiah whistled, long and low, "that's what folks mean when they say, "bat outta hell." I'll admit, I was curious—what makes a guy like you leave a place like this? What even brings a guy like *you* to a place like this to begin with?"

Reeve stepped back. The implication was clear. His limbs were weighed down, but by what, exactly, he could not name. Although it had been hot in the club, the winter air began to chill his sweat against his skin.

Zebadiah drew closer, smiling. "Now, what'd that poor girl ever do to you?"

Then there were hands pulling his arms back, and Reeve saw in his periphery that Hoyt had materialized behind him. He didn't struggle. This conversation—whatever it was—felt inevitable.

Zebadiah walked up to him and pivoted to face Hoyt as if to speak with him, but it turned out to be a feint, and he instead reared back to sucker-punch Reeve hard in the gut. All the breath left him in a strangled exhale, and the shock got him weak in the knees. He sagged forward and was kept upright by Hoyt's grip alone.

"Damn, you really do make this easy," Zebadiah remarked, tugging Reeve's head up by his hair to make eye contact. "Ain't you gonna say something for yourself?"

He sounded just like Ephraim. *God, you always fall for this shit*, his brother had said, and he was right.

The words hit a wall in his throat. "Nothing I could do will change what'll happen here," he said after a long moment, voice hoarse. "Not anything at all."

"Aw, well, had to try."

Hoyt, whose breath was warm and wet against Reeve's ear, laughed and shook him. Zebadiah punched him again, this time in the face. His lip split and tannic flooded his tongue. The ground beneath him was insubstantial, his legs wavering.

"I watched you walk in here, skittish, to a place I know you ain't never been before. You were alone. And there was this look on your face I didn't understand. It was weird, a little sad. I asked myself what could do that to a man. It wasn't too hard to figure out.

"I see you every day. I have to, with us being neighbors and all. I don't much care for it. You don't have friends, or family, or even a wife. There's just that Jew and your new buddy. He's a funny one. Thinks he's a cowboy or something. I'd tell you to watch yourself 'round him, but I'm not too sure you want to.

"It's not much of a leap from that to what you did in there. Those things tend to go hand and hand, don't they? Being so twisted up you can't tell your left from your right."

He gestured for Hoyt to let go, and Reeve dropped to his knees. There was no point in running off. This was his neighbor, his coworker. Where could he go? They circled each other's lives each day.

Hoyt wrested Reeve by the shoulders and kicked him in the stomach, and not long after Zebadiah descended on him, too. Reeve folded his arms over his head and curled into the fetal position, trying not to think, not to feel. To withdraw from this moment until it passed him by.

"It's just…" Zebadiah pressed on, licking at his lips, "so sick, y'know? That people like that are out in the world. Even here. It ain't far to Elohim City. They got it right. Took up for themselves and everything. You spurn us Adamites and spend your days with Cain's children and dirty mutts—fine, that's your choice. But don't expect to have a good time. Not in the least. For Christ's sake, the only thing worse than being a faggot is getting on your knees for something beneath you.

"Explain to me why a kike's life matters. Tell me what good either of them got to bring into this world. Whatever it is, it's less than what we do.

The cross is old school. But I've found that it's the image that matters to people, what really sticks with 'em. Blood, soil. Think about it, Scarlet," he confided, breath hot against Reeve's ear. Then he spat on the ground near his head.

And with that, the two men laughed and walked back into the club, leaving Reeve alone in the alley. Their voices carried into the night. The door opened, closed. It was silent again.

He felt as though his guts had been picked over. They knew about Neal, his feelings for Reeve, and had punished him for it. Characteristically, he'd done nothing for his own defense, but he'd kept quiet on Maze and Neal, too, which felt to him far more like betrayal.

Sit. Heel. Roll-over.

They didn't have to say those words for him to understand the message. The dog was a creature to which submission was in its nature. They were trained all their lives to obey. Therefore, he needed to fall in line.

Reeve licked at the blood on his mouth. It was darkly wet, as he imagined a fox's snout would be after a successful hunt. Reeve exhaled and watched his breath frost the air. His eyes were damp.

He could not recall the last time he cried. Had it been at Ephraim's funeral? Or during one of the endless nights thereafter spent curled up alone in what had been their room, staring at a bed that never needed making, clothes no longer in use, toys gathering dust on the floor. Now, though, Reeve reckoned he was allowed some pity. The jagged images, sounds, and smells that comprised nearly all memories of that day intermixed into one large smear of unpleasantness.

Reeve lay there and looked up at the sky, the moonlight that trickled down past the Blue Room. The stars tangled in darkness. It was beautiful. He felt nothing. It meant nothing to him.

He was trapped and could not summon the will to move, or turn, or even let his lids close. When the tears trickled down his cheeks, he shuddered at the wet slip on skin, but this time it was not just because of the past. This trauma was the present. He wanted to stop thinking. He wanted the constant buzz in his head to subside. He wanted to not be on edge every moment of his waking life, and for his heart to leave his throat.

The cold eventually forced his hand, and he staggered upright, disoriented enough to where each movement was akin to the shift of tectonic plates.

Reeve examined his palms, which were now soaked in rainwater. There were tiny specks of gravel embedded in the flesh that glittered beneath the streetlights. He wore his own blood like a second skin.

A modulated male voice moaned in the distance, the music from the club seeping out. It faded in and out.

He drank it all in with eyes that had adjusted to the dark.

He shivered and whimpered through his gritted lips. The pressure in his head was fast approaching maximum capacity. He could even imagine the steam, the kettle-like whistle warning before his brains boiled over. The shrill reverberation within his mind.

Go home, his mind shrieked, strained and guttural. *Leave. Check the locks. The doors. Get in the shower. Punish yourself.*

Then came the rain. It fell in freezing sheets around him, plastering his hair against his brow and saturating his clothes, which were stained with dirt and blood. He grit his teeth and uttered a low groan. *Why,* he thought. *Why-why-why?* But the question answered itself with one name, one face: Ephraim. It was the image that emerged each time water struck his skin. He'd once been resigned to it, but now things were different. His life was not his own; his body was not his own; even his memories did not belong to him entirely.

He stood there, bathed in shimmering rain and neon light. The puddles around him were distorted mirrors, and his image was reflected in each one. Black eyes, white hair. And blood, blood, blood. Distantly, he heard more thumping bass bleed through the club's walls and out across the lot. The bouncer would not look at him.

Reeve's feet found their way to his car, the beautiful and terrible Laguna, and he peeled out from the lot in a daze. The road disappeared beneath his wheels, and the gloomy chat mounds rolled by under the cloud bank.

Where could he go? This—Neal's love, his lust—would follow him anywhere. His knowledge of it seemed to be writ into his face. Something about himself had changed after his confession, of that much he was certain. How else could Zebadiah and Hoyt see what was between them? Reeve dug his free hand into one of the scratches they'd inflicted on his forearm. It hurt. Oh, God, it hurt.

Then came a voice, eerily like Ephraim's. *Don't lie to yourself—the pain can make you come. If given by the right person, that is. You need it.*

He didn't want it to be true.

Reeve drove and kept driving. He let the blackness consume him. His radio edged in and out as he swerved through the empty stretch of road that separated Carthage and Maidenhead. There was no rhyme or reason to his wanderings; he merely felt lost, unmoored. His brain was full up with Neal, Zebadiah, Hoyt.

The word love rattled around. Reeve could not recall the last time anyone had said that to him. His father, Amon, had been a man of few words—not unlike himself. His mother had been absent for a majority of his childhood, calling him epithets like "sweetheart" or "honeypie," but never saying "I love you." Ephraim, *hah.* The more he contemplated it, the more he realized there was hardly a kind word exchanged between them.

So, who else was left but Neal?

He'd been there, gone, and was here again. Many details about his current situation and the intervening period between their time together and now were undisclosed. Reeve was smart enough to pick out the silences, the omissions, in his language. That should be enough for him to walk back their friendship, let alone whatever Neal wanted it to be, right? Any sane man would dispose of the situation and its trappings before things got further tangled.

But Reeve was not just any man. And he wasn't particularly certain he was quite so sane anymore, either, if he ever had been.

Neal called to him. His breastbone ached with it. It was a connecting line spanning the many miles he had driven, terminating at both ends. His want expanded outward, up, until it reached his molars and rattled his skull. *Neal.* He needed to see Neal. Somehow, seeing him would resolve his confusion, despair, everything. Never mind that he'd run from him for the same reasons only hours earlier. He needed to be fixed that badly.

Reeve slammed on the brakes and pivoted, car kicking up dust around him. Then he sped back from whence he came. In the distance, obviated by chat mounds, clouds, was Carthage's miserly jewelry-box lights, as his mom had liked the call them. Two-bit emeralds, rubies, and diamonds. It was there that Neal was, alone, thinking that Reeve hated him or didn't care for him no more. Maybe he had even left already after he'd ditched him earlier.

His stomach twisted. The thought of Neal leaving was more anathema to him than the wonder-terror of the confrontation to unfold. His grip on the wheel tightened, and the urge to exit his own skin magnified tenfold, leaving him tearing at his cuticles and scratching himself to hold on before he spun out into space.

Neal. Neal. Neal.

He loves me, Reeve thought hysterically. *My best friend is in love with me. He's loved me for as long as he's known me.*

Very sweet, Creepy Reevey. But don't you remember? Ephraim's voice replied. *You can't fix what's inside. And sooner or later, your boy's gonna figure it out.*

MAZE IV

Maze heard the girl before she saw her. The entire house had been saturated in bass, and she could feel it pulse and vibrate through the walls even upstairs. There was the occasional outbreak of laughter, too, often chased by the sound of broken glass or a high-pitched shriek. She took a drag from her cigarette.

Maze wasn't drunk, and she wasn't sober. She had arrived at that unpleasant midpoint between the two, when the world hadn't yet descended into unreality but had started to lose focus at the edge. She'd retreated to this sad little corner to try and rid herself of the building pressure behind her eyes.

It was the noise, she thought. The noise and the people.

Even this far removed from the speakers and kegs, the hall was still populated by two couples—a pair of what looked to be freshmen, their bodies inexpertly pretzeled together, and a guy she recognized from her stats class with a nervous hand shoved down his girlfriend's jeans. Maze was alone. Oralene had parted with her on bad terms earlier, and now she'd been left to seethe in silence.

The night had started off tense.

Maze was made to wait longer than usual to sneak out, and her long skirt caught on the sill when she climbed out the window, sending her into a sprawl across the hard-packed dirt outside. The wind left her chest instantly, and she cried out more from shock than pain, taking care to shove a hand in her mouth while she waited there, rigid, listening for the telltale creak of a floorboard inside. Nothing.

Maze relaxed and muttered a low, "Dammit." Then she closed the window and darted across the lawn to where her car was parked, bump starting it to let it coast down the driveway until she was far enough down the street to bring the clutch up in gear.

The clouds were a deep slate, voluminous. In the distance, the chat piles were backlit by lightning. Even the new Black Sabbath tape, *Dehumanizer*, did nothing to sate her unease.

Oralene was reclined on her front steps by the time Maze pulled up. Her lids were caked in shadow, which shifted silver under the porch lamp. The Kennedys didn't care whether she went out, and her parents waved goodbye through the lace curtains. Maze wished—

"Nice outfit," the other girl said as she climbed in.

Maze glanced down at herself. Yeah, she'd tried to put in some real effort for once. No jeans, no boots. Just a flannel and a droopy purple shift. But she was already regretting the heels, even with how short they were.

"You too," she said, then checked her watch. "Gotta make one last stop before Lee's. Shouldn't be too long, though."

Oralene groaned at the reminder. "I can't believe they let Cricket in on this. The hell are they thinking, letting her come?"

"I dunno."

There was an unpleasant twist in her chest at the reminder. Maze had an idea as to why and could tell her friend did too; they both knew the invite wasn't serious. Not after Lee's past remarks or Tandy's trash-filled excursion to the Pit.

But she didn't have it in her to break it to Cricket. Neither, it seemed, did Oralene. The look on her face had been so open, so pleased. Naïve, somehow, even despite everything. To kill that light seemed almost cruel to Maze. It was cruel in a way that turned her stomach.

Sheriff Fields' place was two blocks over, and he walked Cricket to the station wagon with a tentative stride. He was still in uniform, ginger hair gelled close to his scalp. His daughter's curls were equally bright and pulled back with plastic clips, leaving the ends to spill across her shoulders like red ink. Her lip-gloss was pink to match her dress, and it made her mouth stick a little when she opened it. There was a silver butterfly necklace looped around her sternum. Cute, but real grade-school shit.

"Sheriff," Maze said, rolling down the window.

"Girls," her dad said, "curfew is at eleven."

"You got it, Sheriff. We'll get her back on time."

He nodded, then turned to his daughter. "Corliss, you enjoy yourself, now," he told her.

"Thanks, daddy."

Oralene looked like she was trying not to snort at the exchange. Maze didn't mind it so much. The sight of Sheriff Fields' broad hand on Cricket's shoulder, his thin-lipped but genuine smile—it was nice. He loved his daughter.

But she had to wonder what Cricket had told her dad to sell him on this, and where, exactly, he thought she was going. Maybe he needed to believe it would be good for her. He had this excited desperation about the whole thing that made her sick.

Then Cricket climbed into the backseat, and an awkward silence fell upon the cab that did not dissipate, not even after they pulled up and disembarked, and Oralene was knocking on Tandy's door. They were swept up into the crowd at once when it opened, with Lee, Tandy, and their friends pulling Cricket into the crowd and pressing a drink into her hands.

Everything was both strange and familiar. The music was discordant, rough, and the uncoordinated roll of bodies around her verged on the claustrophobic. There was a lit joint in Maze's left hand and a warm, overfull cup of beer in her right soon enough. Maze tipped her head back and tried to be overcome.

Not too long ago, she'd enjoyed this. It loomed in her mind as a visceral release. Being with people, she thought. Belonging.

But wherever that girl had gone, she did not resurface. Maze went through the motions—smoking, drinking, swaying to the syncopated rhythm—only to turn at the wrong time and see herself reflected in the sliding glass door or a window, where she was met by an unsmiling face. Her eyes were like gutter slush. Dirty.

Maze turned away, unable to bear her own reflection, only to be met by a familiar figure. Her old dealer had turned up, and when he saw her, he knocked shoulders with her and winked. Maze could feel that he'd slipped something into her hand. Upon closer inspection, she realized it was fry.

"On the house," he said. "You look like you need it."

"Maybe I do."

Then she flicked him, and he disappeared back from where he came, laughing. Her fingers tightened around his gift. She'd always felt weird about smoking a joint that had been dipped in the shit they used on dead bodies, always declining when offered, but tonight was as good as any to try something new. If she could work up the courage, that was. A bad trip was one more problem she didn't need.

Maze soon sought refuge in the kitchen. It was cooler, and she ducked beneath the tap to let the water sluice across her cheeks. The nausea didn't subside, though, and the prospect of reentering the mass made it worse. Her tongue darted out to whet her throat. When she reemerged, she saw that Oralene had joined her.

The atmosphere between them was strained. Why that was, she couldn't place. Maybe it was the culmination of the past week, or everything that had happened since the spring. Either way, Maze felt further from her friend than ever before.

"It's warm in here," Oralene remarked.

Maze tried to jump through the rote conversational hoops. "Yeah, I'm sweatin' like a whore in church."

"Synagogues don't count, Maze. Beer's alright, though."

"It's... PBR."

"Got me there."

There wasn't a lot more to say. Maze tried to dredge up the words. *I'm having a great time, really. Wouldn't trade it for anything.*

All she ended up doing was mutter, balefully, "This party is bogus," and ground out the roach into the kitchen sink. It was her last, meaning all she had left was fry.

Oralene clicked her tongue at that. "Seems alright enough to me," she said. "Music could be better, though."

There was now a slowed-down mix playing. Lee had some cousins visiting up from Houston, and they'd brought CDs with them. Everyone seemed into it. Not as good as *Slayer,* though, but what was?

"I guess."

They lapsed into silence for a moment, leaning back together on the laminate countertop, until Oralene's expression brightened, and she raised a hand in welcome to someone in the crowd.

"Hey, Bliss, over here," she called out.

Three girls made their way to the kitchen, each just as blonde and pretty as Oralene. It was almost like they'd been manufactured in a lab. The one in front—Bliss, Maze supposed—pulled Oralene in for a hug.

"It's been a while, Ora. I didn't know you were friends with Lee's crowd."

"Oh, we go way back. This one, too." Oralene gestured towards her.

"Hey," Maze said to them. "How do y'all know each other?"

"I ran into her at a cheer competition, and we just clicked. Me, her, all the girls here. We still see each other every now and then."

"*Interesting*," Maze said, bored.

Bliss turned to the side. "Now, Oralene, you gotta catch me up," she said.

Maze rolled her eyes and kept quiet while the others talked. They went to school in Maidenhead and were juniors, too, and did nice, normal things like attend homecoming and cheer at football games. Just perfect.

"My boyfriend's here, yeah—"

"—cute."

"Haven't seen it—"

Their voices faded into the background, and the cup crackled between her fingers. Her gaze drifted away from the group and towards the living area, which was crawling with bodies. Among them was Dean.

He was everywhere. His dark head, his dark gaze. He soon dominated her thoughts without even trying, and she hated him for it. That, and his palpable intent. Their conversation from earlier that week haunted them both. He orbited around her, watching, always watching.

"—right, Maze?"

Maze jerked back to the present. Oralene and the other girls regarded her with expectant looks. Fishing for a response, she said the first thing that came to mind.

"Sure."

Oralene's jaw worked. "Sure?"

"Yeah," she said. "Sure."

"*Sure* you dated Dean?" Oralene asked. "You got something else you'd like to talk about?"

Maze sighed. What was the point? Of being here? She wondered. Or trying to reclaim this part of herself? It was like pressing a thumb to a fresh bruise.

"It's just—why are we here?"

"To have fun. See people. Relax. It doesn't really need explaining."

"You know what I mean."

Oralene scoffed. "What I know is that you've been a real piece of work tonight. If you didn't want to come, you should've said something. I could've hitched a ride with Tandy."

"I wanted to come. I wanted to feel—" *Normal again,* she didn't say. *Like my old self. Even for an hour or two.* But the words perished, and instead she said, "Nothing. It doesn't matter. None of this does."

"Nothing?" Oralene scoffed, looking hurt. "Not even me? I'm trying, Maze. I'm trying as hard as I can to be here for you, and you won't even put on a smile for one night."

Maze felt her face heat. Oralene seemed to be waiting for an apology, something to placate her with. But for Maze, this felt to her like things were rapidly escalating out of her control, and she couldn't make herself say anything in response.

Oralene laughed. The sound was loud, sharp. "Actually—I know what this is. You think you're better than me. Dean, too. Guess what, you're not better than us. I got problems, too. I think about things. Fucking some creepy older guy doesn't make you mature or special. It just makes you gullible and a slut."

Maze reared back, stricken. The cup was garroted in her palm. Then she started talking and couldn't stop, saying in a rush, "You think you got problems? You don't know shit about real problems. You're the one watching tragedies on the news. Me, that's my fucking life. So. Fine. Think what you want," she spat.

Oralene's face twisted in something almost like regret, but whatever Maze had seen was quickly replaced by spite. "I will, then," the other girl spat.

Maze stormed off and returned to the crowd, searching for Cricket. It was futile. The other girl had disappeared. Maze didn't really care what she was doing, but she didn't want to up and leave her either. Not after the sheriff's warning about Cricket's curfew and the gleeful way Tandy and Lee had spirited her off.

Her presence had not gone unnoticed. Dean, who'd been keeping his distance before, now tried to push through the crowd towards her. Maze wasn't up to facing him, so to escape his pull Maze went to seek out the least obtrusive place she could find.

There was a soft groan from behind her. Maze was slouched beside the upstairs guest bathroom and had been putting her cigarettes out in an empty beer can for the past twenty minutes. No one had entered or left since. Maze had assumed it was empty. She turned to listen. Nothing. Then she heard it again; a choked-off intake of air. It was almost lost to the ambient grind of music. If she hadn't been so close to the door, she would have missed it altogether. Maze knew that sound, though. Too well. The blood drained from her face.

She pressed her ear to the door. It was quiet, at first, so much so that she thought she was mistaken. But there it was, that soft, near-wet inhalation, followed by a low grunt. Her hands clenched, and when she swallowed it was dry. There was someone in the bathroom, and they could not breathe.

Her dad had sounded the same.

Maze shuddered and glanced back down the hall. The couples remained unaware, lost in each other, and she realized then that she was alone. If she were to leave, whomever was in the bathroom would be left to their fate. Whatever that was. And she feared that trying to convince people to help would take too long. Fuck. The knob was locked, but the door hadn't been closed entirely. Maze ignored the tightness in her chest, how her hands trembled when she pushed it open.

It was dark inside, and hot, like a mouth. There was a leg slung over the edge of the tub by the far wall, half-obscured by a shower curtain. Above the person was a jagged, dark shape she couldn't quite discern.

Maze fumbled for the switch. The bulbs above the mirror flickered and lit up. They had been replaced by party lights that bathed the walls in deep, lurid red. Dread gripped her. It was quieter here, but not by much. The bass intruded still.

There was something she could not name constricting her chest. Maze swallowed; it was sour. Her tongue felt thick and sweat gathered at her temples. She was shivering and didn't know why. Maze wanted nothing more than to leave. To have never involved herself in this at all. The gasping continued, though, and the shadow seemed to undulate back and forth. But when she drew back the curtain, there was a loud shout and the shape revealed itself to not be a shadow at all, but rather a familiar figure.

It was Lee.

He jerked back at her arrival and pulled down the curtain rod as he fell out of the shower. His eyes were unfocused, and his pants were pooled around his ankles. He hurriedly tucked himself back in, but Maze's gaze was drawn back to the tub.

There was a girl sprawled in it, her ginger head haloed in half-empty plastic cups. Vomit threaded her lips and pooled in her throat. *Cricket,* she realized with slow-dawning horror. This was where she'd been.

Her eyes rolled and she convulsed around another aborted breath. More sick spilled down her front. Her hair curled damply around her ears, and Maze could see her nipples through the sheer fabric of her shirt. Her bra— small, pastel pink, with a delicate bow on the front—had been unfastened and discarded beside her body, while her skirt was shoved up around her stomach. Her panties, gone.

Maze hated this, suddenly. Everything. The party. Cricket. What had been done to her. That she was even here. But Maze hated how she sounded most of all; like she was drowning. Maze wondered if it felt that way, too. If it hurt. Her dad had hurt. He'd heaved like this, too, when he'd—

Her brain stalled at that. Maze had no words to articulate what she felt then. Misery came the closest to it, she supposed. Maybe she just stood there in silence because she was trying to make sense of everything, or maybe she was shocked, so shocked her feet wouldn't move her forward, and her lips parted only to breathe. But there was no time to spare for it. Her attention was sublimated by a hyper-focused urgency that screamed at her to *fix this, now.*

"Maze," he slurred. "It's funny, right? Me and Cricket."

Lee tried to smile at her. It was the same smile he used to disarm people both in school and out. But here, in this place, it just made a certain resignation curdle in her gut.

Maze said nothing in response. Her arms shook from keeping them at her sides. Her teeth ground against each other.

"It's just a joke. Don't you get it?" Lee continued, huffing out a strange laugh as he slid his belt back into place. The *clink* of his buckle made her jerk. "It's funny 'cause she's such a tight-ass."

The night made more sense in retrospect. Lee and Tandy had invited Cricket here to get her drunk, Maze realized. Drunk enough to do something stupid. Yeah, sure. Everything was always a joke to them.

Maze put out her cigarette on the wall and crumpled the can. Her hands curled into fists. *Want.* That was what this was all about, wasn't it? Those looks in school. Him calling Cricket a dyke or a lesbo. It all came back to want. The memories rolled unpleasantly in her head.

Maybe he wouldn't have gone this far if he hadn't been drunk, or high, or both. But he'd done it. Lee felt like he was owed something from Cricket, and he turned out to be just a few drinks away from taking it by force. How many other men were like this? It was probably more than she could ever stand to know.

Lee was still talking. "I mean, she was so drunk she couldn't help herself. It's alright, y'know? I was good to her. I even got her off, too."

All the rage left her body in one guttural exhale. "You're so… selfish," she said at last.

"Selfish?"

"Don't you see how pathetic this all is? The drinking, the games. I mean—haven't y'all done enough to her?"

"*Pathetic?* What's pathetic is you being here, Maze," he spat at her. "I saw the way you were around Dean, y'know. Like he'd ever get back with you. Not after what you've put him through. You didn't just burn bridges; you burned the whole damn house down. So, you wanna know that I think? I think the only reason he ever wanted you was 'cause you put out."

"Yeah, sure, that's why. No one else is fucking or sucking 'round here besides me. I'm the *only* option for a guy like him. You're as much of a slut as I am. You stick your dick in any girl with a pulse."

He scoffed. "You stop by this party, a party thrown by people you're too good for, apparently, and start talking to me about things you don't understand. You're outta your damn mind to be acting like this."

"What's there to understand?"

"That she wanted it. That she could want it. That she knew what she was in for when she came here tonight."

Maze remembered how nice and neat Cricket had looked, all done up in her pretty dress and hair clips. The glint of gold along her collarbones. Sheriff Fields' proud expression. It made her get this sick, sinking feeling in her gut.

"Look at her—how could she even want anything right now? She's just too drunk to fight you off. She didn't before, either, and that's the problem you got with her," Maze said, hoarse and somewhat hysterical. It was the shock, she reasoned. The beer didn't help, either. "That's always been the problem."

Lee's face twisted. Faltered. It wasn't in remorse for what he'd done, though. That much was clear. He was sad and desperate because he'd been caught. More than that, he'd been caught by someone who wouldn't give him a pass. Then the impotent anger returned. He was being denied again.

There wasn't anything he could say or do to make this better. It had been too late since he'd brought Cricket up to this bathroom. Wordless, queasy—Maze had no way to describe the shock from taking this all in.

"Girls like her, they just need a taste to get that they're wrong. She needed me all along."

"If you think you're so right, why the hell are you tryin' to justify this to me? She's chokin' on her own sick and you can't give less of a damn. It was just about what she had that you could take," she said.

"I—" Lee began, but she cut him off. Maze couldn't bear to hear him continue to speak.

"You're disgusting. That's what you are," she said.

He had expected no witnesses and no consequences. He'd never had to face them before, so why would now be any different? The only obstacle here was her.

That got his attention. "What did you say to me?" Lee said. He moved closer to her, shoulders pulled taut.

Maze met his gaze. *This* was the line she'd crossed, telling him he was disgusting? Not the rape or the selfishness or the fact that Cricket could have died with him inside her. And she was still over there, right now, aspirating on her own puke while they got into it with each other.

"I said you're disgusting, you selfish sonuvabitch, and I'll do it again. You're disgusting. *Dis-gus-ting.* Now get outta my way."

He stood between her and the tub where Cricket continued to seize. Even listening to her made Maze tense up, ride the narrow edge between now and then. Her dad's slack face flashed in and out each time she blinked. Maze had to get serious about this, but it was so hard.

"And you'll do what—make me?"

"Yeah, I will," she bit out.

"Don't kid yourself, bitch," he said. "I don't think you want to mess with me, not really. How 'bout this: I'll let you by if you tell me you're sorry.

That I was right. That Cricket will thank me for showing her what she was missing out on."

Maze recoiled. He had this funny glint in his eye. It was the same one he got whenever he crossed a line with his pranks. The one where he was the only one laughing anymore.

The sight made her feel nauseated, and even less at ease than before. But beyond that, there was this inclination towards violence that she felt in her teeth. The hate she experienced then was so visceral she shook with it. Not even her clenched palms could quell the need to lash out, to be the person who dealt out pain rather than take it.

I'm done with this, she thought. *I'm done with him*. Her body grew taut with anticipation. Maze watched Lee recognize what she was about to do, dismiss it, and grin at her. *You think you can take me?* It seemed to say. *You're nothing.*

Maze let out a strangled shout and lunged at Lee, sucker-punching him in the gut with as much force as she could manage. Lee took the body shot straight and stumbled back into the counter. He groaned and wrapped an arm around his middle, followed by a wheeze that made him spit bile all over his shirt.

The next wild lunge had her knuckles catch him across the jaw, and she felt a finger dislocate on impact. The pain was distant, muted, but it slowed her down enough for Lee to recover. He grabbed Maze by the hair and smashed her head-first into the wall.

He wrenched her back and did it again, and Maze felt her left temple grow damp. Her ears rang, and something hot and thick filled her mouth. Lee smelled like bad weed and booze. The scent was physical, heavy. Lee had lowered his jaw to the crook of her neck to bite out slurs as he ground her face into the wall.

He was screaming and shaking his head like a rabid animal, and she thought that might be enough for someone to come help her, but at that moment, someone downstairs turned the speakers up until they were submerged in bass beyond recognition.

Was this how Cricket had felt with him? Helpless. So, so helpless. Maze held the distant and somewhat futile hope that she'd zoinked out long before Lee ever came across her. Her vision grew dark at the edges, and she could feel how matted her scalp had become with her own blood. Maze recognized it for what it was, defeat, and not only her own but Cricket's as well.

No. If she started this, then she damn well was going to finish it. Maze reached out blindly for something, anything to give her enough leverage to get him off. Her hand found a cylindrical object—a towel rod, she realized—and she jammed her foot on the plaster and pushed herself backwards at the same time she wrenched it away from the wall.

It separated from the base with a metallic shriek, and the recoil sent her and Lee into a rough sprawl across the floor. His grip eased with the fall, and Maze seized the opportunity to twist around and face him, the rod now poised above his face as though it were a club. The smirk melted off his lips as it connected.

Maze hit him and hit him until there was red everywhere and his eyes fluttered open and close. It was unconsciousness, she realized. He was about to pass out. But she couldn't have that. Not yet. Not while her rage still burned this hot.

Maze stood up. "I need you to get what you are," she spat at him, pressing a shoe to his neck. "You think the world owes you somethin.' That *she* owes you somethin.' You don't deserve anything. Not even shit."

Then she smashed the rod onto Lee's face for the last time. He didn't cry, or moan, or utter anything at all. He just went limp. The anticlimax left her even more on edge than the fight.

It had been short, brutal, and left Maze nerve-wracked from the adrenaline rush afterwards. The pressure behind her eyes had worsened. It felt like old grief and darkness. Her anger had hardly abated. It had just grown listless and ill-defined without a target.

When she moved, everything ached, and she whimpered despite herself. Maze collapsed next to Lee's prone form, which bent at an uncomfortable angle. He wasn't dead, though, thank fuck; his chest rose and fell, and she could see movement beneath his lids. There was something in his back pocket, she noticed, a pink glimpse—

Behind her, Maze heard a noise that sounded like a moan and a death rattle rolled into one. Her heart stuttered. Cricket. The focus had been lost somewhere in the fight. Maze stifled her lingering disquiet and twisted to face the other girl. It was difficult to even look at her. The slackness with which her body was positioned. How she struggled less and less with each passing moment. The slow-deadening crawl from the extremities inward as she began to give in.

Maze wanted to be brave, to reach over and help her without fear. But it lingered, sour, within her, and the solution seemed to be a little liquid courage. She downed the contents of the cup nearest to Cricket's head. The drink was unusually thick and sweet, with a flavor like grape coke, chased by an aftertaste she could not quite place. The bite made her more alert. *Yeah, she told herself, you can do this.*

Maze turned Cricket on her side, then depressed her tongue with her fingers and scooped out the bile. Her palms were unsteady. They refused to be subdued. It took a moment for Cricket's chest to even out. The other girl did not wake, but she was alive. Maze put her hand on her neck and slumped back when she found a steady pulse.

The relief she felt was a little like pain.

Why'd you have to be so stupid, Cricket? Maze thought, wishing she could shake some self-preservation into her. *So easy for it? Look at yourself. You didn't help yourself at all. Not one bit.*

Maze remained there, arm posed at an angle behind her to rest on the other girl's breastbone, her heartbeat its own reassurance. It was done, she thought. Cricket was fine. This, here, wasn't at all like what happened last time. But guilt unfolded with her, heavy, sinuous.

The memories that had haunted Maze since she first heard Cricket's cries now overtook her, and so too did the inevitable slide into entropy that accompanied them. Maze could no longer keep still, nor exile her dad's face from her mind.

Blue. That's what she recalled. The color blue.

It dominated everything about that day. The clear, cloudless sky as she'd walked home. The paint on the walls in the living room. His skin, lips. If blue had a flavor, it would be salt, she thought. Like tears. How the eyes drowned in them. Flooding the mouth with bitterness as they rolled down the cheeks.

Maze had found her dad in the garage with a cord wrapped around his neck. They were alone. It had been late in the afternoon, right after school. His boots were planted on an old desk chair they'd stored there for years. He said nothing when she stumbled across him, just got this panicked look she hadn't seen before or since. They stared at each other, open-mouthed and tense, until he kicked the chair out from under himself.

Maze recalled being so shocked she couldn't move. It was just—she couldn't understand it. That it was happening.

There had been a wordless scream trapped in her throat that refused to be let out. All she could do was watch as he hung there and died. It wasn't quick. The bones in his neck didn't snap on impact. He clutched at the rope and made these raw, guttural, wounded animal sounds. Death noises that crawled and skittered. His legs twitched. His fingers scrabbled for the noose. It took forever for him to go.

Yes, his expression had been agonized—oh, those eyes, his eyes—there had been a light in them, an almost-satisfaction.

Maze didn't know what to make of it then or now.

There was no note. No final declaration. He'd been silent. Even now, she hadn't divined the reason as to why. There were no debts, or mistresses, or lies. No secrets, period, other than his death wish. Her dad had been, for the most part, no different than any other man. He'd even been happier than usual in the weeks leading up to that day. Happy in a way she hadn't seen him be in a long, long time.

And so, she was left to wonder. Maze thought that it was at times worse than the pain of his death. The not knowing. The *whys* of it all.

Maze wondered if their life had been so bad. What she and her mom had done to make him hurt that much. Maybe there was just a crack in him that had grown worse with time, and that they were entirely irrelevant to his suffering.

But he wasn't irrelevant to hers.

His continued absence was a phantom limb: something she felt but could not see and would not be separated from her. It was hard to reconcile the man who'd once held her so gently, and regarded her with such affection, with the person who left so abruptly and without cause.

Your death is my death! She'd wanted to scream for months.

Maze still remembered what it felt like to hold him for the last time. Maze hadn't been allowed to touch him for fear she'd contaminate any evidence they might find before the medical examiner had a chance to determine the cause and manner of death, so she'd had to embrace his body bag.

All she could think about were these horrible things she saw on the news; people crying and begging and shooting at each other and fires and mass graves. Those were worse, right? People who weren't ready, people who died in senseless, horrible ways. The world kept turning. So, why couldn't she move on from the one person who'd made the choice to go?

A strangled whine jerked her back to where she belonged. Now. The house. Cricket, Lee.

Her arm began to protest its current position, and Maze removed it with some lingering trepidation. Then she wiped the vomit from her hands onto her skirt and got to her feet. Maze wanted another cigarette, badly, but now wasn't the time. And she couldn't just ditch Cricket. That much was evident. Maze's gaze drifted back towards her, and Cricket almost looked as though she could have been asleep. When she woke, that peace would be gone.

Maze's skin felt too tight for her face. There was an itch beneath it, too, something that urged her to get out and run away until all this became nothing but a bad dream. She couldn't be here anymore. Maze couldn't do this alone. Not again. Oralene, she thought. They needed Oralene. But first she had to find her in a house infested with people. It was a task that seemed more daunting by the moment.

Exhausted, bloodied, and soaked in vomit, Maze could do nothing but lay there, splayed over the tub's edge, for several long, torturous moments. When she shifted, she felt the joint move in her jacket pocket, and the realization burned a hole in her head.

Maze tilted her head back, reached inside, then considered the fry. If there was ever a time, Maze thought to herself, now would be it.

What better way was there to push herself from her own brain? She'd seen this shit make people freak out like nothing else—the kind of hallucinations that made you think they were on PCP or something like it—and never forgot. Maybe if she just smoked a little, it wouldn't be too bad…

She pulled out a lighter and lit it before she could chicken out. The first hit scorched her mouth and throat, and Maze coughed her way through a few more before stubbing it out on the counter and pocketing what was left in her flannel.

Things were better and worse; the pain in her hand and head seemed to subside, but she couldn't stop coughing. Maze coughed and coughed until she could taste blood.

Expletives rattled around in her brain while she staggered upright, kicking Lee in the crotch as she stepped over him. But when she turned to grab Cricket, the door was pushed ajar.

"Hey, Lee," a familiar voice called out. "Are you in here, man?"

It was Dean. Even half-immersed in shadow, Maze recognized him at once. He tensed the moment he noticed her and the two bodies by the bathtub. His expression was sad-sad-sad. Maze wanted to peel it off his face. Her nails bit into her palms. Maybe there had been something in the drink, too? Maze tongued her lips and tasted bitter sugar. It was too late now.

"The hell happened?" Dean asked. He stumbled a little when he tried to get nearer. He reeked as much as Lee did. Maze licked the air and tasted how fucked up he was. Dean couldn't help them. He couldn't even help himself.

"Why d'you care?"

"I'm a fucking human being."

"He was," she began, searching for the words, "having sex with Cricket while she was blacked out. Didn't take too well to me telling him to stop."

Dean flinched. "No—he wouldn't do that. I-I know him. I've known him my whole life."

Maze wanted to scream. There was this desperation, hot and acidic, burning a line up her back. All she wanted was for someone to understand what was happening. Why was she still so surprised by all the different ways people could disappoint her?

"Don't bullshit me, Dean. There's knowing and then there's *knowing*," Maze said. Her voice sounded strange and unreal. It was getting harder and harder to remain coherent.

"He doesn't need to do that to get chicks. 'Sides, maybe Cricket came 'round to the idea and just had too much to drink."

"Cricket don't like to drive stick, if you get what I mean. So she won't come 'round to shit. And if you like suckin' your friend off so much, then go get on your knees and have fun. It would put that hole in your face to better use. I'll even give you the room. 'Cause it's fine if he ain't awake, right? Maybe he just needs to be taught how to love a man," she said, throwing Lee's own twisted logic at Dean. He squirmed beneath her scrutiny.

"So, why are you takin' up for him? You never stood up for me when it all went down last year. Y'all talk about what it means to be a real man. But you ain't brave. If you were, we wouldn't be here. Things would be different," Maze said. "We might still be together.

"And because you did nothing, and because you're defending him even now—you're a part of this. So, quit acting like a coward and stand up for yourself. I thought you were better than this. One day, what you're doing now won't be enough anymore. You'll stop being "one of the good ones" and they'll turn on you. It's only a matter of time. They ain't your friends, Dean. Not really. So, take a damn good look at yourself!"

They were closer now. To her left, reflected in the mirror, Maze saw how the shadows stretched behind her like wings. Makeup was smeared in glitter-flecked streaks up and down her cheeks.

She raked a hand through her damp curls. "Get your head outta your ass and—and just think for a sec, alright? This ain't about you, or me, or even him. It's her. So please, just help me."

Dean deflated. "Jesus, yeah," he said. "Okay."

He appeared to contemplate whether to move closer, and when he did, Maze felt a cold thrill run through her and stumbled back. Dean's eyes went wide and fearful, more at himself than her, and he flinched. Maze wiped at her cheeks and forehead, sweaty and clammy and tense. The walls rippled and sagged inward. Oh. *Oh.* She could no longer stand to be in the same room as these people, the same house, breathing the same air. It seemed to cling to her, settle on her skin like disease.

The urgency she'd felt before did not slip away, not entirely, it just changed course. Dean's mouth opened, closed, but his words were each just heaps of broken syllables, and each expression he made its own broken image. With every moment that passed, Maze felt herself slipping away. Soon, the pain in her head, her heart, were just dim impressions.

"Help her. Call the cops," Maze forced out, sidestepping him. "I... I can't. I need to go."

Dean made a plaintive sound and reached for her, but Maze was already gone. She stumbled into the hallway and felt it shift around her. She could not stand straight, her feet unsteady, and she fell into the wall. The couples stared, wide-eyed.

The girl who'd gotten fingered earlier came up to her and said something, yet what that was, she couldn't say. There was a burst of noise from behind her in the bathroom.

Maze paid it no mind and headed towards the stairs. She was a slow-moving comet in a house that oozed music and sweat. It wasn't until the last few steps that she tripped, one of her heels snapping off. The living room was hot and packed with people, their undulating silhouettes wreathed in smoke and colored light as they danced. Back upstairs, she could hear Lee and Dean yelling at each other.

He'd woken up. Maze started moving faster, quicker, the momentum to leave there but distant. She took her shoes off and bled into the crowd. There was a ripple in it behind me, and I turned saw that the two boys were descending in a violent flurry of movement. The yelling began in earnest, then, and Maze knew she had to leave. The front door was too far away; she'd have to leave out the back.

The thrashing mass undulated around her, side-to-side, people drunk and lolling their heads like a many-headed monster. Darby and Everett, two members of the girls' and boys' varsity basketball teams were grinding on each other, only to be disrupted when Maze got caught between them.

"Hey!" The pair chorused.

Maze mumbled out a "sorry" and continued, bare feet slipping and sliding across the carpet, which had become saturated in sweat, drink, and who knew what else. The living room may as well have been a sty or a stable. Then the mass tapered off, and she fumbled her way into the kitchen were the girls she'd miserably spectating before—the visual distortion that comprised the past thirty minutes, hour, two hours skittered into being—who all stared and began speaking in unison. It was akin to a flock of agitated birds cawing at her. Oralene was among them, her eyes large and luminous in this light.

Too caught up in the group, Maze ran face-first into a football player with bullish features, catching herself on his shoulder before then barreling into three tittering horse-faced cheerleaders, who were stolen away from their arm-candy to collapse in a tangled pile at her feet. Hillary, head cheerleader and top dog senior, shrieked and came at Maze, who was so disoriented she got snagged on the chunky belt the other girl had slung over her dress. Eventually, it snapped, and Maze fell back with its remnants caught in her hand.

From there, she navigated her way to the back door, dragging it open while the jocks and burnouts and preps stampeded in her periphery, shouting about Dean and Lee's knock-down, drag-out fight that had at last spilled out into the living area.

The outside wind was bitter; Maze lapped at the air to taste it. Tongue still hanging out, she scoped out the backyard to find the space completely fenced off. Her only means to leave would be the apple tree in the back corner, dead now but laden with golden fruit in the early fall. Maze clambered over and scaled it, flopping over the fence and onto the surrounding shrubbery.

The fall knocked the breath from her chest, and she groaned at having taken another hit so soon. Maze allowed herself a moment to simply be a worthless lump for a moment until she regained the ability to stand.

Maze ran across the grass and onto the road. It was an evil winter night. Cyanotic cloud cover obscured the slivers of moonlight visible from down below. There was no point in going for her car since she couldn't even walk straight right now, let alone drive. Waylon's place wasn't too far, she realized, impulsively deciding that was to be her destination.

He's my man, Maze thought. *He won't mind.*

Then she ran and ran and ran.

The syrup-slowness dissipated the closer she got to Waylon's, and as the high faded, everything became realer and realer. His front door marked the return of her sober brain.

Waylon answered her rapid knocks with an easy grin, catching her in his arms when she lunged at him. He laughed nice and easy when she curled up into his arms, swaying back and forth while she cried. It was such a release that she shuddered in pleasure at being seen and heard by someone. His touch didn't even bother her like Dean's had. Maze was so glad she came here.

Her boyfriend massaged her back gently while she worked the tears out, murmuring into her ear, "You think you're so tough," he said, "but you're soft. Look at you."

That gave her pause. Maze disentangled herself from him and examined Waylon more closely. Maybe it was because of what Oralene had said to her earlier, or maybe she was just stuck in her own head, but she was somewhat taken aback by his demeanor.

"What d'you mean by that?"

"You act tough for everybody else, but not for me. I see where you're all soft inside. That's only for me."

"Um, okay," she said.

"Let's sit down and get some rest," he told her, leading Maze into the bedroom. "You staying in that getup?"

Maze, who didn't feel much like being any more vulnerable than she already was, nodded, but splashed some water on herself in the bathroom to clean up. When she returned, she found Waylon flipped back onto his unmade bed with his body curved into an open parenthesis. He beckoned for her to join him. Maze obliged, seeking comfort but nonetheless unsettled from her earlier encounter with Lee, so she faced away from him.

Waylon cut the lights and sidled closer. "So sorry you had a bad night, baby," he said. "Let me help you feel better."

Maze shrugged him off. "I-I can't, Way. Not tonight."

"You always let me have this. What makes now any different?"

"'Cause I don't want to. I'm not feeling it."

"C'mon, Bright Eyes."

"Look—can't you just, I don't know, hold me?"

"Yeah, alright, c'mere," he said, and folded her into his arms.

Maze settled into the embrace and tried to find comfort in it. The high was receding, and with it reemerged the pain in her hand, her head. But it wasn't long before Waylon's touches grew more insistent, and he rubbed himself up against her.

"Quit that," she said, only to have him breath hot and wet against her neck, and for his nails to dig into her hips. "I'm on my period," she lied.

"I don't mind."

"Well, I do."

He sighed. "I don't get why you can't give me this. You're being selfish."

"I don't feel well. I just want to be with you."

"Then *be* with me."

Maze squeezed her eyes shut. She wished she could up and disappear. It felt like everything she touched turned to ruin; the people in her orbit, their relationships with her, and him. Why couldn't she just give him this? Waylon was right. He didn't ask for much, and he'd been there for her when no one else was.

"Do what you want."

He smiled against her skin. "There's my girl."

Then he pulled down her jeans, her panties, and she heard the crinkle of a condom wrapper. Waylon pushed inside this side of too dry, and she shifted with discomfort. His breath washed over her. She gagged; he needed to brush his teeth. As he grasped at her sides to ruck up her shirt, she noticed how his hands were clammy, soft. It was all wrong.

Despite the times before when they'd done this, when it had been okay, Maze couldn't relax. Cricket's face flashed in her mind. She could not dispel it. The tears slipped through. Hot, unrelenting. They pooled in her open mouth and imparted it with the taste of salt. Her stomach roiled.

"I love you," she said suddenly, as though that would make him pull back or murmur the same words into her ear.

"Oh, Bright Eyes," he said, smiling at her, "thanks. Thank you so much."

It looked like Lee's smile. And soon the familiar amusement was all she could see. Feeling humiliated and used-up, Maze remembered what Oralene had told her earlier that night:

Fucking some creepy older guy doesn't make you mature or special. It just makes you gullible and a slut.

"Hey, can you walk home from here? I don't want my car being seen near your place. People might get the wrong idea."

Maze nodded and accepted the perfunctory kiss to her neck.

"I'll be seeing you, Bright Eyes."

The worst part was that he was right.

***

Later that same night, Maze wandered alone through Carthage. Thinking, she was thinking. The events unfolded like a terrible dream in her brain. More than anything, though, she contemplated Waylon. He'd told her all the right things, but did that even matter?

Malicious, selfish, thoughtless. It—this—hadn't really meant anything to him. Oralene had been right. She was just a stupid slut. Maze had her head so far up her own ass for so long, she'd been shit-blind to the truth. She was no better than her mother. She was no different than Cricket.

It was then she noticed her wanderings had led her to the Pit, but it was so dark out that she didn't see the edge until it was too late. Maze plunged forward and tumbled down to the bottom, rolling into a sad heap at the bottom. Above her, the walls stretched up and out for what felt to her like infinity.

169

And in that moment, she'd transcended her pain, her hatred, and her grief; there was just this feeling, this being, and the body it happened to inhabit. Nothing else seemed to matter.

The shame, the misery, the fear—they were being excommunicated from her. They were in each breath that exited her lungs, the sweat collecting along the divots of her collarbone, and her own stuttering groans.

Maze wasn't scared anymore. She wasn't anything.

Was this how low her dad had felt? Was it like this for him all the time? If that was true, then maybe she shouldn't blame him for wanting to die.

NEAL IV

He'd put his fist through the wall when Reeve left. Neal was—God, he didn't know what he was. Gutted, maybe. Like someone had shoved their hands into his insides and rearranged them. He'd wondered whether the truth would be less painful than his silence; but now, left with that final, terrible image of Reeve's disgust, his fear, there was no question. Neal wished he had lied. His want sickened him. It had ruined everything; it always did.

And now he was here again, back where he'd started, wondering what the hell it all meant. *Don't you see me? What do I look like to you?* He needed now, more than anything, to not be himself. To go and be someplace else. His keys were in his hand before long.

Carthage's bleak, pockmarked landscape welcomed him as he left the motel and pushed his car through every backstreet and road he knew, desperate and trapped. It began to rain. His thoughts turned once again to Reeve. He couldn't leave. He had to make things right. To say something that would kill that look on Reeve's face and resurrect fondness. The words died on his lips, though; even in practice, and when he saw a familiar car parked outside the Blue Room Club, he became so singularly devastated that at last he understood his love had been real.

There it was again, the familiar anger.

I've never told anyone besides my mom I love them. There had been a time when he hadn't thought he was capable of loving or being loved. But Reeve—Neal thought he could be the exception.

He then could not keep from driving to the last place he knew he should be. The Liquor King's sign—a smirking, cherub-faced boy with a paper crown perched at a jaunty angle upon his head—mocked him as he pulled up. Neal didn't blame him. He was throwing away seven years of sobriety over one man. A man who was cold and cruel and strange. He had to be out of his goddamn mind, losing it over him. But, Jesus, he just needed to not think for a while.

Neal was about ready to vibrate out of his skin by the time the clerk handed him the bag, and he had the cap of the first whiskey bottle unscrewed before he even slid back into the Road Runner. The smell turned his stomach.

He was going down that same dark hole again, the one that could only be found at the bottom of a bottle. The burn down his throat was welcomed and despised. He was back where he belonged.

From there, the hours became shapeless, ill-formed; "Helter Skelter" by the Beatles twisted throughout. He tore open the glove compartment at some point and took Reeve's evil book in hand. The words dribbled and smeared down the page in a miasma.

Ezrah sat stooped over another journal, scribbling furiously. The skitch of his pen over paper was the only sound in the room aside from their breath. This—the poetry—it was less something Eliot understood or sought out, and more that he appreciated his friend's ardent passion for the craft. And as Ezrah's sole friend, he saw it as his duty to support him in this. After all, he was certain Ezrah would do the same for him when the time came.

His work was laden with sadness, suppressed feeling, and Eliot figured that was because he was someone with one foot in two worlds and unwelcome in either. His grandparents were cruel and distant; his mother a blank-eyed doll; and his dad had long been sent away.

Eliot only wished he could do more than listen.

His poem read:

In the Lethe

To bathe in the Lethe
is to forget the living,
to leave what lingers,
to accept annihilation,
and then, in submersion,
destroy the self utterly.

At dusk, I wander alone
beneath a haze of virgin stars,
would-be kings and princes
who rule in finite ascendancy,

looking for the buried path
to find the end of all things.

All are welcome in the fade:
those who eat raw their fear,
melancholy, lurid nightmares
like filaments of glass, gravel,
that work open the throat
whenever their thirst is slaked.

Apotheosis is upon me, now,
the final letting go, collision,
but as I enter, drowned at last,
I cannot help but wonder
if my next incarnation will—

Their friendship was one pursued in secret. Ezrah's family sought to hide him from the town, still ashamed, though his birth was an open secret. The fact that they had ever chanced a meeting felt to Eliot a little like fate, who had come to care deeply for his companion. He brought him trinkets when he could; candies wrapped in glittering wrappers, toy soldiers, and used books.

His older sister, Eudora, tall and handsome for a girl, would help him evade suspicion when she was able. Their mother could not know because she would not understand. Sometimes, Eudora's gaze penetrated him after a favor had been asked; Eliot had never mustered the courage to inquire with her about the nature of these heavy looks. He was not sure he could bear whatever it was she had to say.

He fell into uneasy slumber, Ezrah's handsome, open face haunting his dreams. And when he woke, the prospect of an impending rendezvous at their hiding place was sure to distract him throughout the morning hours. This imposed, necessary separation was one he understood but despised.

Ezrah was his best friend.

Ezrah, God—it hit too close to home. Neal grunted and angrily threw the book on the passenger seat. Why the hell was he reading anything that bastard had given him? He took another swig and hid the evidence under the passenger seat so we wouldn't get nabbed on the way back to the Mirage.

The world around him fell away piece by piece until he realized he was back at his motel room, viciously packing his bag and throwing anything breakable he could find at the walls or on the floor. His seven-year chip burned a hole in his back pocket. Maria Goretti wept around his neck.

By the time he heard a knock at the door, Neal was wreathed in the remnants of his own ruin. Broken glass and ceramic crunched underfoot as he moved, and when Neal wrenched the knob open, he wasn't sure what he'd expected. An irate neighbor, maybe, or the night manager, there to toss him out on his ass for making such a damn unholy racket at this hour. It wasn't for Reeve to be hunched on the threshold, soaked in rainwater and dead-eyed, hair and clothes matted with blood and dirt. His glasses were cracked, tie askew. There were fresh bruises all over his face and neck.

He smelled like heavy rain—oh, what was the word he'd used? Petrichor? He was bathed in it. That goddamn *petrichor* scent radiated off him and into the room.

"The hell d'you want," Neal slurred.

He should reach out, ask what happened. The water would usually render Reeve insensible. Yet his spite held him there, torn somewhere between concern and vindication. He wanted Reeve to suffer like he had. And it was such a terrible thing, to feel that way. Neal was once again the guy who lived up to every bad thing ever expected of him.

Reeve was quiet for a moment. Then he said, "You're drunk." It was delivered with the same flat, mechanical intonation he so favored these days.

"Really?" Neal remarked sarcastically, holding up the near-empty bottle of whiskey and squinting at it. "Are you sure?"

"I thought you were sober."

He sighed, sinking into the doorframe. "Yeah, Red. So did I."

When Reeve lingered at the threshold, still wet and twitching, Neal sighed and waved him in. The other man's dark gaze roved over the room, its destruction, and then, finally, settled on the packed bag. Never on Neal, though.

"You're leaving. Why?"

Neal's levity evaporated at that. "Why? You're asking me *why?* That's funny. It really is. I'm leaving because you walked out on me. I saw how you got when you knew what I wanted. Now you won't even look at me. How's that for why, you fucking machine."

Reeve swallowed and struggled to speak; his tremors were violent. "I-I never hated you. I don't want you to leave. I don't want you to be in pain."

"Well, you did this, Reeve. You made me love you. And nothing good will ever come of it," he accused, laughing bitterly, then threw the bottle at the wall, where it fractured with a tremendous crash.

Neal wiped at his eyes. They were damp. He was so, so drunk. *That road is a dead-end, son,* his dad had said. *You'll think you're in love. Maybe you even will be. Whatever the closest thing you people have to it. But there's no future there, boy. There's nothing.*

"You did this to yourself," Reeve said, looking at the broken bottle, "But that's okay, I think. I did the same thing."

His throat closed up. "What?"

"I never stopped thinking about you. I thought we were friends, y'know. That I loved you like a brother. But I had a brother, and he died. And I realized then that maybe there were different kinds of love."

"You don't know what you're talking 'bout," Neal said.

He had the ugly insight that Reeve could be lying. Neal was his only friend in the world apart from Maze, who was just a teenager. It could be that he thought this was something he felt he had to give Neal to keep him. This was worse, somehow, than whatever he'd thought before.

"I—"

"God damn you, Reeve. Just—just shut your mouth and let me get you cleaned up. You're bleeding all over the floor."

"No."

Neal grit his teeth. "You trying to get worked over twice tonight?"

"You've got it in your head that you know what I mean. Maybe you're wrong. Ever think about that?"

"I can't figure you out," Neal said at last. "I want to, but I can't."

"Then leave it."

"You say these things like they're so easy. They're not. At least, not for me."

Reeve stepped closer, so close that Neal could smell the cigarettes on him, and beneath that, aftershave, see where the water pooled near his brow, how his lower lip had been split down the middle. His eyes were dark, wet, glittering with something not yet identifiable to him. Neal found that he couldn't move. It hurt even to speak.

It was difficult to be in the same room with him, breathe the same air as him, stand in intimate proximity with him. Neal couldn't keep from wanting, selfish as it was. He didn't know how to make it stop; he had never known.

He swallowed. "Who did this to you?"

"I don't really want to talk about it."

This time it was Neal who looked away, but by now there was not enough space between them to do even that. Reeve's lips brushed against the corner of his mouth, and oh, it was good, it was perfect. He tasted metal, then salt. Neal's breath hitched. His lids shuttered. God, yes.

He'd always wanted what it would feel like to kiss it. That scar. Maybe he could turn it into something good for them both.

"Red," he said when they parted, voice hoarse, "let me clean you up. Please." He wanted to

"Fine."

Neal led him to the bathroom, gait unsteady, and sat Reeve down on the closed toilet lid. He looked behind the mirror for a complementary first aid kit, and finding it spare, figured he'd have to make do with what he had on hand. It wouldn't be the first time.

Neal changed course and retrieved a roll of floss and a needle from his duffle, as well as the second whiskey bottle he'd purchased earlier. But there was so much blood, dirt, and, upon further inspection, gravel, that he couldn't tell precisely where the wounds were. He wet a washcloth and moved to press it to Reeve's forehead, then hesitated.

"Is this…" Neal trailed off. *Is this okay? Can you handle the water? I know you got caught in the rain, but still—*

"I'm already wet."

"I get that. I'm drunk, not blind."

Reeve slumped. "I meant that it's too late. It can't get worse, I don't think. So, you might as well."

He sounded empty. It explained the tremors. His unease was palpable.

Neal wondered if Reeve was reminded of his brother again, like he so often was when they were younger. The water. It was always the water. The last person Neal wanted to think about right now was Ephraim Scarlet.

"I'll be careful."

Neal got down on his knees. He dabbed the cloth at his head and moved down from there. Then he picked out the granules as best he could from where they had become lodged beneath the skin. He saturated a wad of toilet paper with the whiskey and went back over every open cut until he was sure they were clean, then sterilized the needlepoint the same way. By the time he'd spooled the floss through, Reeve had gnashed his teeth and nodded for him to go on. The first pass through was bad; his hands were shaking, and distantly Neal realized that he shouldn't be doing this while drunk. But the familiar rhythm took over, and soon he'd tied off the last stitch.

He motioned for Reeve to take off his overcoat and untuck his shirt. Neal swallowed and wet his lips. "I'm going to check your ribs. See if anything's bruised or broken. Tell me if it hurts." He grazed his hands up Reeve's sides, making a conscious effort not to linger. He was clammy from the cold and the rain, but it was still Reeve, whom he'd loved for years.

"It's nothing. It's just skin."

"Good. That's, uh, good. Yeah."

He'd spent enough time putting himself back together growing up to know there was nothing he could do for the bruises, which would have to fade on their own time. But even though he knew it was time to pull away, make Reeve leave before he'd do something they would both regret later, Neal found that he could not do it. He leaned forward and put his head on Reeve's thigh and breathed in the scent of him.

He was shameless. He was so shameless it made him sick.

"This is a bad idea," he whispered.

"Maybe."

"Then why did you run?"

"Because I wanted the same thing you did. And it scared me because I'd never known that about myself before."

"That you're, what, gay?"

"I like both, I guess. Men, women."

Bisexual, Neal thought. Then he asked, "Bisexual?"

"Sure."

"Have you ever—"

"No. Not with anyone."

"Never?"

"Never."

He dragged his cheek up along the inseam of Reeve's slacks, even though he knew it was a bad, bad idea. "No one's ever made you feel good, then?" Neal asked.

There was a low intake of breath. "No one."

"I'd be the first."

"Yeah."

He went for the button to begin with, then the zipper, and mouthed at the tented boxers underneath. Reeve groaned. Neal pulled away. "You're hard," he said. The knowledge was an exquisite relief.

"You didn't think I could get it up?"

Neal recoiled. "No. Jesus, I don't know what I thought."

"I'm not quite that selfless, Neal," Reeve murmured. There was a funny look on his face as he said it, like he was in on some joke at his own expense. His lips quirked into an enigmatic half-smile. "Now, c'mere."

Neal eased their lips together. "We could, y'know, if you want," he offered after he'd manage to withdraw, and Reeve said nothing to that, just nodded and fed Neal more of his tongue.

It was uncoordinated, inexperienced. Edged with teeth and little sweetness. Neal exhaled and opened up for him, running his hands through Reeve's hair to draw him in deeper. The press of their mouths sounded obscene in the quiet room, and Neal was ready to go before long. He helped Reeve to his feet and backed him onto the bed. Above them, reflected on the mirrored ceiling, their counterparts did the same. The sconces reached out towards them as if in want.

There was a staggering intimacy between them, and it was a feeling Neal sought to instinctively retreat from. He felt like a child shying away from a wooden spoon, understanding the punishment to come, but shook it off; he gave into it instead.

No, he thought. *I can't ruin this. I need this. I need* him.

They had been headed here, to this place, ever since that bitter January morning so long ago. Their suffering, separation—it had to have played a part in this culminating the way it was, and the idea made Neal choke.

He didn't want to ruin it. He wanted nothing more than to preserve this moment forever. He stared at Reeve with open-mouthed wonder. The other man's presence was heavy, inexorable.

They helped each other out of their clothes and kneeled together on the bed. The light was low and played across Reeve's austere features. He'd discarded his glasses, too. It was better than he'd ever dreamed. Neal licked his palm, got it real wet, then took them both in hand and pumped. It was slow, intimate. Reeve let out a rough, broken noise and tipped his head back. Neal kissed the base of his open throat.

It was falling into something new and old at the same time. And despite what Reeve had divulged, his movements were uncertain but no less passionate for it.

He laid back on the bed and pulled the other man on top of him, then dug his heels into Reeve's back. It was then that he had the sense to recall that Reeve had the shit kicked out of him earlier, and that his entire torso was now a crime scene.

"Sorry," he breathed.

"No, it's alright."

"Yeah?"

Reeve scraped his stubbled jaw along Neal's own. It was a pleasant burn. "Yeah," he confessed, breath hot, "I like the pain. It makes me feel real."

Neal didn't know what to say to that, so he kissed Reeve as gently as he could. It was sweet, almost chaste. Then he scored his nails down Reeve's back and set his mouth upon the other man's neck. Reeve's hands twisted in the sheets by Neal's head.

He wanted to have protected the boy Reeve had been. To stay the horrors his future had wrought. But the past was immutable. And Neal wondered whether they would have even become friends otherwise.

Their cocks dragged together. The spit wasn't an ideal lubricant, and the friction burned, but the pain was secondary to the feeling of completion—of having Reeve with him again. There would be time later, he hoped, to go further. To be inside each other. To do everything two men could in bed. But this was good, too. It was everything.

Reeve came with a strangled moan, and Neal followed not long after. He couldn't last. Not when he had wanted this for years.

After, they curled up on the bed together. Their breathing was labored, bodies slack and satiated. Reeve traced Neal's tattoo with a calloused finger. It was the kind of moment that made Neal feel exposed, laid bare. His own flushed face stared down at him from the mirrored ceiling. The Doppelganger's eyes were wide, pale, secretive.

His tongue sat heavy in his mouth. He recalled what Maze said about telling him the truth, all of it, and how more lies or omissions might be the end of them. Maybe it was the booze, or the sex, or even this place itself, but he felt compelled to let slip the truth.

He was imperfect. Reeve was unsympathetic, thoughtless, and couldn't tell a joke to save his life. But he could also be kind, in his own way, unselfish in the extreme, and good to those who took the time to know him.

"You remember my dad?"

He felt, rather than saw, Reeve turn towards him. "Yes," he said darkly.

"Did I ever tell you 'bout him?"

"Some."

"Not enough, I guess. He, uh… he told me he loved me, but he hit me. He did a lot of things because he loved me, I guess. And I love him still. Even now, after everything. Even though I never liked him. It's senseless. It'd be easier if he'd just been bad, but there were good times, too, despite him being so… angry.

"I used to be angry all the time, too. You keep saying you don't remember it like that, but I do. And I ended up like him because of it. I was mean. I did bad things. Horrible, horrible things. I didn't want you to know this part of me 'cause I don't want you to look at me different. But I have to. I want to lay it all out on the table. I-I haven't been honest with you."

Reeve stilled, broad hand warm and welcome on Neal's shoulder. "You don't have to tell me everything."

"Maybe I want to stop lying for once in my life."

"Then that's your choice."

Neal closed his eyes. Choice—what a goddamn funny thing to say. Choice made and broke him. It brought him here, to this moment, and to Ruth and Joseph, too, but it was his choices that first took him down what seemed to be an unendingly dark path.

He had been in the pen for five months when he got the first letter from Ruth. It was immaculate, with delicate script written on near-creaseless paper that smelled faintly of jasmine. When he opened it, Neal realized at once where the letter had come from; or, rather, *who* it had come from. He dropped it like he'd been scalded, then shoved the package beneath his mattress. It languished there until he mustered the nerve to read it in full a week later.

The letter read—

Dear Mr. Vásquez:

I never set out to write this letter to you. I wanted to forget you, that night, and what you've done. But I couldn't. I see you every day in my husband's suffering. I see your face in my dreams.

Let it be clear: you've managed to somehow stay in my mind long after the sentencing. I thought things would be easier now. You're in jail. My husband is in physical therapy. I'm seeing a counselor. But I can't forget you. You looked so young there, back in that courtroom. I felt bad for you, despite everything.

Maybe it was because I could tell you knew what you'd done was wrong. You admitted to everything on the stand. You plead guilty. You didn't drag this out.

Joseph Banks—remember his name. Don't you let yourself forget it, young man, just like we won't let ourselves forget you. You're in pain. You're hurting, and you're taking it out on everyone around you. It's on account of this that our paths even crossed.

You made a mistake. You've hurt a good man more than you will ever know. I see your grief. It's real—it's plain as day. But what good is it if you do nothing? It sits inside and rots. What happened can't be changed. That's something I've had to come to terms with. It was brutal. I cried for weeks. I couldn't even look at Joseph. I got lost in myself. I was in pain, but I was selfish, too.

I have prayed about this. I have turned to the Blessed Virgin for help. Forgiveness is not supposed to be easy, but I have suffered and struggled so much these past few months to lift this weight off my heart. And I thought that by writing this to you that it might help. I don't know if it will or won't, but here I am, trying, and I have enclosed something to aid you in your journey as well, if you so wish.

This is a medal of St. Maria Goretti, patroness of poverty, purity, and forgiveness—all things I believe you to seek. Let her guide you, if you so wish.

Her prayer is as follows:

O God, author of innocence and lover of chastity, who bestowed the grace of martyrdom on your handmaid, the Virgin Saint Maria Goretti, in her youth, grant, we pray, through her intercession, that, as you gave her a crown for her steadfastness, so we, too, may be firm in obeying your commandments.

Regards,

Ruth Banks

Neal's hands strangled the paper. They were the same hands that had paralyzed Ruth's husband. The envelope wasn't empty, though. The guards had gone through it, like they did all their inbound and outbound mail, but allowed it to remain. When he fished out the object, he realized it was the saint medal Ruth had mentioned in her letter. Inmates were allowed one religious medallion apiece, so he supposed that's why it hadn't been confiscated.

The chain was gold, burnished with age, but no less beautiful for it. Neal clasped it around his neck and rubbed a thumb over the icon. No matter how bittersweet the correspondence had been, this was... God, it was more than he deserved.

Ruth came to visit him not long after he responded. Her eyes and skin were a deep ochre, warm and inviting. Dark coils of hair were pulled back into a colorful headwrap printed with tropical flowers. The way she looked at him was exactly how he wished his mom had when he was a kid.

He sought to be worthy of that kindness.

Now, in bed with the love of his life, Neal caressed St. Maria again. He reached inward for the right words to explain his journey here.

"Reeve, it—it was bad. I was in prison. I hurt someone. And I deserved everything I got because of it," Neal said. Reeve shifted. He said nothing. His expression was characteristically inscrutable.

"Joseph, my business partner—the guy I told you about. It was him. I put him in a wheelchair, and his wife, Ruth, wrote to me while I was in there. Then he did, too. Told me they forgave me. And when I got out, they took me in. We started North Metro Windows and Glass together. My parole didn't end 'til about a couple months ago. I came to see you as soon as I could, I promise. I just didn't want you to know why it took me so many years. I wanted you to have this—idea of me, I guess, that I was a good man."

Reeve's dark gaze appraised him coolly. "I would have rather known that than be left to wonder if you'd forgotten about me. Or that you were dead."

"I get that now. I just—I just wanted to be the kind of man…" *You could love. You'd be proud to come home to.*

"It's easy to realize what we should have done differently. There's a certain—clarity, I s'pose, in retrospection. And we all hate ourselves for it," Reeve mused, and wound their hands together. The name *Ephraim* went unspoken between them. "It's funny, you know," he continued, after a moment.

"What?"

"I don't know what it feels like to get what I want. Never. But I have you here, and I don't know what the hell to do with myself now that I do."

Neal agreed.

"It's weird when you're not used to it. Feels almost like a dream. Like you're an imposter in your own life."

"Neal, what do you feel for me?"

Neal searched for the words. Love, he wanted to say. Devotion. But those were difficult to articulate, make known. They also seemed too simple to distill all his wants, feelings, desires into.

"It goes all the way through me," is what he settled on.

Reeve exhaled, looking stricken. Then his features cleared and returned once more to their stoic rest. His mouth quirked upwards. This was his reciprocity, Neal recognized, at least as much as he was capable of showing.

Neal cleared his throat. "It doesn't matter how long ago this happened, or that you've been singled out for his death because of it. Maybe he wasn't a good person. The grief is still there. I feel like I can even see it. This smudge. A darkness. It's something you can't quantify or compare. You're allowed to be sad, Reeve. It's okay."

"A darkness," he echoed, "sure."

It was late, and an ache had formed within Neal's skull. He was tired. How could he not be? It was from an entire lifetime of bad nights, empty pockets, and grief, he thought. He said something to that effect to Reeve and pulled him closer just because he could.

Neal drifted off into an uneasy sleep under Reeve's scrutiny, and woke to morning's blue murmur, with the other man draped across his chest. His mind felt clouded, thick, and the shame from falling off the wagon had set in for real. But there was Reeve, in his arms. That was its own satisfaction.

He must have moved too much because Reeve made a low sound and shifted. His pale hair was mussed, still crusted with dried gore in some places, and his lower lip was swollen. Not to mention the twisted green stitches over his right eye. Neal was struck by the visceral urge to take him far away from this awful place. Carthage was a sickness, and he had the awful inkling that Reeve understood but did not care.

It was like he'd admitted the night prior; he was a masochist.

Neal didn't know what to make of it. Reeve's inclination to pain disturbed him. But he wanted it, inexplicable as his explanation had been, and Neal could not deny him anything. The things he sought were strange, discomfiting. But he didn't want to judge Reeve for it and had never been able to deny Reeve anything, besides.

He looked even more gaunt in this light, bruised, and smelled like sweat and dried come. His variegated blond and gray hair was a tangled nest.

"Morning," he said.

"It's Friday," Reeve ground out, then, "what time is it?"

Neal had no idea. The clock had been the first thing to go in his rage. "Early?" He ventured.

"I have work."

"Yeah, Red, I get that."

Reeve crawled out of bed and walked into the bathroom. Neal watched him do this with unrestrained hunger. His back flexed as he leaned over to search through the pockets of his coat, and when he turned, Neal saw that the flat planes of his abdomen and prominent ribs were mottled in scarlet marks that looked to him more like shoe impressions by the minute. The item in his hand was revealed to be a wristwatch, which he inspected by the closed window.

"It's only six."

"Must be why I feel like shit," Neal said, trying for levity.

"I have my own reasons," the other man said, thumbing a bruise.

"Maybe I could make you feel better?" The come-on felt forced, made him feel a little self-conscious, but Reeve seemed receptive to it.

"How do you want me?"

"God, um, on your back," Neal said, then rolled over to make room.

Reeve spread himself out on the bed, arms behind his head and legs splayed. He was so, so handsome. Neal settled between his thighs. He—Jesus, he was unreal. The hair that started beneath his navel darkened as it reached his groin. His cock was limp. Neal spat into his palm and worked the base, then lowered his mouth to the head. Tasted its salt and sucked a little. Soon it was red, hard, and slick. Neal took him further into his mouth and relaxed his throat around the intrusion. Reeve moaned deep and low. The knowledge that he was making Reeve feel that good got him hot, real hot, and Neal ground his hips against the bedspread.

He pulled off with a wet pop, and searched Reeve's features. He'd bitten into his busted lip, and there was blood all over his chin. His fingers were fastened around the headboard.

Neal was disturbed by his own arousal at this, by the blood on his face, and how much it seemed to get Reeve off. It made him feel like he'd lived up to every ugly, sick thing people thought of men like him—*them*—and it turned his stomach. But he was so hard, and Reeve was beautiful and right there. Neal was helpless to his pull.

"I'm going to—" Reeve gasped.

Neal worked him up and down. "Do it," he urged, bolder than usual, "on my face. C'mon."

"Neal, fuck," he said, finished, his hips stuttering as spine bowed away from the bed in what looked to be pleasure-pain.

Reeve then yanked Neal up by the hair and kissed him almost savagely. He licked himself off Neal's face and jerked him until he came. Neal collapsed on his side, exhausted, and Reeve followed suit. He balled up a pillowcase and used it to wipe the mess off. Jesus. It was everything he'd dreamed about. This was the fantasy that had exhilarated and tortured him since he was a boy. His dad had been wrong. He was the closest to complete he'd ever been.

Then he glanced at his friend. Reeve was looking past him at the ceiling. He had this terrible, faraway look in his eyes. Neal's hips stuttered.

"Look at me," he said. "Please, look at me."

Reeve shuddered. "I'm trying," he confessed.

"Where were you?"

"I'm right here."

"Tell me what's going on in there."

"You moan like a whore," was all he said.

The comment was so absurd that Neal let out a strangled laugh. "You've got a real way with words, Red. Is this your version of dirty talk?"

"Whores are professionals."

Neal grinned and grinned, smiling so wide his cheeks hurt. The admission shocked a laugh out of him. "So, it's compliment?"

"I s'pose."

"I don't mind."

"You're smiling."

"I'm just so happy."

"Good," Reeve said, low and almost tender. "I don't understand what it means to be gentle," he confessed, "but you make me want to learn."

But his buoyant mood diminished as more light filtered through the blinds. There was something liminal that hovered, intruded into the room. The inexorable return to normalcy. It was the understanding that Reeve had work, his routine, and that Neal was due back in Des Moines in two days.

"You'd better get dressed," he said.

Reeve touched him once, fleetingly, then went to collect his clothes. It became apparent not long after that his suit was ruined from whatever had happened before he'd come here. Neal's chest constricted. He had the blind desire to lash out. To make whoever had done this hurt. Reeve was not one to divulge such things, though, not even to him. He had it in his head that he deserved everything he got, and Neal knew better than to ask again.

"Here, you can use mine," he said, and upturned his duffle.

Neal rifled through the pile and unearthed a Henley, dark jeans, and a black satin bomber jacket with red lining. There were two white open-mouthed serpents embroidered on each cuff. He'd been given it by Ruth as a gift when he got out.

It fit Reeve like a second skin. Made him seem more himself. Beyond that, it got his dick to reconsider being spent. He was wearing Neal's clothes. He'd touched him like a lover. He was looking at him with want. This was—

"You'll be here tonight?" Reeve asked, throwing his coat over the jacket. There was an unsmoked cigarette fixed between his lips. He'd managed to scrub himself clean for the most part. His glasses were folded in his shirt collar.

"I will."

"I could stop by again."

"I, uh, wouldn't mind," he said.

But as he watched Reeve linger on the threshold, he saw this same scene play out a dozen times over: himself, observing with slow-pooling dread as Reeve returned once more to a place that sought to devour him. It was untenable, he realized. Neal would not survive the other man's self-destruction; Reeve would not survive Carthage. He needed for him to get that through his damn head before he was consumed entirely.

Neal swallowed. "I'm still leaving on Monday," he continued. "This won't change that."

Reeve was silent. The tendons in his neck were pulled taut. "I understand," he said, then, with more ferocity, "why would you say that to me?"

Neal was torn between despair and rage. How could he be so blind to what was happening? That what he had now was little more than a half-life? The sheer damn senselessness of what he was doing? He got to his feet and stalked over to Reeve. He had a sudden nasty, panting urge for a fight.

"'Cause we all have choices to make, Red. I've made mine. I'm leaving, and I ain't never coming back to this godforsaken place again. I only did it this time to set you straight. I owed you."

"No one owes me anything."

"I did. For the longest time, you were the only person who'd given a damn about me. I wanted to give that kid everything. But I don't see him in you. Maybe a shadow. Mostly, I look at you now and see someone who's waiting. But for what? I know what I want. Do you? Do you even know yourself at all?" Neal asked desperately.

Reeve's expression twisted. "You'll hand me this just to take it away?"

"I—"

"You don't. 'Cause if you did, you wouldn't make me suffer like this. You're too decent for that."

"If you think I'm decent, you must know me less than I thought you did."

"I—"

"*Nothin,'* that's what. You're so gone on this place, and your own misery, that you don't even dream anymore. It's like loving a dead man. It's the saddest fuckin' thing."

Reeve stepped forward. "I can't change."

"Am I the same to you? I've worked so hard to be more than I was. All just so I could try and be a good man. And to tell me that you can't change—that people can't—is like spitting in my face. I opened myself up for you."

"You are a good man. I never thought otherwise."

Neal was so moved by this that he could not keep from wresting Reeve's coat by the lapels and dragging him in for one last bruising kiss. He tangled his hands in his hair and leaned down to whisper, "I won't wait forever," into his ear.

"Keep me," Reeve begged.

"I wish I could."

"You can. You're choosing not to."

"Sometimes... sometimes I think I don't know you at all. And others, it's almost like I never left. Tell me, Reeve, what will you do?"

He was looking everywhere but Neal. "I've lived in Carthage my whole life. I don't know anything else."

"Well, what the hell is here for you? The people who hate you? That damn trailer? Do you really need to suffer that much? Just don't make me have to end it like this. 'Cause I will, I'll—"

Part III

The Theory of Forms

REEVE V

"—leave, and you won't ever see me again," Neal ground out, his turbulent blue-green gaze sparking bright and troubled.

Reeve believed him.

He opened his mouth to let him know this wasn't about him, to beg Neal to reconsider, but he felt bloated by air and apt to asphyxiate on anything that emerged. Even had his tongue been able to part his lips, Reeve found he had nothing concrete to say. Nothing at all.

Neal regarded him with desperation and released his coat.

The other man made a shocked, dismissive sound. "God, what's got it into your head that things hafta be this way? Don't you want more? Anything? Anything at all? Answer me, goddammit!"

The grief was plain on his face.

Neal was asking for something Reeve couldn't give him. Not now, at least. He couldn't think past the horrible insect noises his brain was making.

There was this static *sktch-sktch-sktch*, then the familiar turning, and since he did not have it in him to speak, he just jerked his head in a nod and left. The motel door shut behind him before he knew what he was doing, abruptly truncating whatever the other man was about to say next, and when he started the Laguna, it was with a violent twist. His tires blacked and devoured the road as he accelerated away.

The wheel labored under his death grip; his knuckles were blanched from how tight they were wound around it. Soon, the Mirage Motor Inn regressed into a dark smear behind him, disappearing entirely when he made the next turn. Its image endured still.

In those walls, Reeve learned how it felt to be wanted for the first time in his life. His only coherent thoughts had been *it's good, it's great, it hurts, it's perfect.*

His head pivoted back to Neal, his parting remarks. *I'm going to leave. You won't ever see me again. What the hell is here for you?*

Reeve heard the words echo throughout him, his emptiness, and grit his teeth. It was what had been said to him countless times. *You're alone. You don't have anything. Nothing.* But that was wrong; he'd always had Neal one way or another, at least until today. Neal had made his opinion pretty damn clear.

Reeve had slept so well last night he could hardly believe it. The sex, Neal's arms around him, his even breaths—it was intimate. His nighttime visitations to other people's lives could not begin to compare.

Did it really take so little to hook him? Was he that pathetic? It felt like the truth, he thought. There was no coming back from this. Not ever. It was evident that their sex had been a disaster of many dimensions. And suddenly he was furious with the other man for doing this to him, for making him know what it meant to want, for teaching him what it felt like to have and be had in turn. Before this, *him,* at least Reeve hadn't known anything different. But now...

He knew intimately what he could have and chose to let slip away: Neal's skin, his mouth, his cock. His love. Neal told him he wanted to be a good man; to Reeve, he'd never been anything else.

His final turn was executed with the same vicious precision as those that preceded it, and he spin-drifted into his parking space in the empty lot. Everything was still, silent. The sky was gradated in washed out blue. This morning could have been any other. It wasn't. His clothes were not his own, he was behind—he checked his watch—by fifteen minutes, and the Laguna occupied the Civic's usual place.

Nothing was as it should be.

Suddenly, the stress from yesterday's beating, his subsequent breakdown, and his fight with Neal set in all at once, and Reeve completely lost his shit.

He let out a strained groan and bit at his hands until he reopened the scabs there and blood dripped down his knuckles in livid tributaries. The feeling sated him briefly, grounded him in the moment, this place. But when he let go, nothing had abated.

There was this pit in his chest, an emptiness. He could add buckets to it, but it remained unchanged. Reeve could feel it like a physical pain, the not-hunger, and it gnawed at him without pause or hesitation. He groaned, twisted his hair between his fingers and rocked forward. Unease radiated from him like heat off asphalt.

His head was so full he thought it would pop. It was impossible to ignore, and his corrupt brain demanded to be itched, for its folds and furrows to be plied open, its insides exposed to hungry hands and rearranged. He sat there, twisted up, wondering what this said about him, and what, if anything, it meant.

People liked to imagine souls, anthropomorphized as little diaphanous white lights or such, couched in each other's insides. They didn't like to think about the fact that they were no more than gray matter talking to other gray matter about the weather and what they'd like for dinner after work. Because what was a man, really, if not a series of disconnected images and sensations?

There was no way to explain this feeling. Everything was being pulled beyond his grasp, the little intimate components of his life turned over, exposed, disarticulated. He'd felt at first that if he regained control, then he could remake it all in his head. It wasn't *working*.

Reeve set his head between his hands and set his nails into his temples. He needed a plan, to settle himself. Yes, that was good. He'd go inside, clean himself up—since he hadn't had time to go home and change—work until six, and return once more to this still, silent lot and his still, silent home. That was the way of things. The prospect appeared to soothe his racing thoughts, and Reeve marginally relaxed back into his seat. Reeve dug his fingers into his scalp until pain shot through him. He could have moaned with relief. It was real. Realer than the noise, his compulsions, and even the parking lot before him. Maybe this was his peace; the ability to think in silence.

Why he needed this, the pain, the sameness, he wasn't sure. Maybe he'd become addicted to the routine, its familiar grooves and turns. He'd had nothing else to hold onto for so long. As for Neal, Reeve wasn't sure he was a certainty, no matter what he'd said or moaned into his skin last night, that morning. He'd left before, and he could leave again.

Yet Neal lingered inside.

Reeve's skull couldn't breathe. It was full up with *Neal Neal Neal*. Neal, who was going to leave him. He couldn't stop it. His bags were likely already packed. The Road Runner would be a glittering speck on I-44 as Neal returned from whence he came.

Even if he let himself give in and drive back to the room, take the other man into his arms like he longed to do, what good would come of it? The thoughts ratcheted up and spiraled out. It seemed to him like everything he wanted slipped through his grasp as water would through a sieve. So, it had been easier not to want at all. But Neal... he wanted him too badly to deny himself.

You couldn't take anything from a man with neither friends nor possessions. But then came Neal, and with his arrival something in Reeve woke that he'd long assumed dead. If he allowed himself to have this, it would be taken from him. There was nothing to be done. He was clutching at nothing, at air.

He'd been a fool; he prized Neal above all else.

And Neal was going to leave him. He couldn't stop it. He couldn't—he had to do something. He replayed the night's events over in his head. The boots on his chest, Neal's kindness, and his own delectable pleasure-pain. If he could just focus, then maybe the lens would clear, and things would disentangle themselves.

Then I could—

His thoughts could not complete their planned revolution. The first few cars had meandered into the lot, and the noise his coworkers made as they filtered into the building crowded out all else. There, near the front. It was Hoyt.

His attention refocused on the man, who was made a sallow, nebulous blob in the early light. He laughed at something another coworker, Ashley, said. It wasn't too far from how he'd laughed at Reeve in the alley.

Just give me a reason.

He felt apt to ooze through his own skin, seething. Reeve bit deep into his wrist to keep from losing it. Metal dribbled down over his tongue, and he chewed at the skin for a little longer. The pain was so clear, so hot; it was what he imagined being high was like. *Ah.* There, much better. He stemmed the flow with tissues and rolled his sleeve down over it. And with that, he dragged himself inside.

When the entry door shut behind him, and Reeve strode past reception and into the office proper, all heads turned towards him on arrival. He did not flinch. Reeve let his eyes drift towards Hoyt, who looked shaken by his injured countenance. It was funny. He'd had no issue with it the night before.

But Hoyt was alone now, in a way, and maybe that mattered more than Reeve had initially understood.

He chose then to bare his teeth at Hoyt in a thin facsimile of a smile and sat down at his desk. The lingering persisted through morning and into the afternoon, leaving Reeve keyed up and uneasy. He kept waiting for the vertigo, the longing, to subside. He sought comfort where it could no longer be found. This—his routine—did not quell the unease twisting his insides. Everything had been disrupted, and the need to conform, to fix this, was a constant itch beneath his skin. He staggered to his feet and made a break for the restroom, pacing around restlessly before coming to a stop by the sink. He needed—

Reeve fit a cool palm to his throat over the bruises and squeezed. It hurt so good. The pain when he'd been given them had been acute, brutal, like he was a fucking animal. Maybe he was one. He recalled the dark, desperate, beautiful sounds Neal made as he came. Reeve wanted to hear them again. He never wanted them to stop.

Everything had been quiet then, even for a moment. The pain was louder than everything else. It made him come. He had *felt* something. Reeve held himself in self-bondage but considered winding the belt around his throat.

His mouth fell open and he uttered a low moan. Why he needed this, he wasn't sure. Maybe if he had left with Neal all those years ago, he would be different, better. But he didn't, and he wasn't. It could be that he'd have wound up the same anyhow.

The creak the door made before being thrust ajar was the only warning he had to release himself. He turned. It was Hoyt.

He appeared drawn and sober, with wax-like skin and faint perspiration upon his brow. Their eyes did not meet as the other man strode over to the urinal to relieve himself. The tension in his shoulders was evident.

The faucet continued to weep. Reeve's knuckles were blanched from how tight he was gripping the sink.

Not even the water could distract him. He thought back to the exquisite pain the rainstorm brought, letting it edge from memory into present. Could it be Neal? Could it be that he associated it now with his gentle embrace rather than Ephraim's death? Was such a thing even possible?

Drip. Ephraim's bloodless face. *Drip.* His mom collapsed on the side of the road, unseeing. *Drip.* The exhausted hiss of an oxygen tank as a nasal cannula lay abandoned around a dead man's jaw. *Drip*. Himself, the asphalt king. *Drip*. Neal's smooth, brown back; his parting words, "You won't ever see me again."

Hoyt had beat him. He'd beat him, mocked him, and now, when confronted with what he'd done, he couldn't even spare Reeve so much as a single glance. *Look at me,* he thought. *Look at what you fucking did.*

His molars ground against each other. He twitched. The ringing in his ears intensified. Before him in the mirror stood a man he hardly recognized. His hair fell in a ragged sweep across his brow, and the ends were still faintly crusted with blood. The twisted sutures rendered him monstrous.

Hoyt buttoned his slacks and flushed the urinal.

After he finished, there was no other sink but the one adjacent to Reeve's for him to use. He noticed Hoyt look at him and then away before reluctantly walking over to the tap. The spray could not have sounded louder in the room's abject quiet.

His patience flatlined. *Pathetic*, Reeve thought. Then he felt the words leave his lips. "Pathetic," he said.

Hoyt pivoted to face him, almost surprised. "What was that?"

So, he can speak.

Reeve straightened to his full height and moved closer. He had a good few inches on the other man, he realized, now that he wasn't slouching. Hoyt shrunk back. *And he thinks I'm weak?* The notion was laughable. Reeve felt something stir in his gut. It was retribution, he realized. Some damn real anger. Reeve would not stand and cower from this silly little man.

"You're pathetic," he said again.

How was it that men like himself—gay, bisexual, whatever—were called weak for being what they were, when Hoyt simpered and did whatever Zebadiah told him but could not face Reeve in the cold light of day?

For once, Reeve wanted to be seen. *Look at what you did. Don't act like this isn't what you wanted.* They had dredged up something raw and mean last night. It turned, tortuous, in his gut, surfacing in his throat. Neal had soothed it, laved at the open wound with gentle words and rough hands. But he wasn't here now.

Neal's exodus was imminent. Reeve had chosen this over his love.

"That, coming from you? A faggot? A dog-fucking—"

Reeve reacted before the intent was more than half-formed in his mind, arm darting out to grab Hoyt by the hair and smash his face against the mirror. It shattered into a radial fracture, smaller pieces breaking off and clattering to the floor. Each shard became its own distorted reflection, his own watchful black eyes all fixed on Hoyt. He ground the other man's head into the glass.

"God, it hurts! Make it stop. Make it stop, please!" Hoyt blubbered out, words mangled by the blood slicking his mouth. His breath emerged as a wet gurgle when he inhaled, and each successive *pop* grated on Reeve's nerve. "Please—what do you want?"

What do you want?

Not too long ago, the answers would have come easy. *Things I can't have. A different past. To be dead. Gone before I ever hurt anyone who mattered.*

"Nothing you can give me," Reeve said at last. He ground Hoyt's head into the glass again. "I'll tell you this, though. Remember the glass when you look at me. Keep my name outta your mouth. Keep *his* name outta your mouth."

"You fuckin' psycho, you can't get away with this—"

Reeve released him, and Hoyt collapsed back onto the tile in a heap. He touched a shaking hand to his forehead.

"I'm bleeding. Jesus, I'm bleeding everywhere."

"I'd be more worried about my blood. Y'know what your people say about my "kind," after all. And your hands were covered in it last night. Maybe you've already got the bug. Could be that I've already killed you. But I own you because I spared you," Reeve said, voice a slow, patient threat. "You're where you belong—at my feet. Tell people what happened here, and you'll find I'll have my own take on things. I'll say you came onto me. That you asked to suck my cock. Maybe they won't believe me. Maybe they will. Either way, there'll always be that... doubt. An idea. It'll never really leave. This is something I know well.

"Like you said before, there's nothing worse than being a faggot," he continued, removing his heel from Hoyt's throat. "So go on and be a fucking liar. It's the only thing you've got now."

Hoyt was all cracked open now, eyes bright and furious, mild features shame-warped and gnarled by impotence. That deer in the headlights type of look.

Reeve pressed forward. "You had an accident."

"I-I had an accident."

"There you go."

Reeve turned his back on him, cleaned up, and smoothed his hair down before exiting the restroom. It was loud outside, louder than usual, which is why nobody had noticed what was going on. Word had spread about some teenage house party that had gotten busted up by the cops the night previous. A truly interesting development.

About five minutes later Hoyt emerged, limping out into the office area. The conversation died with a gasp, and the people closest to him converged like concerned vultures.

"Oh, no! What happened?" A woman cried.

"Tripped and fell," he said through gritted teeth. "Clumsy me."

Another man said, "You look awful, man. Let's get you to the hospital."

Three left with him, carting Hoyt off to the ER in Maidenhead. Reeve waited to feel bad, or sorry for what he had done, but neither came upon him. He could think only of the word "faggot," what Hoyt had said about Neal, and his own wounds. What little empathy he'd once possessed seemed to have dissipated.

Reeve left alongside the others that evening, unable to sit and work any longer, and made a detour on the way home. It was not to that little dog's grave, no; instead, Reeve went to his family's plot in the cemetery their old apartment had long ago overlooked. It was less a conscious decision he made than him winding up there, idling in his car outside its perimeter. The complex still existed, albeit more dilapidated than before, a shroud in the evening.

He ghosted along the dead grass and towards the little rows, some with flowers, some without, and some with headstones, some without. Ephraim had his own plot and the best gravestone they could afford at the time. Reeve had not come to see it in years, but he found the same words waiting for him as always.

Ephraim Raymond Scarlet
1965 - 1976
Blessed are the pure in heart, for they shall see God.
– Matthew 5:8

Reeve stared. He tried to muster the horrible tar-like grief that lurked within and found the well empty. *Am I so far gone that even this is beyond me now?* Reeve was suddenly, briefly furious at Neal for doing this to him, for ruining everything. Then the feeling died just as quick. Neal hadn't made him do anything. Reeve had only himself to blame, as always.

He turned back to his brother's grave.

Would Ephraim even appreciate his penance? In Reeve's memories, his brother had been a purveyor of wisdom, older than his years, and ultimately loving in his own way, despite his rough edges. Why else would the town hate Reeve so much for what had happened in the pool? Why else would it hurt so much for him to die? Why else would his parents split up over him?

His thoughts pivoted back to that day with the mutt. He remembered what Ephraim had told him after the knife parted his lips, murmuring, "Now they'll always be able to tell us apart." *Yeah*, Reeve thought hysterically. *They will. Because you're dead and I'm not.* Bizarre laughter welled up inside. He laughed at the epigraph and the idea that Ephraim was in heaven.

His brother was dead. He'd borne that guilt and its punishment for eighteen years, laboring under its dark weight. Now, Reeve realized, he could be honest with himself—he was glad. Ephraim never got the chance to be a man, something which his mom and dad had mourned to their graves. He hadn't been good or kind or anywhere close to it. He was a liar. He lied just to lie. He lied like he breathed.

So, what was the truth, really?

Ephraim didn't need a reason, and that took him the longest to understand. And Reeve was done pretending otherwise. He felt tears slip down his face. He'd bought into his own myth. To move or do anything for himself was to accept a return to misery. He thought he deserved to suffer.

Everything that had been true about his life up until that moment was no more. He thought he hadn't chosen this, that the town made the choice for him; he was wrong. Reeve leaned in close to the grass marker and whispered, "I'm not sorry you're dead anymore. If there is a hell, you're burning right now. Enjoy it."

He abandoned the marker and spared only a passing look at his parents', too keyed-up to handle it. Reeve then returned to Lazarus Street in a daze. Everything looked and felt the same, he thought. It was him who had changed.

When he pulled up to the tailer, Maze and Neal were locked in a heated argument with Heddie and Zebadiah on the lawn. Looking behind them at his trailer, Reeve realized what, exactly, had precipitated it. "FAG" had been spray painted on his front door in block lettering colored a dirty scab red. He wanted to scratch at the paint until it ran like blood into the streets.

The argument was scattered, pieces drifting in and out as he parked and began to approach the group. Neal's presence made the hair on the back of his neck stand up and his vision fog with anger and want. He elected to ignore him altogether.

"Go on back to your jank-ass trailer. Don't you have kids to feed? Don't you got anything better to do than mess with him?" Maze was yelling at the pair.

Her temple was bandaged, and he could see a splint glint on her left hand as she gesticulated wildly to Heddie, whose arms were crossed over her chest. Zebadiah's attention pivoted to Reeve the moment he saw him.

"*You—*" He began, only to be cut off.

"This is my property," Reeve said.

"So?"

"So, leave."

After the words left his mouth, he saw Zebadiah's face twist. It was quick, infinitesimal even, but enough to see ugly displeasure well up from within. The crack in the man. He bled, he feared, he hated. Like Reeve, he could feel.

He recalled the press of a boot to his ribs, his throat, and asked himself *why*. Did Zebadiah and all those other people, whom, over the years, had poked and prodded at his pain, even look at Reeve as human? He'd tried discussion; he'd tried to be civil. Yet Zebadiah would no more be moved by his words than Reeve would his.

"I warned you," Zebadiah said.

"You did."

"Hoyt called me, let slip your little stunt at the office. I s'pose you didn't learn anything from last night."

Reeve licked at the crusted-over cut on his mouth. "Maybe just not what you imagined," he said.

"Is that so," he said, more to himself than Reeve, before continuing. "Are you a violent man, Scarlet?"

"I'm not sure."

"And it jokes, too. You want to know what I think?"

"I have a feeling you'll tell me no matter what I say."

"I think you, that mutt, and the girl need to learn y'all's place."

"And where would that be," Reeve asked, soft, "at your feet?"

Zebadiah grinned. "That's a start, yeah. I'd be happy to introduce you."

"Do it." The *I dare you* went unspoken.

Zebadiah's fists were fisted tight at his sides. He looked about ready to rush him, all pretenses be damned. But Reeve felt ready now in a way he hadn't before, and he almost welcomed the chance to fight back.

Touch me again and I'll kill you. The thought emerged unbidden, but Reeve, with a sudden and unusual clarity, realized he meant it.

Zebadiah rocked back on his heels and reschooled his features. "This is just the way it is. You shouldn't get too mad. Maybe you'll even learn something this time," he said.

Reeve felt his expression curl, turn feral. "It's funny, y'know, real funny—this so-called concern. It's funny because it's so sudden, and because I don't remember it being there last night. I don't remember it being there any time we've been neighbors, or when my dad died. I guess I gotta ask myself, then, where this comes from.

"You talk to me like you're gonna change my mind. As if you could do that anymore than I could change yours. There ain't nothing you can say to me that'll make me stop. I won't stop. Not ever. And certainly not 'cause of you."

"This, here," Zebadiah spat at him, gesturing around, "it ain't for you. There is evil in the world. I've seen it. And I'm seeing it here, too, right now."

"I don't care where you're from. Your story," Reeve told him. "Maybe your daddy pushed you around as a kid. Maybe he gave you these—ideas. Or maybe there was no saving you. I've seen the evil you're talking about. People think we all come into this place innocent, that we can't be born wrong or bad. I know that's a lie. I've lived it. So, whatever it is that's brought you here—it doesn't matter. You've done what you've done, and I won't forget it."

"Don't worry," Zebadiah said to him then, stepping back. His face settled into something strangely calm. "Fire destroys everything."

"You can hurt me," Reeve said. "That's it. That's all."

"It's a lot more than you think it is," Zebadiah said, giving Reeve a significant look before walking back to his trailer, Heddie close behind.

"Jesus, Mary, and Joseph," Neal groaned.

"A Catholic," Heddie spat, twisting back to face them. "I should've known."

"All this dirty talk is getting my nipples hard," Neal drawled. Then, he said, louder, "Come find me if you're looking for something longer than three inches. And by that, I mean my rosary. Bitch."

Heddie and Zebadiah paid him no mind, the trailer door clicking shut behind them.

Maze turned her attention to Reeve. "Oh, your face," she said, making an abortive gesture at him. She wanted to... *comfort* him. He was so touched he leaned into it, carefully enmeshing her hand with his and laying it against his temple.

"I'm having a hard time," he admitted.

"Yeah," she said, face crumpling. "Me too."

"Your mom?"

"A little. It's... it's him. Waylon, my boyfriend. He hurt me real bad."

He released her but remained close. "This?" Reeve asked, motioning towards her splint and swollen black eyes.

"Nah, that was something else. I took care of it, believe it or not. Waylon did worse. At least it feels like that to me."

It took Reeve a moment to divine her implication, but when he did, he was startled by how angry he became. His hands closed into fists at his sides.

Neal seized the opportunity to cut in, gripping Reeve's shoulder. "Maze, what're you talking about?"

"Not talking to you, Neal," she said without heat. "Reeve, I-I just don't know what to do."

Reeve had some idea as to what he would do if ever saw Waylon. But like himself, Maze wanted to deal with this on her own. Instead, he posed the question, "Does he have something he cares about?"

"I'm sure there's something," she said, rubbing her arm. "Just not me."

"Find it, whatever it is, and take it. Ruin him with it."

"Take it?"

"He took something from you, right?"

"You ain't gonna tell me to move past this or forgive him?"

Reeve smiled an unpleasant shark smile. "If you think that, then you don't know me well at all."

Maze went silent at that, and her features did something complicated. "You're one spooky sonuvabitch, you know that? But I get what you mean, I think. So, uh, thanks for that."

"You're welcome."

"Yeah, I really am," she said. "Mind if I hang around for a bit? I need some time to, uh, think."

Reeve nodded and watched her walk to his trailer. Neal took the opportunity to get a word in, chin angled down and shifting his weight from foot to foot. He was impeccably dressed as he tended to be nowadays, though his demeanor came off as ruffled and less confident than usual.

"Don't you have somewhere to be?" Reeve asked.

"I got lots of places to be, Red, so you'll have to be more specific."

"As in not here."

"Guess my itinerary changed once I saw your house was fucking vandalized," Neal snarled. "Sue me for giving a shit about you, even after you left this morning."

Reeve jerked his head towards his front door. "Let's take this inside," he said, not looking back to see whether Neal had followed.

Neal lingered in the foyer. "Hey there, friend," he said eventually, unsure and awkward and not at all like himself.

"I'm not your friend," Reeve said. "I don't think we're even close to being that anymore."

Neal let his tongue slip out and drag across his lower lip. "No?" He said, voice strangled.

"No, and you've known that for a while."

"Maybe."

"Tell me how long."

The other man stepped closer and tucked his face into Reeve's neck. He welcomed it. "Will you think differently of me if I do?"

"I already think differently."

"Not bad different?"

"No."

"Then… uh, well, from the start, I guess. You were kind to me. You didn't ask for anything other than my company. When I saw you beneath the bleachers for the first time after you helped me out with that piece of shit car, I thought to myself that I had to know you."

Where before the idea of their friendship having been clouded by Neal's desire would have troubled him, now it made Reeve feel wanted, possessed. He never imagined how sensual possession would be. He pulled Neal closer.

"Even then?"

"Even then."

At this, Reeve could not keep himself from groaning hungrily and wrenching Neal's head back by the hair to pry his hot, welcoming mouth open with his tongue. They both moaned soft and held each other close, parting only for air.

"You want me?" Neal asked.

"I want you however I can have you," Reeve admitted, "but I shouldn't. I know I shouldn't."

"It'll be good," he said. "It's us."

"I'll ruin this. You. Everything," he said bitterly. "I always do."

"It's okay."

"No, it's not. But I don't think I can keep away from you any longer," Reeve confessed, splaying a long-fingered palm on the wall by Neal's head.

"Can't argue with that."

He would try and make Neal happy for as long as he was allowed. Reeve was starved for it, this, his love. When they were together, his head was quiet. He imagined this was what normal people felt like.

"It could be like this forever, if you'd let it."

Reeve licked his lips, leaned in. "Do you always understand how you feel?"

"I-I, uh, no. I guess not."

"That's why I needed to think about it," he murmured. "But don't mistake what I mean—you're mine, now. If you'll let me."

Neal paused. "Been yours for a long time," he said finally, ducking his head.

Reeve regarded the other man with open affection. He caught his jaw in hand and dragged a calloused thumb along Neal's lower lip, met by a red, wet tongue that darted out to taste it. They remained like that for a long while. It was somehow better, more important than the sex.

"This makes it real," Reeve said.

"Yeah, it does."

"I'm not afraid anymore."

"I know."

"Good."

Reeve leaned in closer, almost conspiratorially. "Y'know… people talk about being happy like it's some foregone conclusion. Like it's easy. But I don't even know what it looks like for me. Maybe I never will. All I know is I'm not as empty when I'm with you."

Reeve removed his hand in a slow, easy caress, then parted to join Maze in the kitchen area, certain that Neal was behind him.

Her head was pillowed on the small table, idly tracing patterns while she waited. This close, she looked even worse than before.

"You look terrible," he informed her.

Maze let out a weak laugh. "Way to make a girl feel special, old man," she muttered into the laminate.

"It's the truth."

"Reeve," Maze began, tense, "I don't know what the hell I'm feeling right now—just that my mom wouldn't understand. I guess I thought you would."

"Did I… help you?"

"We'll see," she said, staying a little while longer. She wolfed down the pizza they ordered and even met the delivery driver for him.

He allowed himself one piece, one drink, and then more. The food had real taste and texture. It was terrible; it was wonderful. Just like so much else had been these past two weeks.

They spent another hour together, most of which Neal and Maze spent bickering with each other until it was well and truly time for the girl to go. Reeve watched her dark figure weave through the hoard until it disappeared around the first turn with trepidation in his gut.

After Maze left, Neal began rifling through his dad's old record collection until he pulled out a 45 bearing the title, "She's My Witch." When he slipped it from its cover and set it on the record player, an eerie, jagged riff crackled through the speakers. Neal beckoned for Reeve to join him in what passed for the living area. His feet led him there before he could even really think about it.

"C'mon," Neal said, "One dance."

"I don't dance," he said, even as he took the outstretched hands.

Neal pulled him close, smiling big and wide like he couldn't quite believe any of this was real. There was still a nervous glint to his eyes, one that Reeve sought to wipe away. He wanted, irrationally, to protect him from guilt, or pain, or suffering; Neal had known each long before they had even met. If his daddy hadn't been locked up, then Reeve would have put him in the ground himself.

"Now you do."

"Now I do."

He led them both in a slow shuffle, their foreheads pressed together. The chords and vocals rattled him down to the marrow, immolating him from the inside. When the song ended, it soon started over again since the player was an auto-repeat, and this time the other man sped up the pace until they were doing a fast-tempo swing—the jitterbug, Neal told him—that had them weaving in and around each other faster, faster.

There was sweat on his brow, in his hair. He felt his lips turn up. This was exhilaration. Raw energy. He knew it. He just hadn't thought it would be something he'd become acquainted with again. His mistake.

It drawled to an end once more, and he saw Neal begin to slow. No, he thought, that wouldn't do. Reeve was the one to grasp him then, embrace him chest-to-chest, and lead them through the motions he'd at first only stumbled through. Each revolution grew in confidence, their spins becoming complicated and expanding outward to eat up whatever floor their shoes found purchase on.

They danced and danced to that same damn single for the next hour, and when they finally did tire of it, Neal pulled out another record at random and switched them out. Their strange courtship persisted through Screamin' Jay Hawkins' "I Put A Spell On You / Little Demon" track, the dark and brutal blues thumping out a hypnotic voodoo rhythm.

He liked it—and what a strange turn that was. Maze's affinity for music that seemed to claw its unfreedom from speakers, sounding more animal than man, he understood it now that he felt this animalism himself. It slaked a thirst he hadn't realized he possessed.

He didn't stop, couldn't. Not until the sun dipped behind the horizon to shroud the mobile home in darkness. It felt like velvet, sublime. His chest constricted around something deep, something buoyant and sad in equal measure. Reeve's mouth went dry.

Neal left the record on, and its notes still thickened the air.

He didn't bother asking himself what he was feeling. It was known to him now. *Want.* It was a word, a feeling, he'd long intertwined with possession and not satiation. He wanted to leave Carthage; he wanted to quit his job, work on cars; he wanted his family to have loved him; and now, more than anything it seemed, he wanted Neal by his side.

He sought to know, to feel, and, more than anything, to reach beyond these people, their borders, and from there into places unseen. Even outside Carthage, he'd long suspected everyone would still look at him and somehow see the blood on his hands. He felt it himself like a stain that refused to be washed out. Now, though, when he imagined those towns and their anonymous profiles, he thought maybe it wouldn't be that way at all. Nothing. They would know nothing.

It was strange to him how resistant he'd been to this. Not even Neal had been able to persuade his purpose. But now, he understood what it meant to go without.

"I enjoyed that," Reeve said.

"Yeah?"

"It was groovy."

"I figured the earth would quit turning before you ever let on about liking music, Red."

"Until recently, you'd have been right."

Reeve's thoughts skittered towards the wasteland the preceding years had been, how empty he'd truly felt.

"Hey, don't go," Neal said. "Where d'you go when you leave like that?"

"I went to see my brother today," Reeve replied, changing the topic.

Neal stilled at that. "What?"

"I saw him. And my parents, too, for a little bit."

"How, uh, did that go?"

"Fine."

"Alright."

"Neal, did you ever know Eph? Before all of it."

Neal ducked his head awkwardly. "I mostly kept to myself, but I saw him around. He'd be out messing with folks, running with his crowd, and generally raising hell wherever he could. I didn't wanna get caught up in that, but I reckon people thought he was just horsing around. That it was what boys got up to, y'know?"

Reeve was surprised by the sharp noise that left his own mouth at that, something that settled somewhere between humor and pain. "Thank you for being... honest with me, Neal. I'm sick and tired of everyone pretending like he was a good person just 'cause he's dead. Ephraim was a bad kid and a worse brother. That's the truth. I know that now. I've finally come to terms with it."

Neal's eyes widened. "You—what?"

"I hate him. I realized that today."

"I've hated him since I got to know you," Neal choked out.

"Good," Reeve said, tangling his hands in Neal's hair. "Cause he can't have you."

The pair migrated to the garage that had been outfitted as his bedroom, hand in hand. They twined themselves together on the pallet, sharing the same air and touching as much bare skin as possible. Reeve felt no need for sex, and it seemed that neither did Neal. The salt and sweat and musk on their bodies intermingled, filtered in through his mouth to settle on his tongue. Cale Yarborough presided over them like Jesus on the Cross.

With Neal curled up against his chest, Reeve drifted off into an unusually easy sleep. As he did so, he searched for the right term to describe this situation: entropy—when all orderly systems descended into chaos.

He found he didn't mind.

MAZE V

When Maze stumbled back home in the early hours of the morning, still walking off the fry and booze and hurt, her mom, who had been up watching TV in the living room, took one look at her before hustling Maze into the car and rushing them off to the hospital.

"Hezyr, what have you done?" Jessica shouted, strangled, driving with one hand and stroking the hair back from Maze's forehead with the other. "Baby, no, don't go to sleep. Please, baby. You gotta stay up, 'kay?"

Maze only groaned in response but managed to keep her lids slit open until the neon-bright ER entry flashed into view. She leaned on her mom until the nurses took over, rolling her onto a stretcher and wheeling her through the double doors.

The first nurse flashed a light into her eyes. "What happened?"

"Got drunk. Fell down the stairs," Maze slurred, more exhausted than anything. When the nurse looked skeptical, she continued. "Was on some fry, too, and something else, but I dunno what."

"Jesus, hasn't the school told y'all about how dangerous that stuff is? Never mind—Susan, let's pump her stomach and follow concussion protocol."

Between having a tube shoved down her nose and deep throating it until her abdomen clenched and constricted around nothing and being woken periodically by the nurses, Maze was near delirious by the time they actually let her sleep.

Maze later woke sometime in the afternoon, taking the fact that she hadn't been handcuffed to the bed as a good sign. It was pretty much the only thing she had going for her, especially considering her swollen face and busted hand, which was now in a splint. She couldn't shake the feeling she was caught up in a streak of bad luck and didn't know how the hell to extricate herself from it.

It was there, in the sterile hospital bed, that Maze stared at the ceiling and tried not to think about anything. Her dad's image emerged anyways. Being here, funnily enough, was the closest she'd felt to him since, well— everything.

Maze had barely been able to get out of bed after he'd died. She failed all her classes. Lost the finals against Sulphur Creek. Had any potential scholarships go up in smoke. Was that what it had been like for him all the time? Just this… smoke in his eyes.

Dying held no real appeal, but neither did living. Maze drank and smoked because she could be here, physically at least, but her mind was freed from all the bad stuff associated with her body. An escape, at least for however long either lasted.

It felt as though there was no going back; not to the way things were or who she'd been before. This was the point of no return. Had Reeve felt like this when he'd exited the pool that day? Swept up in something beyond his control? She'd been so angry for so long, and she realized now it had sustained her, because in its absence she was just scraped raw. There was nothing else left inside.

"These are just things that've happened to us, I think. It's not who are. And it's not forever," Neal had had told her that night in the parking lot, she recalled. But he was tragic and handsome and intelligent, equipped with deep-felt words and an earnest disposition; Maze, for her part, elicited no sympathy with her ugliness, bad temper, and selfishness. They were more different than she thought he understood. Beautiful people were always like that.

Maze screwed her face up and tried desperately to reach for that same self-assurance, to feel anything other than the heavy and impossible weight everything seemed to hold over her, bearing down harder and harder until she would become little more than a pathetic lump. Her mom, her dad, Waylon—

Their relationship had been something that had once looked like love to her. But now it had turned, twisted. Or maybe she was just now seeing it for what it really was. Desperation, maybe. Control. She wasn't dumb enough to mistake fucking for loving, but he'd held her after, talked about things she cared about, made her feel wanted. Fuck. Had any of it ever been real?

The prospect shifted, sinuous, inside her, so heavy and encompassing that she felt tears prick at her eyes. They were the same. She was no better than Cricket. Just more deluded, maybe.

"That bastard," she said to herself. Then, louder, "That dirty damn bastard!" Maze was seized and released by this newfound energy quickly, and she sagged back into the scratchy hospital pillows.

The quiet did not last long, as her mom soon rushed into the room. Maze reckoned she must have heard the commotion. Jessica looked at her, then away, repeating the motion while she paced around the room.

Not facing her, her mom hissed, "How could you do this to me? After everything I've been through with your father."

Maze opened her mouth to respond but let it fall shut. *This isn't about you. So for once, just be my mom. Just hold me. I just wanna be held.* She imagined being loved for who she was, rather than someone she could be or had been.

Jessica continued, "Not to mention the girls. They would've been devastated."

The girls, Maze mimicked dourly in her head. By that, she clearly meant Thursday's group. "Those people don't care, mom," she said, voice punctured. "They didn't give a damn about us then, and they don't give a damn about us now."

"Dammit, Hezyr! Don't you know how to be grateful?"

Maze felt her expression twist up. What did she think those days and nights spent at Gould's pixelated altar meant, or the weekly excursions to a church she didn't belong to, or the extra cash in her purse that Maze had set aside for tithes and bills? That was her gratitude. It went beyond words, beyond even like.

"Yeah," she croaked out at last, "sounds like me."

Her mom looked stricken for a moment, almost regretful, as though the resignation in Maze's voice had touched something deep inside, but then it passed again, and the pinched line between her brows returned. Maze couldn't decide which was worse—the idea that her mom was ignorant to her pain, or knowing what she'd done, how much she could hurt her, and still doing it anyways.

It hurt because it mattered. Her mom did, that was. Even after all that had happened between them. Blame needed a home, whether she liked it or not;

her mom's had taken root inside her long ago. It didn't matter. Maze didn't know if she would ever stop loving her mom.

"You're grieving. You're lost. I can't carry either of those for you," she told Jessica. "And I don't want you to carry mine for me. How many ways can I ask you to be there when I need you? I'm not just a soft place for you to land."

"I-I just don't understand what it is you want," her mom said, deflating. "I don't get you."

"I want to be held. I want to feel like someone gives a damn about me. I feel like... I feel like it shouldn't be that hard. But it feels impossible. More and more every day."

"You're gonna be okay, baby."

"Maybe one day," she whispered.

"But... don't you want to feel like everything'll be fine? Even just for a little while? Even if you know it's a lie?"

"Sometimes, yeah, sure. But like you said, it's a lie. And I don't think I'd make it through losing it all again. So, can't you just meet me where I'm at?"

"Maze... you can't change what's happened. And I don't think I'm ready to forgive you yet. But that doesn't mean I don't love you or care 'bout you. It just means it's harder—harder than I ever wanted it to turn out," Jessica said.

Maze found herself searching for something—more regret, maybe, or pity—in her face but saw only the same disdain that had lived there ever since her dad's suicide. What would it take, she thought, for her to see? It felt no more within her reach than the stars.

"Get out, mom," she said finally.

"I-I, uh, I'll be outside. You got Oralene waiting for you, so I'll let y'all talk for a bit after the nurse checks in on you."

"Yeah, okay."

Love and like didn't feed her. They didn't clothe her. But they were nice to have, at least every now and then.

Her next visitor was more welcome than the first.

Oralene had heard what happened—or, at least, some version of it—and had stopped by to check in as soon as she was allowed. It proved an awkward reprieve from an even more awkward stand-off between Maze and Jessica.

The other girl's blonde head peeked in first, hesitant, and was soon followed by the rest of her when Maze didn't start cussing her out on sight.

Oralene was wearing a mismatched pajama set and last night's makeup. Her eyes were red, like she had been crying. Strangely, Maze found that comforting; it was proof someone still cared about her enough to cry.

Oralene collapsed at the chair near her bedside. When she extended her undamaged hand towards Maze, Oralene pressed it to her forehead and leaned forward into her own lap. Maze could feel her shaking, hear her half-muffled sobs. She teared up a little bit at this, mouth filled with something bittersweet, and she squeezed Oralene's palm even tighter.

"I leave you alone for one night," Oralene said eventually, not looking up.

Maze took this as the apology it was intended to be. "Maybe you should invest in a leash, then."

"Not really my thing," she gasped out between sobs.

"Cricket—is she alright?"

"Depends on your definition of alright."

"So, everyone knows."

"They'll believe whatever they feel like believing."

"Lee's coming up on top then."

"Looks like."

Maze swallowed. "Do you believe me?"

Oralene nodded. "Yeah, I do."

"Then at least the people who matter know."

"I saw you last night. Cricket and Dean, too. There's... there's just no faking that. Besides, I, uh, know you well enough to know better. Or I should, at least."

Maze cracked the first real smile she'd had in what felt like ages at that. It sobered after she thought about how many times her friend had covered for her when it came to Waylon despite her reservations.

"You were right, y'know."

Oralene carefully did not react. "About what?"

"Him."

There was only one *him*.

"What'd he do?"

"He really was a creep."

Maze turned away as she spoke, throat pulled taut. Her fingers twisted in the sheets until the dislocated one protested, and even then, she did not abate.

"Did he—?"

"Something like that, yeah," she murmured. "I don't want to talk about it."

Maze had been bigger, stronger, and more athletic than him. She'd had every advantage. So why had she felt so powerless? Maybe that was the game, his game. Being able to drag someone down beneath him who might otherwise be fine.

Maze abruptly changed the topic. "Did Dean ask about me?"

"He called me right after. Wanted to come by and everything, but I could hear his parents yelling in the background. All in Vietnamese, of course. The cops came by, I think. They're trying to keep him outta this whole mess. For his sake and theirs."

Why had the police even talked to Dean? Was it just because he'd been with her at the party or had Lee ratted him out? If he got popped for this, his basketball career would be over before it had even gotten off the ground. And Maze couldn't ruin things for him.

She shot forward in bed, gorge rising from the stress. "Shit, Oralene, I gotta go talk to them, tell 'em what happened."

"You're no good to anyone right now, Maze. Bev and Pete won't let anything happen to him. And he didn't really do nothin' wrong, besides. Stay quiet 'til Fields or whoever comes and talks to you. In the meantime, think about what you want. For real. You going off half-cocked ain't helping nobody."

"I want to be happy," she confessed, somewhat hysterically, "but I don't think I can anymore. When something good happens to me, it's like I can't even enjoy it. How could I? I'm supposed to be in mourning, thinking about the person I've lost and feeling like shit. My dad is dead. He's dead and I'm laughing at some joke you told me or smiling because it's a nice day outside. Those things still exist. Him being dead didn't make them go away. I'm stuck in the middle of everything.

"And it's terrible, 'cause now I have to deny myself. I have to be miserable. It's the only way for this to be real. For me to honor his memory. But it's so hard. I can't fucking cope with the sadness anymore.

Maze wiped at her face. "You've got better things to be doing than stay here with me. Go and see about the boys. Meet me at my place tomorrow."

"Gimme your keys, and I'll go pick up your car and drop it off later. Same with your homework and copies of my notes," was all Oralene said, face schooled into something tender and fond.

Maze's lower lip wobbled, so touched she could only nod in assent at her friend as they clasped hands while exchanging the keys. She hoped she conveyed how grateful she was for everything with her eyes, how much she loved Oralene, and how even though her life had taken a nosedive, she still had the time to appreciate things like this.

Oralene departed, leaving Maze and Jessica to check out with the charge nurse. Now that she was more coherent, the prospect of having to pay back however much this was going to cost made her sick. The floorboard would end up emptier for certain. It might take years of schlepping at the Burger Barn to pay off. A problem for another day.

Maze swore under her breath.

Her mom's mouth pinched into a frown. The skin around her eyes was pulled tight, ringed in purple bruises. The frustration she felt was palpable. But she said nothing, and neither did Maze.

They were interrupted by a service call over the intercom, jolting Maze back to awareness—specifically the awareness that Cricket was likely here, at this very hospital, and that she had been too caught up in her own problems to spare her a thought.

"Hey, ma'am," she began, turning to face the woman behind the desk, "can you tell me if Corliss Fields was admitted here today? Last I saw her, she wasn't doing too good." Too good was an understatement.

"You know I can't tell you that, hun."

"Please, she's my friend, and I'm worried about her."

"Hezyr, stop," her mom said sharply.

The nurse leaned in, sympathy flashing across her face, and informed Maze under her breath that, "She's out now, got checked out by her daddy not too long ago. You're right, though, that girl went through something bad. Glad to see she has a friend like you in her corner."

Am I even her friend? Maze wondered. Nothing she did until last night even spoke to any real friendship. And it still wasn't, she thought, because what she did was something she would've done for any girl, any woman. In a way, that made the shame worse. It was almost like what happened to Cricket was a personal failure.

They drove home in silence.

Her mom had barely pulled into the drive when Maze hopped out, limping off and into their house. Her whole body felt like one big bruise, but she knew she couldn't handle being cooped up in here with her mom. And who knew how long it would take for Cricket's dad to come by or for Waylon to call her up? She may as well spend her final hours as a free woman in the company of people she actually liked. This, naturally, being Reeve, and maybe even Neal if the latter happened to come by.

"I'm heading out," she announced.

Jessica glared up at her. "The hell you are, Hezyr. You're grounded for... I don't even know how long."

"And how are you gonna stop me?"

"I'm your mother; that's how."

"Oh, so now you wanna start acting like it? Where was this the last few months? Get outta here," Maze snapped, gritting her teeth. "I want to leave, mom. I'm going to leave. I can write it down if that makes it any clearer for you."

"You're sixteen. You don't know what you want."

"You're almost fifty fucking years old, so what's your excuse?"

And with that parting blow, Maze slammed the door behind her, shedding yesterday's outfit and exchanging it for something comfortable, familiar. She needed comfortable and familiar, as nothing else in her life seemed to be. And because she couldn't handle another confrontation with Jessica, she slipped out the window and found her car curb-parked with the keys tucked into the shade, already knowing where she was going to end up: Reeve's place.

Neal was already there (of course) and caught up in some kind of argument with Reeve's neighbors. Maze had almost forgotten that Heddie lived next to him, too used to seeing the woman in her living room watching *Courageous Grace*.

The couple and Neal were at each other's throat, and upon closer inspection, Maze could see why. Someone had defaced the trailer by spray painting "FAG" on the front façade, impossible to look away from or deny.

The urge to lash out was so strong it led Maze to realize just how much she had come to care for Reeve.

She rolled up and stalked over, uncaring at this point as to what anyone would think about her being there.

"Maze," Heddie said without affect, "you're here."

"Unfortunately for you, yes. Now I don't suppose you know anything about this, uh, art piece?"

"I'd never," she said. "The only reason we're even involved is because this—this *thug* won't leave us alone."

"Oh, sure," Neal sneered, practically vibrating with anger.

"Speak to her like that again, and you'll live to regret it," her husband said with a light tone, expression strangely calm.

His aggressive verbiage recalled to mind Lee's, though, and it immediately set Maze on edge. She straightened herself up to her full height and got all up in his business, forcing him to tip his head back to make eye contact. His expression didn't change, not until another car pulled up the street, stepping back from the teenage girl he'd been in a standoff with.

For her part, Heddie tucked herself in close to her husband, discoloration around her eye socket even more obvious than usual in this light. Maze wondered why no one would say anything about the fact that this woman was being smacked around, then realized there was nothing, really, to do or say. Heddie didn't seem to want it anyways. Maybe she'd made her peace with it. Maze didn't think she would, if given the same situation.

Their attention shifted with the arrival of Reeve, who, much like her, had seen better days. More than that, though, there was this disturbing air about him. That otherness to him, how he filled up any room he entered like a vast shadow, invading, inescapable.

Following a tense, subtextual-laden exchange between him and the neighbor-man, Heddie's sicko husband Zebadiah, Maze took the opportunity to get to talking with Reeve while she could. She was in desperate need of advice. Maze wanted someone who wouldn't judge her for being wrong or bad, who'd give her a fair shake before telling her what to do about it. A guy like Reeve, really. He'd seen shit, lived through shit, and wasn't afraid to set her straight.

Reeve regarded her with a dark, speculative look. He was mulling it over. He used to give her this—stare. Like he was looking through her. Like she wasn't even there. It had passed the longer they knew each other, replaced with the cool tolerance she'd come to associate with him. Neither were there now. No. Now there was a look in his eye that made her uneasy. It was the look a dog got when it had been kicked one too many times. The look it got when it was about to turn on its masters.

His advice regarding her situation was as morally vacant as expected, effectively boiling down to *if they won't take the high road, why should you?* Yet if last night had taught her anything, it's that violence wasn't really a solution, at least not long term. Maze was here, beat to hell and probably going to be arrested, all while Lee got to play the victim because she'd gone and made him into one. That didn't mean she regretted putting Lee in his place, not at all, only about the consequences thereof.

Decisions, decisions.

Thoughts of Waylon wormed through her brain again. Maze could still feel his hands on her, his dick inside her, the warble in his voice as he whimpered. Disgusting and pathetic. And she just let him do it, even if it felt like she couldn't do anything about it at the time.

Later, inside, she had gone red up to her ears at the whispered promises and moans coming from the entryway between Reeve and Neal. When they emerged, trying to play it off and clearly unaware that their voices had carried, Neal looked ecstatic and had a healthy flush to match his good mood. As for Reeve, her beloved weirdo, he could almost have passed for happy. They may as well have been sharing the same skin.

They ordered pizza and talked about nothing important for an hour, after which Maze knew she had to leave. Not just because she needed to head home, but because those two needed to get a room.

She returned home to an empty house, thankfully, and cobbled together some stovetop mac n' cheese to quell her empty belly. The relative peace didn't last long. Her mind turned over the names Dean, Lee, Cricket, Reeve, Neal on repeat.

Maze's impromptu dinner was interrupted by a knock at the door. Immediately, she knew who was on the other side. It was a sharp, authoritative knock, the kind of knock that cops on TV used when picking up suspects.

Sheriff Fields stood across from her on the threshold. "Please step outside," he told Maze.

He looked like he'd aged a decade overnight. His grief was palpable, and he gnawed on the chew tucked into his cheek. Maze complied, holding her hands out like she'd seen suspects do on TV.

"Just get it over with and cuff me already. Lee went and complained, didn't he?"

"Yeah, he did. But I ain't here for that. You're momma ain't even around, either. And I'd want her present for something official. This is between me and you.

"Dean Nguyen came by the station earlier this morning. It's funny. He told me he's the one who beat the hell outta that Lyons boy, not you. That Lee ain't remembering right. And that Lyons—he, um, hurt my Corliss. That he's the reason she's in the hospital."

His drawl mangled "Win" into "Nuh-goo-yin," and tripped over the word "hurt." As if "hurt" could encompass what had happened to Corliss, to herself. Even though their situations had seemed so different at the outset.

"Sheriff, that's not true. I did it, me."

Now Dean had gotten caught up in everything through his misguided attempt to be a hero in the eleventh hour. She wasn't going to let him do that to himself or his family.

"Between you, Kennedy, and Nguyen, I've started to get a picture of what occurred at that party. The nurses ran tests, too.

I know what happened. So do you. But there's your word, and there's his. Corliss—she don't remember much beyond riding there with y'all and having that first drink. Then the hospital. I s'pose it's for the best. I hope she never remembers.

"No one saw him do it but you. The kid wore a condom. It's your word against his. Lord knows how that'll play out. What's gonna happen now is that Nguyen and him'll get their charges dropped. You'll stay away from the Lyons boy. And everyone keeps their mouths shut. We push this, and he'll get a hall pass. This'll be played out as a "boys'll be boys scenario." I'm not dragging you two down 'cause y'all tried to do the right thing."

"Aren't you gonna try and fight for Cricket? She's your baby girl!"

"Her name's Corliss, not 'Cricket,' goddammit!" Fields exploded, before sucking in a deep breath and running a hand through his hair to calm himself down, "Look, I'll tell you this once, Maze. There's a place for people like me in this world. I'm trying to help you here, I really am. And I'm trying to help your friend, too. But I know the law; I know what happens to people in these cases, especially people that don't exactly fit right. So don't act like I don't care about you, and don't you ever question my love for Corliss. That boy will get his due, one way or another. My eye'll be on him 'til he's six feet under. Now, are we clear?"

All the air left her in a rush. "Crystal."

"Corliss… I wish she were different. Not to say I'm ashamed. Not ever. Not once has the thought crossed my mind. But for her own sake, I mean. I just want her to be happy. It ain't an easy life, is all. No one'll care that this happened. Just me, my wife, and you. Maybe it would be more of a tragedy if it happened to someone else.

"Her pain is something I can't change. I can't change it because it doesn't exist, at least not in a way I can touch. This'll follow her forever.

"As for what's gonna happen for her," he began, "she, uh, won't be around no more. There's this all-girl's school in OKC that's a better fit. Things'll be tight but worth it. She needs it more than I thought. Maybe more than I ever knew. I'm just glad someone gave enough of a damn about her to step in. I just wish it happened sooner."

"Can I see her?"

"It's better that you don't."

Maze lowered her gaze and scuffed her shoes in the dirt. "Yeah," she agreed.

The older man turned to leave, but as he did so, she remembered something. Back in the bathroom, after she'd wrestled Lee down to the ground. The pink glimpse she'd seen on him, Cricket's bare lower half. It was starting to come together.

"Hey, Sheriff," she called out. "Did y'all check his pockets, save anything for evidence?" Fields shook his head. "I remember seeing somethin,' uh, panties I think, in Lee's back pocket. Crick—Corliss.' Think that might help with settling this?"

He looked stricken, then contemplative. "Maybe."

And then he left for real, and with his departure she expected to feel relieved, but instead Maze was left with more questions than answers. Her heart was still lodged somewhere up in her skull, turning the day's events over and over. More than that, Corliss' sightless, slack features were burned into her memory, made worse by Fields' pointed remark about his daughter not having someone in her corner sooner. How many opportunities had Maze had to step in? Would it have changed anything in the end? Was she, in a way, responsible for every horrible thing that had happened to Corliss?

The screen door slammed shut behind her. Maze staggered through the living area and ate her now-cold dinner directly from the pot. Heat pricked behind her eyes, and she suddenly was struck by how overwhelmed she felt.

Not too long ago, she'd been excited for basketball games, dances, and college. Things were tough but normal. Now, though, the future made her feel panicked and sick. Maze couldn't see beyond tomorrow.

Usually when she got like this, she'd go and see Waylon, but things were different with him now, terrible, and that they'd never be the same again. The conversation she'd had with Reeve turned itself over in her head. Maybe violence was the answer. Or, at least, it was the only language they understood.

Her hands clenched and tears pricked at her eyes, which she hurriedly wiped away. Maze thought about Lee, his glittering eyes. The way his smile had cracked open his face. It was starting to set in that even though her and Corliss' situations were different, the end result had been largely the same. And wasn't that just so funny? All this time, she thought she knew more about the world than Corliss, was in on how things worked, and that she was so mature, so above everyone else because *she* was the one with the older boyfriend, and *she* was the one who'd been through shit.

I've been so stupid, she thought. Then her thoughts pivoted back to Waylon and what happened the night before. *You tricked me. You won't ever trick me again.*

Her keys were in her hand before she thought about it, and the station wagon's wheels skidded across the pavement as she pulled out. Maze drove to his place without her usual subterfuge, so beyond caring whether people saw her that she almost welcomed the attention. His car wasn't in the drive, which left her pacing around and getting progressively angrier at everything until she boiled over and let herself in with the key Waylon kept under the mat.

Being inside didn't help. The distorted lens she'd seen it through the night prior dominated every good memory she'd made here. Laughing at Waylon's corny jokes, hearing him say, "Thank you, Bright Eyes," after she'd confessed her love; the intimacy they'd shared together, the unwanted ache between her legs that persisted even now.

At this point, she wanted to fuck him over. Make him hurt. Maze wanted to make him feel like he'd lost something important. That something clearly wasn't her, however, else he wouldn't have done—that to her.

I want you to never have a moment of peace again.

Waylon was going to get back soon. When exactly, she wasn't sure, but she knew she needed to be fast. The carpet seemed to move beneath her feet until she got to the bathroom. He always came here when he hid his weed stash. It only took a few passes for her to figure out that he was hiding it in the ceiling, noticing the discoloration around the light and how it was reattached off-center. Maze unscrewed the light fixture and fished out a couple grams, shoving the baggies in her coat pocket. She left the rest behind but made sure that it was a little messy. A nice slap in the face for Waylon.

The next thing she needed was in the living room.

The front door slammed shut, startling her as she was setting the lamp back into place. A cold sweat formed on the nape of her neck. "You can do this," she whispered to herself, cracking her knuckles compulsively. "What can he do to you that hasn't already been done? Nothing." Then, louder, "Hey, Way," she announced, voice strangled.

Waylon seemed surprised to find her there at first, but then he smiled. It was intended to be inviting, she supposed, forgiving. In that moment, Maze was just sickened.

"I knew you'd be back, Bright Eyes," he said, stepping closer.

"Did you now?"

"Yeah," he said easily. "Course I did. I know you."

You don't know me at all. If you did, we wouldn't be here. And I wouldn't do what I'm about to do.

"I guess you do," she said, turning her back on him to examine what she'd come here for. Her neck prickled under his gaze, her own vulnerability in this position obvious.

The guitar regarded her with an imperial air. Like always, it was mounted on the stand near the coffee table—the most visible post in the entire apartment. Waylon had once told her that it resembled a woman with its sensuous outline. That all good guitars did.

"Lucky's all curves," he'd say. "And when I hold her, it's as if I'm holding a beautiful girl in my arms."

The irony of this sentiment was not lost on her, especially considering what she was about to do. *Sorry, Lucky,* she thought.

The vintage baby blue Fender Stratocaster had been given to Waylon by his dad, who had passed three years ago in a car accident. It really was beautiful, she thought, so much so that it made him seem unworthy of this instrument.

Waylon's knuckles ghosted along her nape, dipping a little beneath her shirt. Maze froze at first, helplessness descending on her briefly, fleetingly, before it was sublimated into hate and fear and sadness. Her mouth opened into a silent cry; she reacted almost without thinking.

Maze slammed his head against the wall, and when he collapsed, stunned, retrieved the guitar from the stand and smashed it against the coffee table until both were eroded into splintered wood and glass. For his part, Waylon lay splayed on the ground with a look of abject horror on his face.

"Oh, blow it out your ass, Way," she said, panting, with a strength that surprised her.

"How could you—"

Maze cut him off. "If you don't know, then you're even more of an idiot than I thought."

That shut him up real quick. His eyes darted around, seeking purchase for something, anything to hold onto. It seemed he found it when he ground out, "That guitar was worth a fucking fortune. What's to stop me from going to the cops?"

"I'll snitch on you for dealing. They'll test you, search this shithole and your car, too, and find your stash. Maybe you could go and dump it, but I doubt either your supplier or your customers would be happy about that. You could go and flip on them to save your own ass, after all. Maybe I'll even let it spill that you did."

Waylon looked murderous at this, red-faced, and his hands clenched into fists. Maze swallowed her instinctive fear and stood her ground. The stalemate between them lasted for a minute before he broke and spat out a venomous, "Fine. But don't you ever come by here again. I was sweet on you up 'til now. I won't be so sweet next time."

"Like I'd ever stick around," Maze said, backing away from him slowly. Then, just to twist the knife a little, she pulled out a baggie and shook it at him. "I'm taking this, by the way."

The door slamming shut behind her was near euphoric, and Maze exited that dismal apartment complex feeling something between elation and a horrible, gut-wrenching emptiness. It hadn't done anything to erase the pain, fix her problems. Maybe he'd think twice before doing it again. Maybe he wouldn't. There was even the chance he'd come after her someday. But that was the future, and for now, she'd take the win.

Home was still dark when she returned.

Maze collapsed on the couch and curled in on herself. Sleep came fast but was an uneasy tumult of images. She woke to pitch dark and ate cold leftovers.

When her mom came home from wherever she'd gone out to, Maze had to resist the urge to flee from the confrontation that would doubtless occur. Jessica dropped her purse on the counter and levied a dark look her way, but Maze was too drained to rise to the bait. By the time her mom really got into it, Maze had checked out and let her voice wash over her.

Jessica snapped her fingers three times in Maze's face. "—even listening?"

"No, I wasn't," she said.

"What the hell is wrong with you?"

"You want a list?"

"This isn't funny! I feel like I don't even know you anymore, and it scares me. I am so scared, Hezyr."

Join the club, she thought. *There's more to be scared of in this world than I ever knew.*

Jessica whispered, "Give me something to work with, at least. Please."

Maze regarded her mom, feeling so… detached she couldn't muster the will to exculpate herself or blunt her words. *Now you're concerned? That's real funny. You want the truth you said you were better off not knowing.*

"I got into a fight at a party, okay? I had a boyfriend, too, but I broke up with him 'cause he's different than I thought he was. And I've been hanging around Reeve Scarlet and Neal Vásquez. I don't know if I'd call us friends, but we're something, that's for sure."

Jessica looked as though this information hit her like a physical blow. "Boyfriend? No, that can wait. Reeve Scarlet? That man ain't just "mixed-up," no matter what anyone says. Maybe Vásquez is, but not Scarlet. He's bad all the way through. That creep killed his own brother. And you've been 'round them without me knowing? You, a sixteen-year-old girl. Don't you have any idea how—how weird that is?"

"You asked, mom. And this is the truth you hate so much," Maze ground out. "What can you do about it, anyways? What's happened is done."

There was a certain finality to her last statement, one felt by both women. Jessica collapsed onto the couch next to Maze and leaned back into the cushions. Her expression was far, far away. "What can I do?" Her mom asked finally. "What can I do about this?"

"I don't even know, mom. There's no magic fix for anything."

Jessica closed her eyes, completely deflated. Never before had she looked so old or so sad, and it touched something in Maze. Even despite all the bad between them, Jessica was still her mom, and Maze was still her daughter.

Maze sighed. "I'll go with you," she offered, leaning onto Jessica's shoulder. Then, to clarify, "Tomorrow."

"Really?"

"But I want my friends to come."

"If it was Oralene, you know you wouldn't need to ask. So, um. The two grown men you've been spending time with behind my back. Those friends?"

Maze nodded.

Jessica looked like she was fighting off a migraine. "Fine. It'll probably benefit them," she said, before muttering, "If anyone needs Jesus, it's those two."

That got a laugh out of her, and when Jessica's mouth quirked up, it felt to Maze almost as if things were back to normal between them. She knew she was only kidding herself. Nonetheless, she nodded in assent after her mom asked whether she was up for watching a *Fantasy Island* rerun. Maze couldn't help but lean into Jessica's side, cocooned in womb-like darkness when she closed her eyes, drinking in whatever comfort she could glean from her mom. She worried that this would be one of the few times things would be this familiar between them.

In that moment, it felt like something precious slipping through her fingers.

NEAL V

That night, in bed with Reeve, Neal contemplated his past and everything else that had been unearthed with it.

His dad used to say, "If you loved me, you'd stay. If you loved me, you'd never even think of leaving me." Loving him had never been in question; like, however—well, that was a different story.

Neal couldn't quite remember when, exactly, it was that he began to despise those words. They had been a part of his life so long he couldn't disentangle them from his dad, his so-called "love," the blood that bound them.

It was funny, in a way. If Gabriel was all about love, then his mom had been the opposite. She'd longed, he thought. She'd longed for things. That was what Neal remembered most about Irena. And it went far deeper than she talked about, even through his child's eyes.

He saw it in the lingering glances at new records, dresses situated in storefronts, fresh-baked goods when they had only budgeted for canned or frozen that month. Neal sought to wipe that almost-sad look from her face and ease the tension in her shoulders. But it felt so impossible, and he didn't even know where to begin—the money? His dad? The town that judged her for being a black woman married to a light-skinned man? Now, as an adult, he realized he'd never really known her at all.

Irena had been adopted out of foster care, that much he had known. What came prior to and after was shrouded in mystery; it was a mystery she perpetuated and delighted in drawing out, dangling scraps of information before Neal throughout his childhood for him to pant for like a dog.

When pieced together, Neal could form a somewhat coherent outline. Irena Angelique Vásquez, by her own words:

"They took me. I was taken away from my mother, my father, so I could be given to a nice white family that dressed me in their clothes, sat me in their pews, and taught me to put my past aside. It was a daylight crime, early morning. Legal because it'd been written into their laws.

"It's strange, you know... I don't understand why it hurts me so much. Not leaving my family, no—everything else. Things weren't so terrible, I s'pose, but they were wrong, somehow. Wrong in a way I couldn't figure out for a long time.

"I had my mind wiped. I was made to forget everything that came before and be—I don't know—paraded around to their friends so everyone could tell them what a good job they were doing with me, how kind they were for taking me in. Like I was doll, something to look at but not speak to. I chafed at this. I hated it. I'd take being an atheist over praying to their god. That "Sky Daddy" ain't done nothing for me.

"I didn't have the words, then; the words I'm telling you now. I'd tried to find them. Unfreedom, maybe. The slow death. It wasn't 'til I read *On the Road* that I finally got to understanding what I needed to do. It was leave or die. I met your daddy on that road."

Irena hadn't said where she'd been before meeting Gabriel or how long she'd stayed with her white family. As a kid, he hadn't really thought to ask. But now, back here in Carthage again after so long, he wondered whether she'd ever tried to find her home again, the real one, her birth family; or maybe there had been some childish part of her that had blamed them for letting her go, and she never tried going back. But if not there, then where? Where could she have possibly gone?

Did it even matter anymore? Irena had abandoned him that horrible summer day back in '82. She could be dead for all he knew. The thought persisted, though, and were she alive, Neal asked himself what his mother would think of his confirmation? His time with Ruth and Banks. Not only that, but everything leading up to it. The booze, his time behind bars—all of it. He caressed the Maria Goretti medal. Would Irena have resented him for loving their God? That "Sky Daddy" she hated so much.

He would tell her what it had been like. The shame and the anger and the despair had not left him when his dad got put away or even when he'd found God after prison; he had just learned to carry it better.

He still remembered how it felt to be that boy, the one who couldn't meet his dad's eyes without feeling sick. They were X-Ray eyes, he'd think to himself then, trying not to avert his gaze. Eyes that could see right through him.

Gabriel was impossible in a different way.

His dad had made it easy to want to believe him. That he was good, and it was Neal or Irena that had wronged him. Gabriel could convince them of anything: in his world, the sky was green and the grass blue; down was up; and if Neal tried to say otherwise, he was somehow made out to be the fool.

He remembered how it felt when his dad looked at him, assessed him— and for what exactly, Neal wasn't sure for the longest time. Not until he was older. It was something he did often, and it made him squirm inside beneath the scrutiny. Neal would think to himself, *when he looks at me, I can tell he sees everything about me that makes me worthless. Everything that makes me nothing. And he knows that I know. That's the worst part.*

He'd never felt like a victim, not then. Not of abuse or violence or anything else. To him, everything was just what it was: his parents, his life. Neal just happened to be the unlucky bastard born into it. After he got paroled and met people on the outside, real good people, friends who supported him and cared about how he felt, Neal understood better.

Ruth put it into perspective when she asked him once, "If this was happening to a kid right now, and you knew about it, how would you feel?" He didn't know why things were different when it came to himself, or how to explain it, but they just were. It was as though letting himself say it was abuse would somehow make it more real. Neal didn't want to feel like a victim when he'd done so much wrong in his life.

Even more confusing was the fact that things weren't black and white. Sure, there was ugliness, uncertainty. But there were also moments that were so good, so wonderful that Neal sought to do whatever he could to sustain them. And when his family rode that high, it was almost like nothing had ever happened and everything that came before was little more than a bad dream. But it never lasted. Gabriel would always turn on some invisible axis point and revert to the hateful man who raised the hair on the back of Neal's neck every time he so much as looked his way. He didn't know if he'd ever loved his dad, or whether he'd ever really wanted him to be happy. Maybe he'd just wanted to stop being in pain for a little while.

Yeah. He'd had a real rough go of it. He and Irena—they were so eaten up by each other that it wasn't until much later they'd seen everything for what it was. God, how they'd danced for Gabriel. They were so desperate to be loved by him they'd do just about anything. It made him sick.

Neal sighed, pinched his fringe between his fingers, and stared at the figure in the mirror. Before prison, he'd kept it buzzed. His dad preferred it that way, and Neal had never really thought about why until later. Could be that Gabriel didn't want him walking the streets looking like a fucking pansy or flower child. Or maybe it was due to the curls that formed with any real length, a trait that carried Neal over from "racially ambiguous" to "straight up black."

For his part, Gabriel had passed as white. Neal sometimes wondered if that made all the difference. His dad had light skin and cool green eyes. He went by "Gabe," not Gabriel, in town. His grandma had been Swedish, his grandaddy from Guatemala. They were both long dead. He'd never known them, even in that dreamy, half-forgotten manner children sometimes had with grandparents.

Neal wondered how a man who so desperately sought to be anything but what he was ended up with a brown wife and an even browner son. Was his dad reminded of everything he wasn't each time he looked at them? He put on a mask, wore a pale face, but the real whites would never see him as their own, not really. How that was evident to Neal and Irena but not Gabriel was almost a little funny to him.

Spanish was not spoken in the house. Neither was Swedish. They were strangers to each other in every way. Their home was haunted by people who possessed no past.

Neal thought about his love for his parents, its twisted roots, and asked himself how this hurt still felt so recent. Maybe some things never went away, no matter how old you got. Or maybe being back in Carthage had reopened more wounds than he'd suspected. He'd been taken from Reeve, after all; Neal never would have left him willingly.

***

Gabriel had made some comment, Neal recalled. A comment that led to everything falling apart. They had been at home, in the living room, when his dad said it. The word escaped him now, and he couldn't pull it from his memory. He just knew it wasn't even that bad or mean and could have been another blip in their history. But it wasn't, for whatever reason, and it was from there that everything spiraled out of control.

His mom stiffened, tensed up like a spooked cat, and fisted the dishtowel in her hands while she let out a loud exhale from between her teeth. Her back bowed over the sink, hair spilling long and dark across her forehead.

"We're done," she whispered. Then again, louder, "We're done."

Neal froze where he was on the couch. Irena had never talked to his dad that way before. Not for herself, and certainly not for him.

He cut his gaze over to his dad, who was reclined on the couch watching TV. The lights danced across his features. The actors' voices were muted, unintelligible. Gabriel had gone still after her comment. It was instant, eerie. Then he smiled.

"What was that?"

"Y-you heard me," she said. "We're done."

"You'll never be done with me."

"You don't want us here. I don't know when that happened, but it did. I see it. I feel it. I have to hear about it, over and over. It's… it's every day."

Neal watched as a tendon in his dad's neck pulled taut, but he kept quiet. He got that look about him where he was deep in thought. "He's my son. You're my wife. That won't go away. Not ever."

"I want things to be better. *I do.* I'm trying so hard. So's Neal. You're the problem, Gabriel. You. Not me or him. You act like we're—toys."

"I love you," he told her. "Isn't that enough?"

"I used to think so. Not anymore."

"Where will you go?"

"I don't know. I'll figure it out."

"I've looked after you longer than anyone else has."

"Yes, you have. I get that. But I can't take this anymore."

Gabriel didn't look at her. He angled his face towards Neal while he spoke. "You can divorce me. You can even file for custody. But you can't change what's happened."

Irena trembled. "I know."

"You want to take everything from me."

"If that's what you want to call it."

"It's what this is."

There was no response. His mom dropped the towel and grabbed her purse, eyes darting nervously between Neal and Gabriel as she made her way to the door. She even grabbed Gabriel' keys. Then she gestured for Neal to follow.

"We're, uh, going out to eat. Just us. You know, to give you time to think. We'll hit the Dairy Queen in Maidenhead. I'll bring you back something."

"Fine."

"Good. That's good," she said, grip white-knuckled around the purse strap. "Now say goodbye to your daddy, Neal."

"See you, dad," he forced out.

When the door shut behind them, the noise cracked through the air like a whip. Neal started at it and stumbled down the steps. His mom was walking towards the car without breaking stride, and when he hesitated, she slammed a palm on the horn.

He couldn't believe she'd done that. Said those things to him. He'd expected his dad to yell or maybe even hit her. This indifference weighed heavy in the air, swollen with something that felt almost like anticipation.

The Dairy Queen was familiar enough to settle him a little, and the two sat quietly beneath the fluorescent lights, eating their food together in silence. They lingered until the workers pointedly started to mop up and count the cash in the register, shooting them dirty looks until the pair were chased out.

The sweltering heat had persisted into night. Neal thought he would have been sweating regardless, though, with how goddamn sick he felt at the idea of going home. His knuckles were pulled white with how tight he gripped the seat on the drive back.

The house was near-dark, submersed in shadow and dwindling evening light. Gabriel was seated at the kitchen table, jaw pillowed on one hand while he seemed to examine something on the laminate top. As Neal drew further into the room, the object took on a more recognizable shape. Jesus God. It was a gun.

Neal stuttered to a halt and braced an arm out to stop Irena, who let out a soft gasp when she saw what had caught his attention. His dad said nothing. He just picked it up and cocked the hammer with casual ease.

"I told you I'd do this if you left."

Kill myself went unsaid. Irena lurched forward at that, and Neal had to practically grab his mom to hold her back. "I-I don't believe you," she hissed at him, voice cracking despite her outward composure.

Gabriel pressed the barrel to his temple. His mouth was slack, almost sad, but her flinch at the motion made his eyes glitter with hunger. They were so green. The same blue-green as his own.

"I'm serious," he said.

There was a moment when nobody moved or made a sound after that. They had each become statues, calcified in place, and the house was soundless apart from the cicadas outside and their own syncopated breathing.

"Don't expect me to tell you to stop," Irena said at last. "Do it. Do us all a fucking favor and just pull the trigger. Because I can't take it anymore. I'll die if I spend one more night in this place!"

His dad caressed the handle. "I asked myself what I did wrong and have no answers."

"*Answers?* You—"

"You're ungrateful. I don't understand it. I gave you a home, food, love. I gave you a son. I provided for you. And here you stand, looking at me like I locked you in a cage. You've made this here bed. It used to be enough for you."

"I've given you everything I have. You want more and more and I'm— I'm withered up now. There's nothing left."

He met her gaze evenly and pulled the trigger. Neal and Irena recoiled on instinct but heard only an impotent *click* as the cylinder rotated in the revolver.

"*Ah*," Gabriel remarked, steady, "no bullet. There's one in here somewhere. Guess I'll have to keep trying."

"You're crazy. You're fucking crazy," his mom said, nails biting into Neal's bicep. They were holding onto each other now.

It was different now. He could sense it somehow. Neal was too on edge to even move. His shirt was damp with sweat. He could taste its salt on his tongue.

It had never been like this before

His dad fixed Irena with a cold, unblinking stare. He stared and stared. It was laden with something impersonal, disappointed. There was nothing behind his gaze. Nothing at all. Emptiness.

Then he fired again, this time at her. Irena shrieked and jerked back, hands flying up to cover her face. But there was just noise. No shot, no blood. Fingers shaking, she lowered them and blinked over and over, whimpering.

"Gabriel," she moaned, "why?"

"I told you."

You're taking everything from me. That's what he'd meant, Neal realized. Them, his things.

That's why his mom called them "toys."

Neal tried to swallow but couldn't. Had his dad ever really cared about them? What about the flowers, the trips, their gifts? The lighter weighed heavy in his pocket. Didn't any of it mean something? Maybe there wasn't anything else. No hidden love or comfort to motivate him, no warmth in his blood.

"I've got four more shots," Gabriel said. "Someone's going to go tonight. It doesn't have to be me."

"Jesus Christ. You maniac. Oh, God. Neal. Neal, get out!" Irena yelled and shoved Neal to the side.

He heard the gun click two more times as he fell onto the coffee table, which buckled and splintered beneath him. His side lit up in pain, and it felt like the breath had been gut-punched out of him. He groaned and sat up, so disoriented that it took him a second to register the noise.

Gabriel had fisted a hand around his mom's throat, who was shrieking and scrabbling at his fingers. "I've tried to make this work," he said to her, almost gently. "I didn't even ask for much. But you and that kid just can't listen. The thing about it is that I've been so good to you. I made you my own."

Irena spat on his cheek, which got the first real reaction out of him that evening. His eyes lit up in anger, and he shook her. He walked her back towards the wall and slammed her back against it. He did it again and again until she could only gasp instead of scream.

"I didn't ask for much, did I?" Gabriel murmured, leaning in close and pressing a chaste kiss at the corner of her lip. When she didn't respond, he squeezed harder, and Irena jerked her chin in a nod.

"No," she said hoarsely, "you didn't."

"That's right, dear," he said.

He continued to squeeze.

She's going to die. God, she's going to die here. I have to—I have to do something. Neal managed to get his feet underneath him and crossed the room in two strides, unthinking, just an object in motion.

Neal tackled his dad and made a play for the revolver, but the older man was too strong. Even though he'd neared adulthood, Gabriel was still so much stronger than him. They wrestled with each other on the floor until Gabriel stomped on Neal's chest hard enough for him to go limp, then pistol-whipped him in the temple with the gun, finger catching on the trigger. It went off for real that time, right by his ear, and blew one of the windows out. Glass sprayed everywhere.

His dad hit him in the eye after, and it hurt so bad he cried. He tried not to, but he did. The wetness burned, and when his lid shuttered open there was now a weird glare that obscured his dad's furious expression.

This was it. This was how he was going to die. And the thing about it was he'd never realized how badly he wanted to live until that moment.

"Be a man for once," his dad spat in disgust. "I asked for so little. For a son I could respect, a wife who would listen. And I got neither, nothing."

"Dad—" He began but cut himself off.

In his periphery, Neal could see his mom's blurry figure approach the kitchen counter and pick the vase off it, then smash it across Gabriel's head. The pieces skittered across the floor, insect-like, until they collided with the wall and fragmented further. His dad collapsed onto the tile next to Neal, moaning, clutching at his hair.

Neal tried to stand up, get some distance between them, but staggered backwards and had to brace himself on the kitchen table or he'd wind back on the floor. His stomach turned, and he retched all over his front. It burned going up and out. When he placed a palm to his mouth, Neal could see blood mixed in with his bile and snot.

He still couldn't hear or see properly. His parents' voices were an echo, the house blurred and distorted. His mom's figure shifted, and he could see her raise her leg up, down, until his dad went quiet.

Irena moved towards him, cradled his face like a child. Her palms glistened wet and red after she withdrew. At first, she seemed to stare at them in horror until her expression grew flat, near empty.

"Neal," she breathed. "Baby."

He tried to embrace his mom but succeeded only in slumping onto her shoulder, chest hot and tight. "Is he... is he dead?"

"Maybe. I don't know."

"I don't know," sounded a lot like "I don't care." Neal wasn't sure whether he wanted it to be true or not.

They stood there, hanging onto each other, until Irena's chest stopped heaving and she'd calmed enough to stumble over to the phone and call the police. When she let go, he was overcome with a sense of loss he could not explain; that embrace they'd shared was the closest he'd ever felt to her.

"Poets are damned... but see with the eyes of angels," she murmured after abandoning the handset, nonsensically, then barked out a little manic laugh, to which Neal could say nothing in response.

Irena didn't touch him again, not even when the cops and the paramedics came and took them to the hospital. He couldn't bring himself to beg for comfort.

That night, while Neal was worked on in the intensive care unit, and his dad kept for observation, she left. Irena just left. The social workers told him that there was security footage of her walking towards the service entrance, where she disappeared out the door without once looking back. The next day, Gabriel was cleared and taken to the county jail. Neal never saw his mom again.

They'd tried to find her. It didn't matter. Irena got what she always wanted—a way out, the open road. Like her friends Sal and Dean. Neal didn't know if Irena had even carried that dream by the time she'd left, but he wanted the girl she had once been to return, be excavated from whomever it was he'd known. She'd cared enough to save him, but not enough to stay.

Hers was a life with no room for him.

Neal was sent to emergency foster care, then officially placed with a family outside Carthage while his dad's trial dragged on. He barely had any time to gather some clothes and lose the pigs long enough to bury the things that really meant something before they sent him away. There was this baseball field near the high school, a place that he and Reeve hung out at on occasion. He'd thought about using the bleachers, but the area around it would be too easy to disturb, even underneath.

Neal dug that hole with his bare hands, still bandaged and aching from the beating his dad had given him. He cut himself on the glass and ceramic shards, reopening them until his blood had mixed with the soil, gotten lodged beneath his nails.

In the box was everything he'd been back then: a broken watch, his mother's copies of *On the Road* and Ginsburg's "Howl," a picture of the three of them, posed in front of the double-wide with matching smiles—he'd scratched out his dad's face—and, finally, one polaroid of Reeve, leaning back with a book in hand while he regarded the camera coolly. It was the only one Neal had; he had none of them together because there had been no one to take it.

He went to the police station and let social services come pick him up, then stared, unseeing, while Carthage faded into so much country. They told him it was shock. Why he felt so dead, numb. One step removed from the shitshow that was his life. The thaw didn't come until he'd curled up in bed at the first foster home, leaving him with a swooping vertigo, destabilized, wondering how the hell things had gone so wrong.

He was crying so hard he couldn't catch his breath, dry-heaving and stomach churning with nausea. It was all so bleak he couldn't understand it. The fear, the pain, the loneliness seemed to descend on him; where before he'd been near-numb with shock, he now felt everything all at once. Neal twisted his fingers in his hair and pulled at it, eyes burning from his tears.

There was no going back. What little he'd had in his old life was lost to him. It made him feel like the most loveless person in the whole world, and he'd wake up with a singular plea in his throat, wondering, "How can I show you I'm worthy of your love?"

Maybe there was another Neal out there in some alternate universe, one that never knew what it meant to feel this way. He thought about what it would be like to live in that other world, be that other man, the one who was hand-fed love and comfort. But he was just himself. Neal knew only what it meant to live in this skin.

He went back to testify against his dad in the trial, and Gabriel wound up being sentenced to ten years, with parole eligibility for good behavior at eight. His dad spoke to him for the final time in the courtroom during the sentencing phase. His words held no apology, no substance.

Neal didn't know what he'd expected. People in movies and TV shows always seemed to feel some kind of relief or vindication when the bad guy got put away, but he got zilch out of it besides a reminder of Gabriel's unrelenting, unapologetic *meanness*.

He was left underwater and adrift. And when Neal cycled through the next few foster placements, everything that he struggled with before only seemed to get harder, not easier, despite not having Gabriel breathing down his neck. Eventually, Neal's grades got so bad he knew he wouldn't graduate or even qualify for a GED, so he skipped town instead. He hitchhiked around, hustling pool and rolling drunks for cash. Neal even did some under-the-table labor jobs when he could, glad for distraction and the money in his wallet.

He had next to nothing, drifting from place to place, unhappy no matter where he went. He'd thought things would be different. In many ways, they were the same.

Later, he'd touch the faint scars around his socket just to remind himself that it had all been real. Neal was sometimes overcome with the irrational notion that he'd fabricated the entire thing with his dad, mom, his own exodus from Carthage. Built it up in his head over the years until it became more than what it was.

Had it been so bad? He'd had a place to lay his head at night, warm meals in his belly more days than not, and best, those beautiful—interludes, he supposed—together. They felt so real. Realer than everything else. He'd provoked his dad, and his mom did, too. Maybe Gabriel had been right. If they had just tried harder, done what little was expected of them, then maybe they would still be a family.

These thoughts would twist in his chest, leaving him caught in the weird gradient between hate and loyalty. At least, that was, until he pressed a palm to his left eye. The blurred edges and dark splotches that would bloom under his ministrations reminded him who his dad really was.

The scars were proof that his pain had merit.

Ruth, Joseph—that's how family was supposed to act. He shouldn't have to be on edge, trying to anticipate when things would turn on a dime. He didn't deserve what had happened, but he'd be reminding himself of that for the rest of his life.

Ruth had taken his face between her hands one night after he'd confided in her while doing the dishes together. "Life is dark, but that doesn't mean it's hopeless," Ruth told Neal seriously, gripping him tight. "You have this—

this idea about yourself, about who you're supposed to be. There's more out there for you, Neal, I promise."

"Maybe one day you'll see yourself the way I do. The way your friend did."

Neal shifted beneath her kind gaze. "Maybe," was all he said.

But even their regard for him wasn't enough. Neal wanted to belong to somebody, and ever since he was a boy, he'd wanted that somebody to be Reeve. He'd been thinking about it for so long, and even in the abstract it proved torturous. And yet the reality was better than he'd ever imagined. He'd had no idea. It was so good. He'd fucked both men and women, but nothing compared to this.

What he felt for Reeve—the longing, resentment, desperation—was different. It was love. He'd always needed others more than they needed him, but Reeve had rose to match his want. No longer was love an idea or owed to other people, nor a just thing he could only observe through windows and glimpses as though it were a sought-after toy in a storefront; no, he could cup it between his hands.

Reeve's companionship was something whose value had taken him years to understand. He didn't know what he'd had until he'd lost it. Then it became just another thing out of reach, at least until—

He cut his eyes to the sleeping figure next to him. This is my lover, he thought. Mother Mary, his lover. Lover—the word lingered on his tongue, bittersweet and strange. It promised sensual destruction, rebirth, his personal apocalypse. He'd wanted him for so long that he didn't know any other way to be.

Neal cut his gaze back to *Prometheus in Exile.* While his copy languished in a drawer back at the motel, Reeve's was set atop the milk crate masquerading as his side-table. It was clearly well loved, with dog-ear indentations littered throughout and cramped notes scribbled in the margins.

Eliot was a supplicant, inverted shape on the cover, bathed in cyanotic shadow with his hands held out seemingly in prayer, from between which two voyeuristic slits were gouged into his skull in place of eyes. It was a sight that arrested the gaze and made him wonder, not for the first time, what Reeve saw in the book.

He idly flipped to a page near the end.

Isaiah's return had not gone unnoticed or unremarked upon. Night descended upon Scythe like a blow while men took up torches and rope in the street. Eudora's face was among them, pinched pale and solemn as she was carried along by their neighbors. Eliot watched from his porch, frozen in place, as the group approached the Bell House. Their hoods pierced the horizon like church spires, eyes ragged cutouts. Eliot wondered, then—who was the real spook?

Jude's voice was cold and clear. "You can come out, Isaiah," he shouted, "or we'll burn it all."

There was no response from inside. There was only one light on, and it was in the upstairs bedroom. Ezrah's bedroom. Jude repeated himself, this time echoed by the men and women at his side, but still received no answer. The silence was ominous, heavy.

Eliot was suffocated by panic. He couldn't do anything. There was nothing he could say to make them stop, go home, and let the Bells be. Neither could he get through by force. He was but one man, and they were many. This was what became of children born into the land of burning crosses and closed doors.

Such a cross was soon erected on the lawn, saturated in shimmering gasoline that was led towards the house in a glistening trail. When Jude struck the match, he didn't hesitate before tossing it, and the wood erupted into flames almost instantaneously. Eliot was shocked by how quick they cannibalized the cross, the grass, the first floor. The Bell House was soon silhouetted by smoke. But the light in the window did not waver.

He fell to his knees and uttered a wretched moan once the fire reached the second landing. No one emerged, and the snap-crackle of the blaze was the only sound for some time. Why, *he thought,* why won't you leave? Why won't any of you try and save yourselves? *But even if they managed to find an exit, where would they go? The lawn was ringed in white figures that spiraled out into the street.*

Three shots rang out, then, each with terrible finality. Eliot jerked back in horror, and even the townspeople seemed somewhat taken aback. But that was only an interlude; the jeers soon returned and escalated in volume.

By this time, the roof was enveloped in its entire, and embers floated into the velvet sky like despondent lightning bugs. Eliot watched with dread as the house slowly worked itself to ash. The air was thick with smoke and hate and grief. The burning cross remained fixed on the lawn like an unholy beacon.

Eliot stared up at the Bell House. There was still a light in the window. The light endured, even as the rest was consumed by flame and smoke. It was white hot, shimmering in the heat. A light that never went out.

Eliot stumbled back inside and uttered a low sob. Ezrah was dead, of that he was certain. All that remained were his words. The letter he'd refused to read because he'd been so furious with him for wanting to leave. Now he never would.

Eliot went upstairs to his study where he'd abandoned the envelope just the night prior. He clutched the paper in his hands. They couldn't seem to stop shaking. When he at last opened it, Eliot closed his eyes. He didn't know what the contents would mean.

But standing there, blind, he realized how stupid it was to think he could pretend. He was a coward. Ezrah had always been the brave one. Perhaps… it was finally time to join him.

Eliot,

We're leaving tomorrow. All of us—me, mom, and dad. My real dad, not Jude. We'll be going west to California. I think I'll be happy there. Them, too. Things should be better. Don't go worrying about me forgetting you, though. We're brothers. Blood. Your name is in my stars, and I hope mine is in yours.

I'll see you soon.

Yours,
Ezrah

The grief at these words was akin to a physical pain. His chest constricted. I'm not your brother, *he thought.* I'm… Don't you realize what I am to you? The depth of my regard? I suppose it doesn't matter anymore. We're nothing to each other now.

He could see indentations on the page and turned it over to see what else Ezrah had written. It was a poem, he realized.

Blue Interlude

I've oft wondered what a denouement
would feel like—
the pleasure-pain of climax, or
more akin to the cadence of decay, entropy?
Yes, that's the word.
Entropy:
the point where all things begin to unwind.

I am familiar with loose threads,
their twisted ends,
unpleasant feelings and bitter regard.
This is the time the magpie comes home to roost.

I wonder what will become of us:
her—the asphalt queen,
on her knees, her back, cleaved open for public use.
I imagine his oil-slick heel stroke her pulse;
mother licks his boot and rejoices.

Him—
the coldest god I've ever known,
and we his acolytes, supplicants at the fetish-wrapped
altar of his being.
The beseeching banshee-moans we utter
are prayers sent unto Nyx
so the night may grant guidance, humility to
those yoked to
this man, the head, with
the shrapnel mouth and voyeur's liquid heat gaze,
who seeks naught but possession.

He is addicted to the lash.
Perhaps she is, too,

and the once most hated thing
now becomes whatever paradise
one could envision as
his counterfeit reach outstretches and envelops
like a shadow would the sunset
or the flame its candle.

The exhibition is final, the ringmaster says,
a consensual murder-suicide!
The given tickets are finger-traps wrought from
used rubbers and Tijuana bibles and thick, porous grave dirt.
My nails are caked in it.

Myself—
I atrophy to the low, slow tumble
of my lover's prized record, *Saxophone Colossus,*
which buzzes through my head in exquisite revolutions
as I lay alone in bed dusk after dusk.
This apathy, it withers me,
allayed by scraps secreted through
cracked windows, doggy doors, slantwise spaces,
but such glimpses are far from euphoria
as I am learned longing; the difference between have and have-not,
love-paupers and kings.

I wish I could call this courtship
an intimate mystery,
but its ways are known to me—
how easy the descent is into terminal rhythm.
I will thus compose an aubade for the addicts,
and another for their impending overdose.

I give it a name:
Blue Interlude—
the recurrent lapse between the splinter and the baptism,
brief home to uneasy bliss,

where lovers desperate to sustain themselves seek respite
and recover salt when it comes time to turn.

As for I, the unwilling passenger,
jazz and exile are my accompaniments to this
byzantine spiral, uninterrupted
as still
no one comes to knock.

If Eliot were a dreaming man, then he sought to picture Ezrah elsewhere. In a beautiful place. A landscape to inspire the mind. His parents would live nearby in wedded bliss. Somewhere, he thought. Somewhere in California.

He figured that world may be as real as his own. Because he'd come to understand one thing about this life in the past day—it was unpredictable. This was a blood lesson.

Eliot clutched at the paper and let himself turn over one thought, one idea that was at once both alien and familiar.

Everything is immaterial.

REEVE VI

REJOICE, FOR HE HAS COME TO SAVE YOU FROM THE END. SEE
REVEREND AARON GOULD LIVE IN CARTHAGE: 11/22/92. The man of
the hour's round, insincere face smiled down at Reeve and the rest of the
townspeople that had gathered that day to see him from his station on the
billboard.

Reeve's mouth flatlined in distaste.

The large sign mounted outside the fairgrounds was crisscrossed by red
tape that bluntly stated, "SOLD OUT." Reeve leaned back on his heels to
look at the tent they had erected for the occasion up and down. If the preacher
and his lady were so intent on circle-jerking it to their own magnificence,
then he figured white was the appropriate color.

Reeve's ticket had just been acquired and now lay crumpled in his pocket
to be checked by the two moon-faced teenagers out front that bore an
uncanny resemblance to Gould. He'd come alone with the expectation that
Neal and Maze would meet him there. He didn't have to wait long.

Neal stepped up from behind Reeve and gripped his shoulder. He was
beautiful in the sunset, smiling wide and bright. Men didn't usually like to
be called beautiful, Reeve thought, in a rare moment of insight. However,
what other word could so perfectly encapsulate everything Neal was?

"Hey there, losers," a girl's voice called out from the crowd.

Maze still looked as though she had seen better days, bruised and swollen,
but Reeve could tell she had pulled herself together as best she could. Her
hair had been braided back from her face in two twists, exposing her broad
forehead and the jagged, dark streaks of liner that angled upward from her
eyes like war paint; likewise, her painted mouth was set in a grim, sarcastic
line.

Maze's mom—Jessica, he recalled—examined both him and Neal with
extreme distaste as they entered and took their seats. He supposed he
couldn't blame her. They were two adult men whom her daughter had

befriended against her express wishes and were now intruders in her place of worship. Their respective reputations in the town canon weren't even worth mentioning.

The older woman said nothing to them, merely sighed at Maze and then gestured for them to follow her inside, where people had begun to slowly filter in. He, Maze, and Neal conversed for a moment before following. He recognized most faces and noted their apparent confusion as to why he had come. Reeve hadn't set foot in a church since his mom left.

Zebadiah and Heddie were there too, as expected. The other man's gaze lingered on him, acidic, and Reeve met it with equal intensity. It was only Neal's hand on his shoulder that made him break contact and turn away, allowing himself to be led to a row nearer to the back of the tent.

"This is awkward," Neal said, knocking shoulders with him as they sat down.

"Yes," Reeve agreed, eliciting a fond grin from his friend.

"Guess we gotta make the best of things, then," Neal said, "considering we're committed to staying and all."

Reeve nodded but found he had little to say. In the interim, Neal began conversing with Maze, heads ducked low together, and whatever they said to each other caused the pinched expression on Jessica's face to deepen.

Any other day, he was sure this event would have proven to be an exercise in boredom, but the Condors kept him occupied even when the spectacle proved to be less than spectacular. There was a weird tension between them, a low thrum, buzzing just beneath the surface; it was strange—they should have been elated to be here, not looking like they were ready to bolt at the soonest convenience.

Huh.

Anticipation, he realized. Theirs was an atmosphere of anticipation. And it couldn't be for Gould, this event, or what might transpire later in the evening—no, that wasn't it, not when their attention was directed at the watches wrapped around their wrists, the half-open tent entrance.

His reaction was both visceral and inexorable; Neal's presence at his side could not quell his interest, nor Maze's sardonic commentary, and so his eyes remained riveted on the couple throughout Gould's introduction.

As for the man in question, Reeve was unimpressed and paid him little mind. Aaron Gould was everything he'd come to expect after Maze's stories:

an unpleasant, self-important grifter who excelled solely at sleight of hand. His motives held little interest for Reeve, despite how much he seemed to at once vex or beguile everyone around him.

"Mass is a lot nicer than this," Neal whispered when he leaned over. "You always know what to do and how long it'll take."

Despite Neal's defenses, Catholic Mass did not appeal to Reeve in the least. He knew he could probably be convinced by Neal to attend in the same manner he'd been convinced to attend this farce.

This close, he could smell the deep, heady scent Neal's cologne carried. It was smoke and spice; it was tobacco and vanilla. He glistened with a faint sheen of sweat. Distantly, Reeve realized he was going to get hard if he pursued this line of thinking.

How novel. For the vast majority of his life, he'd been indifferent to self-pleasure. It served only as a function of the human body, a momentary distraction. He'd rejected his own capacity for enjoyment in all things. Now he knew what he was missing out on, and the experience had awoken some slumbering beast inside him. He was more aware of his body and its proximity to others than he could ever remember feeling before.

Zebadiah and his wife were two additional presences he was attuned to, albeit for very different reasons. He continued tracking them from the corner of his eye. They were growing agitated, checking their watches and muttering to each other when there was a rise in Gould's volume or the crowd bursting spontaneously into song. Eventually, these interactions culminated in the pair begging leave, navigating back through the crowd and out the door.

Reeve couldn't explain why, exactly, he felt compelled to investigate, but knew there was something about their exit that didn't sit right with him. They were supposed to be pious. "Supposed" being the operative word, of course.

Not following them out was excruciating; however, Reeve had promised this time to Maze, and the thought of separating himself from Neal for their company repulsed him. He sat back in his seat and compulsively picked at his nails, watching Gould's spectacle but looking through him. Eventually, though, his restraint broke.

He stood up. "I have to go."

"What? Reeve, you promised you'd be here for me," Maze hissed at him under her breath. Her mother was still fanning herself, feigning obliviousness.

"Neal will stay," he said, then set a hand on her shoulder. "And I'll be back soon."

Maze appeared shocked at the voluntary contact, the gesture, and so too did Neal, who turned to the girl and said with a smile, "Don't worry, I'm in for the night." He lowered his voice, and said a little conspiratorially, "Bring on the circus."

This seemed to appease her for now, so he twisted away from the group, only to feel a hand close around his wrist. It was Neal, he saw when he looked back, and the other man had nervous slant to his mouth.

"Watch yourself, Red—whatever it is you're doing."

"Enjoy the show," was all Reeve said before drifting through the tent, through the opening, and into the outside world.

The good weather from before had dissipated. It was a dusty evening, cold, with an ugly sky saturated in thick clouds. Still, the Laguna glittered invitingly in the low light. He couldn't spot their truck; they must have already left. Where would they go?

Reeve turned around in a circle, inspecting the comings and goings around the lot, searching for a glimpse as to their direction. He was momentarily paralyzed with indecision before settling on the most obvious choice: home.

Sliding into the driver's seat, he cut a clear path back to his neighborhood, all the while burning with instinct. The closer he got, the longer the Condors were away, the more ominous the atmosphere became. And when he got there, it was worse than he could have ever imagined.

His trailer wallowed in black smoke. His neighbors' home had met a similar fate, though it appeared to be further along than his own. He could still see the word "FAG" on the façade, even through the thick gray and black clouds billowing out.

Reeve felt something constrict in his chest, then break. His dad's things were in there; so were his own. Every careful arrangement of records, newspapers, VHS tapes, all of it, was going to burn. The Cale Yarborough poster was soon to be ash. How much, if anything, could be saved was likely negligible. He looked at the remnants of his own home, slowly being worked to pieces at his feet, and was struck by a feeling he could not quite name.

His breath guttered in, out.

Heddie and her kids were gathered outside, wet-eyed and dusted in soot. Her ankle was fixed at an odd angle. He could hear their dogs, still chained, barking in the distance. They had been left to burn alive. His own strays, being cats, had been smart enough to flee when the fire took over. Selene, the black tabby, wound herself through his legs.

"Please," Heddie called out when she noticed Reeve's approach, "God, please. You gotta help him! He's in there!" She pointed at Reeve's trailer; her voice was hoarse from smoke inhalation.

Ah, he thought. There could be only one *him.* Zebadiah was the one who'd done this. It was no surprise, really. And yet Heddie had the nerve to ask him for aid.

"Why?"

"'Cause it's the right thing to do."

How was it that he was expected to be the better man here and now? No one else seemed to have risen to the occasion. Not her, not anyone nearby either. Wasn't he born under a bad sign? The man who murdered his own twin. He'd been convicted of fratricide without a trial. Never before had he been given the benefit of the doubt. Never before had he been given a second chance. Never before had he gotten anything more than scraps. At least until someone needed something from him.

"I get you're angry, but—"

"I'm not angry. I'm not anything."

"I don't believe you. But please, do something. My husband's gonna die; their daddy's gonna die!"

He turned away from Heddie, who had now begun to sob in earnest, Reeve wondered who had really died that day? Him, or Ephraim? He wasn't sure.

"God, please! Please!"

Now the woman was tugging and pulling at him, the fag who was previously so low, so disgusting that he'd required a lesson from her, from her husband. But fortune had shifted since then, and the pair needed to be rescued from a mess of their own making. Reeve brushed her off.

He thought back to Hoyt's sniveling face, how small he'd seemed in that moment, and saw that same weakness in Zebadiah now. He just put on a better show.

These people—Zebadiah, Hoyt, Heddie—they were the debased ones. Not him, and certainly not Neal. Stooping so low when he'd done nothing to deserve this. Any of it. Not the insults or the beating or the fire blazing around him. They were worms.

Heddie's moans reached dog-whistle level.

It was not morality or compassion that ultimately moved Reeve to action. Interest was probably more accurate. Interest in seeing what had become of Zebadiah. He approached his trailer with measured, easy steps, felt the intimate heat. Was the other man still alive, trapped and burning? Or was he simply reveling in the destruction of all that Reeve owned? Either way, it would serve him well to know.

The front door was ajar, and Reeve ducked inside, met by heavy smoke and flame. The origin was concentrated deeper within the trailer, so it was safer to navigate this section. The towering stacks were almost labyrinthine in this context, but it was nonetheless the place he'd lived for nearly his entire life, so his feet retread the familiar path, its jagged grooves and eddies, until he approached the moaning and grunting noises within. It was the part of his living area where he and Neal had danced earlier.

Zebadiah was squirming and gasping on the floor, torso mangled by the capsized section of the hoard that had collapsed atop him. The grind of bone against bone was coupled with the lick of flame. He ceased movement when he realized he wasn't alone, fixating now on Reeve's form.

"Thank God," he cried out. "Get me outta here! Jesus, God, I'm dying!'"

Reeve felt no urgency. He merely stood there, staring down at the man who'd defaced his home and beat him about the face and chest not two days ago. His things continued to burn.

Zebadiah gaped up at him. "Are you just going to stand there?"

Reeve surprised himself by saying, "Yes." He didn't even realize he'd decided to do nothing until that very moment.

The other man's eyes went wide, bulbous, and he could see a very real glint of fear in them. He'd expected more from him. Why, he wondered. Zebadiah thought him to be a sick freak and a killer—what psycho would go out of their way to save anyone, let alone someone who'd tormented them?

"Do you know what it is to be terrorized?" Reeve asked calmly. He thought about how best to put that hovering, omnipresent fear into words. It seemed almost unable to inhabit sentences. Zebadiah's mouth hung open like a fish. Reeve's anger at the man's disbelief compounded. "I do. I know it well."

"What the hell d'you want me to say, huh? Sorry? Is now really the fucking time?"

Reeve appraised him coolly in response. Zebadiah squirmed under his gaze, face red and glazed with sweat. He panted, contorting his torso to try and extricate himself. It wasn't working.

Eventually, he cracked. "Jesus Christ! Fine! I'm sorry I kicked your ass and graffitied your place, man. Now get me the hell outta here. I don't wanna die!" Zebadiah shouted.

"I reckon you expect me to be ashamed," Reeve said by way of reply, "but I'm not. You can't make me feel that way. You have no power."

"It's not too late," the other man pleaded. "You can still do the right thing."

"Yes, it is."

It had been too late from the moment Zebadiah threw his brother's death in his face. From the moment his boot left an imprint on his throat. From the moment the slur appeared on his house, and the moment he said those horrible things to Neal, it was too late.

Whatever that thing was, the thing that made a person value human life, it was gone. Reeve knew it was wrong; he simply didn't care.

"You can't leave. You can't! You gotta help me. I can't die in here like this," Zebadiah hissed out. He jerked and thrashed against the numerous objects piled atop him.

"And why's that?"

Zebadiah looked like the question hadn't even occurred to him. He'd operated under the assumption that Reeve would be the better man; he was mistaken.

"Your children are outside. I saw them crying. Your wife, too. Maybe she knows why you're in here. But *they* don't, and I hope they never do."

"Don't they deserve a dad?"

How many people wondered what they'd done to warrant the parents they had? Neal and Maze did, that was certain, and who was to say Zebadiah's kids wouldn't feel the same way one day. It could be that he'd be doing them a favor.

"You did this to them," Reeve said.

"You'll go to hell for this," Zebadiah spat, voice hoarse and sclera bloodshot from the smoke. He'd seemingly caught a last-minute second wind. "You're going to fucking hell, Scarlet! What's gotten into you, huh? Ain't you supposed to be innocent or something? Better?"

Reeve could have laughed. *And here I thought I was headed there anyways,* he thought wryly. *Guess we'll be seeing each other again.*

"I've lost my fucking mind, that's what," he informed the other man with an inflection that almost bordered on gleeful, the tone a foreign shape in his mouth. It seemed like something either Neal or Maze would say.

Then he retreated and watched as the flames ate at Zebadiah's face, his skin splitting open like overcooked meat. He continued to scream, rough and desperate, as he was consumed by the same fire he'd created. It was neither quick nor silent. Reeve felt nothing; he was no more or less moved by this sight than he was by an overcast day or a scuffed bootheel. *Oh, well, that's that.*

He watched the fire grow, evolve, its movements rhapsodic as the smoke thickened inside. Soon, he couldn't see the other man at all, and those *tht-tht-tht* sounds he made were subsumed into the snap-crackle of flames and the haunting, siren-like crooning of the record player, the 45 still spinning, warbling darkly out into the night air. The blues were beautiful in death.

The smoke in his lungs was a revelation, and Reeve emerged from the burning remnants backlit by an orange haze. His hands were clenched into fists, and he felt grime between his lips. *Ashes,* he thought. *Human ashes.* There was bone meal in the smoke, and in the softly descending embers, as though a massive urn had been overturned onto the lawn.

He thought, at last, he understood why this kind of movement appealed to people. It was in the energy, the outward projection. Reeve felt himself pulled into a shuffle as he exited, feet casting circles on the carpet, pavement, and then dirt. It was almost as though the music he and Neal had danced to earlier had never ended, and that it followed him out rather than into the flames. The real music, though, was the B-Side of the '45 that had been left on earlier—Screamin' Jay Hawkins' "Little Demon."

Reeve's head rolled in time with the beat. There was something wired wrong in his brain, something that couldn't be untangled or rearranged, only coped with. He could live, or he could wither. At least being in pain could be erotic, the antithesis to apathy; it meant he could still feel. The emptiness inside him no longer felt like hunger or longing. No, it was freedom.

He pulled out his pack of cigarettes and lit one.

This feeling, these compulsions—they were the closest thing he'd ever had to a God, he supposed. Everyone had something or someone that ruled them, and maybe this was it for him. And Neal was as much a part of it all as he was.

It was done; all was dust, shadows. And Reeve didn't have it in him to feel bad. Maybe Heddie was crying, and maybe her kids were, too. The woman collapsed when she saw he was alone, hands clutched to her face as she sobbed. The children were wet-cheeked and wide-eyed. Why she spared tears for a man who'd brought nothing but obligation and pain into her life, Reeve couldn't begin to guess. It was another human mystery.

People wrote about the world like it was beautiful. But blood was just blood. Red was no more than red. And death was neither dramatic nor peaceful—it was nothing. An end to the pain, maybe. Zebadiah learned that lesson tonight.

He knew he should have felt scared, maybe, or guilt-ridden, but he didn't feel any different than he had before. A little happier, he thought, now that a problem in his life had been removed. This feeling, this openness—it was as destructive as it was purifying, glittering like blood, like dawn, and the light and heat from the pyre was a comfort to him.

Neal saw a person who was no longer really there. He'd searched for that boy in himself and found only echoes. The Reeve who'd shed tears over that poor, whimpering mutt was dead. The door he'd opened when he walked into the trailer tonight was one he couldn't close.

There was no dignity for people in death or pain. It was ignominious. Pathetic. He'd seen it firsthand. He recalled what Ephraim had told him so long ago, that everyone was just piss and shit and mud. That nobody was better than anyone else because animals would never be more than just that— animals.

The town then became little more than a backdrop to this arson, which to him had devolved into something new, dark, and important on a level that extended beyond his own possessions. But how could anyone know? Their attention was elsewhere: their visitor; their husbands, wives, children; their lives' little intricacies. Reeve had never empathized with such things before, never known what it was like to be so entangled in another that they became an obstruction to the senses.

It was like he'd risen from his own dark age.

Neal's figure appeared in the distance, followed soon by Maze. They had seen the smoke, he supposed, and had left the encampment to investigate what was happening.

He heard the incoming sirens, the flames behind him, and the shrill crescendo harmonized by Heddie, her children, and her dogs' screams. Yet they were soon enclosed by the fade, by Neal's arrival, and he could think only about how humanistically beautiful the other man was. The fondness he felt for the other then was intense, and emerged, unbidden, from somewhere deep in his chest.

And suddenly, there were police and firemen everywhere, converging on the two burning trailers, comforting and then cuffing Heddie after she sobbed out what she had done—"God, Jesus. We burned them. We burned them! We just wanted the insurance payout!"—while Reeve remained where he was, pleasantly warm and satisfied, greeted soon by Neal and, later, Maze, whose steady, gray-eyed gaze followed him keenly.

Familiar arms encased him. He turned his head into Neal's neck, let Maze dig her fingernails into his shirt collar. There was desperation and relief and care laden in these motions, encompassing him.

He knew this wasn't love, not yet, but it was close. And maybe even someday soon, he would feel all that Neal felt. It would unfurl, he thought, within him, like light, liberating and beautiful in its truth—an end to ignorance. *I want to be your blood. The food you eat. The air in your lungs.*

It became obvious, then, the difference between Neal being here and Neal being gone. Reeve breathed air. He woke each morning. But he did not live.

He felt as though he were hurtling towards something final, an end, maybe not to this life or him, but to his time here.

Turning to Neal, he let himself lean into his body. Their eyes caught, and the other man's vaporized iris had become a galaxy in this light. He was more beautiful for having been broken, Reeve thought. He was better now than he had been before. They belonged to each other.

He tucked his head into Neal's collar; to anyone looking at them, it may have appeared to be one man just comforting another, or so he hoped. But when Reeve closed his eyes, everything was blue, blue, blue.

MAZE VI

The good weather felt like an insult.

Maze slit her eyes against the sunset. The sky was as sheer and gauzy overhead, smeared with orange-hued cirrus clouds that seemed to regard the procession of people into the tent with mild benevolence. *It figures,* she thought sourly.

At least she came equipped for the occasion. Maze was armored in one of her dad's old plaid button-ups, a purple t-shirt, and ragged jeans. Her parka was tucked under her arm in case the temperature turned again, and a pair of tiny sunglasses were slung low on the bridge of her nose, showing off the twin shiners Lee had given her. When she adjusted them, her splint glinted in the early evening light.

"Are you really wearing that?" Jessica had asked her when they left the house, giving the outfit in question a perturbed once-over.

"Mm. I think it shows how badly I need to be saved."

Her mom said nothing to that in response; she just made a soft, exhausted sound and handed Maze the station wagon's keys.

Gould's team had set up in an abandoned industrial space just outside of town. It had been used as fairgrounds once upon a time, Maze recalled, before the EPA began sniffing around and taking samples. Loose dirt caught on the air, skittering across the pockmarked earth and colliding with people, cars, and the tent itself.

There was now a massive white monolith dominating the area. It towered among even the chat mounds—a grand edifice to Gould's ego, she thought. *Edifice.* It was a word they had learned in English earlier that week. Little Miss Kelly would be ecstatic to learn that something she taught them had been useful for once.

People she recognized from school and work were there, too, milling about outside while they waited in line to get in. There were others she didn't know. Maybe from Maidenhead or another nearby town that was full up with good little boys and girls who had nothing better to do.

Louisa from Stats class was huddled close to a guy she'd hooked up with at the party. Heddie and her weird, white trash husband were tailgating with some familiar faces she recognized from her mom's meetings. Three of her coworkers from the Burger Barn sat chain smoking beside their cars. Dean laughed at something his sister said.

Maze tried not to look at him.

The crowd shifted, and that's when she saw him again: Lee. He stood stooped beside his mom and dad, head bandaged in gauze. His face was swollen, mottled skin stark against the familiar red of his oversized Carthage Lions hoodie. Maze went *huh* to herself at this. That night, he'd been otherworldly, violent—like a man. Here, in this moment, he looked… normal. No more than a boy who'd lost a fight. And pretty badly, at that. It was somehow worse than if he'd turned out just as big a boogeyman as she'd made him out to be.

Lee seemed to notice her then, and the reaction was visceral and immediate. He stiffened and glared at her, cheeks purpling with rage. *There you go*, she thought, *look at me*. If he expected her to back down, he'd been mistaken. Maze held his gaze and bared her teeth at him.

Do you remember what you did to Cricket? What you tried to do to me? More than that, do you remember what I did to you?

Maze shaped her fingers into a gun and pointed to her temple; it was the same spot where she'd beaten him over the head with the towel rod. The splint dug into her skin as she mimed shooting one, two, three times. Enough for him to get the picture. *Don't fuck with me or mine.* Lee went pale and averted his eyes. The way he melted into his parents' embrace and disappeared into the crowd said everything she needed to know.

Message received.

Then she saw the two people she actually wanted to spend time with and called out, "Hey, losers."

"Hey, kid," Neal said.

"Neal, Reeve—you really came," she exclaimed, smiling for the first time that day. Maze hadn't understood how much she needed them here until that moment.

Neal cut his usual handsome figure, well-attired and hair slicked back. Even his cologne smelled expensive. It was deep and spiced. The kind of cologne that made regular guys strut around thinking they had even half his looks.

For his part, Reeve appeared awkward and bored. Maze shared the sentiment. Neal was the anomaly among them, this bright, shining star with whom they both occasionally shared the privilege of spending time with. They, at least, were similarly underdressed, roughed up, and known for being two damn unpleasant individuals.

This close, she could tell there was something dark speckled on his overcoat's lapel. Blood, maybe. He either took no notice or didn't care. Maze wanted to reach out to him, smooth the wrinkles in his shirt, wipe at the stains; it was very motherly. She thought back to when she'd first knocked on his door, about how spooky he'd seemed to her—how cold. The warning she'd given Neal that night out by the Burger Barn. But somehow, for whatever reason, she couldn't imagine him doing anything to hurt her, not ever, at least not intentionally. Maze thought that even if she did paw at him, her strange friend would stand there and accept the gesture for the misplaced kindness that it was.

Life was funny like that.

Jessica coughed. Her mom had moved between the pair and her, regarding the two men with something heavy and disapproving in her gaze.

Off-key instrumentation and gospel song began to emanate from within the tent, and Maze realized they were some of the last still outside. Only the smokers in the lot remained, and she lingered behind the others long enough to make a rude parting gesture at them. The resulting heckling followed her to the entrance where Jessica stood waiting.

"It's time," her mom said.

"I know."

The inside was no better. The crowd swelled and constricted like a beating heart. Their chorus didn't quite line up, words spilling over each other and the music until everything became more feeling than meaning. They had to push people around to get seats, and even then, it was only the relative height of their group that let them navigate the crowd.

When Gould materialized on stage, she'd expected to feel that same presence that had oozed through her TV screen. Real life was different. He was fat, stuttering, and his voice wheezed in and out as he spoke. The contrast between him and his stick-like, angular wife was made even more apparent in person. Maze's eyes tracked them across the dais; back-and-forth, back-and-forth. It was so performative, she thought, and the little cracks in their specialness showed every time the wife uttered another canned laugh or gasp at something Gould said.

Her mom leaned over, breath hot on her neck. "Do you see now, what I meant?" Jessica asked.

"No, I don't."

"Is it… is it really so bad if this brings folks some peace in this life?" *Even if it's a lie?*

Maze didn't respond, and instead let her attention drift towards the other members of their group. In the heat, the wild thrashing and moaning audience, Maze hadn't noticed anyone slip in or out. But Reeve did, apparently, because when she turned towards him, she found the man staring hard at the vacant space that had only just earlier been occupied by his neighbors. He murmured an apology to her and gave Neal a look that he apparently interpreted as significant.

"Good riddance," muttered Jessica.

"Shut it," Neal told her without even so much glancing her way. Maze punched him in the shoulder for speaking to her mom like that, though she privately agreed.

Maze made herself relax back in her seat and let everything wash over her—the voices, the hymns, the swaying—but the longer she sat there, the more unmoored she felt. Her splint dug into her thigh where she gripped it tight. What did this mean? Her mom's point about it not being so bad was one she didn't even bother turning over.

Maze smoldered with discontent, searching within herself for that surety from before, or something like it, and found only an echo. It was enough, she decided. If she knew anything, it was endurance.

I can be grateful, she thought. *And I am. I'm here, aren't I? What's more grateful than that?*

It was laid out before her: the tent's suffocating white folds and arches, the smooth wooden panels beneath Gould's feet, and the congregation's asynchronous voices. Perfect, full of devotion. But at the same time, she saw the sweat beading on foreheads, the loose dust skipping across the ground, and the stink of desperation in the air. Maze had thought them indomitable. An unsympathetic, featureless monolith.

They, this, everything; it had all been built up as a puzzle she couldn't hope to solve. Now that she was here, it was obvious. Desperation, she thought. What they shared was desperation. Desperation for money, community, salvation. They were here because they needed something. And Gould was just a man. No different than those here with him, except he believed instead in the dogma of greed.

Her mistake had been assuming they were rational. That people were rational. They weren't. They were vulnerable, emotional, and selfish. Everything that overrode reason when things got tough or dark. It was the world's cosmic order or something.

Maze swallowed thickly. *They think we live in a world of heroes and martyrs. But there's just us. What we hold in our hands.*

It was funny, in a way; she'd been just as blind to Waylon's faults as her mom was to Reverend Gould's. They both sought to see the best in the men who had given them something to.

Only in hindsight did this feel less like insight and more like a hand wrapped around her throat. They had seen what they'd wanted to see. For Maze, that was love. Her mother, someone who'd promised answers and a denouement to her grief. Two different types of liars. But standing there, surrounded by hostile faces, Maze realized it was pointless.

The events of the past two weeks suddenly seemed to weigh on her all at once. Maze was suddenly and intensely exhausted. She'd been swimming upstream against a current; the town's reality—no growth, only death, stagnation. The material world. Like a current, it was inexorable.

Her eyes skated over her mom and onto Neal. He jerked his head to the exit as if in question, and she nodded. Maze stood up, and he rose to join her.

Her mom's voice was the first to rise in the resulting unrest. "You promised," she said.

"Yeah, and I'm sorry, but I've had just about all I can handle of this," Maze said, holding out her hand for the final time. *Let's get out of here. Leave, and never come back. I need you to say yes. I need you to choose me. I need to be needed.*

Jessica regarded the outstretched hand with a conflicted expression. Her eyes—the same gray as Maze's own—darted around the tent, over the offended faces, and then back to her. Maze could see something waver in Jessica. For a moment, she recognized her mom for the first time since her dad died. Her sadness, her open vulnerability.

It was this look that made Maze deflate. The anger and resentment that had been building over the past six months seemed to seep out, leaving her with nothing but a wrung-out ache in her chest. It was pity, she realized. Pity that it had come to this.

"Please," she said.

Jessica's fingers twitched. Her mouth moved around a truncated inhalation, tongue darting out to wet her lips. There would be no coming back from this. Not for her or her friends in this space. Then she accepted the gesture.

Neal watched them with an unreadable look and began to move towards the back. The derision ascended in volume, sibilant, and as the three approached the exit, Gould's cut through it at last.

"It doesn't matter who you are, or where you've been, because you're here now," he said to them in a grand fashion. "You're here now, and there's still time to turn back. Let me be your eyes." His bloated face and bulbous, ravenous gaze stood out starkly, pinpricks of color amidst the white.

Maze opened her mouth to say something, spit out what she really thought, act like the bitch everyone knew her to be.

Y'know why this isn't working? Because you're just a man. And men die. They fail. They're flawed. If you really had this—connection, something would have happened by now. It'd be happening all the time. You'd be blessing people whenever you could. But this is fake. You're a phony. A big damn fucking phony. So, you say we're being tested. That we need to have faith. That's a non-answer if I've ever heard one. It just means you don't gotta do anything except stand there and run your mouth.

Everyone here will believe whatever you say. They're so desperate for answers, and to have this power greater than themselves touch their lives, that it doesn't matter how delusional you sound. It's like playing the lottery— sad, empty people will buy into it just on the off-chance they'll win. You've got the winning ticket, and you know it.

Then she saw the expression he wore and noticed how similar it was to Waylon's. They both shared the same hunger. Gould was waiting for her to retaliate, she realized. He wanted her to rise to his bait. Maze unclenched her hands, took a deep breath, and counted to ten like all those damn self-help books always told her to do.

I'm denying you, she thought. *I'm denying you my pain, my anger. You don't get to have this from me.*

So, she said nothing. Even as the strange cries from the audience grew louder, and Gould's skin mottled with frustration, and his voice shrieked and arced over the congregation, she remained impassive throughout. After she'd had her fill, all Maze did was smile at him. It was the patented "Bless your heart" smile reserved for every idiot living south of the Mason-Dixon Line. Lips still pulled back, she turned on her heel to continue towards the exit.

By the time she, Jessica, and Neal had reached the end row of the folding chairs, the noise had well and truly become a cacophony.

"You come to this place of worship and spurn salvation?" Gould hissed out through his teeth, expanding outward with anger. "The devil has made a home in you, girl. That much is clear."

"I'd like to see you try," Maze called back, feeling wild. "Do it. Use your powers, your connection—whatever this is supposed to be—and make me obey you. Prove yourself!"

"Heathen! Nonbeliever! Whore! Who are you to tell me what to do?" Gould retorted. "And if I truly am the liar you say, may God strike me down where I stand. Now, I—"

Before he could finish speaking, Maze felt the dirt shift beneath her feet. There was a weird, echoing rumble that resonated throughout the tent, audible even beyond the stomping and yelling.

Suddenly, she remembered the warnings issued by the EPA about the soil's instability in this area, as well as the sinkholes that had been popping up in town the past few years.

Maze reacted without thinking, grabbing her mom by the wrist and dragging her towards the exit even as the woman screamed and thrashed in her arms. Ahead of them, Neal saw this and doubled back to meet her halfway, hoisting Jessica up into a firemen's carry as the ground around the stage continued its collapse. Heart in throat, eyes flooded by sweat, she extended her legs farther and ran faster, faster, until she emerged alongside Neal and her mom in a cloud of noxious dust.

Behind them, the tent began to pitch inward, destabilized, and even seemed to teeter for a moment before its final and momentous sprawl. Maze hacked out a full-body wheeze and trembled from the aborted adrenaline rush. It was just like the party, this feeling, the initial uptick in vertigo and then the sick exhalation that released her pain out into the world.

Fucking hell. The tent was literally sinking into the ground like a mouth to their Christian hell had opened.

When her feet trusted the gravel beneath her long enough to move, she twisted to seek out where Neal and Jessica had gone. It took less than a second to locate them, huddled together a few yards away, her mom's dark head tucked into Neal's shoulder. But he wasn't even looking at her, or the people still clawing their way free from the smothering white folds, or those fleeing the wreckage; rather, his gaze was directed towards the horizon, which was seething with smoke.

The source had to be on the other side of town, far from the main drag and the highway, near the trailer homes. The realization hit her with full force.

"Oh, hell," she said to herself, dumb with shock, "that's gotta be Reeve's place." Then again, stronger now, "That—that's Reeve's place!"

And he'd left early, hadn't he? To trail after that white trash couple who'd been making their lives a living hell. The two being related seemed at first too out there for her, but then she recalled Heddie's knowing smile, and Zebadiah's composure, at last unmade. The "FAG" on the trailer's front door, red like the blood from a torn scab. Her friend's bruises, wounds. No, she realized, it was as possible as the massive fucking sinkhole within spitting distance of her.

The prospect turned her stomach at once, and she staggered towards Neal, extricating her mom from his arms. "We need to roll, old man. Now."

His face did something complicated at that, and he glanced back at the tent. Maze, for her part, felt her sympathy be sublimated by the greater urge to pile Neal and Jessica into her station wagon and peel out, leaving everything as it was to instead go and see whether Reeve, her actual friend, needed them. But when she made to move further in the direction of the parked cars, the woman pushed at her and uttered a shriek. It was a sound that spoke to mindless, impotent terror. The animal cry a doe would make when caught in a predator's hold.

Maze reared back and tried to wrest her mom back into her arms, towards safety, heels biting into the ground. Thrashing and scratching at every glimpse of flesh within reach, Jessica let out a shrill, "No! No! They need us! We need to help them! They're dying. Jesus, please, they're dying!"

Yeah, this was true—even though she could hear sirens fast approaching in the distance, louder still were the screams of those still trapped inside. People whom her mom cared about, and whom Maze had become reluctantly familiar with.

And Dean. She'd seen him earlier, hadn't she? He and his sister both.

Even though she disdained these people, and they her, this was something she wouldn't wish on anyone. It had to have been hell.

Neal was practically vibrating in place with the need to abscond. The hurt in his eyes was evident. He really did give some kind of a damn, didn't he? It made her even more certain he needed to go.

"He better not be dead," was all she told him, then jerked her head in the direction of the fire. "Just go—I'll try and catch up."

Neal grasped her once on the shoulder before darting across the lot until he disappeared from view.

"Let's try and pull some people out," she ordered. Jessica wiped at her cheeks and nodded.

The tent had folded in on itself, now dark and light by the turns of shadows, its posts cracked and inverted by the collapse. The ground was unstable, and Maze had seen enough sinkholes in her time to know she didn't want to be anywhere near it for fear it would expand. But this was her mom, these were people she knew, and they didn't deserve to die just because she didn't like them.

I'm going to be brave this time, she thought, then steeled herself and led Jessica back into the tent.

It was dark and cramped inside. The structure had collapsed almost entirely by this point, and there were people groaning beneath upturned chairs and equipment—or worse, run through by metal spires. There was nothing they could do for most in attendance who hadn't escaped the center pulpit in time, with them either caught beneath debris or at the bottom of the sinkhole.

Breathing heavy and trying not to panic like she had at the party, Maze grabbed the first person she was able to wrest out from an overturned chair and pulled them out. She went back in again and again with Jessica, shouldering others or dragging them if there was no other option. Maze didn't stop until she was coughing so hard she was doubled-over, sick with exhaustion and fear.

They had retrieved everyone they could

The landscape was obscured by dust and studded with mangled bodies. Figures rushed around her in a chaotic tumble. Moans and cries rose into the air. It was a seriously spooky sight. Jessica was full-on sobbing now, tucking herself into Maze's side and grabbing onto her like she was the only thing keeping her upright.

Emergency services soon arrived, but Maze had to bolt before they tried treating her for shock or keeping her around for a statement. She didn't have time to get caught up with that while Reeve and Neal could be in trouble. Several familiar faces were already being led to the ambulance, being tended to by the EMTs. Lee and his family weren't among them. Dean and his sister were, though, and their eyes met just like they had at that stupid party, only this time the battlefield was different.

"Mom," she said, "I'm going."

Jessica nodded dumbly, gaze tracking the spectacle around them like it was a dream. Maze hugged her tight and pivoted to leave. Her mom watched her run off, a despondent, lost look on her face. She did nothing to stop her. *We've got time,* Maze told herself. *Time to work on this.*

Maze didn't know whether this decision was the right one, not when her mom stood there looking so lost. But then she remembered Reeve's awkward kindness, Neal's gentle arms around her as she cried into his shoulder, and her own gutted heart reeling from Jessica's acidic words as she was blamed for her dad's death.

It wasn't good or right, but it was the truth. It was her truth.

Dean had managed to extricate himself from the first responders to intercept Maze on her way to the parking lot. "The hell are you doing by running off, Mazie? You need to get checked out by the EMTs," he told her, panting. Blood was smeared along one temple, and a white bandage peeked out from his dark hair.

"I got something to take care of," she answered, turning around to search for her car in the pandemonium.

Dean reached out and grasped her wrist. "Maze," he began, only for her to cut him off.

"Dean, I don't have time for this. Please, just *trust me*, alright? Trust me like you trusted me the other night."

His hold on her tightened, but it wasn't to keep her in place, but rather to pull her in for a quick hug. It was familiar, comforting, and something she hadn't realized she needed so badly. Maze relaxed into it for a moment before the two parted.

"I trust you," he said. "Find me when this is all over. I'll look after your mom in the meantime."

"Thank you," she breathed.

Then they were drawn in opposite directions, Dean back to his sister and Jessica, and Maze to her friends.

The fairgrounds, billowing dust, and the dead and dying phased by her as she sprinted towards her car, and from there, the fire. It made everything weirdly clear.

The idea that she had no real control used to paralyze her, make grief well up in her throat. Now there was a weird freedom in it. She had no control, no power. But neither did anyone else she knew. Maybe over themselves, sometimes. They had no insight into people's minds or intentions or really even the town around them. Just people swimming upstream, blind together. They were all hurtling towards something—a crossroads, maybe—and she wasn't sure what awaited them.

Maze felt herself give into it.

Yeah, she was starving. Maze wanted attention, sex, love; to be regarded with open fondness; and for her voice to be heard.

But Maze was just a person, no better or worse than those around her, secure in her own forward momentum as anyone could be. She was looking towards the future.

NEAL VI

Neal heard the screams before he saw the fire.

The sky was drowned in red when he and the others emerged from the tent, gaping at the unfamiliar sight of a tree line obscured by smoke. Even though the chat piles obfuscated the horizon, he could still see that it was coming from the south side of town near where the trailer homes stood.

He felt fear stab through him, sharp and visceral. It was somehow worse than the chaos at his back. The warning he'd given the other man was still fresh in his mind, lingering, a phantom thread to pull at until he could no longer abate its unraveling. He'd told Reeve to watch himself, but he knew now that his words hadn't been taken to heart. Neal was never lucky enough to be wrong.

"Jesus, Mary, and Joseph," he breathed. "Oh, God, Red."

Neal shoved a hand in his pocket and clamped it around his keys, then released Jessica from his hold. Rather than turn back like he'd expected, she fell forward into him and clutched at his shirt as she began to sob. He was torn between the innate need to comfort a crying woman and the urge to abandon her in the dirt for getting in his way.

Maze stumbled to a stop next to them, eyes blown wide by the same sight that now had Neal apt to vibrate out of his skin. "Oh, hell," the girl uttered, "that's gotta be Reeve's place. That—that's for sure Reeve's!"

And when she got the idea in her head to go off and help Reeve, Neal could not keep the genuine gratitude he felt for this girl off his face. *Finally*, he wanted to shout. *Finally, someone else gives a damn about him.*

It had been a club of one for too long.

Maze wrenched her mom away and made to follow Neal but was stopped just as he had been. Jessica was still losing her shit, screaming and grabbing at Maze, begging her not to leave, to stay, to try and see whether any more people there could be saved.

"Dammit—just go. I'll catch up," she yelled. ""He better not be dead. Just go—I'll try and catch up."

Then she pushed her mom in the other direction, and the two ventured back into the tent's gaping mouth.

Neal wished he could say he spared her more than a parting glance, and that his thoughts had not pivoted with ease towards the possibility that something was wrong with Reeve, made it out to be more important, more everything than the people hurt and probably dying behind him, but that would be a lie. Neal left the teenage girl and her widowed mother to help while he hurtled away towards uncertainty. Any lingering hesitation evaporated with each successive footstep.

After reaching the lot, he skidded so hard around his car that he lost his footing and collapsed on the dirt beside the driver's side door. There was blood all over his palms and knees where he'd braced himself, and little bits of rock too, but Neal just wiped it off and wrenched the handle open, putting the Road Runner into first and peeling out of the gravel lot, tires kicking up debris as he sped towards the fire. The only light on that side of town, in a neighborhood so far out, came from the flames; there weren't even streetlights installed.

Everyone else was back at the tent.

It's not like there's much else to do, he thought hysterically. Carthage was so starved for entertainment that church and the fried chicken joint were the town's two major hot spots, making Gould's weird setup a natural crowd-pleaser. It was new, and that's all it really had to be. God being involved was just a bonus.

The smoking double-wide soon peeked over the horizon, making Neal bite at his tongue until blood welled up wet and thick as he thought, *I was right. I was right. I was right.*

There was smoke everywhere. The two trailers were charred shells, diseased with fire and fluttering ash. Emergency vehicles were already on site, and Neal could see Reeve's neighbors gathered on the lawn. Wait, no—the husband was gone. Zebadiah. And neither could he see Reeve. His chest constricted at that, and he heaved for breath even before the heavy air began to settle in him.

The blazing dynamo was soon divided, though. It was just a silhouette at first, but soon took on a familiar masculine shape, and soon he watched

Reeve emerge from within. Backlit by flames, he was beautiful and terrifying, and when Neal drew closer, he noticed, nonsensically, that the other man's reserve had somehow thawed, and how now his expression now bordered on satisfaction. He looked, more than anything else, unreachable, a creature of complete sensual impulse.

Neal felt an inexplicable loss at the sight. He recalled Eliot's description of the light, heat, and felt then the overwhelming fear articulated by his voice in the penultimate chapter. *My black-eyed creature,* he'd described Ezrah, and it never seemed more pertinent than in this moment.

Looking at Reeve now, he had to wonder—had he ever really known him at all? When you're a child, you never really know people for what they are. *Look at us,* he thought hysterically, *running around in the dark.*

Reeve slunk across the lawn until he let himself collapse into Neal's arms, coughing and choking but looking lighter than he'd ever seen him before. The neighbors must've known something he didn't, as they reacted to Reeve's arrival like a death omen, sobbing uncontrollably. The woman, Heddie, was particularly vocal, her cries rising above them to join the ash.

The husband's absence from the group became more pronounced, but Neal had no time to contemplate the matter further, as it was then they were put through the paces with emergency services, being passed around as volunteer firefighters worked to put out the blaze before it ate up the surrounding brush and buildings. After a quick inspection, Neal was put aside in order for the medics to attend to Reeve, who was clearly the worse for wear. They checked him out, draping a shock blanket over Reeve's shoulders and administering supplemental oxygen to him through a mask.

The woman, Heddie, sputtered out explanations and apologies until law enforcement led her to the backseat of a police cruiser, her kids being shepherded around by the only other officer on scene. Everyone else must have been at the massive fucking sinkhole. The town probably had no clue how to handle two largescale disasters happening simultaneously.

Neal hovered while Reeve was attended to, wanting to be close but keep up the appearance of "normal" boundaries. The things that came easy to other men but had always escaped him. Eventually, the officer who had arrested Heddie scuttled over to where they were seated by the ambulance.

He withdrew a notepad and pen. "Mr. Scarlet, if I could have a moment of your time."

Reeve nodded in agreement and answered the rapid-fire questions that followed, which amounted to *when did you arrive, what did you notice on scene, did your neighbors say anything to you,* and so on.

Then the officer inquired, "Mrs. Condor said you ran in to save her husband. This true?"

There was a heavy silence. "I tried to save him," Reeve said slowly. "But I couldn't. He was trapped beneath a pile of my things. I had to leave. It was leave or die."

There was something about the expression on his face, Neal thought, that gave him pause. It would have escaped anyone else's notice, but Neal was an expert in Reeve-speak. He was… lying? Why? The only reason he could conceive was so awful, so preposterous that Neal truncated it immediately. *He wouldn't do that,* he thought.

"This seems cut and dry, but I reckon the chief'll call you in later to run everything through again. So, find a place to stay in the meantime and make sure we have your extension," the officer said.

Neal gave him his room number and extension at the motel, which he now needed to extend his stay at.

Any suspicion regarding Reeve that pivoted around who, exactly, he was, had been snuffed out by Heddie's allocution and the ongoing disaster over at the fairgrounds. The pair were waved off by the officer just as Maze's godforsaken beater peeled onto the scene. The girl tumbled out of the car and ran over to pull them both into an uncharacteristically deep and lengthy embrace.

"I can't believe I was so worried about y'all," she said in a rush, arms an iron grip around them. It was her version of "Thank God you people aren't dead."

Neal smiled tremulously, relieved to see her. He was suddenly, pathetically grateful for her presence, and he leaned into it before pulling back. The girl was soot-faced and shivering.

"Go back to your mama, kid," he told her gently. "We're all good here, as you can see. You don't need to worry 'bout us no more today."

"What the hell about this is "good?"" Maze retorted, gesturing at the firefighters shooting water into the base of the blaze. Then, she pivoted to Reeve. "And you, you—ridiculous man. 'Course you'd get caught up in this nonsense."

"The Condors did it. Insurance scam or whatever," was all Reeve said, but his gaze was nonetheless soft when he regarded her. "Not my fault."

"Naturally," she said.

Neal glanced over at the family drama unfolding nearby, the buzz of cops. Heddie had a hungry look about her every time he'd seen her, and so too had the children. They were still wearing it. Hungry for money, for love, for more than what they had. It made sense to him.

"We're good," Neal interjected, then amended, "well, *ish*. So, skedaddle. We can't go anywhere for a while yet, and you've got someone you love hurtin.'"

Maze opened her mouth like she was about to argue, but then she let it fall shut in what seemed to be acquiescence. "Alright, but I'm holding you to that. You can't leave without seeing me first."

Neal squeezed her shoulder and released her, watching as she careened away back to the site of another disaster. They were her friends, but they were fine; her mom had more resembled a bent stick than a human being when they'd fled the collapsing tent, not to mention all the other people she likely knew inside. And it was true that they would be sticking around, especially with what the officer had said about taking statements. He recalled the tedious court process from when he was a boy, and loathe as he was to repeat it, understood that it wasn't something he could run from.

The two men lingered at the scene for a while longer. Heddie was arrested and the kids taken into protective custody. It was very close to a parody of his final night in Carthage as a boy, and he could see his own family superimposed over them.

He knuckled his sockets and inhaled a few gulping breaths. This, the sinkhole, and Reeve's off-kilter demeanor hit him all at once.

"Red, I need to," he started to say, wavering, "not, uh, be here anymore."

"The Mirage?"

Neal nodded and motioned for the other man to follow. They took separate cars, and even that short separation felt anathema to him. When the pair reconvened, it took everything in him not to paw at Reeve while out in the parking lot, waiting until the second the door closed and locked behind him to approach his friend.

Beneath the dim, off-kilter light that bled in off the street from between the blinds, Reeve shed his chrysalis-like layers until he was bare, raw; his un-blunted edges were now exposed to the world. Neal was liable to cut himself on them. He might even enjoy it.

He was drawn forward into the other man's proximity as though magnetized and was then eased into his arms. Embraced by lingering smoke, soap, and heat, Neal allowed himself to be held. It had been a trick of the light—what he'd seen earlier, that was. He knew this man. He cared for him even more deeply. And that had to mean something.

The air was swollen with potential, desire. It was intimate rather than erotic. Their gazes locked, and Neal let his skull rest against Reeve's.

He didn't want to risk asking about the fire. But when he spoke next, because he had to know, the words tumbled out despite himself, "You saw him—Zebadiah. He was alive in there, wasn't he?"

Reeve said nothing at first, then his lips turned up at the corners. "I did," he murmured, "and this time, I'm not sorry at all."

This time.

There was this feeling, Neal thought, like something was slipping through his fingers. It was a loss he could neither describe nor articulate. He swallowed, mouth dry, his tongue a sandpaper rasp across his cheeks. Wetness beaded along his hairline. *Reeve,* he thought. *Reeve. Reeve.*

When Reeve opened his mouth to continue, Neal tensed, almost pulled back, but Reeve's calloused palm was spread across his nape, and he was so warm.

"Stop," was all Neal could muster.

He was struck by the profound certainty that Reeve could have saved him and chose not to. Maybe there was no forethought, no serial killer intent, and maybe Zebadiah had even deserved it on some level, but it was murder all the same.

He wanted power so he could hurt people as he'd been hurt. Not everyone, just those who deserved it. Neal had walked that road, too; he'd walked it right into a cell.

And it occurred to him then that Reeve would be taken from him and locked up forever if he said anything. He choked on that horrible thought. The idea was worse, somehow, than the prospect of being a liar. Neal felt like he was on the ass-end of some cosmic joke.

Reeve didn't say anything to him, not an apology or another remark about the death, and for that Neal felt desperately grateful. When the other man's grip tightened around his neck, he could think only: *what have you done?*

He wouldn't get to have him anymore if he did the right thing. And he was so, so close to getting what he'd always wanted. Neal gripped Maria Goretti and murmured a prayer for forgiveness. He couldn't ask for guidance because he knew already what he was going to do.

I can't let go of him. He's the first person to ever give a damn about me. Even when I was at my worst, I had him.

Neal didn't know whether he hated or loved Reeve in that moment. He didn't know if Reeve loved or hated him either. But both had brought him here. To him, they were so alike they may as well have been the same thing. Maybe it didn't even matter, not when this man took up all the space in his head.

"What am I to you?"

Reeve considered it. "The only person who's ever known me," he said.

It was a little funny that he would say that, Neal thought, because he felt like he'd never known him less in his life. But he couldn't help the soft, almost tender feeling that unraveled in his chest.

"I miss you," he confessed.

"You're mourning me like I'm dead, but I'm still here. I'm talking to you," Reeve told him.

There are some things you can't come back from, Neal wanted to say. *And this is one of them.*

In a rare instance of loquaciousness, Reeve continued speaking. "I told you once that I believed in nothing. Not God, not hell. Just us, this world, and its emptiness; what I can see before me. But now, I know there are things I can't touch. I believe in murder. And in suffering. That pain can bring greater peace than love. How there's a crack in everyone. It's the crack that makes an object broken, and it grows and grows with time, until everything is just... past repair. That brokenness lives inside me, too. It always has, I think. I was made this way. So were you. We fit with each other; I think. Like two shards cut from the same glass."

"You're wrong, Reeve," Neal said, hopping mad, angrier at him than he'd ever been before. "People make their own choices. And sometimes, those choices are just the wrong ones. They got no one to blame but themselves. It doesn't matter whether you believe in the man upstairs, or in evil, 'cause this—all this—it's just us. Those things work through our hands."

Reeve scoffed openly and grasped him tighter. "So you say," he said into Neal's hair. "I think people like that... they're talking at the sky."

Neal closed his eyes and let himself be carried away by their physical proximity to each other. It was easier than the alternative. He was scattered, displaced.

"If you were mine, you'd have a place to belong. You would never be without a home again," Reeve offered when Neal remained quiet.

He could have laughed. It was what he'd always wanted to hear. "Don't you... don't you get it? You're my sure thing. You've already got me in all the ways that count."

"Good," Reeve murmured. "Hold me closer."

Neal's arms strangled his torso, but even that wasn't enough for him, as he asked for *more, tighter, kiss me again, bite me* until they were one vertical line. They had entered into a kind of sensual purgatory with each other, clutching at the other's body, sharing breath but escalating it no further. The grip he had on Reeve's shoulders had to have been painful by now, Neal thought, but Reeve showed no sign of discomfort.

"I—I just want to make you feel good," Neal said, a little helplessly.

"This is what makes me feel good."

No, Neal wanted to tell him. *This isn't. I'm not blind. I can see what you are. You're desperate, lonely. You want so badly to be loved. You want it so much that you need to punish yourself for it. But I love you more than you hate yourself*, he wanted to say. *I'll even act like I hate you if that makes the difference.*

Neal's pain had so often been physical; but Reeve's, it was intangible. People punctured him with their silences and words by turns with their disdain, their suspicion.

"You make me so—crazy," Neal admitted instead. "I'm halfway to being outta my mind here. Are you sure about this?"

"Does it matter?" Reeve countered. "Maybe there's a reason. Maybe not. This clears my head. Makes me want like nothing else. It's a different pain than misery and indifference. It's... good."

"Yeah?"

"Let me give you my skin."

Reeve began to unbutton his shirt, then his slacks, and tossed them both to the side. He wasn't wearing boxers. His cock hung soft and heavy against his thigh, uncut. He moved to the bed and lay down, Neal not far behind.

"You—what do you want?"

"I want to do it for real this time," he breathed.

Neal bit back a moan. His fingers twisted in the sheets by Reeve's head, and he had to close his eyes. The dry heat sparking up his spine was impossible to ignore.

It might hurt a bit, Neal wanted to say. *Just at first. And it's weird when you're new. Then it feels good, so good. But the intimacy, being that close, that comfortable with another person—it's the best part of all.*

"You sure?"

"I want you to have this. You're the only one I want to be good for."

He shouldn't be doing this. Not to Reeve or himself. Love, sex—they couldn't fix people. These things were just bandages on an open wound.

"O-okay," he said, settling back on his knees. "You'll, uh, need to clean up. Probably would be good anyways with the..." *fire,* he didn't say.

"I see," Reeve agreed, departing for the bathroom to shower.

Neal rolled off the bed and went to get the K-Y Jelly and condoms he'd brought because he was a horny optimist. And just to be sure, he rubbed himself down with a couple baby wipes he kept on-hand. It paid to be prepared.

Reeve returned, wet and clean, to sprawl on the duvet like a fallen angel. His eyes were burning coals, the scar on his mouth was a crack on glass. Neal was hypnotized. He prepped him quick and rough, rolling on the condom and settling himself inside probably too soon. Reeve didn't seem to mind.

"Oh, God, fuck," he moaned, voice growing deeper, rougher. "Fuck me, Neal. God. I need it."

Reeve clutched at his back, his sides, nails biting into the skin there until he drew blood. Then he set his teeth into Neal's throat. Neal leaned into it and uttered a noise that he had never heard himself make before. He didn't sound like the man he'd come to know himself to be, and when he glanced at the mirrored ceiling, neither did he recognize the face staring down at him. That man looked rough, wild, and alive; that Reeve looked almost happy. They had to be some other men, living some other life.

He sat back on his heels and dragged Reeve with him, letting him gaze drift over the other man as he changed the angle of his thrusts.

I would let him do whatever he wanted with me, Neal realized. *Anything.* Because Reeve had been in the dark and cold for so long, alone, and Neal wanted to give him whatever he needed to feel warm again.

After Neal finished, he lay on top of the other man for a moment, eyes closed as Reeve carded his fingers through his hair. It was—it was nice. Intimate. The atmosphere in the room was swollen with this intimacy. He felt it everywhere: their twined bodies, slick with sweat; the air that smelled like musk and come. When he finally pulled out, Neal watched lube trickle down Reeve's lean, pale thighs. God. Christ. *This.*

The other man's arm enclosed around Neal and dragged him up towards the headboard, where he was twisted onto his side, ear pressed to Reeve's heart. As it stuttered out its metronome beat, Neal wondered how it was he felt so safe here. Everything he'd ever wanted, he now had, and it was perfect, almost perfect. Maybe, he thought, maybe if he weren't so selfish—

He cut that idea off and tightened his hold on Reeve. No, there was no point in speculating. He'd made his choice. It was done.

They lay together like that for a little while, tangled and sticky, until Neal felt Reeve's cock stir beneath him. He shifted overtop and sucked a wet mark into his neck when Reeve moaned. If he'd really been a virgin before now, it made sense he was on a hair trigger.

"Neal," Reeve murmured, brushing a dry finger across his hole, "can I?"

Even at the short contact, Neal shuddered in pleasure and nodded. He wouldn't get hard again this soon, but he didn't tend to get too oversensitive to where a second round wasn't possible if he were on the receiving end.

Reeve flipped him onto his stomach without hesitation, hands thumbing bruises into Neal's hips. He spread his legs on instinct and rutted against the bedspread, which dragged rough up and down his limp shaft. The other man was a line of liquid heat down his back.

"There've been others," Reeve said without preamble.

"Yes."

"But you're mine now."

"Yeah," he breathed, higher.

"Tell me how you like it."

"I'd lick me open," Neal moaned into the mattress, shifting, "and go in with just spit. It'd be slow, good. It'd be so, so good."

Reeve's palms moved to spread him, and a wet tongue breached him soon after. It was so wet, so good. His mouth was shockingly hot, leaving Neal so turned on he felt it in his toes.

Neal had half-expected the other man to back out upon hearing the request; he was now very grateful he'd taken the time to clean himself up beforehand. He squirmed and panted like a bitch in heat under Reeve's ministrations, voice tapering off into a whine when fingers were added. The twist gut-punched a moan out of him.

"Is this good for you?"

"*Hnh.*"

Like there was any place he'd rather be than here, with Reeve, panting and wanting above him, around him, inside him. Neal worried at his lower lip until it split, moaning around the blood.

He felt the blunt head begin to press inside—Reeve hadn't wrapped it—but catching the bug was the last thing on his mind then. Reeve was unsteady on the first thrust but soon settled into an awkward if syncopated rhythm. He was generous too, adjusting Neal's legs until he found a trajectory that had him drag his cock back and forth across that spot in him that made Neal moan.

Amazingly, he felt his own length grow half-hard, leaking, and began careening towards a long and resonant climax that was practically wrenched out of him. His gut twisted pleasantly. He'd never thought love would ever have anything to do with biology—not like this, at least.

When they were done, Reeve leaned over and licked the tears off his face. The atmosphere was disquieting, sensual. Neal feared shattering it, so rather than speak, he went through the motions of cleaning them both up before settling back down on the duvet to sleep.

Reeve fell asleep first, splayed possessively over his body. It took Neal longer to prod his brain into submission, and even then, his earlier unease lingered and followed him into that strange space between dreams and consciousness.

Almost four years ago now, he'd celebrated Fry Day with Ruth and Joseph, cheering when the news announced Bundy's death. Joseph had called it the "electric chair boogaloo," and had roped the rest of them into following the news coverage.

Neal hadn't felt the same anticipation wash over him. He mostly felt sick. And as he watched the anchors' mouths form word after word, Neal could only think back to Gacy's trial coverage as a teenager.

There had been a news profile he and his dad watched together when he was a teenager, seated side-by-side before the screen, that described the horrific things Gacy did to those young boys and men in Illinois. As if somehow sensing his discontent, Gabriel had leaned over and told Neal about a cousin he had, one that went missing up near Chicago a few years back.

"He was young, y'know, and a little like you, actually. Ran away from home, got some contract work in the area. Then one day he just up and disappears. We start thinking that Gacy got him once they found the bodies in the crawlspace. It makes sense, really, considering. They still don't know who all those boys are, and he'd been a little faggot, too. Just like those kids Corll picked up down in Houston."

He was talking about Dean Corll—a serial killer who'd haunted Houston in the early 70's, doing unspeakable things to guys like him until he got himself killed in '73, thank God. He and Gacy were true-to-life horror stories for him. They were reminders that people like Neal got punished for what they were. He knew about them because his dad made a point of ensuring he did.

Neal remembered sitting there, unmoving, until the program finished.

That same night, he turned restlessly in a bed of sweat, Gacy and Corll's faces drifting in and out of focus before his dream became more concrete, more real, until he was on Corll's rack and being passed between the two as they each took turns torturing and raping him. He woke with a strangled shout, sheets twisted around his calves. Then he cried for what felt like forever, only stopping when he could no longer produce more tears.

After, Neal snuck out into the kitchen and drank from his dad's whiskey bottle until he didn't feel anything.

For the next several weeks, those men haunted him, and even the thought of touching another guy made him nauseous. His desire would ebb into a heavy, tightly coiled thing within his chest, an unwanted longing, one quelled solely by his nighttime torturers.

"You're so tough on the outside, but we know the truth—you're soft. You're all soft in there," they would tell him like a secret, right before cutting into his flesh.

Neal didn't want to be another unidentified body languishing in the crawlspace or basement of an unrepentant killer. He didn't want to be who he was. He would have given anything to be someone who didn't have to worry about these things.

That fear hunted him into adulthood, into prison, out, and back to Carthage. But with each exhalation Reeve uttered into his collarbone and the shift of skin against skin, it seemed to be a fear that dwindled. Maybe one day it would even die.

He shut his eyes.

***

They were permitted to leave a little over a week later. Heddie's spontaneous confession at the scene had done a lot to clear Reeve's name, not to mention the treasure-trove of staged photographs with items they'd returned to various big-box stores across the state recovered from their shed just off the property. After Sheriff Fields took their statements, he let them know they would be asked to testify at the grand jury hearing. The pair didn't need to stay in town as long as they could return when they were needed.

Reeve's things had all burned in the fire. The horde, the records, Cale Yarborough. He had nothing save for his car and what meager possessions were left therein. That, and the demonic stray cat he'd chosen to accompany them. Selene, indeed.

The other man's decision to join him seemed to Neal more and more momentous by the day. *He's coming home with me. I get to have him.*

Their final morning came soon. It was so early the sky outside was still dark and velvet. They invited Maze to meet them early before they had to set off for the first leg of their journey to Des Moines.

Neal looked over at Reeve, silhouetted by a newborn sunrise. His eyes were obsidian, ancient, thin mouth tilted up into a secretive half-smile around his cigarette. He'd become what everyone thought of him.

When Neal let his gaze linger, he was rewarded with a fond look. He felt something like longing sit heavy in his chest. Reeve was clad in his shirt, his jeans, his black satin bomber jacket. It felt a little like ownership.

There was the telltale squeal of tires and accompanying metal music that marked Maze's arrival. As promised by both parties, she had come by to bid them farewell. She disembarked with impressive speed and bounded over to them.

Her eye had mostly healed, though her nose remained a little crooked. The sunglasses today were tinted violet, frameless, and perched low on her face. Her outfit was likewise haphazard: she was bundled up in a long gray overcoat, Dickies, and men's work boots.

"Hey there, Neal, Reeve," she said.

Reeve's expression shifted into something almost bittersweet. Neal would miss her, too, he realized, as bizarre as their brief acquaintanceship had been.

"How's your mom?" Neal asked.

"As well as can be expected, I guess. Coping."

"Think she'll be back in with those, uh, tent folk anytime soon?"

"Somehow, I doubt it. She threw out most of their shit. And we've been spending most days together at the house, talking. Small stuff, I know, but it's on the way to being better than it was."

"That's good," Neal said, pleased. What he knew of Jessica Maze was limited to second-hand knowledge from Maze and their solitary, ill-fated meeting at the fairgrounds.

"I'm trying to just *be*, for once."

"How's that going for you?"

"Better, I guess. I'm trying."

"You see the paper they published about you?"

Maze groaned and went red, which made Neal grin. Several days after that eventful evening with Pastor Gould, the *Maidenhead Herald* published an article about a teenage girl and her mother who rescued nearly a dozen people from the wreckage of a tent after a sinkhole had formed beneath it. The headline read, rather alliteratively, MOTHER AND DAUGHTER DYNAMIC DUO DELIVER DOZENS FROM THE BRINK OF DEATH. Someone had managed to snap a candid shot of Maze carrying out a woman bridal style from the tent's mouth, Jessica not far behind.

Maze's latest "picture day" headshot was featured prominently on the bottom right section of the front page. Her dark hair had been tied into four pigtails, each tied off with a safety pin-adorned rubber band. Likewise, her eye makeup had been caked on in jagged vertical streaks. Just below frame, a Pantera logo on her t-shirt peeked into view. All in all, she resembled the bastard lovechild of Gene Simmons and a Led Zeppelin groupie—otherwise known as every WASP's worst nightmare.

"It's embarrassing," Maze retorted, though she secretly looked pleased. "Can't believe they used that photo."

"I definitely can," said Neal. "You enjoying the infamy?"

"The shitshow will pass, and things will go back to the way they always are 'round here soon enough," she said with a shrug.

"It won't be long 'til you can leave, too," Reeve interjected. "If you want."

"Might not be long. The EPA and the state are in talks to force everyone out, apparently. Guess this place ain't considered safe or something," she said with a sarcastic emphasis before a smile took over her face. "And we're not saying goodbye. Not really," she said. "We're just saying see you later."

"See you, then."

She laughed. "Someday, somewhere besides this speck on the map."

"You've got my info," Neal said, handing her a scrap of paper. There was a phone number and an address written on it. His landline, his home. He flicked her on the head.

"Yeah, I do. Enjoy life with this ghoul," she murmured, jerking her chin towards Reeve.

Neal pulled her close and hugged her, not because he thought she was weak or even really needed comfort from him, but because he wanted to. And to his surprise, she hugged him back.

Maze knocked him on the shoulder as they parted and pulled Reeve in for a hug. He could see her lips move by his ear but could discern nothing concrete.

They watched her retreat into the station wagon and pull out, back to her home, her job, her family. Neal wished her nothing but good things. Whether that included seeing them again one day, he wasn't sure, but he hoped they'd meet again on the other side.

His and Reeve's possessions were already packed into their respective vehicles. The Road Runner, the Laguna. Their fingers brushed against each other before they parted.

"Don't look back, Neal," Reeve told him.

"Okay," he said, then again, "okay."

Around them, the dawn emerged. Cool, welcoming. An end to the night.

EPILOGUE

Blue Interlude

In the summer of 1982, two boys spent their days and nights at the edge of the world. They had retreated there to leave everything behind for a little while. The mine shaft was desolate, a more preferred loneliness.

There was a photograph in the first boy's back pocket. It featured him when he ought to have been a child, tense-shouldered, crooked into the embrace of a Janus-faced woman. Her eyes were two dark polysemous pools. They stared through the fabric to gaze at the sensuous, cobalt-streaked sky. The other had nothing except a scar turning down his solemn mouth.

They reclined back on the hood of the car, which overlooked the mouth to the underworld. It was bright out and pleasantly warm. The dark-haired boy, the one with the picture, had lifted a six-pack from the convenience store for the pair to split, and he clinked his can against the other's.

Their unoccupied hands were nearly close enough to touch. They never closed that distance, not once, but it didn't seem to matter; they were tangled in other ways.

The radio moaned out a murder ballad while the sun descended on the horizon. This warmth, this feeling—it was something that couldn't quite be placed, not in either one, but whatever it was, it was enough.

***

THE END

ABOUT THE AUTHOR

August is an introvert who likes cats and darkness.

Instagram

https://www.instagram.com/funerealpoetry/

Website
https://funereal-poetry.tumblr.com/

Threads
@funerealpoetry